AND THE LAST TRUMP SHALL SOUND

A Future History of America

CAEZIK
SF & FANTASY
ARC MANOR
ROCKVILLE, MARYLAND

SHAHID MAHMUD
PUBLISHER

www.caeziksf.com

"The Breaking of Nations" copyright © 2020 by Harry Turtledove.
"The Purloined Republic" copyright © 2020 by James Morrow.
"Because it is Bitter" copyright © 2020 by Cat Rambo.

Cover art by Scott Grimando, grimstudios.com

ISBN: 978-1-64710-005-6

First Edition. October 2020
2 3 4 5 6 7 8 9 10

An imprint of Arc Manor LLC

www.CaezikSF.com

This is a political satire, and meant to be a parody based on how events might look in the future. Although certain political figures are used as characters in these novellas, there is no attempt to prove or even imply that the situations depicted in these stories represent actual events related to any of these individuals.

As a parody/satire with occasional over-the-top elements, some readers may find certain portions of these stories caustic. But the reader is reminded that this is a satire and neither the authors nor the publisher purport that anything contained in this anthology is either true or likely to happen, or is a true representation of the characters.

CONTENTS

THE BREAKING OF NATIONS

Harry Turtledove

NICOLE Yoshida clicked the remote's channel-up button, first once, then twice. The same story led on Fox News, Fox-CNN, and Fox-MSNBC. At President Pence's order, the governor and lieutenant governor of Connecticut had been remanded to protective custody on a charge of treason for refusing to cooperate with federal court-mandated immigration sweeps.

Connecticut State Cabinet officials had unanimously resigned in protest; the media said they had, anyhow. On a temporary basis—so every network's newscasters assured their audience—the chief of the Connecticut State Police had been appointed acting governor of the state.

The governor of California made a disgusted noise and turned off the TV. She remembered when the news channels each had a different spin on things. She remembered when some of them dared disagree with the federal government, even on important things like the first coronavirus pandemic.

It hadn't been that long ago, either. They'd stayed that way well into President Trump's second term. *The good old days*, she thought sourly. Then consolidation hit television and radio and what was left of the newspapers. That social media had already gone the same way made finishing the job easier.

" 'Therefore never send to know for whom the bell tolls; it tolls for thee,' " she quoted.

Her CHP bodyguard—one of her CHP bodyguards—let out a snort. "Yeah, the whole country is Donne to a turn," Captain Myron Flegenheim said with malice aforethought.

She winced to let him know she'd noticed what he'd done. "How long till the Last Trump blows for me?" she replied, just as maliciously.

His pained expression told her he'd hoped a governor would be above such things, and she'd just disappointed him ... again. "The United States is washed up," he said. Then he added, "Anybody got a cigarette?"

"Go outside," Governor Yoshida told him.

"I always do," Flegenheim said.

And he did. Even almost a third of the way through the twenty-first century, even with vaping driving cigarette manufacturers batshit, some stubborn people with a nicotine jones still got their fix from good, old-fashioned tobacco. Captain Flegenheim was one of them. He was polite about it, but he was.

Being polite helped only so much. People who smoked smelled bad all the time. The odor clung to their clothes, their skin, their hair, their breath. You couldn't tell them so, either. They refused to believe you. They'd got so used to their stink; they were noseblind to it.

Nicole Yoshida wished she were. She'd thought now and then about asking Chief Musavi to take Flegenheim off her guard rotation and to replace him with a nonsmoker. She hadn't done it yet. The captain had a lively, sardonic wit, which was about as uncommon in cops as it was in politicians.

As if to prove as much, he asked, "When the Feds come for you, will they give this office to my boss?"

"They'll be sorry if they do," she answered.

That Ali Musavi—not just a Muslim but a Shiite Muslim—headed the California Highway Patrol, might have been one reason the Feds hadn't tried to seize her yet. That he was further left politically than she was couldn't hurt, either.

"They're never sorry for anything. That's part of what makes them what they are," Flegenheim said.

"I know," she said. "Boy, do I know!"

"How long can things go on like this?"

"What an interesting question! If there are no other questions, class is dismissed," the governor said. She'd taught poli sci at UC Berkeley. She'd got into academic politics there—an excellent training ground, she often thought, because the stakes were so low. But

4

she'd wanted to play the real game, too, so she'd left the university for politics politics.

And here she was, in the governor's mansion in Sacramento. And the game was getting realer than she'd ever dreamt it could twenty years earlier.

Captain Flegenheim made a discontented noise. "Joke as much as you want. They aren't joking in Washington."

"Yes, I know," Yoshida said. They'd been over this ground several—dozen—times before. "Why do you think the CHP is as militarized as I can make it? If I need more muscle, I can call up the California National Guard."

"You can till President Pence federalizes it," Flegenheim replied. "That'll take—what?—thirty seconds, tops, from when you order it to active duty."

"It will if California officers obey the president's order."

He looked at her. She hadn't been so blunt before. Well, things hadn't been so bad before. "Funny, but you don't look like Jefferson Davis," he said, then softened it a bit by adding, "You'd look silly with a little fringe of beard under your chin."

"Heh," she said. It wasn't much of a laugh, but in the year of our Lord 2031, with Mike Pence; star-spangled fascism; and the Father, Son, and Holy Ghost calling the shots from D.C., you took what you could get and were glad to get anything at all. In a different tone of voice, she went on, "Would you step into the outer office for a while, please? I need to make a conference call, and I don't want any witnesses."

"Okay, but do you really think that will do any good if the Feds aim to hear what you're saying?"

Nicole Yoshida only shrugged. Some Silicon Valley people, whose expertise she trusted, said nobody in Washington could crack her encryption. Maybe they were wrong, maybe not. Either way, the FBI probably already had a good notion of what she meant to talk about. As a song older than she was said, you didn't need to be a weatherman to know which way the wind blew.

Occasional horizontal streaks of color marred the images of Governor Ng of Washington state and Governor Lysbakken of Oregon.

5

No doubt her face was similarly streaked on their phones. It was an encryption artifact. They just had to live with it.

"Do you really think it's time?" Axel Lysbakken asked.

Of the three of them, he'd shown the most doubts over the past few years. Nicole Yoshida felt some sympathy—what they were eyeing hadn't been seriously contemplated for more than 160 years, not by sane people it hadn't—but only some.

"If not now, when?" Dakotah Ng said.

She sounded firmer in her purpose than Governor Yoshida did. She'd come to politics from real-estate law, not academia. In a racket like that, you had to sound sure of yourself whether you were or not—perhaps especially if you weren't.

But with or without bravado, the governor of California had facts on her side. "We started this ball rolling down here, remember," she said. "People were circulating a secession initiative for the 2018 ballot here—Calexit, they called it. It didn't get on, but the spirit was willing even that early."

"Secession." Governor Lysbakken spoke the word as if it tasted nasty in his mouth. It probably did, because he went on, "I don't want to be tarred with the Confederate brush."

"Ha! You won't be! I can just about promise you that," Dakotah Ng said with a snort. "Pence won't dare. Half his base—more than half—thinks the nineteenth-century secession was a good idea."

"I wasn't worrying about his base," Lysbakken said gloomily. "I was worrying about mine."

"You can make a good constitutional case that secession has been legal all along. I used to teach that stuff, so I did the research," Governor Yoshida said. "It never got litigated in the courts, though. It got litigated on the battlefield instead. That the South lost, and that it tried to secede on account of slavery, left secession with a permanent bad reputation after that. Until now, I mean."

"A permanent bad reputation unless you wear one of those dumbass made-in-China MAGA caps, anyway," Governor Ng said.

"Yeah, unless," Nicole Yoshida agreed. "But we haven't been talking about leaving the United States because we want to take freedom away from people. We're talking about it because that's what Washington's been doing ever since Trump got elected the first time."

"Washington and Moscow, you mean," Axel Lysbakken said. On the phone screen, Governor Ng nodded. Nicole nodded, too. It was funny how a fellow who'd learned his trade in the Marxist-Leninist KGB turned out to be so good at spreading fascism across the world. It was funny if you didn't have to live with it, anyhow.

"All three of our states have passed resolutions authorizing us to pull out of the Union if things get bad enough," Dakotah Ng said. "We've had them in our back pockets for a while now. How much worse do things need to get, exactly? What happened in Connecticut can happen here, too. And you bet it will, as soon as Pence and his stooges decide they can get away with it. It will if we don't move first, I should say."

"If they do everything they can, we're toast," the governor of Oregon said. "We're a bunch of atheist heathens and queers out here. Everybody knows that. Everybody in Buffalo Poop, Kansas, and Chitlin Gulf, Arkansas, anyway."

"Pence may not care. The people who prop him up and feed him money will," Governor Yoshida said. "But are we agreed? We'll put the ordinance of secession through our legislatures and come out the other side as Pacifica?"

Neither of the other state leaders told her no. Since California had three times as many people as Oregon and Washington put together, she knew she was likely to become the first president of Pacifica … its George Washington, or, as Captain Flegenheim had said, its Jefferson Davis.

On the TV screen, President Pence looked like a man bedeviled by bees. "This so-called Pacifica is illegal and ridiculous," he growled. "As someone before the Civil War said, it's too small for a country and too large for an insane asylum."

He paused for applause. The assembled representatives and senators gave it to him, abundantly. Applause at every presidential pause had been standard operating procedure since Donald Trump got the authoritarian ball rolling. It reminded Nicole Yoshida of the acclamations the servile Roman Senate used to give really rotten emperors in the third century A.D. The way Vice President Lindsey

Graham and Speaker Devin Nunes blistered their palms while sitting behind Pence on the rostrum particularly disgusted her.

Except for Speaker Nunes, only a handful of representatives and no senators from Pacifica sat in the House chamber. The rest were getting ready to come home. The ones who wouldn't be welcome here now were literally men without a country. As far as Governor Yoshida knew, no women elected in California, Oregon, or Washington supported staying in the USA.

President Pence went on, "We will try to resolve our differences with the governments of the West Coast states by peaceful means if that is at all possible. If a peaceful basis for reconciliation is not possible, we will use whatever means we must to show them that our great federal democracy, now and forever, is one and inseparable."

More rapturous applause. Lincoln had said pretty much the same thing. Governor Yoshida had no doubt Lincoln had said it better, too. He couldn't very well have said it worse. Mike Pence was the kind of man who could put coffee to sleep.

Nicole's iPhone vibrated. She checked the text. *Studio is ready for your reply*, her communications director had written.

I'll be there as soon as he finishes, she wrote back. *How much will the country east of our border get to see?*

The reply from Anna Badal came in moments. *Nothing on the networks, of course. We're also streaming on several platforms. They won't block all of them—they aren't as good at it as the Chinese. Yet.*

She had to be content, or discontented, with that. She was glad the studio was inside the governor's residence. That would make it harder for the FBI or ICE to grab her. Getting those people out of the new country would have to be a top priority. So would a million other things. As far as she could see, the biggest roadblock to secession was what a pain in the ass it was.

President Pence called down the blessings of God on the United States—not, Governor Yoshida noted, on Pacifica or its people. Then the screen cut away to the Reverend Franklin Graham. As the capital's favorite preacher was in the habit of doing, he declared that anyone who didn't bow down to Mike Pence and the ghost of Donald Trump was heading straight for Satan's George Foreman grill.

The governor hit the power button harder than she'd meant to. Franklin Graham reminded her of an Americanized German Christian: one of the many Protestant ministers in Nazi times who'd put Hitler ahead of Jesus. Franklin Graham didn't just render unto Caesar. Caesar was the Golden Calf he worshipped ahead of God. He creeped her out every time he opened his mouth and stuck his foot in it.

As she walked to the studio, she understood that she was counting on Mike Pence to show a certain amount of restraint toward the new republic she was about to proclaim. In one sense, counting on restraint from anybody running things in Washington these days was an act of insanity. In another, though ….

If Pence wanted to scramble a squadron of fighter-bombers with orders to flatten this residence, he could chop Pacifica's head off right now. The new nation couldn't stop him or his planes, not yet. One day real soon now, it would have to be able to do that. She understood as much. But it couldn't yet. One thing at a time.

She relied on Pence to understand that killing her and Governor Ng and Governor Lysbakken wasn't the same as killing the idea of Pacifica. Donald Trump wouldn't have got that. He'd thought telling him no was a capital crime.

But the second great COVID outbreak in 2024 had sent him to the hole in the ground, six feet by three feet by six, which was as much as anybody owned more or less permanently. Trump had broken the Constitution's grip on the government by simply ignoring it as much as he pleased. As soon as he was gone, Pence smoothly started to consolidate his party's and his faction's grip on power.

Not knowing or caring how government worked, Trump wouldn't have been so good at that. A bureaucrat born, Pence understood which levers to pull, and when.

To Nicole Yoshida, who'd grown up playing D&D, they illustrated the difference between chaotic evil and lawful evil. Odds were Pence would have called that satanist. In Pacifica, just about everybody got it.

As soon as she walked into the studio, a makeup artist attacked her with powder and soft brushes. "You have to look your best for this," he said.

"Thanks, Jeremy," she answered, and then, sputtering from the powder, "I think." He laughed. She wasn't so sure it was funny.

Anna Badal bustled up: a small, slim, medium-brown woman in a dress somewhere between gold and copper. "The teleprompter isn't loaded!" she exclaimed. "Are you going to wing this?" The prospect plainly horrified her.

"No, no," the governor reassured her. "I have some notes"—she tapped her handbag—"and this is stuff I actually know. I'm not just telling one more lie to get me through one more day, the way they do in D.C."

"All right." By the way her communications director said it, it was anything but.

Nicole sat down at a desk that was a good mock-up of the one where she usually worked. Behind it stood the flags of California, Oregon, and Washington. For the past century and a half, the Stars and Stripes would have been at the right of the line.

Not tonight. Tonight, the world would see the new flag of the new nation of Pacifica. On a background of gray-green—the color of the North Pacific as it washed against these shores—were three gold stars wreathed in concord.

The symbolism seemed obvious. Nicole Yoshida knew at least a quarter of the people who saw the flag would misunderstand it no matter how obvious it was. Human nature worked that way.

She arranged her notes where she could glance at them when she needed to. These days, most people would have had them on their phone. The governor found that writing things down by hand helped her remember them.

When the light under the camera across the desk from her went red, she took a deep breath and said, "Good evening, my fellow Pacificans, people of goodwill around the world, and all the Americans who manage to see this in spite of everything the illegitimate government in Washington, D.C., is doing to keep it hidden from you. That the U.S. government is trying so hard to keep you from learning the truth about what's happening on the West Coast is one of the big reasons it *is* happening. I'll give you some others before long, too."

After sipping from a glass of water—no plastic bottles here—she went on, "As you probably know, the citizens of Washington,

Oregon, and California have all passed, by large majorities, referenda authorizing them to leave the United States and join together to form the new, free nation of Pacifica if their governors determine that abuses by the authoritarian government in Washington, D.C., have not diminished. Governor Ng, Governor Lysbakken, and I agree that, unfortunately, this hasn't happened. Instead, the regime's abuses keep getting worse.

"We firmly believe we have every legal right to take this step. In 1776, in the Declaration of Independence against tyranny from London, the Continental Congress said of the colonies rebelling against England 'that they are, and of right ought to be, free and independent states.' Not one state, notice. *States*. It goes on, 'As free and independent states, they have full power to levy war, conclude peace, contract alliances, establish commerce, and to do all other acts and things which independent States may of right do.'

The Declaration of Independence goes on to say that whenever any 'form of government becomes destructive of the ends for which it was established, it is the right of the people to alter or abolish it, and to institute a new government.'

"What has the illegitimate regime in Washington, D.C., done? It has destroyed freedom of the press. Even in his first term, Donald Trump claimed that anyone who criticized or disagreed with him was guilty of treason. Suppression of opposing newspapers and takeovers of TV news networks that used to question government policy show that dissent is no longer tolerated.

"Neither are personal freedoms. Women are particularly aware that safe, legal abortions have not been available in the United States since the Supreme Court overturned *Roe v. Wade* five years ago. Doctors in Canada and Mexico profit from American foolishness. Women who can't leave the country to end an unwanted pregnancy have gone back to the old days of dangerous illegal abortions. Hundreds if not thousands of them are dying every year from botched ones. And, since a fetus is defined as a human being from the instant of conception, they can face a murder charge if they're caught.

"Outside every city of any size along our southern border are concentration camps. They're full of people who tried to come to the United States because they thought it was still a free country. They're also full of people who dared quarrel with Trump and Pence. The Nazis and the Communists would be proud of us. The Founding Fathers are spinning in their graves.

"The Founders are also spinning in their graves because they respected freedom of religion. They did, but Trump and Pence have trampled on it since the day the Russians helped their regime come to power. In the very first year Trump was president, he showed where he stood. When Nazis held a torchlight parade in Charlottesville, Virginia, and chanted 'The Jews will not replace us!', what did he say? Did he condemn them for rioting, and for running down and killing a young woman? You know he didn't. He said there were very fine people on both sides.

"Things have only got worse since, too. Do I even have to mention the Chattanooga Synagogue Massacre of 2025? The pogroms against Somalis in Minnesota? The ignorant racists who firebombed a temple full of Sikhs in St. Louis because they thought the men's turbans meant they were Muslims?

"And what has President Pence done to stop these abuses? Nothing. Nor has he stopped the growing persecution of gays, lesbians, and transgender people. They're against the principles of his narrow religion, and he thinks the laws of his religion are the laws of nature, or at least the laws of the United States of America. I'm sorry—I *am* sorry—but he's wrong."

Nicole Yoshida took a deep breath. "Some people will say the issue of secession was settled when the South tried it, and we fought the Civil War to hold the Union together. Those people are mistaken, and I'll tell you why. The South seceded because the white men who formed the Confederacy formed it so they could go on holding African Americans as slaves. They wanted to take freedom away, not to spread it.

"Things are different now. The government in Washington, D.C., is stealing freedom of the press, freedom of privacy, freedom of movement, and freedom of religion—plus anything the people in the Cabinet can get their hands on. We want to hold on to our freedoms here on the West Coast. The white men who tried to set up the Confederate States 170 years ago would support the Trump-Pence regime today. Too many of their descendants still do."

Fuck you, American South, went through her head. She didn't care. She'd never run for any office there. And, every once in a while, just coming out and telling the truth felt great.

She went on, "The states of Pacifica would have stayed in the USA if we possibly could. We can't. Freedom matters too much to us. Freedom used to matter all over the United States. We hope what we do here today will also make others think about all they've lost over the past fifteen years.

"We would like to live at peace with the nation we've just left. We won't start any fighting with the USA. But we are a country of our own now, with the same rights and duties as any other country. If the United States attacks us, we'll defend ourselves.

"People of the United States, we're your neighbors. We want to be your friends. Your own government will start lying to you about us as soon as I finish talking—maybe even sooner. Don't believe it. Lies are the only way this regime holds on to power. People started counting how often Donald Trump lied after he became president. After a while, they gave up—he lied too often to keep track of.

"Things haven't got better since he died. I'm not telling you anything you don't already know. I'm just trying to explain why Pacifica can't stand it any more. Thank you, and good night."

Governor Lysbakken came on right after she did, and Governor Ng after him. They both kept their speeches short, saying their people had approved the same kind of secession resolutions as California's, and that California's governor had outlined their reasons for leaving the United States.

Dakotah Ng quoted the Nazi-era German minister, Martin Niemöller: " 'First they came for the socialists, and I did not speak out—because I was not a socialist. Then they came for the trade unionists, and I did not speak out—because I was not a trade unionist. Then they came for the Jews, and I did not speak out—because

I was not a Jew. Then they came for me—and there was no one left to speak for me.' "

The governor of Washington looked straight into the camera. "The best time to end evil is when it's still small enough to stop. We never should have elected Donald Trump to begin with. But even if the country as a whole is too frightened or too drunk on the sweet wine of hating everyone who doesn't look just like them, the states of Pacifica aren't. Good-bye, United States, and good luck. You'll need it."

Nicole made air-clapping motions at the monitor. She'd stuck it to the old Confederacy (even as she'd cribbed a bit from South Carolina's Ordinance of Secession). Governor Ng had flipped off the whole rest of the United States.

How many of President Pence's pink, corn-fed, Evangelical supporters liked what they heard from her (assuming the U.S. government let them hear it at all)? How many of them enjoyed it even less because they heard it from a golden face with narrow eyes and a low nose? Quite a few, unless Nicole Yoshida missed her guess, and wasn't that exactly the problem?

Mike Pence needed almost an hour after Governor Ng went off the air to come back on himself. That took him well out of prime time back East. The announcement that Pacifica was going its own way couldn't have been a surprise. He should have had a response canned and ready.

He should have, but he didn't. The Trump-Pence regime's trail of blunders was at least as wide as its totalitarian stripe. And it wasn't as if the current POTUS would draft a reply on his own. He needed speechwriters to turn his incoherence into something like English, and he had to call them back from home or restaurants or bars or opium dens or wherever the hell they went after quitting time.

On the screen, he looked like what he was: the baby boomers last try at holding on to power forever. Nicole imagined him coming out of a coffin rather than a dressing room, but admitted to herself she was just being bitchy.

He blinked a couple of times to show he might be human after all as he stared into the TV camera's cyclops eye. "My fellow Americans, this so-called secession by the so-called country of

14

Pacifica will not stand," he said. "The Republican Party, the party of Abraham Lincoln and Donald J. Trump, defeated secession in 1865. We will beat it again if we have to. Democrats led states out of our wonderful Union then, and Democrats are trying to lead states out of it now."

That *Democrats then, Democrats now* argument had smelled like old fish since the GOP started using it in Trump's first term.

Then Pence got down to the nitty-gritty: "To remind the states now calling themselves Pacifica that their duty is to stay in the United States, I am immediately federalizing all National Guard troops in California, Oregon, and Washington. They no longer owe obedience to state authorities, but will take orders directly from me or from appropriate personnel in the Defense Department.

"And I am ordering all active-duty U.S. military personnel stationed in the states calling themselves Pacifica to high alert, and I direct their commanding officers to prepare plans to bring those states back to their appropriate allegiance by whatever means become necessary.

"Finally, to the elected officials in the states now calling themselves Pacifica, I remind you that secession from the United States is treason against the United States, and that treason is a crime with punishments up to and including death. I hope a word to the wise will be plenty. If not, never let it be said you were not warned.

"God the Father, God the Son, and God the Holy Ghost will bring the United States through these trials, as He has brought America through all the challenges it has faced before," the president of the United States finished. "May He continue to bless this land and to keep it safe and free forevermore. Amen."

A commentator came on to explain to the American people what President Pence had just said, in case they couldn't figure it out for themselves. Given the ignorance that had led the country to where it was, no doubt a lot of them couldn't. The blow-dried blonde—surely no worse than second runner-up as Miss Tennessee or wherever she came from—went on to explain that, since Pacifica was full of gay heathens, the president of the USA was really being generous and merciful by wanting to keep those states in the Union at all.

15

"My ass," Nicole Yoshida said sweetly. She took uncommon pleasure in grabbing the control and making the Fox-CNN bimbo disappear.

As soon as she turned her phone back on, she got a secure call from Axel Lysbakken. Dakotah Ng joined the conversation less than half a minute later. "That didn't take long," Lysbakken remarked. Governor Ng nodded back at him.

So did Nicole. She quoted Benjamin Franklin: " 'We must all hang together or assuredly we shall all hang separately.' "

"Heh," Dakotah Ng said. "That would be funny if only it were funny—know what I mean?"

"I wish I didn't," Nicole answered.

Lysbakken said, "If I'm such a goddamn gay heathen, how come I'm not having a better time?" He'd been watching Fox-CNN, too, then, or maybe the identical message had gone out on all the U.S. news channels. It often did these days.

Someone the phone camera couldn't pick up laughed. Governor Lysbakken glanced left for a moment and smiled, so it was probably his husband.

"Hang on," Nicole said. "I've got a couple of texts the phone is flagging as urgent." She checked them. "First one is from the governor of Hawaii. They're with us, but they can't secede yet. The U.S. military sits on them even harder than it does on San Diego."

"Seattle will be that kind of problem, too," Governor Ng said.

"Uh-huh." Nicole scrolled down. "Uh-oh—this one's from Yang Wang, the Chinese consul–general in San Francisco. He says … Holy crap, he says the PRC welcomes Pacifica into the family of nations, and he's been named acting ambassador!"

"Holy crap is right," Axel Lysbakken said. "Is that good news or bad?"

"Probably." If Nicole sounded abstracted, well, she had good reason to. Of course the People's Republic of China would want to stick its finger in the USA's eye whenever it saw the chance. The trade war that had simmered and sizzled since Donald Trump's first term had kept stock markets in both of the world's largest economies nervous.

Businessmen didn't like uncertainty. The only thing you could be sure of about the Trump-Pence regime was that, if it said one thing today, it would do something else tomorrow.

Her phone chimed softly: another high-priority text. She looked down. "This one is from Scotland. It's from Prime Minister Sturgeon herself. Her government recognizes ours and wishes us as much luck with independence as they've had."

"That *is* good news," Governor Ng said. Scotland had left the United Kingdom and retained membership in the European Union after Brexit. More than a decade and a half now after Leave won the referendum in the UK, what was left of Not-So-Great Britain was still trying to figure out what to do with itself. None of the answers it had come up with so far was pretty.

With some concern in his voice, Lysbakken said, "Our National Guard commanders *will* follow our orders and not Washington's, right?"

"The ones in California will," Nicole said. She'd been weeding out officers who wouldn't, doing it discreetly so the Defense Department wouldn't realize why she wanted Colonel A in the chain of command but not Colonel B.

"Same here," Dakotah Ng agreed.

"It's not as if I haven't been getting ready for the day myself," Lysbakken said. "Still, you worry."

"Yeah." Nicole nodded. "You do." She worried about other things, too. Most of California's population was blue, but that blue part was concentrated along the coast. The same held true for Pacifica's other two states. Most of their area, the rural and agricultural parts, was red, red, red. A disproportionate number of ordinary National Guardsmen came from those parts. If push came to shove, where would their loyalties lie?

When she said that out loud, Governor Ng replied, "They're worrying about the same kind of thing in D.C., too—you bet they are. Fifteen or twenty percent of their personnel come from our states. How many of those people want to shoot at soldiers or bomb civilians who may be their friends and relatives?"

"All of a sudden, I have a lot more sympathy for Abraham Lincoln's generals. For Jeff Davis's, too, come to that," Nicole said.

17

"Some of Nancy Todd Lincoln's relatives fought for the Confederacy," Lysbakken said. "I hope we don't find out firsthand just how complicated life can get."

"That would be good," Nicole said. Her phone let out the important-message chime again. She checked. "*Hello*—This one's from the governor of Nevada. He says .... Basically, he says his state's declaring its neutrality. 'No passage of armed military men of any faction will be permitted by Nevada state authorities,' he says."

" 'What happens in Vegas better not happen in Vegas,' " Governor Ng misquoted.

Governor Lysbakken offered a one-word comment: "Kentucky."

"Kentucky?" The governor of Washington didn't get it. Since she'd specialized in real-estate law, there was no particular reason she should.

Nicole spelled it out for her: "During the first days of the Civil War, Kentucky tried to stay neutral between the United States and the Confederate States. Whoever ticked Kentucky off first would lose it, basically. The Confederates did, and they did. Kentucky wasn't happy being part of the Union, and Lincoln had to sit on it with a lot of soldiers, but it stayed loyal. Loyal enough, I mean."

"It would be nice if Idaho and Arizona did the same thing as Nevada," Lysbakken said.

"Idaho won't," Dakotah Ng said flatly. The other two breakaway governors gave identical mournful nods. Idaho was one of the reddest, most Trumpist states in what was left of the USA. It had long been a refuge for American Nazis and Christian fascists and other right-wing wackos. It would give President Pence whatever his wizened little heart desired, and a free order of fries on the side.

Arizona ... Arizona might be trickier for the USA. It wasn't as reliably reactionary as it had been in years gone by. The federal government could have a harder time moving, say, a column of tanks through the state than it really wanted.

Thinking of that reminded Nicole that the U.S. Interstate Highway System, a lifetime old now, hadn't been built to let people drive fast from Los Angeles to San Francisco or Las Vegas or Phoenix. It had been built so the American military could move men and equipment wherever it wanted, whatever the weather. The I-5, which would become Pacifica's backbone, had more in common with Roman roads than with the street you used to get to the mall.

Before she could remark on that, fighter jets roared over the roof of the governor's mansion. By the way their thunder penetrated even the TV studio's soundproofed walls, they roared maybe six inches over the residence's roof.

She wasn't altogether amazed when, within a couple of minutes, fighters also overflew the governors' mansions in Eugene and Olympia. "I think Mike Pence just sent us a message," Dakotah Ng said, sounding commendably unflummoxed. "As long as they don't drop bombs or shoot rockets or open fire, we don't have to listen," Governor Lysbakken said.

"Even if they do," Nicole insisted. "If we aren't in this for keeps, we shouldn't be in it at all." If Pacifica collapsed at the first threat, secession was a joke, and not a funny one. She sighed. "I wish like hell we could do that over the White House."

She did wonder whether Jefferson Davis had had to deal with as much *tsuris* leaving the United States as she did. The Confederate States, she remembered, had had a provisional Constitution ready to roll out before the shooting started and before the permanent one went into effect for all its four years' worth of permanence.

The Confederates had modeled their Constitution on that of the Union, tweaking it here and there with what they thought were improvements. The Confederate president served a six-year term, and wasn't eligible for more than one. Confederate Cabinet members could debate on the floor of Congress, though they couldn't vote. And not once, not twice, but three times the Confederate Constitution enshrined slavery as a permanent part of the law of the land.

Pacifica had tweaks of its own. To form a body of decent size with room for differing views, each state would get nine senators, not two (the number of senators per state would be reduced if more states adhered to the country; the total number of senators would be capped at thirty). That was easy and noncontroversial.

So was getting rid of the Electoral College. The president and vice president of Pacifica would be elected by direct popular vote, nothing else but. If the United States had had that rule, Donald Trump never would have happened. Neither would the second Bush, for that matter. Nobody complained much about that, either. The other big change ….

If Nicole had had her druthers, Pacifica would have made civilian possession of firearms largely illegal. She didn't get her druthers. Other people whose support she needed feared an outright gun ban would touch off exactly the kind of guerrilla warfare a new nation didn't need.

So the provisional Constitution banned semiautomatic rifles of all types. It didn't say anything about going out and hunting down the hundreds of thousands—millions?—of them already in civilian hands. It did say that people convicted of using one in a crime would have an automatic twenty-five years tacked on to their sentences, years not to be reduced by parole.

Nothing was perfect. A provision like that would help crowd prisons. But, with luck, it would deter some crime. And, with import of new weapons of that kind also prohibited, they would fade out of use little by little.

Nicole Yoshida hoped like hell they would, anyway.

Meanwhile …. Meanwhile, she conferred with Major General Malcolm Washington, the highest-ranking officer in the California National Guard. He looked as if, thirty years earlier, he'd played middle linebacker at a medium-good university. As a matter of fact, he had.

"Ma'am, I think we have this pretty much under control," he said. The LED lights in the ceiling fixtures in her office shone off the chocolate-brown skin of his shaved scalp. "We're weeding out a certain number of undesirables who can't stand the, ah, new arrangements—"

"The idea of Pacifica, you mean," she said.

"Yes, ma'am. The idea of Pacifica," he agreed. "Only a few have gone into the stockade, though, for making threats against the new authorities or for plotting against them. Our people are better at monitoring message systems than they think we are. We have some folks in Silicon Valley to thank for that."

20

"We sure do. And up in Redmond, too," Nicole said. Without high-tech backing, Pacifica would have been a no-go. With it …. With it, the new country had a chance. Nicole didn't like the degree to which the cyberwizards could snoop on the citizens, but that wasn't a problem here alone. That one was as worldwide as the Web. *The fault, dear Brutus, lies not in our stars but in our technology.*

"We have other issues that aren't serious yet, but could get that way in a hurry," General Washington said. "Some of our personnel are getting their credit cut off by U.S. companies, for instance."

"That's … not good," Nicole said slowly. Life ran on credit these days; one of the nastiest things the USA might do was cut off everyone who lived in Pacifica. She didn't want to repudiate debts in what was now a foreign country, but she knew she would if she had to. "We're going to have our own currency. That wasn't high on my list—people all over the world use the dollar—but I may need to move it up." She scribbled a note to herself.

"Yes, ma'am," General Washington said. "One more thing to worry about, one more cloud on the horizon." He chuckled on a sour note. "Never thought I'd be a black man fussing about the ins and outs of secession, but there you are. And here I am."

"Here you are. Would you rather be a black man here or back in the United States?"

"You already know the answer to that one, I expect. Only black folks happy with how things in the USA are these days are what I'd call collaborators. Same with Mexican Americans. Same with Muslims. I don't think the white folks in D.C. have figured out how big a problem they've got when something like a quarter of their population hates the government like poison. And I'm not even talking about the woke whites."

"I wish there were more of them," Nicole said. New York and New Jersey and New England were under what came as close to martial law as made no difference. That the Connecticut state legislature had immediately impeached, convicted, and removed the Trumpist governor Mike Pence appointed sure didn't help. Fear the same would happen here had precipitated secession. But white men—and, distressingly, so many white women—in the South and Midwest remained solidly behind the Trump-Pence GOP.

21

"Doesn't make you real happy about how things roll, does it?" Malcolm Washington said.

"Now that you mention it, no," she answered. He laughed again, as unhappily as before.

She continued, "If push comes to shove, how much of a fight can we put up against the United States?"

"Well, we'll do everything we know how to do, that's for sure." Washington let out one more sandpapery laugh. "But if they give it everything they've got, we're whupped. Don't kid yourself, ma'am. They're a hell of a lot stronger'n we are, pardon my French."

"That's not quite what I meant, or not all of what I meant," she said. "With things the way they are, how close can they come to giving it everything they've got?"

"Ay, there's the rub," he replied, and for a moment she let herself appreciate a general who could quote Shakespeare. "To tell you the truth, I've got no idea. It's not just all the Pacificans they've got in their military. African Americans and Hispanics join up more than white folks do, because they see the uniform as a step towards a better life. How enthused they'd be about shooting at people just to make Mike Pence happy, I don't know. Neither does he, I bet, and if I were in his shoes I wouldn't exactly be itching to find out."

"I was thinking the same thing," Nicole said. Everyone in Pacifica who wanted voted to get the hell out of the USA had thought the same thing. President Pence couldn't be dumb enough to order in the tanks and bombers … could he?

How much evidence was there, though, that anyone in a high position in the Trump-Pence regime had the smarts or even the common sense to carry guts to a bear? Common sense generally, as Nicole knew too well, was much less common than it should have been.

She asked, "What *do* the high-ranking officers in the U.S. military services think of the civilian leadership they've had the past fifteen years? Will they follow whatever orders they get?"

"You know the right questions, ma'am, for sure. I only wish I had answers I was sure of for you," General Washington said. "Early on, I'm pretty sure they were as grossed out as everybody else. Trump named General Mattis Secretary of Defense, remember, and when Mattis quit he told Trump where to go and how to get there."

"I do remember. And Trump was too dumb to figure that out for himself till people drew him a picture," Nicole said.

"Yes, ma'am." This time, Malcolm Washington's laugh actually seemed amused. But mirth didn't last long; he went on, "You've got to remind yourself, though, those guys have been in power a while now, like you said. They've had time to move their people up the chain of command, and to weed out folks they don't like or to just ease them out through retirement. So maybe if Pence says, 'Hop, frog!', they'll just ask, 'How high?'"

"Good Germans," Nicole muttered.

"Yeah." Washington sounded as disgusted as he looked. "Do you have any idea how sick it makes me to see Germany doing a way better job at this whole democracy business than the United States is—I mean, was?"

"I think I may, General. And just in case I don't, I promise you Myron Flegenehim does."

"Who's he?"

"CHP captain. One of my bodyguards. May head up my Secret Service when I decide I have to have a Secret Service. Member of the tribe."

"Okay. Gotcha." Washington nodded.

Growing up in Southern California, Nicole Yoshida had gone to school with a lot of Jewish kids. She didn't know where the general had learned what Jews sometimes half-jokingly called themselves, but he had. In California—in Pacifica—Japanese Americans and African Americans and Jews and most other kinds of Americans got along with one another pretty well more often than not. Nicole had a Jewish sister-in-law and two half-Jewish nephews.

Trump and Pence, by contrast, had been pitting white against brown, brown against black, straight against gay, ever since their gang swindled its way into the White House. The way they'd talked encouraged Aryan cockroaches to crawl out from under flat rocks with AR-15s and shoot up synagogues, and Christian zealots to do the same to mosques. *Divide and conquer* was Rule Number One in their marching orders.

"General, are we making things better or worse?" Nicole asked. She'd been asking herself the same thing since she decided she couldn't stand to leave her state in the USA any more.

"I hope we're making 'em better, ma'am." Malcolm Washington did her the courtesy of not taking the question lightly. "Every time they go and do something horrible back East, I think, *Well, they can't sink any lower than that*. And then they do. They always do. So if we wind up in a concentration camp together, better we wind up there for trying to make things better than for sitting back and letting 'em happen."

"Thanks," she said. "I feel the same way."

Every day that passed felt like a day won to Nicole. Most of the senators and representatives who came home to the West Coast from Washington, D.C., got heroes' welcomes when they did. And most of them would go back into Pacifican politics once elections here got off the ground—of that, the acting president had no doubt.

Along with the Speaker of the House and the House majority leader, the handful of other Republican representatives from rural districts stubbornly stayed back East. "I am an American first and an America Firster. America First is what we should all be about," a congressman from Oregon thundered on the steps in front of the Capitol. All the Fox feeds in the USA played up his speech. "America First, America forever, America right or wrong! I love my country! I love my president! God bless the United States of America! Nobody can tell me I'm not an American any more! This stupid, evil rebellion against the country and against the president will fail, and the people who started it will get what they deserve!"

That congressman, or somebody, had assembled quite a crowd to listen to his rant. Nicole wondered how many of those people—almost all of them white, in a capital mostly black—were there just because they felt like hearing a speech, and how many were getting paid to show up.

She also wondered whether you could still ask that question in the USA without seeing the inside of a jail cell. The press there remained theoretically free, but theory was wonderful. Ever since the *New York Times* got shuttered for "deliberately spreading slanderous lies and misinformation about the administration," theory and practice walked diverging roads.

24

The people in the crowd whooped and hollered for the Oregon congresscritter. A lot of them, men and women, wore red MAGA caps. "Make America great again! Make America whole again!" they chanted in suspiciously good unison.

After the speech ended, a Fox-MSNBC reporter stuck a mic in front of one of the red-capped faithful. "My name? I'm Dave Phillips, from Lansing, Michigan. I'm in Washington on business, and I just came here to listen to democracy in action," he said. "God will help President Pence bring those crazy people out West back to their senses. He says it, and Reverend Graham says it, and I believe it."

"You believe in Reverend Graham, do you?" the reporter asked.

"Yes, ma'am. Sure do," Dave Phillips answered. "God talks through Franklin Graham. You can tell. Anybody can tell."

Paid or not, certainty gleamed in his gray eyes. Nicole turned off the TV. She needed to watch it to keep up with what was going on in the country formerly hers, but more than a few minutes at a stretch made her want to grab a shotgun and blow the big flatscreen to kingdom come.

Maybe the news feed on her iPad wouldn't be so hideous. Or maybe it would. The second story from the top was headlined *Technical difficulties continue to limit BBC access in USA*. The BBC wasn't what it had been, either. Since Britain pulled out of the EU and Scotland took back its independence, the Beeb had swung hard right, too. But it still showed more freedom of action and thought than any U.S.-based news network.

Which was bound to be why it was having those "technical difficulties." Mike Pence and his minions didn't want anyone in the USA getting anything but their predigested pap.

Pacifica still had free speech, or as much as anyone did in this electronically politicized age. Nicole wondered what she'd do if swarms of MAGA-friendly news outlets suddenly started cropping up in places like Fresno and Bakersfield and Pendleton and Clarkston. If they were genuine local efforts, Pacifica might do better ignoring them. If they ran on outside funding, though ....

How could you know for sure? Those operations had got smoother with practice. Everyone would start screaming "Censorship!" if she shut down outfits like that.

25

How much do I care? she asked herself. Then she thought, *In cyberspace, no one can hear you scream.* When she started riffing on taglines from movies that came out about the time when she was born, it was time to go do something else. So she did.

The governor of California—now the acting president of Pacifica—traveled to official functions in an electric Lincoln limo only a little lighter than an armored personnel carrier. Green ... after a fashion. Normally, guests rode in another equally humongous green vehicle. Since her guest on this trip to the Bay Area was her husband, they shared the limo.

That did only so much for the environment. The CHP cars escorting the Lincoln all burned gasoline. For range and pedal-to-the-metal performance, they still topped electrics. The gap had narrowed, but it remained there.

Brent Yoshida sighed as he stretched out in the back seat with Nicole. "I could get used to this First Man business," he said. The Lincoln was about twice the size of the Hyundai he drove to teach his econ classes at Sacramento State.

"I wish I were still just governor. I wish the United States weren't so awful we had to pull out. I remember when it wasn't," Nicole said.

"So do I," her husband said. The Lincoln got rolling. His eyebrows went up. "Quiet in here."

Nicole nodded. "It is." Electrics *were* quiet. And the limo kept outside noise out, too. Not all its weight was in the batteries. Some came from soundproofing. Quite a bit also came from bulletproof glass and armor. The Lincoln probably wasn't so well protected as Mike Pence's fancy ride, but it was in the same ballpark.

Red and blue rooftop lights blinking, the Chippies (only that stupid, ancient TV show ever called them Chips) cleared the path for the limo. It was about ninety miles southwest down the I-80 to San Francisco: a little more than an hour without traffic, probably more like an hour and a half even with the fancy escort.

"It'll be good to see Jacob," Brent said.

"Uh-huh," Nicole said. Their son was at Berkeley, working on a doctorate on the reign of the Holy Roman Emperor Frederick II

Hohenstaufen. He seemed cheerfully resigned to the idea that he might never land a job teaching what he'd studied. His older sister Joyce was more practical. She was doing an oncology residency at a hospital in Spokane.

Once onto the interstate, Nicole idly wondered how people in places like Kazakhstan felt about using leftover Soviet infrastructure. One more thing she'd never figured she'd worry about.

They'd gone past the 505 shortcut up to the 5 and were almost to Vacaville—halfway to San Francisco, near enough—when a thuttering roar penetrated even the limo's soundproofing. It seemed to come from everywhere at once. "What the devil is that?" Brent said.

"Oh, good! I was gonna ask you the same thing," Nicole said.

Their driver, a CHP sergeant named Eric Mendoza, said, "Ma'am, we've got helicopters landing on the freeway in front of the motorcade. I think maybe you and your husband better sit tight. This is liable to be trouble."

Nicole's angle of view from the back seat was a lot narrower, but she saw them a moment later. The cop cars in front of the Lincoln slowed to a stop. So did the limo, and, Nicole presumed, the CHP cars behind it. Were more copters landing in back of those cars? She twisted in the seat to see out the rear window. Sure as hell, they were.

These weren't the black helicopters right-wing conspiracy maniacs babbled about. They came close, though: they were a dark, menacing green. And they didn't come from the UN. They had the American star-in-a-circle-with-bars painted on their flanks in slightly lighter green. When Nicole saw that, she realized what kind of trouble they were liable to be in.

Brent was thinking along with her, as he so often did. Thirty years of marriage helped that happen. "Psychiatrists must love those people," he said. "Everything they claim the other side is guilty of, they do themselves. Trump was the biggest crook in the world, so he had the MAGAts yell, 'Lock Hillary up!' The people with the tinfoil hats wail about UN helicopters, and look! American helicopters! Projection, I think the shrinks call it."

"Yeah," Nicole said tightly. "And *I* think we're about to have one of those 'unfortunate accidents' that happen to people they don't like. They learned that one from Putin. You never saw so many peo-ple have unfortunate accidents as the ones in Russia."

"Sometimes they were nine-millimeter accidents," Brent re-marked. He still sounded very calm. Maybe he couldn't believe things like this happened in what had been the United States of America. Nicole only wished she couldn't.

Men started jumping out of the copters and trotting purpose-fully toward the motorcade. *They* wore black from head to toe: only the skin around their eyes was visible. And they carried weapons.

The Chippies in the cars (or maybe some belonged to the Na-tional Guard; Nicole hadn't worried about the arrangements, though she realized she'd have to start doing that if she ever got another chance) didn't wait for the SEALs or Special Forces guys or what-ever they were to get close. Some of them hopped out and opened fire. Others started shooting from inside their vehicles.

A moment later, two bullets starred the front windshield. Nei-ther got through. "Holy fucking shit!" Brent said. Nicole couldn't have put it better herself.

"Get down, goddammit!" Sergeant Mendoza explained loudly.

Nicole didn't, not right away. One of the people who'd got out of a CHP car didn't just have a pistol or an assault rifle. He carried some kind of fat tube. Crouching behind the passenger-side door of his ve-hicle, he aimed it at the closest helicopter and did … whatever he did.

Whoosh! Trailing a tail of flames, some kind of missile or RPG flew on its short but merry way. It slammed into the copter just be-hind the cockpit. The copter turned into a fireball.

"I hope we have some more of those!" Nicole said. People had just died in that fireball. She was amazed how little she cared. They were people who were trying to kill her or kidnap her or do some-thing else horrible to her. As far as she was concerned, that shoved them right out of the sympathy bin.

Something slammed in through the rear window's bulletproof glass and showered her and Brent with shards. It slammed out through the windshield, too. "That was a fifty-caliber round," Men-doza said. "Will you get the fuck down now, *please?*"

Nicole got the fuck down. So did her husband. "I'm supposed to protect you," he said. "I don't even have a pocket knife."

"I don't think a pocket pocketknife would do you a whole lot of good right now," she answered. "Under the circumstances, I mean."

The sergeant opened the side window partway, quickly fired three times, and shut it again as fast as he could. The noise of gunfire from only a few feet away was staggering, stunning. Nicole's ears rang, the way they would have after two hours at a concert with the amps cranked up to eleven.

"Got the fucker in the face." Sergeant Mendoza's voice sounded as if it were coming from a long way off, but she could make out what he said. "They can't armor that."

"Good!" Brent said. He also seemed convinced the people from the not-quite-black helicopters weren't on the side of truth and justice, no matter if they thought they were following the American way.

After what seemed like forty years, but couldn't have been longer than two or three minutes, the din outside died away. Like a submariner wanting to surface, Nicole asked, "Can we come up now?"

"Hang on." Instead of a 9mm or a .45 or whatever the pistol was, her driver pulled out his iPhone. He had to dial two or three times before he got somebody. When he finally did, the conversation seemed at least half obscenities. He stuck the phone back in his pocket. "Yeah, come up. The bad guys are all down, and we've got help on the way. They underestimated the stuff and the kind of people we have with us."

"Do they have help on the way, too?" Brent asked as he scrambled back onto the rear seat. Nicole wished he hadn't. She could too easily imagine one more helicopter hovering half a mile off to one side and ripple-firing rockets from pods on its wing stubs.

All Sergeant Mendoza said was, "Let's hope like hell they don't." Maybe he was seeing the same thing in his mind's eye. He didn't seem to like it much, either.

Nicole looked ahead, behind, and off to the side. What she saw put her in mind of hell or a Jerry Bruckheimer movie, assuming there was a difference. Helicopters and CHP cars burned, sending clouds of thick, greasy black smoke into the sky. Bodies in black and bodies in khaki sprawled on the interstate. They bled a lot more for real than they did in pictures.

And the Sacramento-bound side of the I-80 was another sub-urb of hell. How many drivers had got caught in the crossfire? A couple of cars over there were burning, too. More had crashed into one another.

People on that side who weren't trying to help the wounded or call 911 were taking photos and videos with their phones. No doubt they were uploading their images to Twitter and Zeep and Instagram and Facebook2. These days, U.S. social media got censored almost as tightly as Weibo in China, but sometimes a word like *almost* mattered. People outside of Pacifica would get to see some of this.

Which reminded Nicole. She fished out her own phone, took a brief video, and uploaded it to Twitter with the comment, *The USA just invaded a foreign country at peace with it. Is President Pence after his own Fort Sumter?*

Somebody tapped on the limo's side window. Nicole looked over in alarm, but it was only Captain Flegenheim, a cigarette dangling from the corner of his mouth. She hit the switch, and the window went down. The people who'd built the Lincoln did good work.

"Glad you're all right, ma'am," Flegenheim said. He had blood on his tunic, but it didn't seem to be his.

"Glad you are, too," Nicole said. With the windows down, she smelled more smoke and charred meat than she had through the bullet holes. She smelled some other pretty basic odors, too. Why she hadn't crapped or pissed herself, she couldn't have said, but she hadn't … quite. Others had looser sphincters.

"We have a couple of POWs, I guess you'd call them," Myron Flegenheim told her. "Wounded, but not too bad. We're going to question them, if that's okay."

"No rough stuff," Nicole said. Washington, D.C.'s, twenty-first-century infatuation with concentration camps and torture was not the smallest part of what had driven the West Coast out of the USA. "No, ma'am, none of that," he agreed. And maybe he was sin-cere, and maybe he was telling her they wouldn't do anything where anybody could see. She couldn't read his face.

"I mean it." She wanted to say more, but left it there. These peo-ple had just been through a firefight to keep her alive and free. Some of them were wounded, too, and some dead … for her. She couldn't make herself warn them about their jobs.

He nodded, less mechanically than he'd spoken a moment before. *We're all in shock*, she realized. "We know what the rules are. We'll play by them. We aren't Homeland Security goons," he said.

"Okay." She nodded. Myron Flegenheim sketched a salute and went back to taking care of whatever needed to be taken care of. Ambulances screamed up. So did more CHP cars and cars and vans full of ordinary cops. No, not ordinary cops—SWAT guys tumbled out of them, with assault rifles and body armor and, no doubt, other toys, as well.

"Is this an act of war?" Brent asked.

"I don't exactly know. Depends on how much deniability they've got. But I'm going to try to find out." Nicole dialed the White House switchboard. "This is the acting president of Pacifica. I want to talk about Pence's an attempted murder or kidnapping just now."

"The president of the United States does not recognize any entity by the name of Pacifica," the flunky on the other end of the line said primly.

Nicole almost told her where to stick her headset, and how. But that wouldn't have been diplomatic. And, during the Civil War, Abraham Lincoln and Jefferson Davis had played these stupid prestige games, too. Sighing, she said, "He will. But tell him the governor of California is on the phone, then. He's not too pure to talk to the governor of California, right?"

"Please hold."

She waited. The hold music played things like "Onward Christian Soldiers" and "The Battle Hymn of the Republic," all done by 10,001 strings. If she had to listen to it for very long, she thought she might use a 10,0002nd one to string herself up. But Pence came on the line fairly fast. "Governor Yoshida!" he said. "What do you claim happened to you just now?"

"I don't claim it happened. It happened. You landed some army copters in front of my motorcade and behind it. The men who got out of them didn't intend to invite me to church." Yes, that hold music had got to her. "Luckily, my bodyguards were loaded for bear, too. There's a hell of a mess on the I-80, but your people

31

didn't get to assassinate me or fly me off to a prison or a concentration camp."

"I don't have any idea what you're talking about, Governor Yoshida. Nothing like this was done at my orders. Please believe me when I assure you of that." Mike Pence sounded sincere. He was good at it. He was also good at lying through his teeth—maybe not quite so good as Donald Trump had been, but plenty good enough to keep enough people in the USA enthralled.

Not Nicole. "They call that plausible deniability, don't they? Except it isn't plausible. The army wouldn't do anything like that without orders. We have prisoners, by the way. We'll see what they tell us."

"You must believe I had nothing to do with whatever happened to you, nothing at all," Pence said.

"Sorry. I don't believe it at all." She thought of Henry II growling, *Who will rid me of this turbulent priest?* Not a direct order, but a couple of tough guys with swords hopped on their horses and Thomas à Becket wound up dead. Henry cried crocodile tears afterwards, which did Becket no good at all. "Are we at war?"

"Not unless you want us to be."

"I don't," Nicole said quickly; she saw the teeth in that trap. "All I want is for this new country to stay at peace with everybody else—and that includes the United States."

"You can't make a new country by saying you have," Pence replied.

"You can't kill a new country by killing its acting president," Nicole said. *Not when your plot goes haywire, anyway.*

"None of these unfortunate events—which I'm seeing for the first time on my computer as we speak—has anything to do with me. No one can prove it does," the POTUS said. With that last sentence, he might have begun to approach something resembling truth. He was careful about covering his tracks. Trump had barely bothered.

Nicole wagged a finger at him even though they had no video link. "Your Uncle Vladimir will be disappointed in you. When he sets out to murder people, they stay murdered."

"Good afternoon, Governor Yoshida. I think we've said everything we have to say to each other," Pence said, and the line went dead.

"He denies everything?" Brent asked.

"Of course he does." Nicole didn't bother hiding her scorn.

Her husband said, "I texted Joyce and Justin. They know we're in one piece—and he knows we'll be late getting into the Bay Area."

"Good. We're lucky we're not late, period." Nicole gave her attention to Sergeant Mendoza. "*Can* we go on to San Francisco?"

"Ma'am, I think so, once the damage-control people deal with the wreckage in front of us and we get some more folks to ride shotgun for you," he said. "I don't think they fired a whole lot at the limo, and only that one .50-cal round got through. Motor and batteries don't seem damaged. The tires are run-flats, so we can get to San Francisco even if they've lost air. Probably ought to have somebody put on a new set before we head back to Sacramento, though."

"Tend to that, please," Nicole said, and he bobbed a nod. Something was coming the wrong way up the road behind the wrecked helicopters that blocked the path forward. Several somethings: red fire trucks and yellow bulldozers. The trucks laid foam down on the copters and on a couple of the CHP cars that had been in front of the limos. Once the fires had been reduced to smolders, the dozers shoved the junk off onto the shoulder.

The asphalt was smoldering, too. The fire trucks doused it. Captain Flegenheim pronounced himself satisfied with the numbers and competence of Nicole's new guards. The revised procession rolled on. It wasn't Sarajevo in 1914—but not from lack of effort.

"Ladies and gentlemen, it is my great pleasure—a pleasure even greater than I thought it would be—to introduce to you Nicole Yoshida, acting president of Pacifica!" the mayor of San Francisco said. She waved Nicole forward.

Applause was a politico's drug. Nicole had got into the game late, so she was nearing middle age before she realized what a rush it gave. She knew it now, though. And she needed that rush. She was running on adrenaline fumes.

"Thank you very much. It's good to be here. After what happened earlier today, it's good to be anywhere," she said.

33

More applause came, loud and fierce and angry. Shouts of *Lock him up!* and *Down with the USA!* rang through the hall. Nothing pumped up patriotism like having your leader shot at.

Nicole said, "I came here to talk about what we need to do to revive the Pacific Coast Stock Exchange as an independent organization. It joined the New York Stock Exchange in 2006, I know. That was fine as long as Pacifica was part of the USA. But an independent country needs an independent bourse."

More applause filled the room. "I was going to talk about all the great companies based in Pacifica that might want to shift their trading to the revived PCSE," Nicole went on. "You know the ones I mean: tech, biotech, entertainment, aerospace. You can name the names as well as I can."

She sipped from the glass of water someone had thoughtfully left on the lectern. The inside of her mouth felt dry and rough as sandpaper. *Amazing what terror will do*, she thought as she set the glass down. Her hand didn't shake … too much.

"I was going to talk about things like that, yes," she said. "I was going to, but I won't now. We are still in great danger, and the USA is every bit as bad as we thought it was when we walked away from it—maybe even worse."

The crowd booed the United States. They knew too well what it had turned into over the past fifteen years. Nicole wondered, though, how ready they were to fight if it came to that. Pacifica would make a perfectly good European-style country like France or Spain.

But Ukraine and Poland might have made perfectly good European countries, too. Russia had nibbled off the Crimea and much of the land in eastern Ukraine, and kept trying to destabilize and gobble up what remained independent. Trump and Pence hadn't let out a peep of protest.

So far, Russia hadn't done more than threaten Poland. But the Polish government, by now, leaned about as far toward fascism as Moscow did. Nicole didn't want to imagine that happening to Pacifica, which would also have a large, aggressive, right-leaning neighbor.

"We'll have to be careful," she said. She hated words like *vigilant* and *resilient*; the U.S. government had used them too much to

34

steal power and freedom from the people. "We'll have to try to stay strong and try to stay free at the same time. It won't be easy. It won't come cheap. We're going to have to make hard choices. We may have to fight. I don't want to. I don't think any of us wants to. But it takes two to make and keep a peace. One can start a war."

Not so much clapping now. People up and down the West Coast hadn't really believed the USA might be willing to kill to enforce their allegiance. Nicole hadn't really believed it herself. She ran a hand through her hair. She still had little bits of glass in it.

"A long time ago," she finished, "a Roman named Vegetius said, 'If you want peace, ready yourself for war.' That's hard, harsh advice. Nobody wants to hear it. Enjoying yourself and hoping everything will turn out fine is easier, cheaper, more comfortable, and more fun. But the Roman Empire fell not long after Vegetius lived. Going on and doing what you please isn't guaranteed. You have to earn it. I'll do my best to make sure Pacifica does just that."

She stepped back from the lectern. Here and there, somebody clapped. A big part of the audience sat on its hands, though. She hadn't expected anything else. People wanted to hear good news from politicians. Telling the truth instead was hazardous to your job security. Right this minute, she didn't much care. If they wanted somebody to take them down the rocky road to independence, she'd do that. And if they decided they'd rather bow down before the all-holy Mike Pence instead ....

New Zealand is still a pretty civilized country. Canada, too, even if not so much as it used to be, she thought, and turned and walked offstage.

Sacramento was hot a lot of the time. The Imperial Valley, down by the Mexican border, was hot almost all the time. When irrigated, its soil was some of the most spectacularly fertile in the world. Most of the people who grew its crops were Hispanics. Most of them had crossed the border to work here, or had parents or grandparents who'd done that. You heard more Spanish than English.

Pacifican flags waved everywhere in the town of Imperial. No place up and down the coast was more eager for independence than this stretch of farm country. Nicole wondered how many of the brown people lining the streets here had relatives in a U.S. concentration camp.

One would have been one too many. The United States had no business building concentration camps to begin with. Nicole didn't realize she'd said that out loud till her driver nodded. "Damn straight, ma'am," he said. "That's why we close this one down, huh?"

"You bet," she said.

"Well, that and to send out the pics that show what a bunch of douchebags the USA's got running things," Sergeant Mendoza added. "Some of the people back East, they still gotta have working consciences, am I right?"

"I sure hope you are," she replied. "I wonder how many of the kids in the camps have working consciences any more, too. Some of them have been inside tents and barbed wire since they were toddlers, and now they're just about old enough to vote. Some of the children in the camps have had children in the camps."

"Can't even do an abortion in there if a fifteen-year-old gets pregnant. It'd be sinful," Mendoza said.

"Right," Nicole said tightly. She did worry about letting camp kids out into the wider world. Sure as hell, some of them *would* cause trouble, and would make people think they should have stayed confined. But if Pacifica *didn't* free children from concentration camps, what kind of country was it? Why had it wanted to leave the United States to begin with?

As for the political prisoners …The United States wasn't supposed to hold political prisoners. It was supposed to free them in other countries. The Trump-Pence regime hadn't read that book, though, or many others.

The motorcade picked up National Guard (only the nation was Pacifica now) muscle as it rolled out of Imperial on Highway 86 toward Calexico, the border, and the concentration camp outside of town. The M-60 tanks were obsolete, but obsolete tanks beat the crap out of no tanks at all. The Bradley fighting vehicles had fought in Afghanistan, probably in Iraq. The M-113 armored personnel carriers might have fought in the first Gulf War, back in the twentieth century. For all Nicole knew, some had fought in Vietnam before she was born. They still ran, though.

ICE had fortified Camp Calexico. They hadn't fortified it to hold off this kind of firepower. Nicole hoped like blazes they hadn't, anyhow.

Getting down to the camp didn't take long. Inside the barbed-wire perimeter, the Stars and Stripes still waved. Seeing the flag she'd grown up loving flown over a place like this made Nicole furious and hideously sad at the same time.

The tanks and Bradleys and APCs fanned out into the desert, belching diesel fumes and kicking up dust and sand with their tracks. This time, Nicole's car wasn't protected by the Highway Patrol. The Humvees with her limo were of the same vintage as the Bradleys, but each of them carried soldiers and mounted a Ma Deuce. Nicole shivered, remembering the fat round that had punched through her "bulletproof" glass as if it weren't there.

She got out of the Lincoln at the gated entrance to the camp. Signs in English, and not very good Spanish, warned about unauthorized entry. They didn't say *All hope abandon, ye who enter here*, but they might as well have. The ICE guys (some of whom were women, which irked Nicole) at the checkpoint looked nervous.

Malcolm Washington hopped down from one of the Humvees and walked over to her. He nodded to the people on the other side of the barbed wire. "Open up and let us in," he said. "First, last, and only time I ask. You won't like what happens if you say no, promise."

"You wouldn't dare!" a woman with captain's bars said shrilly. "This facility is under federal jurisdiction!"

"You should get out of your camp more often. There've been some changes made," Nicole said dryly.

General Washington said, "Lady, you dick around with me, Nacho over there'll put a burst of .50-cal through your brisket and whatever's behind it. He's got a cousin in one of these fucking camps, so he'll smile real big when he does it. And if the balloon goes up, the big guns on the M-60s won't leave enough of you assholes to bury. So what's it gonna be?"

"I comply under protest," the ICE captain said.

"As long as you do it," the general said. "Order your people here to lay down their weapons. Get on the horn with the rest of the camp. Tell everybody to keep away from weapons. If any of you start anything at all, I promise you won't like how we finish it. Got that?"

"I understand you." The captain spoke into a radio. She listened, then spoke again, more sharply this time. Nicole heard "… they'll murder us." After more back and forth, the captain set the radio and her pistol on the ground. "Your orders will be followed. Under protest, like I told you, but they will."

"Good," Nicole said, at the same time as General Washington responded, "As long as they are."

The other ICE personnel at the gate set down their weapons and communications devices. As one of them unlatched the gate, the captain pointed at the Stars and Stripes and said, "Aren't you ashamed to be doing this where that can see you?"

"We could ask you the same question here. As a matter of fact, we're going to be asking you the same question," Nicole said.

Malcolm Washington added, "What's a flag, anyway? Ambrose Bierce called it 'A colored rag borne above troops and hoisted on forts and ships.' It appears to serve the same purpose as certain signs that one sees on vacant lots in London— 'Rubbish may be shot here.' "

"Who?" the ICE captain said blankly. Washington had wasted the splendid quotation on her. She sank even lower in Nicole's estimation, something she hadn't dreamt possible.

Vehicles started entering Camp Calexico. Dismounted National Guard troops took charge of the weapons, phones, and radios the ICE personnel had surrendered. They started frisking them for holdout guns and devices, too.

"What are you doing with us? Uh, to us?" the captain demanded.

"Placing you under arrest," Nicole said.

"On what charge?" The other woman looked and sounded gobsmacked—a telling measure of how FUBAR'd things here really were. She went on, "We were only carrying out the commands our superiors gave us."

"Honey, that defense didn't fly at the Nuremberg trials eighty-five years ago, and it won't fly now, either," Nicole answered. "As for the charge …. If things in there look the way I'm afraid they will, it'll probably be crimes against humanity."

"You can't do that!" the captain said.

"No? I don't know what world you're living in, but it sure isn't the real one," Nicole said, reflecting that that had been the USA's problem since 2016. When she got back into the limo and closed the door, the AC felt wonderful. "Take me to the tents," she told Mendoza.

"You got it, ma'am." Silent as thought, the electric Lincoln limo rolled forward. So did some Humvees and APCs. And so did a couple of Bradleys, for the persuasive power their tanklike looks and the 20mm cannon in their turrets carried.

The tents that housed kids, especially the ones in the middle of the cluster, looked old and weary. The sun had paled their walls and roofs. Here and there, paint that didn't quite match covered up graffiti. Camp Calexico had been here long enough to have settled into an unhappy middle age. It couldn't last forever, but was trying to pretend it could.

Do concentration camps have midlife crises? Nicole wondered. In this case, she knew the answer. Camp Calexico was about to.

Farther on, an internal barbed-wire fence cut the camp in half. The politicals were on the other side. She saw a few men with gray jumpsuits and shaven heads up against the fence, trying to find out what was going on over here.

ICE agents milled around in front of the kids' tents, looking worried and alarmed. The German guards at Dachau and Buchenwald had looked the same way when Allied soldiers got there; Nicole had seen pictures of them online. The inmates at those places had avenged themselves on some of the worst guards. Nicole hoped it wouldn't come to that here.

She'd just opened the door to get out when Malcolm Washington's voice boomed from his Humvee's PA system: "Don't do anything stupid, people! Any mistake you make will be your last one. Cooperate with Pacifica's lawful authorities and we'll do our best to keep you safe. You got that?" He sounded like the voice of God. Nicole wondered if he was thinking about the German camp guards, too.

Behind Nicole, along with heavily armed soldiers sweating in body armor, came reporters and camerapeople. They seemed to worry and alarm the ICE personnel more than the tough guys with assault rifles. A plump ICE sergeant blurted, "No media allowed inside the perimeter!"

"You don't give the orders here any more," Nicole said. "Don't you think it's about time you figured that out?"

Again, the Pacifican soldiers took charge of the ICE agents, searching them to make sure they hadn't stashed any weapons, radios, or phones. More soldiers started going through the administrative tents on this side of the internal fence—the politicals had their own set. Some of the soldiers were ordinary rifle-toters. Despite camo uniforms, others gave off the aura of Silicon Valley. People here might try to delete things they didn't want the outside world knowing about. Nicole would have bet—was betting—they wouldn't succeed.

"You better watch yourself, lady," the ICE sergeant said as she walked towards a tent with C27 stenciled by the flap. "Ain't nothin' but animals in there."

"If they are animals, you made them that way," Nicole answered. He stared at her with no more comprehension than if she'd answered him in Turkish.

A couple of National Guard soldiers trotted past her and went into the tent before she could. That was their job. As soon as they did, and as soon as the kids inside realized they had Pacifica's dark green flag on their sleeves instead of the Stars and Stripes, the tent erupted in cheers.

She went inside. It was as bad as she'd thought it would be. The concrete floor was filthy. The air stank of unwashed people, backed-up plumbing, and stale food. A few fans stirred the air around, but there was no AC. She wouldn't have let half so many people crowd in here. The kids—she didn't think anyone in the tent was over twenty or so—were skinny and dirty and grubby.

Brown eyes stared at her from brown faces. Well, she had brown eyes, too, and if her skin wasn't quite so brown as most of theirs, it wasn't white, either. They chattered together in a mix of Spanish and English. Like a lot of the non-Hispanic Californians, she had acquired bits and pieces of Spanish herself.

One of them asked her the questions that mattered: "Who you, lady? What you gonna do with us?"

"I'm the acting president of Pacifica. California, Oregon, and Washington aren't part of the United States any more," Nicole answered. She waited to see if they were surprised. They weren't, or not very. If you had a phone, you could find out whatever you needed to know. And people had phones, or could get their hands on them, even in places like this. She went on, "We're closing down Camp Calexico as fast as we can. If you're of legal age, you'll be free. If you're not, we'll try to reunite you with your parents. If we can't, you'll go into our foster-care system till you are of legal age."

Kids who knew more English translated for ones who knew less. As they all got the word, they looked delighted. They would have been less so had they known more about California's overstretched, underfunded foster-care arrangements. Then again, compared to the malicious neglect they got here, even foster care might look good.

She ducked out of the odorous, overcrowded tent. Other places on this side she wanted to see were the kitchens and the infirmary. The kitchens seemed to specialize in sandwiches and casseroles that might have started prison riots at San Quentin or Folsom. If *Bad and Not Much* wasn't their motto, it should have been.

An infirmary for kids that had its own maternity ward …. Like Camp Calexico as a whole, it made her sad and furious at the same time. She asked a maybe sixteen-year-old who was nursing a baby boy, "Where's the school here?" The girl just stared at her. She tried in her bad Spanish: "*¿Donde está la escuela?*"

She got an answer, but one much too quick and colloquial for her to follow. The girl in the next bed had enough English to translate: "She says there used to be one when she was little. I remember it, too. But they shut it down a long time ago."

"What do you do with your time?" Nicole asked helplessly. Both girls just shrugged. The babies they were holding gave one answer. But you couldn't do that all the time.

An ICE nurse, who looked as if she wanted to spit rivets at the invaders, said, "This isn't the Hilton, you know."

"Yes, I noticed," Nicole replied. "Not even close. It's not even the Trump Tower."

The nurse gave her a dirty look. "They came here illegally. They can take their chances."

"They're still people," Nicole said. "My grandparents got thrown into camps like this during World War II. That was bad enough. But we're way richer now than we were then, and we aren't fighting the countries these kids came from. We've got no excuses at all

41

for this ... and this is why Pacifica isn't part of the United States any more."

"They came here illegally," the nurse repeated. "What you're doing is illegal, too, and ungodly. All you sinners will burn in hell on account of it."

"When Jesus said 'Suffer the little children to come unto me,' He didn't mean 'let them suffer' or 'make them suffer,'" Nicole answered. "He meant 'permit them to come to me.'"

"The Devil can quote Scripture to his purpose," the nurse sniffed.

"Yes, I've noticed that with Franklin Graham." Nicole turned away.

She'd just stepped out of the infirmary tent when General Malcolm Washington strode up to her. Saluting, he said, "We have Camp Calexico secured, ma'am. No trouble—well, not much. One of the ICE people didn't want to hand over his phone, and two or three of my guys gave him a good, old-fashioned stomping while his friends watched. He's not ... too badly hurt. We're taking care of him. We ought to bill the U.S. government for the cost of patching him up."

"Do it. Anything that gets on their nerves is fine by me."

"Yes, ma'am. And some of the things I've seen here .... The political side is even worse than this. Dachau in the desert, sure as hell. Forced labor and starvation rations."

Wearily, Nicole ran a hand through her hair. "I only wish I were surprised."

"Yeah. I know. When the whole country sees what they're doing here—I mean the whole old country, from sea to shining sea and like that—everybody will know what a pack of heartless bastards they've got running things back in D.C."

"Everybody's known that since Donald Trump gave his inaugural address—at the latest, since he fired his FBI director a few months after that," Nicole answered. "The trouble is, too many people just don't care. And they can see all the horrible pictures of concentration camps we put online, and all they'll say is, 'Those shitty foreigners and traitors deserve it.' In too much of the old United States, if you aren't the right color and if you didn't grow up speaking English, you can't be a human being, much less an American."

"You aren't the right color. Neither am I." Washington spoke with a certain somber pride.

"Yes, I've noticed. An awful lot of people in Pacifica aren't. That worries me, too. It gives the people in D.C. one more excuse to speak stupidly and carry a big stick."

"That isn't quite how Teddy Roosevelt put it," the National Guard CO said with a chuckle.

"You know that. So do I. Those clowns in D.C.? I sure wouldn't bet anything I couldn't afford to lose." Like General Washington, she found herself saying *D.C.* a lot of the time when she meant the capital of the USA. Not only was Washington his name, it was also the name of one of Pacifica's constituent states. *Disambiguation*, she thought: an ugly, bureaucratic-sounding word, but sometimes a necessary one.

The U.S. government condemned what it called the illegal occupation of a federal facility and demanded the immediate release of all ICE personnel taken into custody. Nicole refused. Not only had they treated the kids and politicals in their hands with something closer to active cruelty than neglect, the ex-detainees told lurid stories about drug smuggling and about guards lying down with girls—and occasionally boys—under their control.

Some of the guards' confiscated phones had photos and videos on them to back up the lurid tales, too. "You know," Nicole remarked to Myron Flegenheim, "when I was a kid, back in the twentieth century, most of the time people just *did* things. They didn't take pictures of themselves doing them. They especially didn't take pictures of themselves doing them when the pictures could land them in trouble."

"Nobody'd ever heard of a selfie," the CHP captain agreed—he was three or four years older than Nicole. "Not like that any more, though. And if you're under thirty-five, maybe under forty, you don't remember when it was like that."

"Nope." Nicole tried for a wry grin, but feared she came closer to a sour smirk. "Welcome to Old Fart Land."

"Hey, if your kids are anything like mine, they'll tell you you were born an *alter kakker*." Flegenheim paused. "That's *old fart* in Yiddish, or close enough."

"I've heard it," Nicole said. And so she had, mostly from Hollywood types and from Silicon Valley neckbeards. She knew the literal meaning, too. Knowing it didn't mean she felt like talking about it, so she changed the subject: "You know what else we need to do?"

"No, ma'am, but you're probably gonna tell me, aren't you?" The CHP man had guarded her since she became governor of California. He thought that gave him the right to get snarky with her every now and then. Since he didn't push it, she'd always let it ride.

"You bet I am," she said now. "We need to start getting U.S. military personnel out of Pacifica. Without starting a war, I mean."

"That'd be nice," Flegenheim said, deadpan.

"Which? Getting American troops out or not starting a war?"

"You pick."

Nicole gave him a few syllables' worth of laughter. Then she went on, "Suppose we let, say, the Marines at Camp Pendleton know that if they're from Pacifica, and they'd rather serve their proper country instead of the United States, we won't let the Feds drag them back."

"That'd be about one jarhead in six, something like that," Captain Flegenheim said. Nicole nodded; everyone in Pacifica made that calculation these days. He asked the next relevant question: "Are we strong enough to get away with it?"

"General Washington says that if they start a big war, we'll lose. That's been true since Day One. But God only knows what a big war would do to our economy, or to the USA's. The general thinks we can protect them up to a point."

"He's got his head on pretty straight," Flegenheim said—no small praise, coming from him.

"I think so, too," Nicole said. "It's already happened a fair number of times, even without our pushing. We'd just make more noise about it, squeeze Mike Pence a little harder."

Flegenheim muttered something under his breath. Nicole thought it was *Squeeze the balls Mike Pence hasn't got a little harder.* She didn't want to know for sure badly enough to ask. The captain went on, "Suppose military people who aren't from Pacifica want to join us? Or suppose Pacificans who're stuck in the USA want to come back?"

44

"Repatriation," Nicole said, and Myron Flegenheim nodded. There'd been a lot of that after the Confederacy seceded but before the shooting started. Men who'd been friends and comrades in arms had last meals and last drinks together and then went their separate ways. Pretty soon they'd start trying to kill one another, and often enough they'd do it.

The Southerners, for instance, let William Tecumseh Sherman leave his teaching post in Louisiana and fight for the U.S. Army, and spent the next four years regretting it. And, after Lee turned down the Union's offer to command its armies, they let him go home to Virginia and serve the Confederate States.

Things might not be so gentlemanly now.

And not all the movement during the Civil War was exactly repatriation, either. Some men from the North fought for the South, and vice versa. In time of the breaking of nations, life got … interesting.

She realized she hadn't exactly answered Flegenheim. That was what woolgathering did to you. She said, "We have had some people in the U.S. military go AWOL so they could come back to Pacifica and serve here. Only it isn't exactly AWOL if the U.S. government's authority doesn't run here."

"The Feds won't look at it like that," he replied, which was bound to be true.

Instead of admitting as much, she went on, "Right now, we haven't taken military volunteers from other American states. Immigration issues are going to be fun."

"You think? Maybe a little?" Flegenheim said. Nicole laughed. It was laugh or pound her head on the desk. How many Americans, blue voters trapped in red, red states, would want to go West, young person of whatever gender, go West? And how many agents would the FBI, taking its cue from its Russian chums, plant among them?

Correspondingly, how many people from rural California and Oregon and Washington would want to pull up stakes and move someplace where they liked the politics? The number wouldn't be as large, but it wouldn't be small, either.

"Exchange of populations," Nicole muttered, more than half to herself. Greece and Turkey'd had a big one when they got done fighting each other in the aftermath of World War I. As those things went, it had even worked fairly well. The bigger one between newborn India and Pakistan following World War II, though, had been a blood-soaked disaster.

"We can't hold all the people who want to get out of Trump-and-Pence-Land," Flegenheim said. "Not even close."

"I know." Nicole didn't want to contemplate that, either. The worst thing the USA could do to Pacifica would be to expel all its liberals and say something like, *If you don't want to be here, we'll send you somewhere you do want to be. See how you like it there!*

They couldn't do that. Could they? How many illegal immigrants had ICE and the FBI combed out of American cities these past ten or fifteen years? How many of them were sitting in camps on the Mexican side of the border right now? Too many had nowhere else to go. Give those camps a couple of generations and they'd be just as horrible as the ones that warehoused Palestinians.

"You know what it looks like to me, ma'am?" Myron Flegenheim said. Nicole raised an eyebrow and waited. She didn't need to wait long: "It looks to me like this is one of those damn stories without a happy ending anywhere."

"It better not be," Nicole said. "If we can't find a happy ending here, nobody's going to find one anywhere. You have to try. Trying, sometimes, means more than doing."

He didn't answer. Considering what he probably would have said, that was bound to be a kindness.

Nicole had occasion to remember the conversation with the man who'd become her boss bodyguard a few days later. The people in Pacifica who liked Trump-and-Pence-Land better than the new nation in which they found themselves called the Fresno Convention. If Pacifica had seceded from the USA, they were damn well going to secede from Pacifica.

She thought about West Virginia at the start of the Civil War. It hadn't been a state then, just a poor, backward part of Virginia. Hardly anyone in what became West Virginia had enough money to buy slaves. So it seceded from Virginia's secession, and the Union promptly admitted it as a state of its own. And it had been a poor, backward part of the USA ever since.

Was that what the people going to the Fresno Convention wanted? To be poor, backward parts of the USA instead of staying attached to the rich but—gasp!—liberal Pacific Coast? Or were they stooges acting on orders from Trump-and-Pence-Land or from Russia?

When that occurred to her, another name popped into her mind: Konrad Henlein. Nobody'd ever heard of Henlein till his *very* well funded Sudeten German Party started dinning Nazi propaganda in the ears of all the ethnic Germans in the Sudetenland, the western fringe of Czechoslovakia, during the run-up to World War II. And, as soon as Hitler got the Sudetenland and, shortly thereafter, Czechoslovakia with it, no one heard of Henlein or the Sudeten German Party again.

So that kind of movement, when backed by a powerful neighbor, could do a lot of damage. Nicole wasn't the only one who realized as much. She got worried calls from Dakotah Ng and Axel Lysbakken.

"Those people are getting too frisky," the governor of Washington said in worried tones. "There are places near the Idaho border where the State Patrol has to go in three-car convoys. Everybody in the cars wears body armor and carries an assault rifle, too. That's the only way they can stay on even terms with the militias—and the sheriffs and some of the small-town cops, too."

"It's the same way some places here," Nicole said. "We have the coast and the main highways. Away from them? Not so much."

"Are we smart to let them hold their miserable, stupid convention, then?" Governor Ng asked. "All kinds of trouble are liable to come from it."

"The U.S. government is holding down the whole Northeast the way we're holding down our rural areas," Nicole said. "And we're liable to get in even more trouble suppressing free speech than we do if we let it go."

"You sure?" The other Asian American woman sounded dubious.

"Well, I do have a little something else in mind," Nicole admitted.

"Like what?" Dakotah Ng asked. Nicole told her. By the way the governor of Washington laughed, she was out of practice.

47

Most of the would-be secessionists who flooded into Fresno made themselves obvious. They were overwhelmingly male, overwhelmingly white, and either elderly or, well, rustic. A lot of them wore camo. A lot of the ones who didn't wore MAGA hats. They wanted to be recognized for what they were; they were proud of it. They expected to be welcomed with open arms by fellow believers.

But a surprising number, a very surprising number, had trouble with their hotel reservations. Those had vanished from the system or their credit-card company was reporting a problem. Nicole watched video of conventioneers pitching hissy fits when they couldn't get rooms. That rainbow-clad counterprotesters waltzed right by them and to the elevators only pissed them off more.

"I'm sorry, sir," the desk clerks—East Asians, South Asians, Filipinos, Armenians, Hispanics—kept saying. Most of them didn't even smile. Some of the language the MAGA crowd threw at them was filthy even by the standards of America almost a third of the way through the twenty-first century.

"What kind of shithole country do you damn greaseballs come from if you don't know a reservation when you see one?" shouted a man whose jowls, in fury, were nearly as red as a baboon's. He waved a sheet of paper in the air.

The desk clerk—by his looks, a Hispanic—stayed cool. "I'm sorry, sir. I'm very sorry. I don't know why, but the reservation you *say* you have—"

"Say I have?" the secessionist howled. "Sonny, you bet your lazy, worthless ass I've got it! Here it is!" He slammed the paper down on the front desk.

He didn't faze the clerk a bit. "The reservation you say you have, sir, isn't in *our* computer system. I am sorry, but I can't honor something I can't find." Helpfully, the man added, "The computers this hotel uses are made in China, sir. Just like your hat."

There were a lot of counterprotesters in the streets of Fresno. Not all of them wore the rainbow of LGBTQ folk, by any means. More were in ordinary T-shirts and jeans or shorts. And some, like some of the secessionists, came ready for trouble ... and ready to start it. Antifa black was their equivalent of the other side's camo.

Nicole happened to know that a lot of the counterprotesters had had their way to Fresno paid for them. She also happened to know the same held true for many attending the Fresno Convention. Some of the money that got them there came from reactionary Pacificans. More flowed into the breakaway country from farther east.

The biggest local arena was the Save Mart Center, where the Fresno State Bulldogs basketball team played in fall and winter. It held upwards of 15,000 people. Nicole didn't think the secessionists were smart to hire a hall on a university campus, but that wasn't her concern.

No, it was theirs. The students jeered them as loudly as the countermarchers in the streets. It was summer, so fewer kids were on campus than there would have been at other times of the year. They used enthusiasm to make up for lack of numbers.

"You're too old!" they shouted. "You're all men! You're too stupid! You're too Christian! You're too white! Go home, rednecks!"

One infuriated would-be secessionist bawled, "You can't be too white! You can't be too Christian!"

"Shows what you know, Grandpa!" a girl shouted back. By her looks on the TV screen, Nicole would have guessed she was Armenian. Lots of Armenians had lived in that part of California since the 1920s. She wore very short shorts and a cutoff T-shirt that clung. As the college kids had said, the MAGA crowd was mostly male. Getting sassed by tempting girls especially pissed the secessionists off.

Cops and those metal barriers, like overgrown combs with feet, channeled the incoming crowd toward the Save Mart Center. The secessionists had private security—conspicuously armed private security—at the doors to the arena. They checked names off a list and made people go through metal detectors so nobody got inside with a gun.

Nicole knew NRA conventions worked the same way. The NRA loved people packing heat … except when those people might shoot up NRA dignitaries. They weren't so fond of them then.

The security guards might have been the lucky ones. It was hot outside. Few places got hotter than Fresno in the summertime, hell possibly not among them. Inside …. Inside, video monitors said WE WILL REPAIR THE AIR CONDITIONING AS SOON AS POSSIBLE. WE APOLOGIZE FOR THE INCONVENIENCE. Men and women in hard hats and Day-Glo orange safety vests bustled around, some carrying toolboxes, others electronic sensors. The AC stayed off.

In the main hall, Colin McCarty, one of the big wheels behind the Fresno Convention, spluttered in fury. McCarty was a longtime GOP congresscritter from rural Kern County. He was less conservative than some; his ideology lay only a little to the right of Attila the Hun's. He'd also beaten several corruption raps by methods that made people think of Bismarck's comments about sausage-making and politics.

Now he was sweating like one of the pigs that might have got turned into sausage. Part of that sweat could have sprung from over-wrought political outrage. Mostly, though, he was shvitzing because it had to be at least 110 in the hall.

"It's a plot! It's a conspiracy!" he shouted to anyone who would listen. "The radical socialists and Reds who want to hijack the three Pacific states of our great Union are doing their damnedest to under-mine the will of the people of California, Oregon, and Washington!"

Only a few hundred people of California, Oregon, and Washington had braved the heat to keep sitting in there to hear him. They applauded … tepidly, under the circumstances. Most of the huge crowd the secessionists had promised came disguised, in the classic phrase, as empty seats. His Internet audience would be bigger. Then again, the stream from the arena had technical difficulties, too.

Nicole took it as a badge of honor that someone like Colin Mc-Carty would call her a Red. That didn't mean he was wrong about the misfortunes attending the Fresno Convention, of course. You could make life difficult for people you didn't like in all kinds of unofficial ways. You could, and Pacifica did.

When McCarty's pickup resumed after another outage, he was shouting, "Do you think it's an accident that there's no room at the inn for so many of us honest, God-fearing folks?"

He paused for a roar of *No!* What he got was much smaller on the Richter scale.

Undismayed, he plowed ahead: "Do you think it's an accident so many freaks and geeks and antifa criminals and queers and fairies have swarmed into Fresno to try to mess us up?"

Again, he got a few calls of "No!" Again, he got fewer than he would have wanted. There were more than before; nothing got the

God-fearing folks worked up like freaks and geeks and queers and fairies. As for the antifa, well, if the "Horst Wessel Song" made you want to stand up and whinny, you weren't likely to care for anybody who opposed fascism.

"Do you think it's an accident that the air conditioning inside this beautiful Save Mart Center doesn't work?" McCarty thundered. "Do you think it's an accident that all these things are happening at once? Do you think it's an accident that they're trying to subvert—"

He had to break off there. Men in the crowd were yelling for paramedics. Somebody there had keeled over, whether from the strength of the congressman's oratory or, more likely, from the sweltering heat. The medical personnel got him onto a stretcher and carted him off.

"If that man dies," McCarty bellowed, thumping the top of the lectern with a beefy fist, "all the traitors who are trying to pull California and Washington and Oregon out of the United States of America—the greatest and freest country the world has ever seen—deserve to be stood up against a wall and shot like the traitorous dogs they are!"

You've got a bad case of redundancy, Colin, Nicole thought. *You wouldn't recognize irony if it bit you in the ass, either.* The Trump-Pence crew had mostly been irony-blind since Day One. That was hardly a surprise; no one with a clue about what irony was could ever have voted for Donald Trump.

But Colin McCarty's sweating partisans whooped and cheered. They stomped their feet on the concrete as if a Fresno State Bulldog had just made a game-winning, buzzer-beating three. No, they cheered harder than they would have for that. A basketball hero was much too likely to be African American, and it wasn't as if they had a whole lot of use for big black men.

A few at a time, more secessionists trickled into the arena. Every so often, somebody who'd had all he could take would give up and go outside for fresh air, or as close to it as he could come in Fresno. Another fellow who looked as if he could afford to lose a few pounds, or more than a few, passed out and got carted away. The speeches went on.

Nicole was sure she listened to them more closely than they deserved. Then again, Hitler had been nothing but a crackpot in Bavaria when he wrote *Mein Kampf*. Had people then paid attention to what he was saying, they would have saved the poor suffering world a lot of trouble later.

All things considered, the national and state politicians seemed within shouting distance of sanity. They liked the Trump-Pence USA better than the new, liberal Pacifica, and they wanted to go back to what they liked and punish the people who'd dragged them away from it. You might find that revolting, but you could understand it.

The small-town mayors and empty-county sheriffs, though .... Some of those men made Nicole think of the saucer loons who swore aliens had given them enemas, of Thorazine and lithium, of involuntary commitment. They were so far Out There, it was a wonder they hadn't died from lack of oxygen.

A deputy sheriff from Modoc County, the northeasternmost county in California (which had 4,200 square miles and right around 10,000 people), got the mic and screeched, "We can't let the Soros cartel internationalize us, turn us into mongrels, and start forcing abortions on our womenfolk! We can't let them take away our logging rights! We can't let them drag us into mosques and make us talk Spanish! If we all have to use euros, what'll we do for real money? Huh? What?"

No one got on his phone to call the nice young men in their clean white coats to come and entangle the impassioned but bewildered deputy sheriff in their butterfly nets and drag him of to a (no doubt Soros-controlled) asylum. He got less applause for his rant than he plainly thought he deserved, but he got some. That alone chilled Nicole.

In spite of all the speeches, or maybe because of them, no secession resolution came out of the Fresno Convention, much less *any* program for carrying out that kind of resolution. In spite of everything McCarty and his friends tried to do to move it forward, parliamentary wrangling over just what the resolution was supposed to say and do kept it from ever coming to a vote.

The most the secessionists managed to accomplish was to agree to meet again at some unspecified time in some unspecified place. Jeered by the jubilant counterprotesters, they slunk out of town.

Nicole was watching a Fox-MSNBC correspondent bemoan the convention's failure to pull parts of the three states of Pacifica back into the USA when her phone rang. She was going to reject the call till she saw it came from Axel Lysbakken.

After the hellos and the usual small talk, the governor of Oregon said, "Well, all that went about as well as it could have."

"What, the Fresno Convention, or as much of it as there was?" Nicole said. "Yes, I think so, too. They were even clumsier than I figured they would be. If you gather to secede, and you can't even pass a resolution in favor of secession—"

Lysbakken's smile made her break off. Most of the time, with his white hair, his pink cheeks, and his kindly manner, he reminded people of their favorite grandpa. Now he put her in mind of a skeevy old great-uncle, kindly grandpa's brother gone bad, the one who'd done time for fraud, drank too much, and tried to feel up women half his age.

"What did you *do*?" Nicole demanded, sure he'd done *something* worthy of that smile. "I mean, you know what I did, but what did you do?"

"I bored from within," he answered accompanying the words with an even more evil grin. "I know the secessionists are all a bunch of bores anyhow, but not all the people who were working to move their resolution forward were really on their side."

"Tell me more, why don't you? I think I'm going to like this," Nicole said.

"Not all these people know each other, not in person. They just talk to each other online all the time," Lysbakken said. "So as soon as they started going on about holding their convention, I slipped in some ringers. With people who know what they're doing, fake social-media profiles are awfully easy to set up. And, of course, people usually believe what they want to believe."

53

"You've got that right. Even people who don't know what they're doing can convince the fools to believe what they want them to," Nicole said. "Look how much the Russians helped Trump. Look how they've kept on helping Pence. And some of their phony 'American patriots' can't even write English."

"Neither can a lot of the real ones," Lysbakken observed.

"Meow!"

He stuck out his tongue at her, then went on, "Anyway, it doesn't look like the Trump-Pence crowd did much vetting on my friends. If somebody said he was on their side, they believed him."

"How many people from their Cabinets have had to quit on account of that?"

"Lots. But my friends didn't want any big, up-front jobs. They worked inside the organization. I think it was Stalin who discovered how much power a general secretary has if he knows how to use it."

Nicole nodded. "I think you're right. And so …?"

"And so, in real life, one of the guys I sicced on the secessionists has been the parliamentarian at the business meeting for the World Science Fiction Convention the past five or six years. What Ed doesn't know about the rules of order isn't worth knowing. Another person has held that same slot for Bouchercon, the mystery convention. And Beth was a woman, God help us, so of course that crowd didn't believe she could really know anything."

"Heh," Nicole said tightly. "I hate to break it to you, but that kind of thing doesn't happen just with the fascist crowd."

"Really? I never would have believed such a thing!" Whatever else you could say about Axel Lysbakken, irony-blind he wasn't. He continued, "And so, for some reason, their motions behind the scenes kept getting things tied up in knots."

"If we had medals yet, I'd give you one," Nicole said.

"No, you wouldn't," he said. "If you gave me a medal, that would mean I'd done something. Since I haven't done anything that shows, some people would start wondering what I've done that doesn't show. They might try to find out what. And, seeing how things are in the virtual world these days, they might do it, too. They won't, though, if they don't have any clue."

"No one who went to the Fresno Convention has any clues. Except the subversives you sent, I mean."

"They may not. Some of their friends in the FSB will."

"You've been reading too many spy novels."

"Guilty," Lysbakken said. "I watched all the James Bond movies on VHS—remember VHS?—when I was a kid. I thought Sean Connery was seriously hot, too, but never mind that now. The movies made me read the Ian Fleming Bond books, and they led me to more, and that's why I'm corrupted the way I am. Only I never really thought it would come in handy till a couple of months ago."

"I don't know whether you saved the republic, Axel, but you sure saved it a lot of trouble," Nicole told him.

"I saved the republic … from the Republicans," Axel Lysbakken said sadly. "And people have needed to do that over and over, ever since Nixon and Watergate. This last time, they couldn't do it back in D.C., so we've got to take care of it for our chunk of America. If we can."

She nodded. "That's right. If we can."

After the United States failed to kidnap or kill Nicole on the road between Sacramento and San Francisco, U.S. military forces in Pacifica stayed very quietly in their bases. Part of that, Nicole knew from people who preferred her country to the Trump-Pence regime, was because U.S. officers weren't sure whom they could trust and how far they could trust them.

And part of it, no doubt, was because even Mike Pence had second thoughts about killing tens of thousands of people to bring the survivors back to an allegiance they didn't want. Abraham Lincoln hadn't hesitated to make that choice. But no one had ever accused Mike Pence of being like Lincoln. World opinion might not have let him get away with it, either. Maybe there had been a little progress since the 1860s, even if Pence and Putin were trying to unwind it.

Still, Nicole understood why Fort Sumter and other U.S. installations in the Confederacy had so annoyed Jefferson Davis. If the country you said you'd left still had bases on your soil, how sovereign were you really?

San Diego had been a U.S. Navy town since at least the turn of the twentieth century. So had Seattle. And so had San Francisco, no matter how much the technosavvy hipsters who could afford to live there these days disliked the idea. If the Marines ever erupted out of Camp Pendleton, Nicole knew they could overrun a huge chunk of SoCal before Pacifica's improvised forces even slowed them down.

She called Malcolm Washington to her residence. "This is our country," she said. "How do we get the United States to understand we don't want their occupation forces here?"

The general ran a hand over his smooth scalp. "Ma'am, that's a tough one. Since World War II, the United States has been a global power. How does it project force in the Pacific if the only Pacific coast it has is up in Alaska? You can bet Pence is asking himself the same question right now. You can bet Xi Jinping is, too."

"He's recognized us," she reminded him.

"Sure. Think he did it because he likes it, or because he wants to stick a finger in Mike Pence's eye?"

She exhaled slowly. "I don't want to be China's puppet—or Russia's, or Saudi Arabia's, or, well, anybody's. I want to keep our foreign policy aligned with the USA's ... with what the USA's ought to be, anyhow. I don't want us hopping into bed with every dictator who stands up straight and puffs out his chest and talks loud."

"And has a lot of folding money to spread around," General Washington added.

"That, too." Nicole nodded. "I hate the way the United States has been for sale the past fifteen years. Some of the coin the payoffs are made in, too ... Pence and his pals aren't as bad as Trump's people were, not about that. They're plenty bad enough, but not as bad."

"They think that kind of thing is sinful. Some of them get off on it more because it's sinful and they're doing it anyway, but you're right—not all of them. If I think I'm doing something wrong, it turns me off, not on. What do I know, though?"

With some regret, Nicole dragged the conversation back to the business at hand. "If we have guarantees of our independence, I'd be willing to let the United States keep some bases here. We're a medium-sized country bumped up against a huge one. We have to remember that."

56

Malcolm Washington chuckled harshly. "Maybe you should talk with the president of Ukraine. You two may have more in common than you think."

"That's crossed my mind, as a matter of fact," Nicole said.

"Could be interesting. I bet I know one thing he'd tell you for sure—after the Soviet Union broke up, Ukraine was dumb to give all its nukes back to Russia. If it had kept them, Putin wouldn't be able to push it around the way he has."

Nicole didn't know how many nuclear weapons the USA kept in California, Oregon, and Washington. Somebody would, though, or could find out in a hurry. And … "Even if they take away all the ones that are here, we can make our own pretty damn quick if we have to. We've got the know-how."

"Germany can do that. And Holland and Belgium. And the Scandinavian countries. Italy, too, I suppose. They don't because the United States has always protected them against Russia, and they've trusted that. They have until these past few years, anyway."

"Yeah. But I don't want to hide under China's nuclear umbrella against the United States." Nicole sighed. The more you looked at things, the more complicated they got. All the countries the general had mentioned had signed the nuclear nonproliferation treaty. If they thought it wouldn't do them any more good, though …. The past few years, some disquieting rumors had come out of Europe. Officially, everyone over there denied everything. The United States said it believed the denials.

Of course, the executive branch of the United States believed the FSB more than it believed the CIA. It trusted North Korea more than it trusted defense intelligence agencies. Professionals back in D.C. were still trying to hold things together. How could you, though, when no one who actually decided what to do would take you seriously?

"If the USA is going to keep bases here, the way it does in Europe, it should pay for them," General Washington said. "That's the best way I can think of to remind those people that they aren't calling the shots any more."

"I haven't suggested that to Mike Pence yet. He wouldn't do it. He'd just hit the ceiling in fourteen different places, or maybe seventeen."

"Yeah. I know." The general sighed. "The worst thing about us leaving is that, without us voting, those rotten sons of bitches can probably win most of their elections even without cheating. I'm glad to be gone, I'll tell you."

"We're all glad to be gone—well, all of us who didn't go to the Fresno Convention," Nicole said. "Sometimes you have to walk away when something doesn't work out."

"Welcome to my first marriage," Malcolm Washington said, which startled a laugh out of Nicole. He went on, "I made the second one fly, though. And we're better off without the bigots and the religious fanatics running things back East."

"Amen!" she answered. That made him chuckle, too.

Despite secession, traffic between Pacifica and the old United States flowed unimpeded. No one insisted on a passport or asked people questions about where they lived and why they wanted to cross from what was now one country to the other. Nicole thought Pacifica gained more than it lost by that.

Mike Pence evidently thought the same thing. The idea pleased him less than it did her. And, one day, unannounced checkpoints popped up just over the state lines between Pacifica and Idaho, Nevada, and Arizona. They were called enforcement areas. Just what they were meant to enforce wasn't spelled out. Maybe that was because the U.S. administration didn't know—a common failing of the Trump-Pence regime—or maybe the lack of clarity was deliberate.

U.S. ICE officials didn't actually stop anyone from crossing in either direction. But they made the process as slow and unpleasant as they could, requiring people to fill out paperwork that gave away more personal information than anyone sensible wanted to do.

The first thing Nicole did was call the governor of Nevada. She wondered if he'd want to talk to her, but he accepted the call right away. "I thought you said you'd keep the Feds from acting against us in your state," she told him.

"For one thing, I said I didn't want the USA sending troops through Nevada. These aren't troops—they're civilian personnel," Heber Wilson said.

"They're ICE. ICE is how you say Gestapo in American," she replied.

"You can argue that both ways. I don't want to fight about it now," Wilson said. "And I hadn't finished. They didn't tell me they were going to do it, either. The westbound jam on the I-15 stretches almost all the way back to Las Vegas. Everybody who's stuck in it is just as happy as you are."

He was a Mormon, but he was a practical man, too. If people had trouble coming to Vegas from Los Angeles, they'd stay home, and that would cost Nevada money, lots of money. Nicole said, "Have you pointed this out to the folks back East?"

"I'd just got off the phone with them when you called," he said. "They … weren't very reasonable. They talked about punishing the West Coast. They don't seem to understand they're punishing us, too."

"They don't care, you mean."

"You said that. I didn't." Wilson sighed. "They don't always have a full understanding of what things are like here."

"Can you get them to take down the barriers if you push them a little?"

"Push them how? By saying I'll start bringing Nevada into Pacifica if they don't loosen up?"

She echoed him: "You said it. I didn't."

"I think Pacifica would be looser and freer than the United States," Heber Wilson said. "I don't think the difference is big enough to make up for everything secession would cost us, in terms of trouble with D.C. and in terms of trouble with our own people."

Nevada's political geography mirrored those of the states in Pacifica. Las Vegas and Reno held most of the people, and would have fit into the West Coast republic well enough. But the rest of Nevada—a small minority of the people, a vast majority of the area—was overwhelmingly reactionary.

Still, Nicole said, "If you can't handle your own people, why are you governor?"

"When I ran, I thought I'd do the state some good. So did enough other folks to send me to Carson City," he answered slowly. "This is the start of my second term now. If I'd known then what I know today, I suspected I'd still be back on the Reno city council. I also suspect I'd be happier today than I really am."

Yes, he did seem an honest man. If he didn't seem strong enough to suit the times …. Well, a lot of people were guilty of that. Nicole often worried she was one herself. She said her good-byes and got off the line.

Then she called Dakotah Ng and Axel Lysbakken to let them know how the conversation had gone. "So much for neutrality," Lysbakken said. "He's a weak reed. He'll break and pierce our hand." He chuckled sourly. "See? Mike Pence isn't the only one who can quote from the Bible when he needs to."

"Wilson can quote from the Book of Mormon, too. The Constitution? Forget it," Dakotah Ng said.

"To be fair, I haven't heard him quote Franklin Graham," Nicole said.

"That's not the point," Lysbakken said. "The point is, Pence thinks he's got a direct line to the Big Guy who wrote the thing. I know better, or I sure hope I do. It's great literature and all that. It's got some good advice about how to live your life, and some really dumb stuff in it, too. And when the people who wrote it squatted down to take a dump, it wasn't angels that fell into the chamber pot."

Nicole felt the same way. She was sure Governor Ng did, too. You could think such things—you could even say them out loud—and still get elected here on the West Coast. California, Oregon, and Washington weren't so secular as broad swaths of Western Europe, but they were gaining on it.

She tried to imagine a candidate for governor in, say, Kansas or maybe Mississippi coming out with the kinds of things Axel Lysbakken just had. Losing the election would be the least of his or her worries, a long way behind murder. Of course, Axel had come out himself. You could do that here and still succeed in politics. An openly gay man or a lesbian would have a much rougher time in most of what was left of the United States.

"Do you have any good news from your talk with Wilson?" Dakotah Ng asked.

"Only in the sense that, once you've cleaned up all the horseshit, you know there's a pony *somewhere*," Nicole said. "The pony here is,

Pence and ICE and I suppose the U.S. military aren't shooting at us. They're just making themselves into gigantic pains."

"They've been gigantic pains for years. If they weren't, we'd still be part of the United States," Governor Ng replied. "They're getting less and less shy and more and more proud about showing it, though."

"That's what fascism runs on. Performative cruelty is its gasoline," Governor Lysbakken said. On that cheerful note, they all seemed to decide the conference call was over.

Something as close to open rebellion against the U.S. government as you could come without lots of people dying broke out in New England, New York, and New Jersey. State officials and most local governments completely stopped cooperating with federal authorities in any way at all. The governor of Massachusetts declared all federal laws passed since 2017 null and void because Trump and Pence hadn't been legitimately elected.

"We stand with our brethren on the West Coast, and regret how far we are from civilization, and how close we are to the jackboots," he said.

After some delay pretending nothing was wrong and some trying to calm things down, Mike Pence went on TV to rally the parts of the country that still wanted to listen to him. Nicole turned on Fox-CNN to see what he'd say. Pacifica didn't block programming from the USA, even if the reverse wasn't true.

Despite the best efforts from his makeup people, Pence looked old and tired. Nicole wished baby boomers would just shut up and go away. Even the youngest of them were hitting retirement age … except for politicians. People who'd got their habits before computers roamed the earth had no business trying to run the modern world.

"My God-fearing, God-loving fellow Americans," Pence said, "I come before you tonight to warn you of a plot against the very soul of the United States of America. Radical socialist activists in the so-called country of Pacifica are plotting with related elements in the Northeast to stir up disorder against the legitimate, constitutional government in Washington, D.C."

He paused to sip from a glass of water on the Oval Office desk. The more trouble the USA blundered into, the louder the regime trumpeted its legitimacy. So it seemed to Nicole, anyhow. *The Prexy doth protest too much, methinks* ran through her head and made her wish she lived in a little hamlet someplace where she didn't need to worry about such things.

Putting down the glass, the POTUS continued, "Disrespect for federal rights and powers cannot be tolerated. I warn the self-proclaimed government of Pacifica that encouraging revolutionary, anti-government sentiments within the territory of the United States of America is an action no sovereign state anywhere would tolerate. We have been patient, but our patience has an end. If you keep doing this, we will punish you.

"And I warn state and local authorities in impacted areas of the Northeast that you cannot get away with defying the national government. Accordingly, I am ordering all National Guard units in the states of New Jersey, New York, Connecticut, Massachusetts, Vermont, New Hampshire, and Maine into federal service, effective immediately. Any contrary statements from local leaders are inoperative. You will cooperate fully and completely with ICE and Homeland Security. If you fail to comply, you will face the maximum penalties the law allows. I want to be very clear about that.

"To loyal citizens in the impacted areas, don't let your misguided leaders drag you down the path to socialism and anarchy. Let them know you stand up for the United States, the greatest, freest country in the history of the world! Don't let them get away with this misguided protest."

Socialism *and* anarchy? Nicole didn't see how you could have both of them at once, but then she'd actually studied poli sci. To someone who stood far enough to the right, they both just meant *bad*.

"To citizens outside the impacted area, stay calm and loyal," Pence went on. "Let your elected Republican representatives, and your ministers of the Gospel, hear from you. Pray privately and publicly. Beg God to return unfortunates in the impacted area to their senses. And believe me when I tell you, we will do whatever it takes to keep the country united so everyone can go forward together into new freedom and prosperity. Thank you, and God bless the United States of America."

A Fox-CNN talking head came on, praising the president's wisdom and mercy and strength. "I'm sure Donald Trump is looking down from heaven on President Pence and smiling at how he never stops working to make America whole again!" the man gushed.

Half an hour later, Nicole sat in front of a TV camera herself. "Hello and sympathies to the people in the United States who are still allowed to see me, and to the people who manage to see me whether they're allowed to or not," she said. "I just want to state on the record that Pacifica has nothing to do with resistance to the Trump-Pence regime and its illegal power grab in the Northeast. We had a bellyful of that itself, so we left the USA. If the Northeast wants to follow our lead, D.C. shouldn't stand in its way. As someone reminded me not long ago, sometimes breaking up a bad marriage is better for everybody than staying in it. Thank you. Good luck to you all."

After the red light went out, her husband said, "Now Pence will blame you for encouraging New England and New York to secede."

"And New Jersey. Don't forget New Jersey," Nicole said.

Brent Yoshida rolled his eyes. "If it wasn't for that stupid MTV show way back when, everybody would have by now. Good God, Trump managed to make a casino in Atlantic City go bankrupt. How do you make a casino go bankrupt? Casinos are designed so the house can't lose."

"Donald Trump had all kinds of unexpected talents," Nicole observed.

"He sure did. He screwed up the whole United States. How many people can say that?"

"Walt Disney?" she suggested.

She won a snort from him, but he plowed ahead anyway: "You know what I mean. Pence carries on Trump's legacy the best way—I mean, the worst way—he knows how. But without Trump to give him room to stand on the whole country, Pence would just be a little wannabe *Führer* running one state into the ground."

"I only wish you were wrong. And I'll tell you something else: any time you want to teach my political science courses after all this is over, be my guest. You know which end is up, that's for sure."

"Talk dirty to me some more," Brent said. Nicole giggled. She couldn't remember the last time she'd done that. It felt amazingly good.

Had her husband lived in biblical times, Nicole thought, there would have been an Old Testament Book of Brent. He foretold exactly what President Pence would say about her speech. Elijah? Isaiah? Jeremiah? They had nothing on him when it came to prophecy.

"The so-called country of Pacifica encourages radical uprisings elsewhere in our great United States of America," Pence said somberly. "They think rebellion here helps them there. I am here to tell them they're wrong. If they keep interfering in American constitutional law enforcement, they'll be sorry. I'm here to tell them that, too."

Nicole got a text from Dakotah Ng. In its entirety, it read, *No good deed goes unpunished.*

Ain't it the truth? Nicole wrote back, and poked the SEND button on her screen.

Myron Flegenheim asked to see her about something he didn't want to discuss on the phone. He didn't do such things if he didn't think he had good reason to. When he came in, he said, "If we can keep him safe, one of the senior FBI guys down in Los Angeles wants to, wants to …."

"Defect?" Nicole suggested.

"There you go," Flegenheim said. "He knows things, this guy. Not only that, he's got a flash drive full of stuff he wasn't supposed to copy."

"That could be interesting. What kind of stuff?"

"He didn't show our people everything. He isn't dumb enough to do that. But the secretary of Homeland Security won't last two days if some of what they saw is legit."

"That … could be interesting. It would be for sure, if the people who run things back in D.C. cared anything about their flunkies do except follow orders." Nicole scratched the side of her jaw, considering. "Do you think whatever this guy has is hot enough to cause a lot of trouble?"

"Based on what I've seen, based on what I've heard, based on what I've been able to find out about his past, I'd say yes," Flegenheim answered. "He's one of those straight-shooting FBI agents who's never had more than one drink on any day of his life, and it seems like he's been disgusted with the Trump-Pence clowns and everything they stand for ever since what's-his-name—Comey—got canned, if not before that. So yeah, if he thinks we're honest, he'll give us what he's got."

"You never did tell me his name," Nicole pointed out.

"I kinda got used to not saying it." Flegenheim chuckled sheepishly. "The code name we've been using for him is Raw Milk, but his folks called him Patrick O'Donnell."

"Okay. Thanks." Nicole smiled a little. Back in the day, people had tagged the FBI "the Irish Mafia." Even Trump had noticed it and scorned it before shuffling off this mortal coil. So code name "Raw Milk" was a leftover from those days, was he? She nodded. That made things more interesting, not less. "Let's do it."

Trumpeting O'Donnell's decision to change sides to the heavens would have raised expectations higher than he might be able to fulfill. There was no point to keeping quiet about it if Pacifica meant to use him to poke the U.S. government. And so small press releases and small online and print stories announced that senior FBI agent Patrick O'Donnell had renounced his affiliation to the United States and been granted asylum in Pacifica.

Nicole wondered whether D.C. would respond at all. The Trump-Pence regime had always been good at ignoring news it didn't like or news that made it look bad. Trump started calling stories like that fake news even before the Russians helped him slink into the White House.

But she got a phone call from the White House less than an hour after the story broke. "President Pence wishes to speak to the governor of California," the senior aide who actually placed the call told her.

"In that case, you've got the wrong number," Nicole answered cheerfully. "Miguel Narváez succeeded to that position weeks ago.

The lieutenant governor takes over for the president the way the vice president takes over for the president. Mr. Pence should know all about that, shouldn't he?"

The aide let out an exasperated snort. "Will you accept the call or not?"

"As governor of California? No. Good-bye." Nicole enjoyed hanging up.

She wondered whether they would try again. But another call from 1600 Pennsylvania Avenue came in twenty minutes later. This time, speaking carefully, the aide asked, "Am I talking to the person who calls herself acting president of Pacifica?"

"That's right." Nicole noted the people back in D.C. didn't admit she was any such thing. But they acknowledged that she claimed the title. For the moment, it would do.

"All right. Thank you. President Pence would like to speak to the person who calls herself the acting president of Pacifica."

"Put him through. I'll talk with him."

A couple of clicks and pops later, Mike Pence said, "Good afternoon, Mrs. Yoshida."

"Good afternoon, Mr. Pence." If he wouldn't say her title, Nicole was damned if she'd say his, especially since hers was bound to be more legitimate.

If he noticed—and he probably did; he was narrow-minded and bigoted, but not stupid, unlike his predecessor—he didn't make an issue of it. "Mrs. Yoshida, you are harboring a fugitive from justice. The attorney general has issued a warrant for Patrick O'Donnell's arrest. The charge is unauthorized disclosure of classified documents vital to the national security of the Unites States."

As had been true since the very early days of the Trump-Pence regime, the U.S. attorney general seemed to do the president's bidding, not the law's. Nicole said, "Mr. O'Donnell has asked for and received political asylum in Pacifica, Mr. Pence. We have no extradition treaty with the United States, and even if we did, we'd be unlikely to send back someone who faced sure conviction in one of your kangaroo courts."

"That is an unfair and unjust characterization of the juridical process here," Pence said.

"How many people do you have locked up right now for what you call national security violations? How many thousands? How many tens of thousands?"

"I'm not going to argue semantics with you, Mrs. Yoshida," he replied.

Nicole concluded that meant he either didn't know or didn't care to admit how many people were jugged in the new American gulags. One of the politicals freed from Camp Calexico might have been able to tell her.

Pence went on, "I didn't call to do that. I called to demand O'Donnell's immediate return, and also the return of the data he stole and any and all copies of it you may have made. You have no right to hold that highly classified material."

That was interesting. Mike Pence sure didn't want the outside world seeing any of what O'Donnell had on his precious flash drive. Which argued it was as hot as the defecting FBI man claimed it was. Nicole said, "I already told you, we won't hand over Patrick O'Donnell. As for the data, we're a sovereign state. You don't make demands like that on us. You make requests, through the proper channels."

"Mrs. Yoshida, I've had about enough of this nonsense. The United States will consider your keeping O'Donnell and his stolen data a hostile act. We will respond in whatever way we find appropriate, up to and including military action. Is that clear?"

Are you really sure you want to fire that cannon aimed at Fort Sumter, General Beauregard? Nicole hadn't imagined Mike Pence would escalate so hard so fast. If he wasn't scared, he was doing a hell of a good impression. "If you don't want O'Donnell's information published, Mr. Pence, you'd do better not to attack us," she said carefully.

"If you publish anything that man has pilfered, we will take it as an act of war. Is *that* clear?"

"No one would doubt what you mean. Why you're so upset about all this, though—that's a different question."

"Because I take American national security seriously, that's why. Someone has to, what with things the way they are."

"Are you talking about national security or about hushing up things that will make even the people you've oppressed for so long want to march on Washington and string up everybody who ever had anything to do with your regime?"

Pence didn't answer that, not directly. All he said was, "I called to warn you, Mrs. Yoshida. You'll take the warning or you won't. Good-bye." He broke the connection.

Nicole hung up, too. She stared at the telephone on her desk, feeling like someone who'd gone out to catch herrings and hooked a great white. One thing seemed pretty clear—she needed a good, long look at everything Patrick O'Donnell had lifted and brought to Pacifica.

The flash drive was a big one: 512 GB. Nicole plugged it into a Mac that had had its WiFi disabled. She wasn't going to let anything get onto and possibly corrupt Pacifica's government network if she could help it. The external drive icon came up on her desktop. So far, so good.

When she opened it, she found the folders were arranged in chronological order. She started looking at documents from even before Trump first ran for president. She found money transfers from Russia to Switzerland and Cyprus, from those places to Deutsche Bank, from Deutsche Bank to the Trump Organization. O'Donnell had more details than the old, underused Mueller report showed, but this wasn't new news.

Trump's ties to Jeffrey Epstein weren't new news to her, either. When they came out, he'd just laughed them off, the way he laughed off so many things. The press let him get away with it far too long. He made good copy. A clown like that couldn't possibly get elected, right?

Well, no.

She found what sure looked like a smoking gun connecting the Trump campaign staff and the Russian intelligence folks who'd fed dirt to Wikileaks. She found records of a guy who was working for one of Putin's propaganda mills at the same time as he worked for a right-wing U.S. TV network Trump praised to the skies.

She found tons of dirt on Russian election interference in 2016, 2020, 2024, and 2028, and how the FSB had hacked voting machines and falsified vote totals. A crack Boss Tweed made way back in the nineteenth century bubbled up in her mind: *As long as I count the votes, what are you going to do about it?* The question seemed as good now as it had more than 150 years before.

The more she looked, the more the Trump-Pence regime (along with fellow travelers like the two Grahams, Vice President Lindsey and self-anointed Evangelical Pope Franklin) seemed to her to be a wholly owned subsidiary of Vladimir Putin and the FSB. She saw that they hadn't caught Pence in a honey trap, the way they had with Trump. Pence really did seem faithful to his wife. But he looked to do what the Russians told him as spinelessly as Trump ever had.

Finding that out took some digging into the more recent documents. A lot of his relatives seemed enmeshed in business deals either shady or propped up with Russian money or, often, both. Parts of that stuff were just embarrassing to him. Other parts might put various kinfolk behind bars for long, healthy terms. Or they might, if U.S. courts weren't yet totally corrupt.

She started copying documents to another flash drive: a representative sample, to give people a nice taste of all the goodies Patrick O'Donnell had compiled. She didn't know how any of it had anything to do with U.S. national security—one more lie from the Liar-in-Chief in D.C. But she could see how it all contributed to Pence's irrational insecurity.

Before any of this stuff went out, she intended to have her infosecurity people do forensics on the flash drive to make sure no malware lurked in there along with the interesting material. *You aren't paranoid when they're really after you* made a pretty good mantra for anyone getting anything electronic from an unvetted source.

Having taken care of that, she called Dakotah Ng and Axel Lysbakken to let them know what she'd found. "It's nothing people haven't suspected for a long time, but there's real evidence here," she said.

"Will anyone care?" Lysbakken asked.

"Pence seems to think so. He came as near as makes no difference to threatening war if we published this stuff," Nicole answered.

The governor of Oregon chuckled sourly. "Why does he even worry? It's not as if the lickspittle Congress he has will impeach him and convict him and throw him out of office on his Christian ass.

And that's only got worse since people from our states came home. He's there as long as he wants to be."

"Not if the Joint Chiefs of Staff get a bellyful," Governor Ng put in. "Do you think they want to take orders from a Russian puppet? Some of them still remember which country they swore their oath to."

"How many, by now?" Nicole wondered. "They've made over the top brass in the military, too."

"I'm not sure how many top soldiers now care more about the country than about the regime," Dakotah Ng said. "It wasn't anything I ever expected I'd need to worry about. General Washington will have a better idea than we do. I can ask some of my own senior Guard officers, too, if you like."

"Yes, do that, please," Nicole said.

"Also might not be a bad idea to find out what Patrick O'Donnell thinks about it," Governor Lysbakken suggested.

"You're right. That's a good idea, in fact," Nicole said. "I may also ask him whether he thinks the United States would make a better neighbor or a worse one after a military coup."

"You'd hope the generals wouldn't hold on to power real long, that they'd restore democracy as soon as they could." Axel Lysbakken sighed. "You'd hope so, but there's no guarantee. Whoever's in charge may decide he can't trust the country not to swing fascist again. Or he may just decide he likes telling everybody what to do. I bet that's why a lot of dictatorships last as long as they do. Power is a drug, same as meth or heroin or coke."

"You make more sense than I wish you did," Nicole told him.

He laughed, again without much humor. "Thanks. They can put that on my headstone."

"As long as they don't put 'shot for treason,' we're golden," Dakotah Ng said.

Nicole found herself nodding.

Myron Flegenheim gave Nicole a thumbs-up. "He's in the waiting room, Madam President. Ready when you are."

"Acting president, please," Nicole aid. "Only I'm not much of an actor, and nobody's given me a script. It's like one of those dreams

70

where you're back in high school, and you've got to take a test you haven't studied for."

"Nobody will know as long as you don't tell," answered the CHP man who ran her security detail. That struck her as sensible advice. He went on, "Shall I bring him in, then?"

"Yes." It sounded oddly formal to Nicole, almost on the order of *The die is cast*.

Flegenheim left her office. He came back with a man in his late fifties, his face lined, his sandy hair thinning and graying. Patrick O'Donnell wore a suit likely bought off the rack at Target. He wasn't much to look at till you noticed the eyes behind the bifocals. They were green as a cat's, and they didn't miss a thing.

After introducing him, Flegenheim went out again. "Sit down, please," Nicole said to the defector from the United States. "Make yourself comfortable."

O'Donnell did sit, but he answered, "I wonder if I'll ever be comfortable again. For all I know, a cruise missile is heading for this room right now."

It wasn't impossible, as Nicole knew. It wasn't even all that unlikely. "Pacifica will go on if they take me out. It will go on if they take you out, too. We've already started publishing some of the more exciting bits from your flash drive."

"Yes, I know. I've seen that. If anything's likely to make the POTUS and his gang of crooks go off half-cocked, it's being exposed. Have you ever watched termites squirm when you lift up their rotten board and the sun hits them?"

O'Donnell had a gift for unpleasant metaphors. Gulping a little, Nicole said, "Ants, yes. Termites, no. The first thing I want to ask you is, do you think the military can control this regime?"

"If they could, they would have done it by now. If they could, and if they wanted to," O'Donnell said. "The military, Homeland Security, the police—most of those people rely on the commander-in-chief because he *is* the commander-in-chief. Never mind if he's a jackass or a traitor. He's the commander-in-chief. Organizations like that draw people who like rigidity and order and doing as they're told and making other people do what they say."

71

"You keep being sensible. Could you cut that out, please?" Nicole thought to make light of things with a joke, but she could hear it fall flat.

O'Donnell gave her a thin, a very thin, smile. "I admire what you're doing here, I really do. I wanted to give you as much help as I could. But I'm afraid the odds are still against you."

"We've struck a nerve in the United States. I haven't heard all the Fox outlets screaming 'Fake news!' so loud in a long time," Nicole said. "And a couple of commentators even said what we were putting out there would be important if only it were true. The implication is that it's a lie, but people can see past that. Some people can."

"People in the Northeast can. African Americans and Hispanics can. Other than that in the United States? Don't count on it," the defector said. "They've got that place locked down pretty tight after fifteen years. That's why I decided to, well, change allegiance. And if they invade, even that isn't a good bet."

"Invade?" Nicole caught herself. Pence had warned her the USA would do whatever it took to suppress the goodies on Patrick O'Donnell's flash drive, including military action. Donald Trump would have telegraphed his punches, bragging about what would happen and where before it did. Pence was smarter than that—praising with faint damn, but there you were.

O'Donnell must have read her eyes. "You see the problem. He doesn't want to go to war, I don't think. He has loyalty issues in the military—you've seen as much. But he doesn't want the information coming out, and he doesn't want you sitting on it, either. You can blackmail him if you do."

"Oh, boy! Us and the Russians!" Nicole said.

"And the oil sheiks, and some other people," he agreed. "That's what happens when you go down that road. How good a defense can you put up?" He raised a hasty hand. "I don't want the details. I know I'm not cleared for them. But generally?"

"We'll fight as best we can. The USA is bigger and stronger than we are, and geography isn't exactly on our side. If the United States pushes hard enough, it can overwhelm us. We aim to make that as slow and expensive as we can."

"Fair enough. My assessment pretty much matches yours," O'Donnell said.

"If things don't go … the way we want, what will you do? You're already a wanted man, which is putting it mildly," Nicole said.

His mouth twisted in what wanted to be another smile but died stillborn. "What can I do? I've burned my bridges with the United States. Maybe I can make it to Canada or Mexico if Pacifica goes under. Even Canada isn't looking so great right now, though. If everything goes wrong … well, I'd sooner check out my way than Mike Pence's."

"Yeahhh," Nicole said slowly. She hadn't wanted to think in those terms, but maybe it was about time she did. Oblivion on her own terms, as O'Donnell put it, might be preferable to a treason trial and whatever followed that. After Timothy McVeigh in 2003, the United States hadn't executed anyone till late in Trump's first term. It had made up for lost time since.

"Sometimes things work. Sometimes they don't." O'Donnell's shrug was a good, game try at nonchalance, anyhow. "You have to be ready either way. Or you'd better be."

"Uh-huh. You'd better be," Nicole said.

No, Mike Pence didn't come out and bellow that the United States would spread fire and fury across Pacifica. But it began to look more and more as if he was getting ready to do just that.

Back in the day, people had managed to take nasty neighbors and rebellious provinces by surprise when they invaded. It didn't work like that any more. Phone calls and social-media posts about troop movements, canceled leaves, and arrests of the unwilling or otherwise insufficiently patriotic began reaching Pacifica no more than minutes after those things happened.

General Malcolm Washington thought it was funny … up to a point. "I bet Pence's generals are tearing their hair, the ones who still have any." He ran a hand over his own bare scalp.

"If we know just what they're doing, will that let us stop them?" Nicole asked.

"Now that you mention it," he answered, "no."

"I was hoping you wouldn't be quite so blunt."

"Sorry about that, ma'am. If it makes you feel any better, knowing what they're up to will help us slow them down—some. But if they hit us hard, we'll fall over. We're too small next to them to do anything else."

As signs of the buildup grew ever more unmistakable, Governor Wilson of Nevada mobilized his National Guard forces and the Nevada Highway Patrol. He went on TV to say, "I told everyone from the beginning of this dispute that I wouldn't let my state be used as a battleground or a highway to a battleground. We will resist, with force if necessary, any unlawful incursions into our territory. Let all sides hear and be warned."

Nicole heard. She wasn't warned: Pacifica had no intention of invading Nevada. She also knew that, if U.S. forces outclassed the ones she led, there was simply no comparison between what Mike Pence had and what Heber Wilson did.

But it didn't come to gunplay, at least not on Nevada's border with Idaho, Utah, or Arizona. The operation that seized Governor Wilson and his lieutenant governor went much more smoothly than the one that failed to grab Nicole. A couple of NHP officers were wounded, but no one got killed. And, quite suddenly, Nevada's Republican secretary of state, a staunch Trump-Pence loyalist, found herself in the governor's residence in Carson City. She immediately ordered the National Guard and the Highway Patrol to stand down.

Federal troops entered Nevada unopposed, then. There were also new encampments near Pacifica's borders with Idaho and Arizona. At least as ominously, two aircraft carriers recalled from watching Chinese moves in the western Pacific stood off the coast, barely in international waters, ready to do whatever the POTUS told them to do. The usual support vessels screened them from harm.

"Can we do anything at all about those?" Nicole asked General Washington.

"Little boats flying drones carrying explosives, maybe. Even if that worked, though, it'd be a suicide mission." By the look on his face, Washington had scant hope for his own scheme.

She made a television and Internet speech to justify Pacifica's cause to the world: a world that had proved largely indifferent to the breakaway republic. "All we ask is to be left alone," she said. She knew she was echoing a Confederate rallying cry, but she also knew most people wouldn't notice. And she knew her cause was a hell of a lot better than the CSA's. She went on, "Our only crime is that we've been telling the truth about the government of the United States to the people of the United States. The men who run the government there are afraid of the truth. They're willing to shoot and bomb and kill to keep it from coming out. That's not a government—that's a crime syndicate. If the United States invades Pacifica, who knows what it will do next? Who wants to take the chance of finding out?"

President Pence went on the air right after she went off. He looked even more stony-faced than usual. "The entity that calls itself Pacifica is in fact the three American states of California, Oregon, and Washington. They are an integral part of the territory of the United States. How we bring them back to their proper place in the country is a purely internal matter and of interest to no foreign government. That is my final word."

Nicole turned to her husband. "So long. It's been fun knowing you. The next sound you hear will be bombers knocking Sacramento flat."

"Don't give up now," Brent Yoshida said. "We've come this far. Maybe we can go a little further."

"Honest to God, I don't see how. The whole thing about seceding was, it would only work if the United States didn't attack us. They're too big. They're too strong." She paused. "Oh—that reminds me!" She sent a text to General Washington: *Make sure you order our people not to open fire on U.S. forces unless they actually cross the border. We don't want to give them any excuse for combat. Let it be on their heads.*

Order already issued. Will repeat. Washington's answer came back in less than a minute—about as fast as he could type it on his phone. She nodded to herself. She'd thought that was the case, but she'd wanted to make sure. In his HQ, Malcolm Washington was probably fuming about what a micromanaging bitch his acting president was. Well, too bad for him.

She hadn't put the iPhone away when it rang. She frowned; this was supposed to be a secure line, and she didn't recognize the number the phone displayed. 206 was the area code for Seattle. "Who is this?" she said sharply.

"Good evening, Madam Acting President." Whoever he was, he owned a heavy Slavic accent. And he turned out to have every right to such an accent, for he continued, "Sergei Khloponin here. I have honor to be Russian Federation's consul–general in Seattle."

"What ... do you want, Mr. Khloponin?" she asked, her voice wary. Maybe the Russians had a way to hack into her allegedly secure line. Why not? They seemed to hack into everything else. "Forgive me, but I'm a little busy right now. We're about to be invaded by your good friend Mike Pence." If she sounded bitter, that was only because she was.

It rolled off Sergei Khloponin like raindrops off an oilcloth. "Maybe. But also maybe not. President Putin is soon giving address on Russian television. RT Network will give for you English translation. You may want to hear."

Hardly any TV systems in Pacifica carried the RT Network. Aside from social media, it was the main way Russia propagandized the English-speaking world. "I can get it online, I guess," Nicole said. "Can you tell me what he'll talk about?"

"You may want to hear," Khloponin repeated. "You call me back when address is finished, yes?"

"Yes, I'll do that." Nicole hung up. She went to the online version of RT just before Vladimir Putin appeared on her phone screen. He was pushing eighty, pouchy under the eyes and jowly. But, as usual, he had that cat-that-swallowed-the-canary smirk on his face. She'd hated that smug look ever since the first time she saw him standing next to Donald Trump.

"And now, here with an important announcement on the urgent crisis in the world situation is Vladimir Vladimirovich Putin, president of the Russian Federation," the RT announcer said.

Putin was surrounded by Russian flags and the bicephalous eagle revived from Czarist days. He probably would have been more comfortable with the hammer and sickle and red banners under which he'd grown up, but he made do. He started speaking

76

in Russian. The translator, who had a suave British accent, followed a beat later.

"I have watched with dismay as conditions within the United States spiraled out of control," Putin said. "I remember how, forty years ago, the United States helped ensure that the transformation of the Soviet Union into its constituent republics took place peacefully and without conflict."

Nicole didn't remember that. As the USSR was going to pieces, she'd worried more about elementary and middle school. But Vladimir Putin was already an officer in the KGB—ancestor to the modern FSB—stationed in what was then East Germany. To him, the Soviet Union's collapse must have seemed like the end of the world.

"Now that the United States has begun the devolutionary process seen before in the Soviet Union, I find it incumbent on me to do everything in my power to make sure the world is spared what could be a large and dangerous war," Putin continued. "I believe regional self-determination to be as important in the USA now as it was then in the USSR. Areas which, for whatever reasons they find good, desire to leave the jurisdiction of the central government should be allowed to do so without restraint or violence."

"Did he just say that?" Brent Yoshida whispered.

"He did. He really did," Nicole said, and then, "Hush! He isn't done."

And Putin wasn't. "Accordingly, I am extending full diplomatic recognition to the republic of Pacifica, and wish it luck and success in the family of nations. I have communicated this to the president of the United States, and have informed him that trying to bring the republic of Pacifica back under U.S. jurisdiction by force would cause the Russian Federation great displeasure and would have the most severe diplomatic, economic, and political consequences."

"Oh … my … God!" Nicole breathed. She wanted to start screaming the way she hadn't screamed since she went to a Backstreet Boys concert in 1995.

But Vladimir Putin still hadn't finished. "Since the region of the United States known as the Northeast is also clearly dissatisfied with rule from Washington, D.C., I have urged President Pence to let it proceed with plebiscites and other measures to determine whether its citizens, too, wish to form a new nation." His smirk got a little broader. Nicole hadn't dreamt it could. "Never let it be said that the Russian Federation stands opposed to the practice of democracy."

"What a hypocritical son of a bitch!" Brent said.

"He sure is," Nicole agreed. "But we get the benefit, and the USA gets the shaft."

Her husband nodded. "Big time."

"I still await President Pence's response," Putin went on. "I hope he will be sensible and reasonable, as Mikhail Sergeyevich Gorbachev was when the Soviet Union grew too unwieldy to continue. If not, we and the world community shall have to reconsider our options. I have also consulted with President Xi of China, who forcefully stated that he shares my concerns. Thank you, and good night."

Another RT talking head started summarizing what Putin had just said. Nicole didn't need to listen to that; she'd heard the speech. She turned on the TV, channel-hopping from one U.S. Fox network to another. Commentators on all of them were going extravagantly nuts. One shouted that he wanted to start a nuclear war with Russia for interfering in U.S. internal affairs. He got yanked off the air quite suddenly.

Before he did, Bryce asked, "Where have you been since 2016, guy?" Nicole thought it was a damn good question.

She didn't want to see Fox commentators, though, no matter how much she enjoyed watching them froth at the mouth. She wanted to see Mike Pence. If he meant to ignore Putin's warnings and threats, he might be strong enough to get away with it.

He stayed off television for an agonizing half hour. While Nicole waited and stewed, she remembered she needed to call Sergei Khloponin back. "Thank you for telling me I needed to listen to that," she said. "It's … very important."

"Is important, yes," the Russian consul–general said. "Before too much time, is possible I am Russian ambassador to Pacifica. Would be great honor, believe me."

"It will be an honor for us to have a Russian ambassador, Mr. Khloponin," Nicole said. That was diplomatic, if you liked. She hadn't dreamt Pacifica might get its independence accepted through

Russian intervention. But the new country was part of the world now, and part of the world's politics.

It was if Mike Pence was prepared to admit it was. He finally came on TV ten minutes after Nicole said her good-byes to Khloponin. If he'd been stony-faced when threatening war, now he looked as if the stone had been hit by a sledgehammer. His pale eyes stared blankly, the way someone who wore strong contacts stared when trying to make sense of the world without them.

"My ... my fellow Americans," he began, and his voice didn't work any too well, either. He took a deep breath and tried to pull himself together. "My fellow Americans, I have been in urgent communication with Russian president Putin. He advised me in the strongest terms against using military force to restore the allegiance of California, Oregon, and Washington. He said the consequences of doing that would be dangerous and unpredictable."

He reached for a glass of water on the Oval Office desk. That might have been a mistake; his hand shook as he raised the glass to his mouth. But he plainly needed his whistle wetted. After setting the glass down again, he went on, "President Putin made a very powerful, very persuasive case. Accordingly, I have ordered U.S. forces to pull back from the border of the three states that call themselves Pacifica, and I am prepared to recognize their independence and to negotiate with them in good faith about the many issues involved in their separating from the United States."

He drank again. Maybe he wished the glass held vodka or gin, not water. For all Nicole knew, it did. He licked his lips before continuing, "I will also place no further obstacles in the way of the northeastern states if they too are set on abandoning the ties that have bound the Union together for so long. We wish to govern no one who does not wish to be governed by us."

"My God!" Brent said. "Putin must have pictures of him with a sheep."

"Not just a sheep. A male sheep," Nicole said. Then she shut up, because Pence was still talking.

"I have no doubt," he said, "that we still in the United States will also be happier with the departure of those people who no longer care to share a country with us. And I have no doubt that all of our land will go forward into the future strong and free, and that we truly are making America great again. God bless the United States of America."

There must have been time for some behind-the-scenes confabs at the Fox networks, because their analysts started praising his wisdom and courage. They talked about what a wonderful nation he still ruled over. "We truly are united now!" a blonde woman said brightly. Nicole wondered how the black and brown people in what was left of the USA felt about that.

She didn't wonder enough to want to keep listening to those analysts, though. After she turned them off, she said, "Wow! Oh, wow! I didn't think the Russians would do that. My guess was, Putin figured the United States getting bogged down in a war with Pacifica would work best for him."

"My guess is, he didn't figure the United States *would* get bogged down fighting us. He figured the USA would win fast, bring us back under control, and scare the Northeast out of making more trouble," her husband answered.

Nicole's mouth twisted; that made altogether too much sense. "You may be right," she said. "If we leave and the Northeast leaves, what's left of the United States isn't just weakened. It's crippled— on the world stage, I mean."

"Do we want independence because of a Russian *deus ex machina*?" Brent asked.

"Whether we want it or not, we've got it. We'll show soon enough that we aren't Russia's friends." Nicole sighed. "And what's left of the USA brought this on itself, the same way the USSR did when we were kids. Without four terms of the garbage everybody's gone through, clamping down on anyone who disagrees, the concentration camps along the border, and selling out the country to the highest bidder, nobody would have wanted to leave. That's what people will remember Trump and Pence for. They screwed things up so hard, leaving looked better than staying."

"What you said before was true, though. The United States, what's left of it, won't be a superpower, at least for a while," her husband said. "Russia will try on that hat. So will China. We weren't great at the job, but most of the time we did it better than other people would have."

"I know. If the folks in what's left of the USA ever get sick of the crooks and thieves and crazy preachers and fools telling them what to do, maybe we can talk about getting back together again," Nicole said. "Maybe."

"What are the odds?" Brent asked. "We're gone. The Northeast is going. In the rest of the country, more people than not *like* what the Trump-Pence bozos have been doing. And if that isn't a scary thought, honey, I don't know what would be. They'll keep yelling 'Make America Great Again!' while the bus goes over the cliff."

Nicole sighed again. "It's their problem. It's not mine, not any more. They think they're the real America. I think we are, and the Northeast agrees. Sooner or later, we'll find out who's right."

THE PURLOINED REPUBLIC

James Morrow

I

LET'S get the snickering over with right away. Yes, I was a porn star. *Nolo contendere.* More cultivated than most, perhaps, and rather too eager to show off her self-education by wafting out Latin phrases. But there's simply no denying that, for well over a decade, skin flicks were my bread and butter. Are we still giggling? I'll wait. Call me patient Polly. My friends do. Patient Polly Nightingale. Have we finished chortling? Good. *Ars longa, vita brevis.*

Show me a movie actress from my generation, and I'll show you a woman for whom the motto "My fortune is my face" strikes a responsive chord. For those of us who specialized in adult cinema, of course, the rest of the package also boasted cash value. And yet, believe it or not, this memoir is entirely (or almost entirely) about Polly Nightingale from the neck up. So if you're a stag-movie connoisseur looking for kicks, you'll have to take your libido elsewhere.

Had Rafael Salazar tracked me down on the set of *Tea and Sodomy* or *Tom's Dick and Harry's*, of course, I would have been mightily embarrassed, or at least taken aback. As it happened, though, I'd retired from the Triple-X entertainment business two years earlier, at age forty (a porn star can sustain her career for longer than a professional athlete, but not *that* much longer). My new life found me organizing a theater troupe, the Two-Bit Players, specializing in avant-garde offerings staged in warehouses, parking garages, and other ready-made venues around greater Los Angeles. Mr. Salazar caught the opening night performance of *The Care and Feeding of Minotaurs*, a comedy I'd written in collaboration with my ex-boyfriend, Julius, all about the challenges the Queen of Crete, Pasiphaë, faced in raising her half-man, half-bull love child to adulthood (the horns, for example, made nursing an ordeal). I played Pasiphaë, reveling in the sexual smorgasbord that constituted her psyche. The cast never got tired of calling me Polymorphous Polly.

We staged our extravaganza on a plywood dais we'd erected in a bone-dry, open-air culvert lined with vaulted passages leading to L.A.'s byzantine sewer system. Near the climax, our master of revels instructed the audience to rise from their folding chairs and follow him deep into an array of torch-lit drainage tunnels: the Minotaur's mythic labyrinth. It was here that the twin sister of the bull-man, of whose existence he was previously ignorant, finally tracked him down, persuading him to abandon his unsavory vocation of devouring Athenian adolescents.

The première had gone badly, with every cast member, myself included, fluffing at least one important line, and I was anxious to go home and console myself with bourbon and binge-watching (I hadn't caught up with the second season of *The Bad Place*). No sooner had I exited the tunnels than Mr. Salazar appeared before me, tall, toothsome, mustached, his lean figure well served by his black three-piece suit. He gave his name, congratulated me on my performance, and identified himself as the Deputy Director of the B.U.G., the Bureau of Undercover Guile, "Pacifica's equivalent of the American C.I.A. and the Russian F.S.B." He admitted he didn't give a rip about Greek mythology. He'd attended the play merely so he could importune me afterward.

"We haven't got the kinks worked out," I told him. "Come back tomorrow, and you'll see a much better show."

"I'll get right to the point. I hope to recruit you for a patriotic mission on behalf of your adopted country."

"My patriotism is pretty rusty these days, Mr. Salazar."

"Call me Rafael. Hear me out, Ms. Nightingale.

"Polly."

"May I buy you a drink?"

"No, but you may buy me two."

I was among those thousands of New Yorkers who, upon realizing that the Pence administration was systematically turning the U.S. into a one-party nation (and that party wasn't the Democrats), emigrated to Pacifica, that brave new republic uniting Washington, Oregon, and California under a single flag, with Sacramento as its capital. While not a particularly political person, I appreciated what President Nicole Yoshida was trying to do with her fledgling country, and so I listened attentively to Rafael Salazar's big idea, which he pitched to me as we sipped our drinks in a Santa Monica jazz club and pot emporium called Reefer Madness.

"I'm not sure if you're a news junkie, but you probably know that Pence's primary foreign policy objective these days is to make life miserable for Pacificans. He'll stop at nothing to punish his secessionist neighbor to the west."

Like many citizens of Pacifica, I had mixed feelings about Mike Pence: revulsion intermingled with contempt. But I had to give him credit for one thing. He and his advisors had figured out how to get around the Twenty-Second Amendment, setting presidential term limits. When it came to the 2032 election, Pence had joined the race on the lower half of the Republican ticket. Two days after President Nunes's inauguration, dependable Devin feigned a mental breakdown and stepped aside. Pence straightaway became Chief Executive, naming *éminence grise* Rick Santorum as Vice President.

"I know what Pence has been up to," I replied. "Slapping stiff tariffs on Silicon Valley imports, banning Hollywood movies throughout the United States, impeding Red Cross efforts to help Pacifica recover from climate-change wildfires. I read the *Los Angeles Globe* every day."

"Our operatives in D.C. tell us more such policies are on the drawing board. Pence's people plan to install an array of gigantic fans between Detroit and Phoenix to blow mercury vapor into Pacifica. They also intend to choke off the flow of low-cost AIDS pharmaceuticals coming down from Edmonton and Vancouver."

"They can't intercept bad drugs at the Mexican border, even with that stupid wall," I mused. "Good drugs from Canada? That's a different matter."

"Here's how we plan to get the U.S. off our backs. Last month in the corridors of the B.U.G. an ingenious scheme took root, Operation Epiphany. Most of the credit goes to my boss, Omoyola Akinwande, but I also had a few fingers in the pie. Did you know President Pence has a personal spiritual advisor?"

"His name is Jesus Christ."

"But also—"

"That hard-ass evangelical, Franklin Graham?"

My drink wasn't so great—I made better vodka martinis at home—but the soloist at the keyboard, a real dreamboat, shared my passion for Andrew Lloyd Webber, so I was in a pretty good mood (even though I couldn't imagine what Pence's spiritual longings had to do with me). Just then the pianist was playing "The Music of the Night" from *The Phantom of the Opera*.

"Graham fell from grace," said Rafael. "Too many visits to Crystal Boinkin's cathouse in Chevy Chase. Fox News gave up trying to flip the narrative. I'm talking about the Reverend Walker Lambert, God's man on the ground in D.C. His official designation is PFC."

"Private First Class?"

"Professional Faggot Crusher."

"Huh?"

"Presidential Faith Counselor. An odd fish, no family, known to disappear for weeks at a time on one-man pilgrimages to holy places nobody else thinks are holy, like Las Vegas. In fact, he's out of the U.S. right now—but not on a pilgrimage. We've got him in a Fresno jail."

"You kidnapped him?"

"We put him in detention, like an eighth grader. Nobody misses him yet—and by the time they do, you'll be there, filling his shoes. Neat, huh?"

"Neat," I echoed drily. "Very *Prisoner of Zenda*. Are you out of your mind?"

"Here's the deal. One of our agents—let's call him Chuck—he's a great fan of your work from … you know."

"My *au naturel* period."

"So we spent a day looking at DVDs of *A Prick in Time* and *All Men Are Beasts*."

"*Apes*."

"And we quickly realized Chuck was absolutely right. Polly Nightingale is a dead ringer for Walker Lambert."

"But I'm not even a *man*."

"That's beside the point. Lambert has all your adorable features—the overbite, full lips, *anime* eyes, high cheekbones. I get excited just *thinking* about him."

"You're gay?"

"Ever since I can remember. Of course, you don't look *exactly* like Lambert, but that can be fixed. We have access to the finest makeup people in Hollywood. For the next year or so, you'll be impersonating Lambert and feeding Pence policy suggestions based on your revelations from On High. Dr. Akinwande has written some great scenarios."

"My jalookies are probably bigger than Lambert's."

"Pence has trained himself not to ogle."

"Give me a break."

"A harness should do the trick, like what Judy Garland had to wear for *The Wizard of Oz*."

I lurched to my feet, intending to make an abrupt exit. "This is the stupidest idea I've ever heard."

"The harness will be engineered for maximum comfort."

"Actually, the premise of *Tea and Sodomy* was stupider." Despite my martini buzz, I executed a deft about-face. "See you around, Rafael. Thanks for coming to my play."

The pianist started on "Memory" from *Cats*.

"Try to see the larger picture." Rafael swiveled on his stool and seized my wrist. "Okay, sure, voters in the rural South and the cowboy Southwest and the reactionary Midwest will stick with Pence no matter what the fuck he does. But once it becomes obvious that the POTUS is out of control, secessionist fever will sweep through Newtopia, a crisis certain to distract Pence from his cold war on Pacifica."

For over a year now, the eight states constituting the so-called Newtopia zone—New York, New Jersey, New England—had been making noises about leaving the Union. Connecticut and New Hampshire had even floated plebiscites on the question. In both cases, the state had come within fifteen hundred votes of seceding.

"It would certainly serve Pence and his Republican zombies right," I said, "if they suddenly found themselves squeezed between two actual, functioning democracies."

"At the very least, Operation Epiphany will create the general impression of an American president gone bonkers." With his tongue Rafael harvested salt from his margarita glass. "Dr. Akinwande believes our little conspiracy might even inspire U.S. lawmakers to remove Pence from office."

"I'm not convinced. Trump's sociopathy never fazed his lapdog senators. They would've sooner removed God from office."

"The Trump administration never had to cope with Polly Nightingale's brilliant impersonation of Walker Lambert."

Without quite knowing why, I returned to my chair, then waved the waitress over and ordered a second martini. "I'll say one thing, Rafael, this isn't a boring conversation."

"Then you'll do it?"

"My voice is all wrong."

"What really won me over was that star turn you did in *The Blow Job Brigade*, the scene where you mimicked Bill Clinton begging Monica Lewinsky for an enema. You nailed his Arkansas accent."

"Southerners are easy to do."

"Walker Lambert is from Tennessee. Plus, we have Hollywood acting coaches on our payroll. They'll teach you how to dial down your tonsils a full octave. Want to hear one of Dr. Akinwande's scenarios?"

"First tell me what this gig pays."

Maybe it was the pianist's poignant rendition of "Don't Cry for Me, Argentina" that made me say "yes" to Operation Epiphany. Maybe it was the second martini. Maybe it was Dr. Akinwande's sample scenario, which had Pence issuing an edict that forbid U.S. Muslim citizens to observe Ramadan and required them to instead spend that same month eating hot dogs, drinking Budweiser, and decorating their homes with red, white, and blue bunting.

"I shall bring all my acting skills to bear on your little hoax," I said.

Actually, it was none of those things. It was Rafael's answer to my question about the money. The federal government in Sacramento was prepared to reward my Lambert impersonation with a cool million, half payable immediately, half when my talents were no longer needed. Even after taxes there would be enough to cover my grown daughter's tuition bills—past and present—and rent a real theater for my troupe. No more sewers for the Two-Bit Players. Their director was headed for Washington.

The Care and Feeding of Minotaurs finished its run before the month was out, and then I threw myself into the B.U.G.'s unorthodox scheme. Although I'd promised to tell no one about the project, I spilled the beans to Celeste, who was thrilled to learn that the albatross of student debt—she was going for a master's degree in sociology at Stanford—would soon be lifted from her neck.

"Mom, I've never been so proud of you," she said with a wry grin, "not since I learned you'd signed to star in *Orgasm Beach*."

"They're paying me well. This could be a dangerous assignment."

"I'm thrilled. Seriously. Who wouldn't want James Bond for a mother?"

"Don't tell your fiancée about this."

Celeste Nightingale and Sharyn November were planning to get married in the spring. I wouldn't be losing a daughter. I'd be gaining a second daughter—and a future anthropologist.

"Of *course* I'm going to tell Sharyn," said Celeste. "She'll keep it on the QT."

The first stage of my transformation occurred at home, in the privacy of my Marina del Rey apartment. Day after day, I alternately tutored myself in the facts of the Reverend Walker Lambert's life and memorized the sorts of Bible passages favored by evangelical Christians (heavy on the Epistles' salvationistic certainties, light on Jesus's teachings). Although the late Donald Trump had set the scriptural literacy bar pretty low, Pence clearly knew his way around the New Testament, and so I'd better be prepared to trade verses with him.

Two weeks later I embarked on stage two, driving daily to Paramount Studios on Melrose Avenue and placing myself in the hands of skilled artisans. The hairstylists shaped my coiffeur into a facsimile of Lambert's and dyed it to from blonde to ginger. The acting coaches had me watch countless hours of Walker Lambert's inspirational videos, giving me pointers for mimicking his characteristic gestures (his mile-wide smirk came naturally), then taught me how to drop my voice into a faux-testosterone zone, move with a male gait, and wear men's trousers comfortably (though I never found my inner Katharine Hepburn). My final sessions were with the makeup people, who affixed a scar to my chin, tattooed my temples with a dozen freckles, enlarged my Adam's apple with latex, and inserted an oral appliance that twisted my mouth into Lambert's famous snarl (imagine a warthog with a burr up its rectum). And so it was that, tic by tic, nuance by nuance, I became a B.U.G. spy with a fluid gender.

Upon declaring my transformation complete, Rafael introduced me to my traveling companion and liaison, Jamaica-born Ainsley Laveau, a svelte and caramel-skinned double agent who'd fooled the American C.I.A. into thinking she was working for them. Her smile was incandescent, her hair a glorious black turban. Dr. Laveau and her husband, another double agent, maintained a private home in Foggy Bottom, not far from where the real Walker Lambert lived, which meant Ainsley and I could have regular furtive conversations at the K Street Starbucks surrounded by George Washington University students whose mesmerizing high-tech tablets and wireless earbuds would keep them from noticing the outside world.

After confiscating the real Walker Lambert's passport, the B.U.G. had cleverly swapped his photo for one of me in disguise. Ainsley, of course, was credentialed up to her eyebrows. Thus it happened that we encountered no difficulties checking in at LAX or boarding our jetliner. I was wearing my full Lambert regalia, boob harness included: a disagreeable contraption, but I figured I'd soon get used to it.

Flight 4022, nonstop from L.A. to D.C., landed promptly at 3:10 P.M. The only dicey moment occurred when the security agent at Reagan International, a bulky Peter Lorre look-alike with dimples, recognized my name and let out a whoop.

"Reverend Lambert, may I ask you a favor?" he gushed, exiting his bulletproof booth through the rear door.

"If you don't mind, sir," said Ainsley in an icy tone, "the Reverend is exhausted from his recent missionary work in Hollywood."

"Will you lay a hand on my forehead?" asked the agent, leaning into my personal space.

I did as he requested. "May the peace of our Lord Jesus Christ be with you always."

"Now may I touch *you*?"

"Anywhere but the boobs."

"What?"

"Sir, I suggest you stamp our passports within the next ten seconds," said Ainsley, "or I'll arrange to have you fired by the President himself."

My liaison and I spent the rest of the day coping with jet lag and moving me into Lambert's brownstone condo. At Ainsley's insistence, we communicated through whispers, pantomime, and scribbled notes. Mr. Pence, she explained, would think nothing of spying on his PFC. She promised to scour the place for listening devices before the week was out.

Shortly after dusk, I began to relax. There were no family dogs on these premises to fool, no Lambert servants, children, wives, or mistresses to deceive. Within the walls of 1745 N Street NW, I was free to be myself.

"Here's your name badge, impregnated with four kinds of security clearance, plus a three-page scenario." Ainsley handed me a manila envelope (at the B.U.G., paper was actually considered a more secure medium than pixels). "For our opening gambit, we're keeping it simple, a mere set of presidential proclamations, including the Ramadan thing."

"How about a presidential proclamation announcing the end of sanctions against Pacifica?"

"We thought of that. Too risky. If Jesus developed a sudden, inexplicable compassion for Pacificans and conveyed his sentiments to Lambert, Pence would smell a rat. Forty-Six is brighter than his predecessor."

"So is my daughter's cocker spaniel."

"Naturally we hope these edicts make the President seem nuts, but each one is really just a bellwether for gauging the current state of shamelessness at Fox News and the hypocrisy quotient of Pence's communications director."

"I'm embarrassed to say I don't know—"

"A congenitally disingenuous vixen from down Alabama way. Last year Mary Lou Peachum inadvertently told the truth to a roomful of reporters. She spun her way out with such dexterity that Pence gave her a raise. That gag you pulled at the airport about boobs—no more of that, Polly."

"I understand."

"Really?"

"Cross my heart. So what's the deal, Ainsley? Do I simply waltz over to the White House tomorrow and knock on the door to the Oral Office?"

"Oval."

"I was thinking of Clinton."

"Try not to."

"Do I knock on the door and say, 'Hey, Mr. President, I'm back'?"

"Before our plane took off, our people in Sacramento sent an email in your name to Pence's chief of staff. After some to-and-fro-ing, they arranged a meeting between you and the President this coming Thursday at two forty-five. Just hunker down in the White House chapel right after lunch. We want you to be at prayer when he arrives—you know, like Claudius when Hamlet comes to kill him."

"Are you saying this assignment is more perilous than I thought?"

"Claudius didn't die—at least not in his chapel," said Ainsley. "We'll meet at Starbucks next week. Let me say something, sweetie. It's not every day that Pacifica gets the services of a citizen spook."

"A well-paid citizen spook."

"I'm grateful to you, Polly. I really am. After this craziness is over, let's think about becoming friends."

There was room for only four short pews, but what the White House chapel lacked in spaciousness and furnishings, it made up for in a glorious past. Researching the facility on the Internet, I learned that American presidents had sought heavenly guidance as a matter of administrative routine. No comparable zone in all of D.C. had sustained so many prayers per square inch.

Within these hallowed walls Richard Nixon had reportedly pleaded for divine assistance in extricating himself from the Watergate mess. It was here that Ronald Regan solicited supernatural permission to ignore apartheid and the AIDS epidemic, George W. Bush received his Savior's blessing to mount an ill-conceived crusade called Operation Enduring Freedom, and Donald Trump was told by three angels that converting the chapel into his private latrine, complete with a solid gold toilet, would not be in his best interests.

I did as Ainsley advised, falling on my knees before the silver cross hanging above the pulpit: a posture I hadn't assumed since completing my confirmation classes at the First Methodist Church of Teaneck. As I fixed on the chapel's solitary window, a sunbeam poured through the stained-glass mosaic—Jesus riding into Jerusalem—and projected the donkey's head onto the white silk cloth draping the altar. Instead of praying, I mentally rehearsed the various revelations I intended to share with Pence.

My first face-to-face impression of the President of the United States was not positive—he struck me as a kind of humanoid weasel—but then I realized this wasn't Pence at all but a Secret Service agent. The Chief Executive entered next. He wore his seventy-eight years well: robust red complexion, bright white hair, clear eyes, trim figure. His demeanor radiated an abiding calm. Against all odds, I liked him.

"Good to see you again, Mike," I said, vigorously shaking his hand while my other hand clamped his forearm (my research having revealed this was standard protocol between Lambert and Pence). "How's life been treating you? Praise Jesus."

Two more Secret Service agents crowded into the room. One of them had a briefcase handcuffed to his right wrist—the nuclear codes, I figured.

"Sorry to interrupt your prayers, Walker," said Pence. "Praise Jesus."

"I don't normally put Heaven on hold, Mr. President," I said (a certain levity was reportedly characteristic of Lambert). "But for you, sir—*anything!*"

Pence laughed. A fourth and fifth Secret Service guy arrived. The chapel was jammed to the walls.

"And two hardboiled eggs," I said.

Pence laughed again. "I get it. *A Day at the Races.* The state-room scene."

"*A Night at the Opera.*"

"If Mr. Trump had made that mistake," said Pence, "he would've arranged for the scene to be inserted into every existing print of *A Day at the Races*."

I'll say one thing for Pence. He had few illusions about Forty-Five. "Most amusing, sir."

"God rest his soul."

"God rest his soul," I echoed.

"I hear you've been doing missionary work in Hollywood."

"An evangelist goes where he's most needed."

"Your email to my chief of staff mentioned a divine dispatch."

"While prophesying amidst the fleshpots of Pacifica, I experienced a cavalcade of visions," I said, inhaling deeply. My spandex harness was tight but bearable (luckily I was only a B cup). "Jesus Christ has special expectations for the tenth year of the reign of Michael Richard Pence. Allow me to communicate our Lord's most fervent desires directly to you." I knitted my brow and rotated my head, training a harsh gaze on each Secret Service agent in turn. "Might we continue this conversation in private?"

Pence nodded to his bodyguards. They picked up the cue and sidled out of the room.

"Mike, is it true you never allow yourself to be alone with a woman?"

"Didn't we have that conversation last month?"

"Sorry, sir. I forgot."

"The thing I liked most about being V.P. was all the Secret Service chaperons, and as President I get even *more*. Tell me what's on Jesus's mind."

"So if I were a woman, we wouldn't be having this tête-à-tête?"

"Walker …."

"Early in my Hollywood mission, I attended an obscene piece of pagan street theater staged in a municipal culvert, all about the Minotaur and his victims. The bull-man's mother was played by the notorious Polly Nightingale, former porn star."

"Is she a friend of Mr. Trump's favorite such actress?"

"No, but she admires and respects Miss Daniels's work. I went to every performance of *The Care and Feeding of Minotaurs*, so I could track down Miss Nightingale afterward and tell her about our Lord. She always invited me back to her apartment in Marina de Rey."

"And did you go?"

"Only because she was hungry for spiritual guidance. Nothing carnal happened between us."

"Good for you."

"I didn't even inhale her fragrance."

"Excellent."

"I grabbed her pussy only once."

"What?"

"Here's the astonishing part: each evening, right before I fell asleep on Miss Nightingale's couch, a voice came forth from a Lucite *tchotchke* she keeps on her end table," I said (confident that vivid details would make my narrative persuasive). "It's actually an award she got for best actress at the Santa Barbara Adult Film Festival. It's in the shape of … I hesitate to tell you, sir."

"A … male member?"

"A vagina. The award also functions as a lava lamp. Industry wags call it the Burning Bush. Every night, the voice from the lamp offered me a new and different revelation. They all concerned hypothetical presidential proclamations. On Thursday, the message was about Ramadan. On Friday, tax reform. On Saturday, Alaska."

"The state?"

"The state."

"I thought maybe the dessert."

"On Sunday, a national holiday. On Monday—well, come Monday night all the theaters in L.A. go dark, just like on Broadway, so I didn't see the play, and I didn't end up in Miss Nightingale's apartment. No matter. She'd already accepted our Lord as her personal Savior."

"What sort of tax reform?"

"Jesus calls it a poverty tax."

"Property tax?"

"Poverty."

"I don't understand."

"Harken."

Authorized Transcript: Michael Pence's Communications Director Fields Questions from White House Press Corps, April 18, 2035.

MARY LOU PEACHUM: Okay, let's get started. Ralph?

RALPH ENDICOTT, Fox-CNN: Could you give us the President's reasoning behind outlawing Ramadan? That lefty newsrag down in Texas, the *Austin Fellow Traveler* ...

(Laughter)

PEACHUM: Don't be naughty, Ralph.

ENDICOTT: I mean the *Austin Gazette*—that paper would have us believe this proclamation is anti-Muslim.

PEACHUM: As everybody here knows, Mr. Pence welcomes all faiths to these shores, with the proviso that the creeds in question are not antagonistic to our values.

(Burble of voices)

BRODERICK GREYBILL, *Atlanta Bulletin*: Mary Lou! Mary Lou!

PEACHUM: Yes, Brod?

GREYBILL: But the First Amendment prohibits government interference in the free exercise of religion.

PEACHUM: No, it prohibits government interference in the free exercise of the *Christian* religion. Read your Constitution.

(Burble of voices)

FLORENCE PRENTISS, Fox-MSNBC: Madam Director!

PEACHUM: Go ahead, Flo.

PRENTISS: Some of our viewers are confused by Mr. Pence's recent endorsement of a so-called poverty tax.

PEACHUM: Contrary to rumor, this proposed addition to the IRS Code isn't about balancing the budget. Social scientists have recently proved that low-income and no-income families have in most cases brought their sorry condition on themselves.

SHOLO SOBOWALE, *Philadelphia Herald*: Can you give us some corroboration on that? You know, a footnote?

PEACHUM: A footnote? No, but I'd be happy to give you *the boot*.

(Laughter)

SOBOWALE: Touché, Mary Lou.

PEACHUM: By making undeserving moochers pay for their antisocial behavior, the poverty tax will inspire them to finally go out and acquire some marketable skills. Everybody wins.

(Burble of voices)

MIKAEL GERASIMENKO, *Pravda*: Question about Alaska!

PEACHUM: Fire away, Mikael.

GERASIMENKO: While Mr. Pence's decision to sell Alaska to the Russian Federation went over well in my country, I've heard that certain presidential advisors and even a few Fox journalists were dismayed by this decision.

PEACHUM: Thank you, Mr. Gerasimenko. No comment.

GERASIMENKO: Perhaps the Fox journalists in the room would like to comment.

PEACHUM: No, they wouldn't.

ERIC SHERIDAN, Fox-PBS: Oh, *yes*, they would.

PEACHUM: Okay, folks, here's the skinny on Alaska. The President got tired of all the whining from Newtopia about the plight of the caribou and the polar bears and the Arctic rattlesnakes and so on. By putting the Alaskan ecosystem under Russian jurisdiction, he's inviting the environmental alarmists to take their case to Moscow. They won't receive a sympathetic hearing, of course, which will only serve them right.

(Burble of voices)

GERASIMENKO: Mother Russia will treat her newly acquired polar bears like royalty.

PEACHUM: How nice for them. Jordan, what's on your mind?

JORDAN AGATHON, *New York Examiner*: Presidential Directive Thirty-Two.

PEACHUM: Refresh my memory.

AGATHON: Making Kristallnacht a National Holiday.

PEACHUM: Now I remember.

AGATHON: How do you answer the charge that this decree partakes of anti-Semitism?

PEACHUM: Mr. Pence has made his thinking on this matter quite clear. During Kristallnacht there were good people on both sides of the windows. Anti-Semitism? Israel never had a better friend than Mike Pence, and you know it. Emperor Netanyahu said so himself.

AGATHON: But Kristallnacht didn't occur on American soil.

PEACHUM: Bite me, Jordan. What do you know of soil? The treaty that led to a permanent ceasefire in World War One was signed in faraway France, and yet for many years this country observed Armistice Day. Don't talk to me about soil.

AGATHON: What's next, Mary Lou? National Jim Crow Week?

PEACHUM: I hope you enjoyed popping that snark, Clyde, because starting today you're no longer a member of the White House Press Corps.

AGATHON: The same to your cat.

(Burble of voices)

PEACHUM: Francine, you've had your hand up all morning. Too bad we're out of time.

My mood was gloomy, my gait lethargic, when I entered the K Street Starbucks. Even the sublime aroma of Sumatra coffee beans and the anticipation of a double espresso could not dispel the darkness. The first phase of Operation Epiphany had evidently been a flop. Despite the aggressive nature of his recent edicts, Pence's favorability ratings remained at an all-time high.

I pulled a copy of the *Washington Observer* from the rack, then shuffled to the sales counter and placed my order. Nobody recognized Walker Lambert, probably because I used my normal voice, wore a Nationals baseball cap, and had swapped the damn spandex harness for a comfortable linen bra. Nobody recognized Polly Nightingale, either. My now defunct fan club never had a D.C. chapter.

Double latte in hand, I approached a small table in the far corner, where Ainsley Laveau was sipping cappuccino.

"Sacramento is pleased with your work so far." True to form, the G.W. students were immured behind glowing tablets and active earbuds, so Ainsley didn't bother to whisper. "President Yoshida said to pass along her personal congratulations."

"Here's what I think went wrong." I plunked down my cup, taking care not to slop espresso onto Ainsley's phone. "When Pence went on TV and announced his new policies, he didn't sound *excited*."

"During your meeting in the chapel, did he get juiced when you first described the Jesus edicts?"

"His eyes lit up as I told him about the poverty tax. But Ramadan, Alaska, and Kristallnacht left him cold."

"Relax, sweetie. For phase one, the B.U.G. was merely feeling out Pence's defenses."

"But as long as he leaves the passion to his Fox cheerleaders and doesn't get worked up *himself*, he seems weirdly innocuous. We need him to act crazy, right? He's not acting crazy. He's just making crazy proclamations."

"Crazy is just around the corner." Ainsley pulled a business envelope from the inside pocket of her business suit and set it next to my espresso. "My bosses have cooked up some real humdingers for phase two."

"Shouldn't you wait for me to accidentally drop my newspaper on the floor?"

"Huh?"

"So you can pick it up, furtively slip the envelope inside, and hand the paper back to me."

"We don't do that shit."

"So I bought an *Observer* for no reason? My daughter *hates* that paper."

"This time around," said Ainsley, "Jesus will want Pence to paint the White House black as a memorial to all those babies who got murdered during the *Roe v. Wade* era." Her enthusiasm sounded forced, like a dog barking on command. "Heaven also expects him to create a new cabinet-level office, the Department of Faith, and to repeal the Endangered Species Act as, quote, 'an insidious form of affirmative action.'"

"Forgive me, Ainsley, but this is penny-ante stuff."

"Rafael and Omoyola tell me they considered having Pence make irony illegal." Her voice was weary. Her face looked like she'd slept in it. "But they never agreed on what that might mean."

"We've got to do better."

Ainsley released a mournful sigh. "You know, honey, you're right."

As if cued by her distress, Ainsley's phone sang out a text alert. She opened the application, read the encrypted message, and scowled. "It's from Rafael. He says to go find a live news broadcast—*any* live news broadcast—pronto."

We turned in tandem to face the Fox-MSNBC monitor mounted over the Starbucks cream-and-sugar station. Frightened children. Weeping adults. Fluttering yellow barrier tape. Stroboscopic lights flashing on police cruisers.

The chyron caption read, MASS SHOOTING AT SYCAMORE ELEMENTARY SCHOOL IN PHILADELPHIA SUBURBS.

"Rafael says he and Omoyola already have a Sycamore scenario in mind," said Ainsley, staring at her phone. "Quote, 'Forget the old phase two. Smart money rides on our new script. Details to follow.'"

"So your bosses are trying to exploit a *school shooting*? Jesus. Can't they leave some things *alone*?"

"Not until the U.S. decides to leave Pacifica alone. All's fair in love and war, Polly. And this isn't love.

II

UNLIKE most mass shootings in the United States, the Sycamore Elementary School massacre was a coordinated operation carried out with military precision. Decency demands that I set down the obscene details. Three classes targeted: Karen Murchison's first graders, Patricia Keane's second graders, Peter Gardner's third graders. Three gunmen: white males in their twenties equipped with a variety of firearms, all hailing from an organization called the A.R.M., the Appropriately Regulated Militia (about four hundred gun aficionados who'd gotten kicked out of the N.R.A. for espousing a variety of nihilism even Wayne LaPierre couldn't stomach). Ninety-two children shot, seventy-four dying instantly, eight expiring in transit, seven surviving with permanent neurological deficits, three recovering in full. As for the teachers and their assistants, five out of six went to their graves that morning.

Because Mrs. Murchison, Ms. Keane, and Mr. Gardner kept loaded Glock pistols in their desks, as required by government fiat (Donald Trump's "packing pedagogues proclamation" of 2024), it was assumed that the attorneys for the gunmen would defend their clients through appeals to the "stand your ground" statute recently enacted by the Pennsylvania legislature. Some Fox News commentators predicted that the trio would never even face prosecution. Whatever the future might hold for Brick Riddle, Duke Fallows, and Leon Ipecac, all three were let out on bail, $50,000 per gunman, a sum posted in full by the A.R.M.

Determined to stick it to the rival organization, Sarah Palin, chief executive of the N.R.A., went on Andrew Schlafly's Fox News program and said, "I'm here to offer a special message to all them grievin' moms and dads out there. Moms and dads, I want you to know our organization is sendin' more thoughts and prayers your way than you'd a-ever thought possible."

At my next Starbucks meeting with Ainsley, she handed me a flash drive containing an audio recording prepared by her B.U.G. colleagues in Sacramento.

"It figures crucially in your next revelation to Pence," she explained. "Rafael and Omoyola believe they can turn the Sycamore tragedy into a victory for Operation Epiphany."

"I don't like hearing 'Sycamore' and 'victory' in the same sentence."

"We're paying you for performances, not opinions."

Ainsley passed me the latest scenario, a double-spaced printout on a sheet of computer paper. She told me to memorize my dialogue, crumple up the page, and eat it.

"You're kidding, right?"

"Eat it."

"Last week you said the B.U.G. doesn't do cloak-and-dagger stuff."

"We like to be unpredictable."

I studied the scenario, wadded it up, and inserted it in my mouth. I chewed. It tasted like seaweed bleached in Clorox. I washed it down with my latte. The G.W. students remained fixed on their lambent screens.

My misery knew no bottom. The lines I was digesting were beyond the pale of the pale. Only the world's greatest actress could perform the new B.U.G. scenario with sufficient solemnity and conviction to keep Pence from suspecting a conspiracy. I wasn't Meryl Streep, but I vowed to give it my best shot.

"The latest piece of the divine plan might surprise you, Mike," I told the President shortly after he and three Secret Service guys joined me in the White House chapel. "There I was, strolling through Constitution Gardens, when the hydrangeas opened their mouths—well, not their *literal* mouths—they don't have any—and sang a message from our Savior. It concerns the Presidential Medal of Freedom."

Pence removed a Double Whooper with cheese from his attaché case and peeled away the brown paper wrapping. "I've heard of that award. My memory's a little hazy today."

"The highest civilian honor the Chief Executive can bestow."

"Marvelous." Pence began chomping his way through his lunch.

"Mike, I'm pretty sure cheeseburgers don't help a hazy memory."

"Donald got me hooked." Pence pulled a bag of French fries from his case. "I'm crazy about these things, too. Want one? Praise Jesus."

"No, thank you. Praise Jesus."

"Brad? Milton? Gus?"

The agents shook their heads.

"According to Executive Order 11085," I said, "the Presidential Medal of Freedom is awarded for, quote, 'an especially meritorious contribution to the security or national interests of the United States,' unquote. It's a white enamel star surrounded by gold eagles. Nixon gave one to the Apollo 13 crew. Reagan pinned one on Mother Teresa."

"Who am I giving it to?"

"Our Lord wants you to honor three men who, by dramatizing the fallacies perpetrated by our country's gun-control fanatics, have greatly strengthened the Second Amendment and, by extension, the safety and freedom of private citizens throughout the nation."

"Let me guess. Sarah Palin, Wayne LaPierre, and Ollie North."

"Brick Riddle, Duke Fallows, and Leon Ipecac."

Pence turned as white as the interior of his hamburger bun. The Secret Service agents rolled their eyes and looked at their shoes.

"The gunmen who murdered all those sweet little children?" wailed the President. "I'm supposed to *reward* those guys?"

"I understand your confusion, Mike," I said, inserting the flash drive in my laptop. "Allow me to play a brief recording. You're about to hear the voice of Sally Balaban, one of the mothers who lost a son at Sycamore Elementary."

Authorized Transcript: Messrs. Riddle, Fallows, and Ipecac on CBS Public Affairs Program, "Face the Fourth Estate," September 8, 2035.

ALAN FLYNN, *Boston Sentinel*: Mr. Riddle, you have identified yourself as the guiding force behind the recent disruption at Sycamore Elementary School.

BRICK RIDDLE: Yep, but I couldn't a-done it without Duke and Leon here, my fellow members of the A.R.M.

FLYNN: Please tell the press—and the nation at large—why you decided to call your plan the Definitive Instructional Event.

RIDDLE: As I needn't tell you, Alan, every time one of these school-type shootings occurs, there's a great hue and cry throughout the land, or at least throughout the pinko northeast, and some socialist lawmaker or other sets out to deball the Second Amendment. And then one day it dawned on me. What we needed was a demonstration that would forever silence the gun-control crowd in one swell foop."

FLYNN: You mean "one fell swoop."

RIDDLE: No, "swell foop," an expression from when knighthood was in flower. I figured that, once people absorb the implications of the D.I.E., America would find herself on a brand new calendar, keyed to B.S. versus A.S.

JORDAN AGATHON, *New York Examiner*: Before Sycamore versus After Sycamore?

RIDDLE: You got it. Mark my words. In the near future, whenever some Marxist-Leninist congressman from Vermont gets out his Constitution castration kit, all a patriot needs to do is spit in his eye and say, "Sorry, Charlie, that foop has flown. You're making a B.S. argument, and this is an A.S. world, so go home to your *kumbaya* garage band and leave firearms regulations to the grownups." Take the seductive notion of criminal background checks. Duke here, who we put in charge of Mrs. Murchison's first graders, has a perfectly clean record when it comes to drug arrests, jail sentences, and straightjackets, but he *still* brought down his targets with his Galil ACE and his FX-05 Xiuhcoatl."

DUKE FALLOWS: I've never even gotten a speeding ticket.

AGATHON: But isn't it a fact, Mr. Riddle, that you yourself did hard time in a New Jersey penitentiary for armed robbery? And didn't Mr. Ipecac, after graduating from high school, spend two years at Cedarbrook Psychiatric Center after burning down his girlfriend's parents' house?

RIDDLE: True enough, but *our* roles in the D.I.E. had nothing to do with background checks. *My* job was to expose the flawed thinking behind leftist enthusiasm for banning automatic weapons. I played my part at Sycamore Elementary using nothing but two single-action, magazine-fed pistols. I deliberately left my Remington GPC at home.

AGATHON: But you hit only half as many targets as Mr. Ipecac and Mr. Fallows, who *did* use automatic weapons.

RIDDLE: True, but they had *different* political points to make that morning. Why can't you people grasp the logic of this? We cast the D.I.E. the way we did for very good philosophical reasons.

LEON IPECAC: *My* assignment was to give the lie to the promiscuous obtainability argument.

DORIS CRENSHAW, *Chicago Inquirer:* Are you referring to the notion that it's too easy for an American citizen to build up a vast private military arsenal?

IPECAC: Right. I ordered my Beretta ARX160 from a sporting goods store in Massachusetts, and you can't *imagine* the red tape they put me through. "Fill out this form in triplicate." "Mail us proof that you passed a certified firearms-safety course." "We need two copies of your birth certificate." "Send us a urine sample." The process took three whole months. I'm joshin' 'bout the urine sample. Finally my ARX came in the mail, just in time for the Sycamore demonstration.

RIDDLE: What Leon's ordeal proves is this: even if you banned all weapons transactions on the Internet—even if you shut down the gun shows, outlawed rifle raffles, confiscated pistol-vending machines, forbid big-box stores to sell firearms, and imposed strict quotas on law-abiding families, say, two assault rifles per household—people would *still* acquire the technology they needed to defend themselves and protect their God-given freedoms from the God-given freedom takers.

CRENSHAW: But isn't it true that Mr. Riddle won his Remington GPC at a Grange Fair bingo tournament? Didn't Mr. Fallows receive his Galil ACE as a door prize at a church social?

FALLOWS: Brick and I weren't in charge of unmasking the anti-obtainability fraudsters. In the context of the D.I.E., it wouldn't matter if we'd gotten our guns out of a friggin' Cracker Jack box. Surely that makes sense to you.

CRENSHAW: I know it makes sense to *you*.

RIDDLE: Before this golden opportunity slips away, Duke, Leon, and me would like to express our profound appreciation to every adult out there who lost a child during the D.I.E.

FALLOWS: Especially if you loved that tyke to itty-bitty pieces.

IPECAC: But there comes a time in a patriot's life when that person must put the Constitution ahead of all other considerations, and every one of you rose to the occasion.

RIDDLE: Duke, Leon, and me also want to state we were in police custody long before any moms or dads arrived on the scene. In other words, contrary to some unfortunate Internet gossip, Angela Martin's father did *not* volunteer to help me reload. He wasn't even there yet.

FALLOWS: And despite what you may have read in *Der Stürmer Online*, Thomas Balaban's mother did *not* tell me, "I won't do any special pleading for my little Tommy over there, because we simply can't let our American way of life fall into the wrong hands."

CRENSHAW: But President Pence said he heard a recording of Mrs. Balaban saying precisely those words. It prompted his decision to award you all medals.

RIDDLE: The recording is obviously a forgery.

FALLOWS: Produced and directed by the Father of Lies himself, most likely.

RIDDLE: In any event, I'm not giving back my medal, unless so ordered by the Commander in Chief.

FALLOWS: Mine's already hangin' on the Christmas tree.

IPECAC: Mine's sittin' on my mom's nightstand in the nursing home.

FLYNN: Thank you for a stimulating discussion, gentlemen. We have to break for a commercial, and then we'll interview George Frye, chairman of the House Pollution Control Abatement Committee."

RIDDLE: We appreciate this opportunity to tell our side of the story.

FLYNN: Before you three leave the studio, let me offer you a quaint benediction I learned at my grandmother's knee. "May the curse of Molly Malone and her nine blind illegitimate children chase you so far over the hills of damnation that Jesus Christ himself couldn't find you with a telescope."

Exactly one week after the *Face the Fourth Estate* broadcast featuring the A.R.M. gunmen, the pollsters released a new set of data. Lo and behold, Pence's overall favorability rating among Republicans had slipped from 98 percent to 82 percent, and his acceptability to Democrats had dropped from 14 percent to 6 percent. What was more, 28 percent of Republicans polled agreed with the idea that, in awarding Riddle, Fallows, and Ipecac the Presidential Medal of Freedom, Pence had gone too far.

Although the Chief Executive didn't make the gunmen forfeit their medals (he was not about to flout a divine directive), he came to realize that the White House had taken the wrong side in the Sycamore controversy. Eventually he tweeted his opinion that Riddle, Fallows, and Ipecac should be tried for murder, "just like a pregnant mother who kills her baby," even if the stand-your-ground defense eventually set them free.

"Now that we've got the POTUS on the run, or at least confused, my bosses want to keep up the momentum," Ainsley told me during our next Starbucks rendezvous. "Phase three will play out in south Texas. It concerns, in Rafael's words, 'an historical pageant to end all historical pageants.'"

She described the event as a four-day-long extravaganza called Carnivaliant, celebrating the two hundredth anniversary of the Texas Revolution of 1836. This epic jamboree was the brainchild of the venerable Sam Houston Society, which the B.U.G. had infiltrated so completely that Pacifica agents were now in charge of the Alamo Reenactment component. Scheduled for the last day of the festival, the pageant would unfold on a facsimile of the famous, repurposed Franciscan mission—a three-quarter-scale replica occupying the Shahan Ranch in Brackettville, adjacent to a sprawling mockup of old San Antonio (both the fortress and the town were originally commissioned by John Wayne for his 1960 Hollywood spectacle, *The Alamo*). All the Sam Houston Society had to do was add stadium seating, floodlights, a sound system, and video screens.

"Okay, but what does all this have to do with making Pence look unhinged?" I asked.

"During the reenactment, the President will play William Barret Travis, commander of the colonial forces."

"Because that's what Heaven wants him to do?"

"Precisely." Ainsley and I traded subversive smiles. For a fleeting instant we savored the image of buttoned-up Mike Pence wearing frontier clothes and flanked by similarly attired Secret Service agents. "The two hundred Alamo defenders will be chosen by lottery from a pool of native-born Texans. To play the Mexican Army, the B.U.G. will furtively select fifteen hundred Pacifica college students. Now here's the kicker. Our moles in the Houston Society will make the world believe that Santa Anna's soldiers were recruited from certain controversial detainment facilities along the Rio Grande." She was doubtless referring to the wretched camps in which the Department of Homeland Security had incarcerated thousands of undocumented immigrants, dissident homosexuals, disaffected journalists, and allegedly subversive Muslims. "What won me over was my mental picture of the President standing on the ramparts and ordering his men to fire on undesirable minorities as they storm the fortress."

"No live ammunition, I assume."

"Correct, but the optics will still be terrible for Republicans."

"Okay, but ending the festival with the Mexican Army massacring the Alamo defenders—won't that be a downer?"

"The B.U.G. screenwriter, Ogden McQuaid, the anonymous author of a hundred anti-Trump videos on QueueTube, thought so, too. After the fortress falls, three angels will use separate winches to hoist William Travis, Jim Bowie, and Davy Crockett into Heaven. This is political theater on amphetamines, Polly, gaudier even than that god-awful military parade Forty-Five staged during his last year. You know about *theater*, sweetie."

Theater. A thrill scurried up and down my spine. Phase three was growing on me. "Let me suggest that, every time a Latinx, queer, journalist, or Muslim in Santa Anna's army takes a bullet, we should see some gore. That way the TV coverage and the home videos will make Pence look like a homicidal maniac."

"McQuaid's script calls for stage-blood packets bursting all over the place."

"Well, not *too* many packets," I said. "The children, you know …."

"Good point."

"The Two-Bit Players would never *dare* attempt anything like this."

"Fortune favors the audacious."

When Pence and his bodyguards entered the White House chapel, I realized that his habitual equanimity had deserted him. Although the man never touched alcohol, he seemed to be suffering from a kind of mirthless intoxication, like Brett Kavanaugh after breakfast. Was it too much to hope that the Battle of the Alamo would lift his spirits?

"I wonder why our Savior didn't warn you that the recording of Mrs. Balaban was a hoax hatched in Hell," he said in a low gravelly voice.

"The Lord works in mysterious ways."

"But surely not in concert with Lucifer."

"Occasionally Christ elects to teach us how clever the Devil can be. That recording was a test. Can the Reverend Walker Lambert spot a satanic snare? I failed miserably. From now on, I must redouble my guard against Lucifer's wiles."

"My approval rating dropped six percent. Do you think I should take away their medals?"

"That horse has left the barn. Might I suggest we put Sycamore behind us? I have a new revelation to share."

Without saying a word, the Secret Service agents sidled out of the chapel. Pence sank onto a pew and buried his face in his hands.

"Maybe I should've remained a Catholic," he rasped. "My mother never got over my evangelical conversion. Catholics have it easy, all those priests and rituals buffering them against God's remorseless glory. But to be born again, Walker—to be *born again* and encounter our Savior *directly*—sometimes it's too much for a mortal brain. How do you *stand* it?"

"I find that Jesus never gives me more absolute knowledge of the universe's inner workings than I can handle. Take yesterday for example. No sooner had I started my daily walk along the Potomac than a golden fish leaped out of the water and landed at my feet."

Pence lifted his head. Awash in sunlight, the stained-glass window painted the Palm Sunday tableau on his troubled face.

"Fish," he muttered. " 'Ichthys' in Greek. Five sacred initials: Iota, Chi, Theta, Upsilon, Sigma."

I had done my homework. "Ichthys, indeed, sir. Iesous, Christos, Theou, Yios, Soter."

"Jesus, Christ, Son of God, Savior."

"The fish told me—well, not 'told,' exactly, more like telepathy—it told me about Carnivaliant. A huge event. Mardi Gras for patriots. Burning Man for normal people. The climax will be a reenactment of the fall of the Alamo staged on a ranch in Brackettville. Gabriel and his fellow archangels have someone particular in mind for the role of William Travis, who co-commanded the garrison with Jim Bowie until Bowie got sick."

"I'm not up on my actors. Is Robert de Niro too old? Surely Heaven wants nothing to do with that traitor."

"*You've* been selected, sir."

"Me?"

"The vote by the Council of Angels was unanimous."

"Sounds like a meaty part."

"The script has you dictating aloud the most patriotic letter in American history, an all-points plea for reinforcements. After narrating how Santa Anna had issued an ultimatum earlier that day—surrender or be massacred—Travis then added, and I quote, 'I have answered the demand with a cannon shot, and our flag still waves proudly from the walls. I shall never surrender or retreat.' "

"I shall never surrender or retreat!" cried Pence.

"You're gonna knock it out of the park, Mike."

"What happened to the fish?"

"It wriggled back into the river, but not before revealing that the Houston Society will cast Santa Anna's regiments by visiting our Rio Grande internment camps and putting fifteen hundred detainees in nineteenth-century Mexican Army uniforms. Can you picture it, sir? Can you see the thundering hordes of aliens, queers, journalists, and Muslims sweeping north from the border seeking to abort the embryonic Republic of Texas?"

"Yes! Yes! My blood is thumping!"

"Come Carnivaliant, the blood of all Republicans will thump in unison! Did I mention that Heaven and the Houston Society will give you a free hand in casting Jim Bowie and Davy Crockett?"

"Wonderful. Er … we all get massacred, don't we?"

"History always bats last."

"Shouldn't the festival end on a more positive note? Can't the Society also do the final battle of the Texas Revolution? Yorktown, was that it?"

"San Jacinto."

"Wouldn't it be nice to see the illegal aliens and the deep-state journalists get their comeuppance?"

"The Society has an even better idea. Travis, Bowie, and Crockett will all wear special harnesses. After they die, they'll be winched into the skies, bound for glory."

"A harness? Sounds uncomfortable."

"I've had experience with harnesses. You'll get used to it."

"I think George Bush would make a terrific Bowie."

"An inspired choice, Mike. A Texan portraying a Texan."

"I've got an even *better* idea for Crockett. You were born to play the King of the Wild Frontier. You've got the Tennessee accent and everything."

"I'm no actor, sir."

"Neither am I. This is going to be fun, Walker. Put on your buckskins, take down Old Betsy from the mantel, and come with me to Brackettville. That's an order from your President."

From: Burgess Armitage <hornytoad@gmail.com>
To: Amos Orloff <deplorablepatriot@gmail.com>
Cc: Slack Kovich <fourthmusketeer@gmail.com>,
    Elton Coates <ladiesman@gmail.com>
Date: Tuesday, February 11, 2036, at 10:44 AM
Subject: An Alamo They'll Never Forget

Amos,

Okay, so our attempt to rig the Alamo Defenders Lottery was not a roaring success. My original plan called for a dozen live-ammo delivery men on the ramparts, but we'll have to make do with you, Slack, Elton, and me.

We can still accomplish the mission, as long as we don't accidentally set our phasers on stun, if you catch my drift.

I assume your submacs (with CRM-114 anti-detection chips) have arrived. It turns out my calculations were correct. A chopped-down Uzi is easier to hide than a loaf of bread. When the time comes, we could try smuggling them inside the mission in knapsacks or tobacco pouches, but that's too risky. Attach the piece to your stomach with duct tape, so it looks like a beer belly.

I sense Mr. Trump is watching over us. Do you feel it, too? He's up there in the sky, shooting the breeze with Jesus and monitoring our every move. He's proud of us, Amos. He's by-God proud.

Karen says she would like Lillian's recipe for shoo-fly pie.

Yours, Burgess

On Feb 13, at 4:55 PM, Amos Orloff <deplorablepatriot@ gmail.com> wrote:

During the reenactment, we'll need monogrammed coonskin caps to help us identify each other through the smoke and the dust. Here's an idea: KAGA.

That is, Keep America Great Always.

Yes, I got my Uzi. A real beaut. Yesterday I snuck it into my son's middle school. The A-D chip functioned perfectly.

The single-shot option is for the birds, of course, but I tried the spray mode last night in my backyard. It didn't overheat or jam. I figure we can each take out 90 undesirables per minute. According to the Carnivaliant website, the invading hordes will carry banners indicating their loyalties. I call dibs on the Muslims.

I tried your duct tape method. A-OK. In your next email, could you tell us the details of the escape plan?

Yeah, I can feel his presence. He's going to be with us every step of the way. Jesus called him home, but his spirit yet abides on earth.

The recipe is attached.

On Feb 16, at 12:19 PM, Burgess Armitage <hornytoad@ gmail.com> wrote:

KAGA. I love it.

Okay, Amos, you do the Muslims. I'll spray the undocumenteds. Slack and Elton, you can work out between yourselves who thins out the journalists and who cancels the faggots.

Concerning the escape plan: once we've emptied our magazines, we'll capitalize on the confusion by skedaddling to the San Antonio mock-up and the parking lot beyond. I haven't decided who should drive the getaway truck. My boy Isaac just got his learner's permit, but we'd probably do better with his mother.

On Feb 20, at 9:57 AM, Amos Orloff <deplorablepatriot@ gmail.com> wrote:

Burgess, have you factored in what it means that the POTUS will be manning the ramparts? It means you, me, Slack, and Elton won't be the only ones who brought real bullets to the party.

I think we can best handle the situation by plugging the Secret Service agents at the outset.

On Feb 20, at 11:00 AM, Slack Kovich <fourthmusketeer@ gmail.com> wrote:

I agree with Amos.

On Feb 20, at 1:09 PM, Elton Coates <ladiesman@gmail.com> wrote:

So do I.

On Feb 21, at 8:07 PM, Burgess Armitage <hornytoad@gmail.com> wrote:

Let me think it over.

Shortly after I returned to the N Street condo from the White House chapel, my daughter texted me to say she was in town. She had a dispensation from the U.S. State Department to conduct research at the Library of Congress (a privilege not normally granted to Marxist graduate students from foreign countries). I figured she must have persuaded one of Secretary Buchanan's underlings that her project was politically neutral and, furthermore, that the Pence administration would benefit from appearing to sanction intellectual curiosity, even the sort of socialist intellectual curiosity they cultivated in Pacifica.

Can I come over? she wanted to know.

I'll cook you dinner, I typed back.

Since when can you cook?

Since I learned about "Smorgas on Board, the App for Discerning Appetites." Traveling alone?

Sharyn's in CA, meeting with her dissertation advisor.

I was still wearing my Walker Lambert regalia—boob harness, fake Adam's apple, dental appliance—when Celeste arrived at my *pied-à-terre,* and she did me the favor of not bursting into laughter.

"Mom, you've been doing a *fantastic* job," she said. "Sharyn wants to reboot the Polly Nightingale Fan Club, though of course that would blow your cover. I gather that Pence's reaction to the Sycamore Elementary horror got scads of legislators in Jersey and Rhode Island drafting articles of secession."

"Darling, Sycamore is not something we want to discuss at dinner."

She leaned toward me and whispered, "Are you saying we shouldn't discuss *anything* at dinner?"

"Don't worry, we're not being spied on. The B.U.G. agents have gone over this place with mic-sniffing beagles. What brought you to the Library?"

"My thesis has morphed into a study of the American passion for ideal communities. The Shaker villages, New Harmony, Brook Farm, arguably Salt Lake City. My working title is *Engineering Eden*."

"I can't wait to read it."

"I can't wait to write it."

The movable feast Celeste and I consumed that night, expertly prepared and promptly delivered, left nothing to be desired. The baked salmon was superb, the roasted vegetables sublime, the mashed potatoes transcendent. The wine I'd laid away for such occasions, a pricey Primitivo from the boot of Italy, gave our little banquet a touch of class.

Upon learning that the Carnivaliant festival would find me dressing up as Davy Crockett and appearing in an Alamo pageant secretly scripted by the B.U.G., Celeste offered up her sardonic understanding of the Texas Revolution. For the rest of the evening, the angels of progressive revisionism hovered over the condo. While I failed to share my daughter's indignation, I admired her ability to look depressing facts in the face. Her father had been the same way. When he'd realized his income would never match his gambling debts, he jumped off the Verrazano Narrows Bridge.

According to Celeste, the Texas Revolution was driven largely by the settlers' devotion to the institution of slavery. The practice of keeping black West Africans in bondage had been illegal in Mexico since 1829, but the country tolerated slavery in its Texas province as long as the colonists called their chattel indentured servants and didn't press for legalization.

"Whatever one thinks of the Alamo defenders," said Celeste, "they were fighting as much to quash freedom as expand it."

A quick tour of the relevant websites revealed that she was essentially correct. Knowing that Mexico's winking attitude toward slavery in its colonies could not last indefinitely, thousands of white, English-speaking immigrants resolved to peel Texas off from the mother country and align it with the United States, where abolition was surely a pipe dream at best.

"I'll bet Davy Crockett was opposed to slavery," I said. "I intend to play him with head held high."

"Mom, you could play Jack the Ripper's press agent, and I would still admire you for helping Pacifica."

"Okay, but I don't want to hear bad things about Crockett. When my grandfather was a little kid, he adored the Disney series. So what can you tell me about Mike Pence's character?"

"He doesn't have any."

"Laughing out loud."

"I seem to recall that William Travis had a slave named Joe with him at the Alamo, one of the few survivors. After the siege, Santa Anna made a great show of granting Joe his freedom. That said, I don't think Travis was any sort of anti-abolitionist, so the part probably won't give Pence pause."

"If Travis *was* an anti-abolitionist, the part wouldn't give him pause either," I observed. "He's especially excited about reciting the colonel's famous plea for assistance." I conjured up the hallowed document on my desktop computer and declaimed my favorite sentence. " 'I have answered the demand with a cannon shot, and our flag still waves proudly from the walls.' " I dropped my gaze and continued reading. " 'I am determined to sustain myself as long as possible and die like a soldier who never forgets what is due to his own honor and that of his country. Victory or death ....' "

"I'm trying to be cynical about those words," said Celeste with a wistful smile, "but I can't quite manage it."

"Your grandfather used to say cynicism was its own sort of sentimentality."

"Whoever plays Jim Bowie won't want to read his biography too closely."

"Pence is hoping to get George Bush."

"Bowie was bad news."

"Careful, dear. My grandfather loved *that* series, too."

"He once bested a rival in a knife fight and disemboweled him alive."

"I don't think CBS ever got around to that incident."

To refresh her memory, Celeste consulted her Samsung tablet. "Bowie kept company with scoundrels like Jean Lafitte, made a fortune from land swindles, and for several years pursued a vocation that can only be called slave laundering."

"Could we go back to Crockett? A genuine American hero—wouldn't you say?"

"While living in Louisiana, Bowie routinely procured slaves from Lafitte for a dollar a pound—yes, we're talking about pounds of human flesh—and took them directly to a custom house in St. Landry Parish, where he claimed he'd wrested them away from smugglers. By a federal statue of 1808, not only had slave importation been outlawed, but anyone who foiled a slave runner was entitled to half of whatever the flesh fetched on the open market."

"Are you saying Bowie informed on *himself*?"

"That's right. Profiles in chutzpah. It gets even richer. He would then buy back the slaves at the custom-house auction, accept a bonus equal to half his investment, and take the now legal chattel to New Orleans, where he would sell those same men and women for triple what he'd paid in St. Landry Parish."

"Otherwise known as St. Laundry Parish."

"Good one, Mom."

"How about we open another bottle of Primitivo?"

"You know how to live, Polly Nightingale."

Much to my disappointment, Ainsley hated the idea of my playing Davy Crockett in the great Alamo Reenactment. She feared that the inevitable high-definition close-ups of the Presidential Faith Counselor would prompt someone to notice that my features and Walker Lambert's weren't exactly identical.

"But don't you love the postmodernism of it all?" I took a swallow of Starbucks Christmas Blend. "A female porn star playing a male prophet playing the King of the Wild Frontier."

"Fuck postmodernism," said Ainsley. "This is the real world."

"If I try to back out now, Pence will get suspicious."

"Our moles inside the Houston Society reached the same conclusion, so they decided to make a virtue of necessity. Tomorrow at noon you'll join Pence in the Rayburn Room, along with some Alamo Reenactment personnel newly arrived from Texas. You'll be measured for your costumes and given your scripts. Just before the big show, you'll appear on the ramparts as the Reverend Walker Lambert, but wearing your Crockett buckskins, and deliver a prayer that's actually a full-throated call for Christian theocracy in America."

"That will surely give Newtopian Democrats the fantods."

"Because you now inhabit Lambert so fully, our moles want you to write the prayer yourself." Ainsley passed me a manila envelope. "Here's your plane ticket to San Antonio and your hotel confirmation. We want you to register as Polly Nightingale, so you won't get mobbed by Walter Lambert cultists. You'll spend Wednesday the fifth and Thursday the sixth at the festival, hiding behind your Nightingale persona and acclimatizing yourself to the Texas denomination of the Church of Pence."

"What if some visitors decide I'm Lambert impersonating a woman to avoid the San Antonio paparazzi?"

"Shame them into respecting your privacy. Whatever you do, turn down any and all requests for TV interviews."

"Lambert doesn't get many of those," I said.

"Yes, he does, but you never see them. On the morning of Friday, March seven, Air Force One will touch down at Del Rio International near Brackettville, Pence having spent the week trying to cheer up U.S. troops in Afghanistan. The two of you will converge on the Shahan Ranch for the rehearsal, along with the two hundred Alamo Defenders Lottery winners and the college kids playing Santa Anna's army. The grand reenactment happens on Saturday, March eighth, beginning at three o'clock."

"But the Alamo fell on the sixth."

"We're looking for ratings here, Polly, not gold stars from the Daughters of the Texas Revolution." Ainsley's phone played "Jingle Bells." She opened the text application and scanned the message.

"Here's the latest from our people in San Antonio. George Bush has refused the part of Jim Bowie."

"Because of the land swindles and the slave laundering?"

"Because of what Trump and Pence did to the Republican Party."

"Maybe *you* should play Bowie, Ainsley. My grandfather taught me the theme song." I stood up and began warbling the lyrics. "Jim Bowie, Jim Bowie, he was a bold, adventurin' man. Jim Bowie, Jim Bowie, battled for right with a powerful hand …"

In perfect synchronicity, the G.W. students lifted their eyes and focused on the singing woman. They gave me a polite round of applause, toasted me with their coffee cups, and returned to their screens.

III

MY trip from San Antonio International Airport to the hotel found me gawking out a one-way window in the back seat of a sleek white limousine. Approaching the downtown area, we cruised past displays labeled CARNIVALIANT: THE GREAT TEXAS REVOLUTION FESTIVAL, including a longhorn steer as big as a locomotive, a twenty-foot-high neoprene balloon representing Stephen Austin, a huge equestrian statue of Sam Houston, and an immense mural depicting the Battle of San Jacinto, the eighteen-minute engagement during which Houston and his army (crying "Remember the Alamo!") trounced Santa Anna and thus secured the sovereignty of the newly declared Republic of Texas. The displays climaxed with three billboards, each featuring a different star performer from our forthcoming *Fall of the Alamo* reenactment in Brackettville.

PRESIDENT MICHAEL ROBERT PENCE
AS COLONEL WILLIAM B. TRAVIS!

FOX NEWS CELEBRITY TUCKER CARLSON
AS COLONEL JAMES BOWIE!

THE REVEREND WALKER LAMBERT
AS COLONEL DAVID CROCKETT!

This was the first time I'd heard that Tucker Carlson would play Jim Bowie. A poetic casting choice, I decided. Carlson had once notoriously insisted there was no serious white supremacy movement in the United States. I wondered whether he thought the antebellum slave trade, from which Bowie had profited so handsomely, qualified as a white supremacy movement.

The portraits all flattered their subjects, especially mine, even though it wasn't based on a Polly Nightingale 8 × 10 glossy but on some Walker Lambert photograph or other. Tucker Carlson's image evoked Hollywood actor Jeff Bridges in his prime. Mike Pence looked like a Greek god returning from a leisurely day at the spa.

After moving into the Hyatt Regency on the River Walk, I changed into my blue jeans and checked shirt, though I didn't imagine I would fool anybody into mistaking me for a native Texan. I decided against taking a guided tour of the actual Alamo, even though the shrine was practically across the street. Instead I put on my Rangers baseball cap, coated my lips with Revlon bombshell red, and hoofed it over to the San Antonio fairgrounds, site of the main Carnivaliant exhibitions.

I paid my general admission, $28 for the day, at a wooden post-and-lintel gate adorned with cattle skulls. Beyond this morbid portal lay an array of livestock pens filled with forlorn cows, pigs, and goats standing around in mud and dung. I hurried past the agrarian concentration camp and entered the midway, where festival visitors could shoot BBs at revolving tin ducks, shatter ceramic plates with skeet pellets, enjoy respites from their kids by putting them on carousel ponies or inside little revolving stage coaches, and test their skills on the rifle range: hit the target on the plywood grizzly bear and win a Davy Crockett T-shirt.

In a matter of minutes my sensorium became overloaded. The heady fragrance of cow manure and the hellish scent of swine excrement drilled into my nostrils. Loudspeakers mounted on stanchions boxed my ears with a chorus singing "The Yellow Rose of Texas." A brass band marched down the midway playing "The Eyes of Texas Are Upon You," temporarily drowning out Lady Rose. Stadium lights spilled radiant beams on some distant event—a rodeo, perhaps, or a demolition derby—so bright they made my irises contract, even as mesquite smoke rising from a nearby barbecue brought tears to my eyes.

Seeking to escape the lights and the noises and the animal odors, I headed for the O.K. CALORIES CORRAL, featuring picnic tables arranged on a flat expanse of buffalo grass and hemmed by vendors dispensing every imaginable sort of protein. Here hungry fairgoers could purchase Alamo Martyrs Sirloin Burgers, Lyndon Johnson Pulled-Pork Stew, Jim Bowie Fresh Butchered Ham Steaks, Rio Grande Footlong Sausages, and San Jacinto Batter-Fried Chicken. Vegetables were evidently illegal in Texas, unless you counted the Presidential Popcorn (an allusion, no doubt, to Mike Pence's primary vice beyond Trumpian cruelty). For $14.95 I purchased a hearty lunch of frijoles wreathing a rib-eye steak as thick as a Bible. A mug of Kavanaugh Lager set me back $6. I declined dessert, but the offerings were plentiful: funnel cakes, vanilla fudge, caramel apples, blueberry pie, cherry pie, Mama Bailey's Apple Pie À-la-Mo.

Sharing my picnic bench with two married, overweight fairgoers—he in a fishnet shirt, she in a hot-pink halter top—I was struck by an irony. On Saturday afternoon the Carnivaliant patrons would heap scorn on invading regiments of undesirable minorities, and yet a kind of low-key rainbow coalition had come together on this San Antonio food court. I counted fourteen Mexicans enjoying burgers and chicken wings, ten Native Americans (Coushattas, most likely, or maybe Kickapoos or Pueblos) consuming the same fare, a young black couple eating cheesesteaks (though perhaps they'd simply stopped here during their emigration to Pacifica), and some two dozen of the picnickers' children satiating themselves on hot dogs and milkshakes. Born-and-bred New Yorkers such as myself reflexively mock the provincialism of the American Southwest, yet a Martian visiting Carnivaliant would not immediately conclude that Texans were hostile to pluralism.

I left the O.K. Calories Corral and proceeded down a walkway lined with booths selling pretty much anything your inner cowpoke desired: real six-shooters in oiled-leather holsters, Stetson hats, gauntleted gloves, red bandanas, string ties cinched with silver horse-head clips. Seized by a sudden urge to become more Texan than the Texans, I tried on a pair of knee-high leather boots tooled with western-style arabesques. I tossed my red flats in my handbag, paid for the boots, and wore them for the rest of the day.

My next stop was the main arena, where a rodeo was indeed in progress, all dust and sweat and *yippie-yi-yo-kayahs*. I was happily surprised to see that a kind of sexual egalitarianism had come to south Texas. Nearly a third of the contestants were women. Although there's a limit to the pleasure an Easterner can derive from watching cowboys and cowgirls rope steers, ride bareback on bulls, and get evicted from bucking broncos, I stayed for the rest of the show.

My meanderings next brought me to a traveling amusement park in the northeast corner—Ferris wheel, parachute drop, Tilt-a-Whirl, bumper cars—but I had no interest in relocating my lunch, so instead I studied the posters nailed to a fence beside the ticket booth. If I came back tomorrow, I could kick up my heels at the Hoot 'n' Holler Hoedown, bust a gusset at the Greased Pig Contest, root for my favorite ruminants at various 4-H Club competitions, gape at the Chariots of Ezekiel Fireworks Display, hear a country-rock band called Moonshine Mary and the Revenuers, another such band called Dog's Breakfast, and a heavy metal group called Honor Among Thieves. I decided I would stay at in my hotel room on Thursday, writing my prayer and memorizing my lines.

Not far from the thrill rides stood a collapsible geodesic movie theater. According to the sign, a patron could see, every hour on the hour, a forty-minute documentary from 2015 called THE STORY OF THE TEXAS REVOLUTION, NARRATED BY CLINT EASTWOOD. The adjacent structure, the Béxar Cantina, advertised itself as an EXACT REPLICA OF THE SALOON WHERE DAVY CROCKETT WET HIS WHISTLE IN 1836. My stomach urged me to go inside. The Béxar Cantina turned out to be a buffet joint, ALL YOU CAN EAT FOR $14.95, BEER EXTRA. I took a chance on the spareribs. Dos Equis was on draft, and I ordered a half-pitcher.

So there I was, sitting at a lone table in a murky far corner, munching on my sauce-drenched beef and pouring myself a third Dos Equis, when an ursine man in a coonskin KAGA hat plunked down his stein and pulled up a chair. "Excuse me, ma'am, but don't I know you from somewheres?"

"I doubt it. Why don't you pull up a chair?"

"Huh?" The gloom concealed the intruder's features (except for the cactus-thorn whiskers on his chin), but I suspected he was scowling. "*Now* I remember. I've seen you in the movies. Polly Nightingale, right?"

I wiped barbecue sauce from my fingertips, making the napkin look like a battlefield dressing. "Anything's possible."

"Pleased to make your acquaintance."

The intruder's hand shot out of the darkness like a moray eel exiting its burrow. His forearm displayed a tattoo of an angry bald eagle. Listlessly I shook his hand.

"Name's Burgess Armitage. I have all your DVDs. My favorite's *Tea and Sodomy*."

"What does KAGA mean?"

"Keep America Great Always. My buddies and I are wearin' 'em to the reenactment."

"Lottery winners, are you?"

"Nah, we didn't even enter. Are you goin'?"

"Haven't decided."

"I'll tell you somethin', Miss Nightingale. If I was on the ramparts, I'd be tempted to fire live ammo at all them illegals and Muslims chargin' up from Mexico."

"Then I'm glad you won't be on the ramparts."

"Do it to them afore they do it to you. That's in the Constitution. I hope you're not a socialist."

"Merely broadminded, as you might expect of a person in my profession."

"Ah, so you *are* Polly Nightingale!"

"From the day I was born."

"My daddy used to say, 'I'm the broadminded sort. I've always got a broad on my mind.' "

"If you would prefer that I not throw this beer in your face, Burgess, you will now bid me *adios*."

From: Burgess Armitage <hornytoad@gmail.com>
To: Amos Orloff <deplorablepatriot@gmail.com>
Cc: Elton Coates <ladiesman@gmail.com>,
    Slack Kovich <fourthmusketeer@gmail.com>
Date: Wednesday, March 5, 2036, at 8:44 PM
Subject: Re: An Alamo They'll Never Forget

Muchas mutual congratulations are in order, amigos. To-day we crossed paths a half-dozen times, and none of us acknowledged his fellow musketeers. Keeping cool is the secret to any successful clandestine operation.

You all looked terrific in your KAGA caps.

I'm sure you'll agree that the Uzis on our stomachs were inconspicuous, given the circumference of the average fairgoer. Just to make sure my piece was secure, I rode the roller coaster (remembered to switch on the safety, whew). The piece stayed put. I've had belt buckles that were more uncomfortable.

He would have especially loved the O.K. Calories Cor-ral—don't you think?—all them burgers and milkshakes. Of course, where he is now, he gets all the beef he wants.

You'll never guess who I ran into this evening at the Béxar Cantina. The legendary Polly Nightingale, star of half the best stag movies made in this century. She looks terrific after all these years. Real friendly, too.

On March 6, at 9:02 PM, Amos Orloff <deplorablepatriot@gmail.com> wrote:

I had an even better time at the fair today than yesterday. Following your example, Burgess, I went on the Tilt-a-Whirl with my Uzi in place. No mishaps. Well, I did lose my KAGA cap, but I found it on the ground.

Turns out I have a talent for square dancing. And that band called Honor Among Thieves is the bug's nuts.

Polly Nightingale, shit, how cool is that? Her DVDs work better than Viagra. I know he had a thing for Stormy Daniels, but if he'd ever met Miss Nightingale, he would've had to pay her plenty of hush money, too.

Have you reached a decision about the Secret Service?

On March 6, at 9:44 PM, Burgess Armitage <hornytoad@ gmail.com> wrote:

Blowing away the T-men seems unconstitutional to me.

On March 6, at 10:02 PM, Amos Orloff <deplorablepatriot@ gmail.com> wrote:

What is this, a fucking suicide pact?

On March 6, at 10:34 PM, Elton Coates <ladiesman@ gmail.com> wrote:

What is this, a fucking suicide pact?

On March 6, at 11:02 PM, Burgess Armitage <hornytoad@ gmail.com> wrote:

You might say the first Alamo siege was a suicide pact. At tomorrow's run-through I'll suss out the T-men and decide on the best strategy.

The high-speed, Brackettville-bound "Revolution Train" out of San Antonio comprised six luxurious coaches filled with all two hundred Alamo Defenders Lottery winners, still in their street clothes. I wore my normal Reverend Walker Lambert costume, supplemented with mirrorshades and a Panama hat to blur my identity. I would have preferred making the trip as Polly Nightingale, but I didn't want some salivating skin-flick fan penetrating my disguise and hitting on me like that oaf at the Béxar Cantina.

A chipper, toothsome filly in a cowgirl suit was waiting for us at the station. She identified herself as Corky, a co-ed at San Antonio State (in Texas, evidently, one still used the term "co-ed"), and handed us each a sheet of paper.

SAM HOUSTON PRODUCTIONS
presents
"THE FALL OF THE ALAMO"

ITINERARY FOR FORTRESS DEFENDERS

10:00 AM–10:15 AM. Take shuttle buses from Brackettville Station to Holiday Inn. Complementary cinnamon buns and Lone Star Bucks coffee in lobby.

10:15 AM–11:00 AM. Check into room, freshen up, review script, try on costume hanging in closet, fill blood packets with water. (Stage blood reserved for actual performance.)

11:00 AM–11:20 AM. Shuttle buses to Shahan Ranch.

11:20 AM–12:00 NOON. Meet & Greet with Reenactment Company in Alamo church.

> Calvin Palette, President, Sam Houston Society
> Matthew Burwell, Pageant Producer and Director
> Virgil Wickensham, First Assistant Director
> Bart Pringle, Researcher and Narrator

12:00 NOON–12:45 PM. Barbecue picnic outside Alamo barracks. Please bring any costume problems to Mrs. Worth in Trailer 4.

12:45 PM–1:30 PM. Musket and rifle replicas issued to all lottery winners. Practice inserting powder cartridge, changing flints, and discharging weapon. Bullets strictly prohibited.

1:30 PM–3:30 PM. First run-through of *The Fall of the Alamo*.

3:30 PM–3:45 PM. Coffee break in church.

3:45 PM–5:45 PM. Second run-through, if needed.

As things shook out on that vertiginously eventful day, we didn't need a second run-through: such was Matthew Burwell's skill as a producer, director, and drill sergeant. Whenever a video screen went blank, a floodlight imploded, the sound system started howling, a technician collapsed from the unseasonable heat, or a fortress defender got a powder burn, Mr. Burwell took it in stride, keeping everybody focused and calm (it helped that the Reenactment Company had retained a crack team of nurses fully prepared to handle our medical emergencies). Dressed in jodhpurs, a safari jacket, and a pith helmet, Burwell reminded me of Eggs Sabatini, who helmed my first picture, *Swedish Nuns*, and made the whole underclothed cast feel at ease. No doubt the lottery winners would've been less biddable had they known that Burwell regularly reported to the B.U.G., but who could have imagined the Sam Houston Society was so vulnerable to foreign infiltration?

When you factored in the mock-up of old San Antonio, the set for John Wayne's *The Alamo* was among the largest ever built, rivaling the Port of Alexandria in *Cleopatra*, the Forum in *The Fall of the Roman Empire*, and the Imperial City in *55 Days at Peking* (epics my grandfather had collected on DVD and watched repeatedly). What most impressed me were the ziggurats of stadium seating looming over the Alamo replica on the north, east, and west sides. The whole complex—tiers, floodlights, loudspeakers, video screens, the garrison itself—resembled an immense athletic field, the sort of place where tyrannosaurs might have gathered to play Cretaceous Football. The south side remained open, so the audience could easily observe the thundering hordes as they swept up from Mexico and advanced on the mission (many ticket holders doubtless believed that an 1836 precursor to Trump's border wall would have given Texas its independence without a single shot being fired). Anchored to the uppermost tiers, an immense steel catwalk ran east to west above the fortress, its platform supporting a triad of winches for lifting Travis, Bowie, and Crockett into Heaven when the time came.

Shortly after two o'clock, we learned that Air Force One had not yet landed at Del Rio International, and for some reason Tucker Carlson had also failed to find his way to Brackettville. Standing erect atop the eastern tiers, megaphone in hand, Burwell filled the time by arranging the defenders in the positions they would assume during the final assault, then teaching them how to perform convincing bullet-wound convulsions and realistic death throes. A young man with a Godzilla T-shirt and a complexion like a pineapple appeared at my side, identified himself as Toby Gitt, the third assistant director, and said he would take me to my mark. I shouldered my Kentucky rifle and followed the AD into the church. Bart Pringle, the offstage narrator, sat before a microphone in the apse, clutching his script as he prepared to deliver exposition and color commentary. Toby led me up two flights of stairs to the roof, where a stately oaken pulpit equipped with a leather-bound Bible and a bottle of Evian water awaited me. He outfitted me with a radio-controlled lavalier microphone and showed me how to turn it on.

From my perch high above the parapets, I could see the first and second assistant directors herding Santa Anna's troops—that is, the Pacifica college students hired to portray the Mexican Army—into four columns about a half-mile outside the Béxar facsimile. By now I was sweating profusely in the hot prairie air. My buckskin jacket was soggy. My coonskin cap was practically afloat. Miraculously enough, my Adam's apple remained glued in place.

Lowering my gaze, I observed the two hundred lottery winners arrayed along the Alamo ramparts, practicing their spasms. One looked vaguely familiar. I thought he might be the Béxar Cantina oaf, but he wasn't wearing a KAGA cap, so I put him out of my mind.

Matthew Burwell decided to start the rehearsal without his William Travis or his Jim Bowie. He cued a brass band seated in the northern tiers, and a spirited rendition of "Deep in the Heart of Texas" resounded through the stadium. As the last note died, the rail-thin Calvin Palette, dressed in the same nineteenth-century military tunic he'd worn at the reception, strutted onto a cantilevered podium jutting into space from the eastern tiers and availed himself of the microphone-equipped lectern.

"On behalf of the Sam Houston Society, I want to welcome TV viewers and live audience members alike to this spectacular reenactment of the most celebrated event in the history of the great state of Texas!"

Palette now summoned to the podium the mayor of Brackett-ville, Hank Wallace, who said too many words (and in a quavering voice, though presumably he would do better tomorrow); next the chairwoman of the Daughters of the Texas Republic, Libby Wright, who said blessedly few words; and finally the manager of the Shahan Ranch, Max Hoot, who waved and grinned at the hypothetical audience and said no words at all.

"The Reverend Walker Lambert," said Palette, "White House spiritual advisor and President Pence's personal pick for the role of David Crockett, will now offer an invocation."

I propped Old Betsy against the pulpit and cleared my throat. Was the rehearsal of a prayer itself a prayer? I wondered.

"Heavenly Father, we ask that you bless this tribute to the undaunted courage of the men who died for the God-given freedoms you gave us."

A high-pitched feedback screech shot from the loudspeakers. A sound technician got on the case, dialing down the amplifier.

"With the exception of some know-it-alls back East, historians generally agree that every Alamo martyr had accepted Jesus Christ as his personal Savior, as did all the Founding Fathers before them, except for Thomas Paine, may he rot in Hell."

"Hosanna!" ad-libbed a lottery winner.

I paused to sip from the Evian bottle. My spandex bra itched. My Heaven harness pinched my waist. The water-filled packets chafed my midriff.

"And so this afternoon, with President Pence's approval, I beseech Congress to acknowledge this great heritage of faith by bestowing on our country a new sobriquet, R.J.C., the Republic of Jesus Christ!"

"Hallelujah!" shouted a defender.

"From that consecrated moment forward, the world will know that U.S.A. means not just United States of America but Unlimited Sanctuary for Angels!"

A burst of applause arose from the lottery winners.

"Let the show begin! Let the cannons roar! In Jesus's name, amen!"

As the band softly played "The Green Leaves of Summer," the hit song from the soundtrack of John Wayne's *The Alamo*, the narrator's disembodied voice poured from the loudspeakers and echoed across the fortress. In stentorian tones Bart Pringle set the scene, explaining that on February 23, 1836, knowing that an advance column of a thousand Mexican soldiers was about to enter the town, Colonel William Travis elected to bait Santa Anna by preparing the Alamo garrison for a siege. The Texans herded longhorn cattle into the fortress and filled the storerooms with eighty bushels of corn found in deserted Béxar houses. Thus did the former Franciscan mission become home to Travis's troops and many of their family members—most notably Susannah Dickinson, wife of Captain Almaron Dickinson—plus Jim Bowie's volunteers and David Crockett's Tennesseans.

At three o'clock, Mike Pence, Tucker Carlson, and two Secret Service agents finally showed up, arrayed in splendid frontier costumes. All four men carried period rifles, though I doubted the bodyguards would pretend to fire theirs during the show (now and forever, their job was to keep both eyes on the President). Shouting toward the eastern tiers, Pence and Carlson assured Matthew Burwell that they were wearing their water packets and Heaven harnesses. As the AD clipped on his microphone, the President basked in the cheers and applause of the lottery winners. One Alamo defender fainted, probably from adulation fatigue.

It was good that Pence had arrived when he did, for the narrator had just cued William Travis's first major action: firing a cannon in response to the Mexicans raising a blood-red flag signifying "no quarter given" if the colonists refused to surrender unconditionally.

" 'No quarter' might be your anthem, Santa Anna, but the refrain belongs to *us!*" bellowed Pence, taking a match to the fuse of the eighteen-pounder positioned on the southern parapet. "Once our reinforcements arrive, you'll be begging us to let *you* surrender!"

As the band played the "Answering Shot" cue from Dimitri Tiomkin's *Alamo* score, a cannonball leaped from the muzzle and landed on the prairie beyond the wall, raising a plume of dirt.

"That's givin' 'em what-fer, Colonel Travis!" I exclaimed in my Davy Crockett persona.

"Well done, sir!" added Carlson. He turned toward Matthew Burwell and said, "How about we give Bowie another line here? 'Hey, Santa Anna, there's a lot more balls where that 'un came from!' "

"Please just stick to the script, Mr. Carlson," said Burwell.

"I'm grateful for you and your Tennesseans, Colonel Crockett, though I must confess I know very little about you," said Pence, sticking to the script. "I hear you carry a whole lotta mythology around with you."

I proceeded to declaim Ogden McQuaid's version of my character's very first speech to Congress. "I'm David Crockett, fresh from the backwoods. I'm half-horse, half-alligator, and a mite touched with snappin' turtle. I've got the fastest horse, the prettiest sister, the surest rifle, and the ugliest dog in Tennessee. My father can lick any man in Kentucky, and I can lick my father. I can wade the Mississippi, leap the Ohio, hug a bear too close for comfort, and eat any man alive who speaks ill of Andy Jackson."

The narrator kept the story moving along, relating how William Travis came to pen one of the most celebrated documents in American history. Seized by patriotic passion and spontaneous eloquence, the colonel dictated to Captain Dickinson's wife a letter that would, he hoped, inspire hundreds of armed volunteers to show up at the Alamo.

"To the people of Texas and all Americans everywhere," recited Pence as Susannah Dickinson took down his words. "I am besieged by a thousand or more Mexicans under Santa Anna. I have sustained a continual bombardment and cannonade for twenty-four hours and not lost a man. The enemy has demanded a surrender at discretion. Otherwise, the garrison are to be put to the sword, if the fort is taken."

"Those words are worthy of golden-throated Cicero hisself," said my Crockett character.

"I have answered the demand with a cannon shot, and our flag still waves proudly from the walls," Travis dictated. "I shall never surrender or retreat. I call on you in the name of liberty, of patriotism, and everything dear to the American character, to come to our aid, with all dispatch."

"I'm gettin' tight in the Adam's apple," said Crockett (evidently Ogden McQuaid was not above making in-jokes).

"The enemy is receiving reinforcements daily and will no doubt increase to three or four thousand in four or five days. If this call is neglected, I am determined to sustain myself as long as possible and die like a soldier who never forgets what is due to his own honor and that of his country. Victory or death!"

"Victory or death!" echoed a lottery winner.

"Here's an idea," said Carlson to Burwell. "At this juncture, Bowie turns to Travis and says, 'Colonel, that's a by-God stem-winder of a missive.'"

"I think not, Mr. Carlson," said Burwell.

The narrator reported that a few days later Jim Bowie was confined to a sickbed in the church, stricken with a malady the garrison surgeon couldn't diagnose. On March the third, the defenders, sans Bowie, watched from the parapets as nearly a thousand Mexican reinforcements marched into Béxar. The enemy army now numbered over three thousand. The following evening, Bowie's cousin by marriage, Juana Navarro Alsbury, approached Santa Anna in hopes of negotiating an honorable surrender. Her petition served only to horrify the general with the specter of a bloodless and thus inglorious Mexican victory. In his fevered impatience, he announced that, rather than waiting for the expected heavy siege cannons to arrive on March the seventh, he would schedule the final assault for the morning of March the sixth.

By now the two hundred lottery winners had all assembled in the central courtyard, along with Travis and Crockett, plus Bowie on his sickbed. With magnificent élan and consummate conviction, Mike Pence recapitulated Travis's apocryphal actions of March the fifth. An attack was imminent, Travis explained, and the garrison was certain to fall. With his drawn saber he scored the earth, then invited "every patriot willing to die for the Texas cause" to cross the line, adding that "any remaining soldiers should join the women and children as they depart the Alamo under Santa Anna's pledge of safe conduct." No shame, he insisted, would adhere to any man who left.

The lottery winners practically fell over themselves rushing to Pence's side. Carlson got his big moment when his Bowie character asked Colonel Crockett and Captain Dickinson to "come lift up my bed, so you can bear my body to Colonel Travis and my soul into the hereafter," and of course the two officers complied instantly. Many in tomorrow's audience would know the whole line-in-the-dirt episode had never occurred, but they would probably cheer it anyway.

By midnight the Mexican artillery had ceased its bombardment, the narrator related, and the weary defenders settled into their first uninterrupted sleep since the siege began. Evidently Santa Anna wanted to give them the rudest imaginable awakening. Under Burwell's direction, the lottery winners stretched out on the parapet walkways, church steps, barracks roof, and dusty earth beside the cattle pen. As the band played "Beautiful Dreamer," the reenactors pretended to sleep.

At five-thirty in the morning, the narrator continued, four enemy columns marched out of Béxar, commanded respectively by General Martín Perfecto de Cós, Colonel Francisco Duque, Colonel José María Romero, and Colonel Juan Morales. In the feeble light of dawn, Mexican scouts approached the Alamo and killed three sentinels, but the fourth survived to raise the alarm.

"Come on, boys, the Mexicans are upon us!" cried Travis, rushing to his post on the south wall. "Give 'em hell!"

The enemy buglers bleated at full volume. Scores of eager troops cried "*¡Viva Santa Anna!*" I sprinted to the south wall and planted myself alongside Pence, the T-men, and about fifty lottery winners. A grand panorama unfolded before me—a jaw-dropping, breathtaking vista certain to elicit boos from tomorrow's audience. Prodded by mounted officers and pacing themselves to the cadence of the snare drums, the enemy soldiers advanced relentlessly on the mission: fifteen hundred undesirables armed with carbines and dressed in Mexican Army uniforms. "*¡Viva Santa Anna!*" they cried. "*¡Viva Mexico!*" Each column carried a half-dozen siege ladders plus a banner announcing its unsavory allegiance. The Alamo defenders would soon know death at the hands of the Veracruz Illegal

Immigrants League, the Coahuila Gay and Lesbian Consortium, the Durango Deep-State Journalists Syndicate, and the Zacatecas Latin-American Muslim Brotherhood.

"Death to the Mexican rapists!" cried Travis. "Death to perverts, enemies of the people, and those who would inflict sharia law on our republic!" At this juncture Ogden McQuaid's script went over the top, but nobody seemed to mind. "Wind their illegal alien bowels around your bayonets! Cut out their homophile hearts with your Bowie knives and stomp on them!"

"Will do, Colonel!" ad-libbed a lottery winner.

"Blow their lying deep-state brains from here to East Jesus!" shouted Travis. "Grind their Muslim bones beneath your boots!"

"We're on it!" improvised another defender.

"Bowels, hearts, brains, bones, you got it!" yelled a third defender.

"Hold your fire," rasped Travis. "Mark your targets. Hold your fire. Mark your targets. Hold your fire ..."

"*¡Viva Santa Anna! ¡Viva Mexico!*"

The defenders on the south wall took careful aim with their muskets and rifles.

"Open fire!"

Flints flared. Cartridges flashed. The air resounded with the crack-crack-crack of detonated gunpowder. Caught by the south Texas breeze, smoke billowed toward the prairie. Water packets burst on enemy chests and stomachs. Over two hundred designated Mexicans tipped away from their columns, hitting the ground like loose fence pickets torn free by a tornado. Tomorrow's version of the opening Texan volley would be more graphic, of course, including gaudy splashes of stage blood speckling the earth like poppy blossoms, but this initial winnowing of Santa Anna's brigades was vivid enough to make the President's heart leap up.

"Well done, boys!" he improvised. "Send those rapists, catamites, liars, and ragheads back to the border!"

When they got within ten yards of the fortress, the surviving members of the Veracruz column broke into a run. Kicking up dust clouds, they charged through the narrow zone between the west wall and the corresponding tiers, then took up positions outside the north wall, even as the consortium from Coahuila, the syndicate from Durango, and the brotherhood from Zacatecas deployed themselves before the east, west, and south ramparts respectively. The mission was surrounded.

While the actual fall of the Alamo was, from the Texas viewpoint, a wrenching catastrophe, the final twenty minutes of the reenactment rehearsal proved relatively free of mishaps. No Mexican invader accidentally toppled off his siege ladder (though there were some well-executed intentional falls). Most of the powder burns proved trivial. Performers who blacked out were easily revived with water.

In accordance with the historians' consensus, William Travis was among the first to die. Pence acquitted himself with great poignancy. Trapped on the church steps, he snarled at a squad of Mexicans as they came at him from all directions with sabers drawn.

Having repositioned himself near the horse corral, Davy Crockett wielded his rifle like a club (his powder and shot were exhausted), cracking skull after skull before perishing in a hail of carbine bullets. My water packets all burst properly.

Jim Bowie was bayoneted in his sickroom, but only after killing a half-dozen Mexicans with a brace of pistols and his famous knife. The video screens displayed Carlson's performance in all its hammy grandeur.

Before the day was over, Pence, Carlson, and I found ourselves suspended from steel cables as three brawny angels, splendid in their feathered wings and iridescent halos, reeled us toward eternity. The band played "Nearer My God to Thee." Swinging back and forth like two pendulums, Carlson and I cursed and screamed (better now than tomorrow, I figured). And yet we all made it safely to the catwalk, and I decided that, if forced to spend the rest of my life cross-dressing my way through ludicrous patriotic pageants, I might even learn to like it.

From: Burgess Armitage <hornytoad@gmail.com>
To: Amos Orloff <deplorablepatriot@gmail.com>
Cc: Slack Kovich <fourthmusketeer@gmail.com>,
    Elton Coates <ladiesman@gmail.com>
Date: Friday, March 7, 2036, at 7:33 PM
Subject: Re: An Alamo They'll Never Forget

I was hoping to catch *Fox & Friends* tomorrow morning, but the damn TV in this hotel room isn't working. Are you guys having the same problem?

Obviously we can't massacre the undesirables after they've surrounded the fortress (we might hit some audience members). Completing our task means standing near the POTUS and spraying the four columns before they go off in different directions.

I'm convinced that shooting the Secret Service agents would spoil the whole KAGA point we're trying to make. At least Mr. Pence brought only two T-men along. The Lord was looking out for us in that respect.

Here's the order of battle, boys. The instant Travis tells the defenders to open fire, Amos and I pull out our Uzis and clobber the T-men. After emptying our magazines into the invaders, we dash down the stairs, run through the postern, and make a beeline for the parking lot. My wife will be waiting with our blue Chevy pickup.

On March 7, at 7:45 PM, Amos Orloff <deplorablepatriot@gmail.com> wrote:

I don't give a fuck about your TV. What if the Secret Service agents regain consciousness right away and come after us?

On March 7, at 8:02 PM, Burgess Armitage <hornytoad@gmail.com> wrote:

Then I say, along with Colonel Travis, "Victory or death!" Mr. Pence's predecessor would say the same thing.

On March 7, at 8:12 PM, Amos Orloff <deplorablepatriot@gmail.com> wrote:

Victory or death, my ass.

On March 7, at 8:22 PM, Slack Kovich <fourthmusketeer@gmail.com> wrote:

My TV is working fine. Come over tomorrow morning at 10 AM. Room 319.

On March 7, at 8:50 PM, Amos Orloff <deplorablepatriot@gmail.com> wrote:

I'm outta here, Burgess. Seriously, man. Fuck this suicide pact shit. I quit. Do you hear me? Quit, quit, quit.

On March 7, at 9:02 PM, Burgess Armitage <hornytoad@gmail.com> wrote:

Have it your way, you traitorous jackass cocksucking coward. Elton, Slack, and me will do fine without you. Three musketeers are as good as four, and he'll be protecting us besides. Right, fellas?

On March 7, at 9:17 PM, Elton Coates <ladiesman@gmail.com> wrote:

Right, Burgess!

On March 7, at 9:22 PM, Slack Kovich <fourthmusketeer@gmail.com> wrote:

Victory or death!

On the shuttle-bus ride back from the Shahan Ranch, I made a point of sitting next to the third assistant director, figuring that Toby Gitt was the least likely member of the Reenactment Company to fill my ear with encomiums to Mike Pence, the late Donald Trump, or, for that matter, the Reverend Walker Lambert. I was right. What most mattered to this young man was the universe of superhero comic books. He wanted to get out of Dodge and emigrate to Hollywood, where he hoped his credit on the *Fall of the Alamo* pageant might lead to a job that would lead to a job that would lead to a job, until eventually he'd become an *auteurist* director of blockbuster movies celebrating the sort of feel-good vigilantism practiced by Iron Man, Thor, Daredevil, and the rest.

I told him my limited knowledge of the movie business traced to my friendship with a rehabilitated porn star who walked away from New York's dying skin-flick industry, worked for awhile in Hollywood's more robust Triple-X factories, and now did experimental theater in L.A.

"Do you happen to know her email address?" asked Toby.

"These days she insists on privacy."

Back at the Holiday Inn, I ordered a room service meal—a beef burrito with refried beans—and ate it while watching Fox-CNN. Climate change had triggered drought throughout the Indian subcontinent. The commentator ascribed the crisis to divine displeasure with the nation's failure to stamp out indigenous pagan cults.

The motel phone rang. I thought it might be Burwell, offering me notes on my performance at the run-through, but the voice on the other end was Celeste's, bearing wildly unexpected news. She and Sharyn November were staying in this very hotel, on the floor above mine. They had two bottles of Primitivo. Might they come over?

By the time Fox-CNN wrapped up its coverage of the India catastrophe, Celeste and her fiancée were in the room, explaining what had brought them to Brackettville (though I'd already guessed). In the name of field research, Sharyn the anthropology Ph.D. candidate had decided to join Santa Anna's columns of undesirables, and Celeste had asked to come along so she could see her mother's performance as Davy Crockett.

"I thought the B.U.G. was recruiting only male undergraduates," I said, sipping my wine. Getting plastered on the night before my big Davy Crockett debut would be a mistake, I figured, so I'd vowed to have only one glass.

"For us they bent the rules," said Sharyn.

Both young women looked magnificent in their Mexican Army uniforms, especially Sharyn, the latter-day Amazon, but I still detested the whole situation, and I told them so.

"Davy Crockett would never train his rifle on a brigade that included his very own daughter and future daughter-in-law!"

"You did so this afternoon," said Celeste.

I took a fat gulp of wine. "But I didn't know you were *there*!"

"So pretend we're *not* there—you know, the way you'll be pretending to have live ammunition," said Celeste.

"Don't tell me I'm going to see blood packets exploding all over you."

"We got permission from the second AD to survive the battle," said Sharyn. "I told him it would make my research easier."

I finished my wine and poured a second glass. So much for my pledge. "I suppose I could ignore the Gay and Lesbian Consortium and concentrate on the Latin-American Muslim Brotherhood."

"No, that's the division we're part of," said Celeste. "The lesbian choice was too obvious. I suggest you focus on the deep-state journalists."

"I *hate* this."

"Loosen up, Mom."

"My dissertation committee practically *insisted*," said Sharyn.

"Know something, Davy?" said Celeste. "When we were milling around in the fake Béxar, getting ready to come on stage, we couldn't hear your great speech introducing yourself to Travis."

"One of the script's highlights," I said.

"If it's effective on the printed page, I'll bet it's *thrilling* the way you do it."

"Any chance you could favor us with a recitation right now, Colonel Crockett?" asked Sharyn.

I laughed, shrugged, and laughed again. I had indeed loosened up, just as Celeste wanted, but it was mostly the wine that did it. "Sure, why not?"

"Pretend to pick off a couple of journalists tomorrow, and you'll be fine," said Celeste.

I cleared my throat. "I'm David Crockett, fresh from the backwoods. I'm half-horse, half-alligator, and a mite touched with snappin' turtle. I've got the fastest horse, the prettiest sister, the surest rifle …."

IV

"**T**HE fastest horse, the prettiest sister, the surest rifle, and the ugliest dog in Tennessee. My father can lick any man in Kentucky, and I can lick my father."

As dependable as a laugh track, the crowd rewarded me with guffaws and chortles. William Travis's explosive riposte to Santa Anna's no-quarter flag had wowed our audience (the roar of the cannon prompting wild cheers and delirious hurrahs), and now they seemed equally enthralled by Davy Crockett's facetious boasting. I had them in the palm of my hand.

"I can wade the Mississippi, leap the Ohio, hug a bear too close for comfort ...." Celeste and Sharyn had talked me out of the rest of the sentence, Crockett vowing to eat any man alive who spoke ill of Andy Jackson. "Ride a streak o' lightnin', outgrin a cougar, and whip my weight in wildcats." At this point in his life, my character and the ex-President were bitter enemies, Congressman Crockett having fiercely opposed Jackson's savage and brutal Indian Removal Act.

The next phases of the pageant stirred ripples of unbridled delight in the stands. Buoyed by adoration, our troupe delivered radiant performances. Travis's naively eloquent letter to the world, his offer to let any man walk away from the Alamo without shame, the legendary saber cut in the earth, Bowie's request that Crockett and Dickinson carry him to Travis's side, the colonel and the captain bearing the sickbed over the sacred line: all these events prompted unabashed sobs from the crowd and glorious histrionics from the cast.

The enemy buglers unleashed their brassy taunts. The Mexican drummers beat out their cadence. I took my place near Colonel Travis (and his Secret Service agents), even as fifty other defenders rushed to join us on the south wall. Undaunted by the jeers, oblivious to the hoots, the enemy columns marched out of Béxar in lockstep, carbines pointed forward, hearts and minds fixed on consummating the siege with a massacre. As the printed banners gradually became legible, and the audience apprehended the nature of the invaders (illegal aliens, sexual deviants, uppity reporters, militant Muslims), a chorus of hisses rose from the tiers and sinuated through the hot March air.

"Death to the Mexican rapists!" cried Travis. "Death to perverts, enemies of the people, and those who would inflict sharia law on our republic!"

"¡*Viva Santa Anna! ¡Viva Mexico!*"

A peculiar silence settled over the spectators. Travis's wrath was not playing well. My admiration for Ogden McQuaid's script increased tenfold, for he'd evidently diagnosed the exact point at which the POTUS's passions would distress even his most ardent devotees. The average *Fall of the Alamo* ticket holder probably had no use for immigrants, queers, reporters, or Muslims, but calling for their extermination was something else entirely.

"Wind their illegal alien bowels around your bayonets!"

Yes, no question: Pence was losing the spectators' sympathy.

"Cut out their homophile hearts with your Bowie knives and stomp on them!"

The crowd grew utterly quiet.

By now I could make out Celeste and Sharyn, marching abreast at the head of the invading Muslims. I did as my daughter suggested, ignoring the Islamic column and aiming Old Betsy at the deep-state journalists. The tactic didn't work. The very presence of my daughter on the prairie had me shivering like a malaria victim.

"Blow their lying deep-state brains from here to East Jesus!"

I stole a glance at my fellow Alamo defenders. Abruptly my stomach seemed to detach itself and plummet into the courtyard below. Today three of the reenactors sported KAGA coonskin caps of the sort worn by the Béxar Cantina creep back in San Antonio.

I fixed on the tallest such defender—his bulbous belly, his prickled jaw, the angry bald eagle on his forearm. Yes, it was he—*he!*—Burgess somebody, the sleazoid who'd told me, disingenuously, that he wasn't a lottery winner.

"Grind their Muslim bones beneath your boots!"

If I was on the ramparts. That's what he'd said, wasn't it? *If I was on the ramparts, I'd be tempted to fire live ammo at all them illegals ....*

"*¡Viva Santa Anna! ¡Viva Mexico!*"

"Hold your fire," bleated Travis. "Mark your targets."

My gaze remained locked on the man from the Béxar Cantina, who in turn kept eyeing the nearest Secret Service agent.

"Hold your fire. Mark your targets."

The tattooed man tossed his musket aside, then reached under his buckskin jacket and pulled out a black, skeletal, strangely sensual device. Christ on a raft. The fucker had smuggled a submachine gun into the pageant!

"Hold your fire. Mark your targets."

"Mr. President!" I screamed. "Mr. President! The KAGA guys have live ammo!"

What would Davy Crockett do?

"*¡Viva Santa Anna! ¡Viva Mexico!*"

Imagining I was a cougar, I pounced on the tattooed man. He discharged his submachine gun, but the spray of bullets went skyward, leaving the approaching columns untouched.

Pence flipped his Kentucky rifle like a baton, so now he gripped the barrel. He pivoted on his boot heel and instantly spotted his KAGA guy, gaunt as a scarecrow, with buck teeth and freckled cheeks.

Machine gun in hand, the scarecrow approached a Secret Service agent with the evident intention of whacking or shooting him. The President swung his rifle in a semicircle, slamming the stock against the scarecrow's skull. The machine gun sailed over the battlement and onto the prairie. The clobbered man spun around, lost his balance, and fell into the cattle pen.

I tore the gun from the first KAGA guy, kicked him in the *cojones*, and shoved him off the battlement. He landed in the courtyard with a thud. At that moment, I wished him nothing but ill. I hoped I'd broken his neck, but any sort of spinal cord injury would do.

Shots rang out. At first I was afraid the third KAGA guy had emptied his magazine into Santa Anna's army, but then I beheld a gratifying tableau. The Secret Service agents—pistols drawn, smoke spiraling from the muzzles—stood over a fat, bleeding, inert body. The domestic terrorist still clutched his gun. Weirdly enough, his coonskin cap remained in place.

I surveyed the courtyard. The longhorns had taken it upon themselves to trample the fallen scarecrow. The Reenactment Company nurses appeared on the scene. Half of them ministered to the tattooed man, while the others extricated the scarecrow from the cattle pen.

"Stop the show!" shouted the narrator.

"The show must go on!" cried Pence. "Your President is giving you a command! It must go on! Open fire, boys!"

A collective ecstasy swept through the crowd. This was how a POTUS was supposed to behave. Kill a terrorist on your lunch break and then get back to work.

"Pence! Pence! Pence!" the spectators cried.

Two nurses appeared on the south wall and carried away the corpse of the third KAGA guy.

I couldn't bring myself to aim and fire my Kentucky rifle, but Pence and the lottery winners had no such compunctions. All up and down the south ramparts, the defenders fired volley after volley. Stage blood erupted everywhere on the prairie, as if someone had ignited a string of red Christmas lights. Smoke thickened the air. Coughing echoed throughout the garrison. Designated immigrants, queers, journalists, and devotees of Allah bit the dust. As the Latin-American Muslim Brotherhood marched past, I waved furtively at Celeste and Sharyn, but they remained in character, eyes fixed dead ahead.

"Pence! Pence! Pence!"

The balance of the pageant came off without a hitch: the valiant deaths of the three colonels, Santa Anna's bombastic entry into the Alamo on a white horse, the raising of the Mexican flag over the fortress, the delivery of Travis, Bowie, and Crockett into the arms of the Lord—everything worked beautifully. As I oscillated on my cable, sweating and gasping, a single depressing thought raced through my skull. In fewer than sixty seconds, Mike

Pence had gone from being a sadist screaming about perverts to the hero of the greatest historical reenactment of all time. There would be no stopping him now.

Authorized Transcript: Michael Pence's Communications Director Fields Questions from White House Press Corps, March 11, 2036.

MARY LOU PEACHUM: Morning, everyone. What's on your mind, Sholo?

SHOLO SOBOWALE, *Philadelphia Herald*: The Pence administration claims that the so-called Three Musketeers who tried to sabotage the Alamo Reenactment were working for Nicole Yoshida's government in Pacifica. Can you cite any evidence for this theory?

PEACHUM: Mr. Pence himself laid out the evidence during his last interview on *Fox & Friends*.

(Burble of voices)

DORIS CRENSHAW, *Chicago Inquirer*: Mary Lou! Mary Lou!

PEACHUM: Go ahead, Doris.

CRENSHAW: What is the health status of the three gunmen?

PEACHUM: I'm told that the late Slack Kovich is still dead.

(Laughter)

CRENSHAW: Another feather in the Secret Service's cap.

PEACHUM: Of the two gunmen foiled by our courageous President, Elton Coates survived his trampling in the cattle pen, and Burgess Armitage will be fit to stand trial after he recovers from his back surgery.

CRENSHAW: Doesn't the video footage show that Armitage was thwarted by Walker Lambert?

PEACHUM: No, it doesn't.

(Burble of voices)

BRODERICK GREYBILL, *Atlanta Bulletin*: Help us out, Mary Lou!

PEACHUM: I'll do my best, Brod.

GREYBILL: We keep hearing different things. Was there a fourth gunman or not?

PEACHUM: His name is Amos Orloff, another Pacifica operative. He backed out at the last minute, but the F.B.I. still tracked him down.

(Burble of voices)

THEODORE GILLIAN, *Boston Sentinel*: How about taking a serious question, Mary Lou?

PEACHUM: How about asking one?

GILLIAN: Why would terrorists working for Nicole Yoshida set their sights on detainees from Mr. Pence's Rio Grande internment camps?

PEACHUM: The terrorists weren't interested in harming the detainees. They were hired by the B.U.G. in Pacifica to ruin a beautiful patriotic pageant.

GILLIAN: Since when do anti-Pence dissidents wear Keep America Great Always caps?

PEACHUM: KAGA stands for Keep Atheism and Godlessness Alive. Now, Ted, where's that serious question you promised us?

GILLIAN: Meh.

(Burble of voices)

PEACHUM: Bring it on, Ralph.

RALPH ENDICOTT, Fox-CNN: Is it true that, at the last minute, the detainees were swapped for college students from Pacifica?

PEACHUM: You'll have to talk to the Houston Society about that. Mr. Palette was probably afraid the rapists and Muslims would abuse their furloughs and run away. Detainees, undergraduates, who cares? The pageant showed—and here's what matters—it showed that hundreds of despicable Mexicans died before the Alamo fell.

(Burble of voices)

AGATHON, *New York Examiner*: Madam Director!

PEACHUM: Didn't I fire you two months ago?

AGATHON: Yes, but my paper didn't. Is the Pence administration contemplating any retaliatory actions against Pacifica?

PEACHUM: I'm not free to discuss them *all*, of course. Okay, it's no secret that California suffers from a plague of homosexuality, so next month we're parachuting seventy-five licensed conversion therapists into San Francisco. We're also planning to abduct ninety-eight Pacifica doctors who provided abortions when they were American citizens and make them stand trial for first-degree murder.

AGATHON: Any truth to the rumors of imminent drone attacks on renewable energy installations in Pacifica?

PEACHUM: White House scientists have recently alerted the Pence administration to the carcinogenic side effects of wind turbines and solar panels. The President feels obligated to destroy all such arrays before the threat reaches our western border. Jordan, you've exhausted your kvetching quota for the day.

AGATHON: I'll be back.

(Burble of voices)

PEACHUM: Go ahead, Kate. Do your worst.

KATE TUCKER, *Hartford Beacon*: Shortly before Mr. Pence foiled the terrorists, he said some things that Democrats in

Newtopia found pretty disturbing. He even raised a few Republican eyebrows. You know, "Wind their illegal alien bowels around your bayonets," that sort of thing.

GILLIAN: "Cut out their homophile hearts with your Bowie knives and stomp on them. Blow their lying deep-state brains from here to East Jesus."

PEACHUM: Mr. Pence didn't write the pageant. The author was a dubious character named Ogden McQuaid. He seems to have gone into hiding.

TUCKER: "Grind their Muslim bones beneath your boots."

PEACHUM: Let's say we stop whining about the script and remember that our President knew his lines cold and delivered them with great finesse. Sometimes I think you clowns are all Pacifica stooges. This meeting is over.

Spring of 2036 had come to the American East Coast, a season that, even in the Anthropocene, had blessed Washington, D.C., with congenial weather, exuberant songbirds, and lilting floral fragrances. For our first meeting in April, Ainsley Laveau and I sat on the patio outside our customary Starbucks. I asked her why we were discussing Operation Epiphany within earshot of random pedestrians, some of whom might be F.B.I. or C.I.A. agents. She insisted our blatant observability was the whole point.

"At the B.U.G. we believe in the Purloined Letter Effect. Ever read Edgar Allan Poe's story? The Paris police inspectors knew that the incriminating document must be in the blackmailer's apartment, but they searched only the nooks and crannies they *themselves* would have used. Poe's hero, Auguste Dupin, finds the document hiding in plain sight—on the blackmailer's mantelpiece."

American citizens streamed down the K Street bicycle lane, variously borne by ten-speeds, recumbents, scooters, running shoes, and, in one case, a pogo stick.

"So you're saying it would never occur to the F.B.I. or the C.I.A. to look for subversives drinking lattes outside of Starbucks?" I asked. "I'd think the lattes alone would give us away."

"Rafael and Omoyola are putting the finishing touches on phase four."

"Where do I send my letter of resignation? Shall I just pass it along to you?

"Please, honey, no hasty decisions."

"Your crazy Alamo pageant almost got my daughter and her fiancée *killed*, for Christ's sake."

"We deeply regret that. But your act of heroism, decking Armitage before he could open fire—that must have been deeply satisfying for you, even if Pence got the credit. You probably saved Celeste's life."

"After your people put her in harm's way."

"In the final analysis, the endless malice of the Republican Party is what jeopardized your daughter."

A bus rattled by, spewing black exhaust per Executive Order 20674.

"Did the B.U.G. really have no inkling those crackpot musketeers might show up?" I asked. "Did you expect potential terrorists to do a Purloined Letter thing and brag about their conspiracy in every saloon from Dallas to Corpus Christi, only instead they outwitted you by keeping their plans under wraps?"

"I understand why you're upset with us, but I can't imagine any future B.U.G. scenario that would threaten your daughter."

"If I quit now, how much do I get from the unpaid half of my salary?"

"Not my department." Ainsley bit into her scone. "Sweetie, I really, really hope you'll see Operation Epiphany through to the end. President Yoshida is counting on you. Your country is counting on you. You probably think the Alamo Reenactment was an unqualified disaster—but it wasn't."

"Pence has become a minor deity. He's inflicting the worst sanctions yet on Pacifica. 'Unqualified' sounds about right to me."

"Here's the silver lining. The President now thinks the Council of Angels cast him in the pageant so he could thwart a terrorist attack and see his approval ratings soar. Ah, but how did those angels communicate their desires? Through the Reverend Walker Lambert, that's how! Henceforth Pence will trust his PFC even when the revelations are utterly outlandish."

"They're *always* utterly outlandish."

"Rafael and Omoyola have concocted a masterpiece. You're going to love it."

"No, I'm not."

A professional dog walker, a white male, cherubic of face and morose of disposition, came stumbling down the K Street sidewalk dragged by a merry pack of four-legged clients. Ainsley and I paused to admire a border collie, a Yorkie, and two golden retrievers.

"We have to move quickly with phase four, before Pence can get his latest sanctions up and running," said Ainsley. "If this new scenario plays out as we imagine, nobody will take him seriously ever again."

"Wasn't that supposed to happen back when he was calling for a poverty tax?"

"Ever heard of Audio-Animatronics?"

"My grandfather loved the Pirates of the Caribbean ride at the Magic Kingdom. Does it still have a bride auction?"

"They got rid of that decades ago."

"Good."

Ainsley explained that, while the twentieth-century version of Pirates of the Caribbean had provided a memorable experience for millions of patrons (Audio-Animatronics being the virtual reality of its day), subsequent generations of design wizards had slowly but steadily improved every such robot in all the Disney theme parks. The newest simulacra appeared completely human and could interact convincingly with tourists. At the turn of the century, a dozen nonconformist engineers broke with the Disney organization to form their own company, Techno-Doppelgängers, Inc., specializing in automatons of dead music icons.

"Their Elvis is amazing. Nobody will ever match their Janis Joplin, Billie Holiday, or Michael Jackson. Last night I received an email from Sacramento with a top-secret video download attached."

"Top secret? So the B.U.G. has posted it on QueueTube, right?"

"For five minutes I watched a flawless doppelgänger of Donald Trump during his last year in office. The voice is perfect, the body language uncanny."

"And what's the purpose of this puppet?" I asked.

"Can't you guess?"

"You want the world to think Trump never really died? That'll be a hard sell, Ainsley. His final days at Johns Hopkins left a paper trail a mile long."

"No, Polly, for this scheme to work, Trump's sorry death must remain as factual as his sordid life. Surely you can figure out what we're up to."

And suddenly it hit me. "Oh, my God. You aren't serious."

"Jesus has already given his approval," said Ainsley, grinning.

"You're going to have Trump come back—?"

Ainsley instinctively lifted an index finger to her lips and released a soft but emphatic *shush*.

"From the dead?" I whispered.

"More than that. We're going to have him *raised* from the dead."

"By whom?"

"Take a guess."

"Good Lord."

"On a Sunday morning in the Washington National Cathedral," said Ainsley. "It'll be part of the liturgy."

A stately Doberman pinscher appeared, walking beside a young woman in a yellow sundress. I'd heard that plans to employ the breed as security enforcers in the Metro stations were scrapped when someone noted that Dobermans scare the bejeezus out of people, but this dog's owner seemed in control.

"This is not a good plan," I said.

"Ogden McQuaid wrote the incantation last week. The doppelgänger will remain active for about twenty minutes."

"And then it will return to the casket?"

"Don't tell Pence, but the robot will bolt the cathedral and start running down Wisconsin Avenue."

The Doberman assumed a defecation crouch between the sidewalk and the street. Mom pulled a Mutt Mitt from her handbag.

"I don't like anything I'm hearing," I said.

"A B.U.G. team will be waiting to throw the robot in the back of a van. Before the day is over, they'll disassemble it and dissolve the pieces in sulfuric acid."

The Doberman pooped on the grassy verge. Mom whisked away the waste.

"What will the robot do during its time in the cathedral?"

"We're not certain."

"*Not certain?* But all its behaviors will be programmed—surely that's the plan."

"Republicans of the Caribbean?"

"Exactly."

"Naturally our first instinct was to script every single moment of the resurrection, but then President Yoshida made a brilliant case for programming only the doppelgänger's departure from the cathedral. Beyond that, the algorithms would be restricted to giving the robot Trump's cognitive habits and personality traits."

"Bottomless narcissism, bedrock loutishness, bloody ignorance, and groundbreaking dishonesty?"

"Uh-huh. The code was a bear."

"I think you're leaving too much to chance."

"Yoshida convinced us that no matter what outrageous actions and speeches Ogden McQuaid and the rest of us might invent, an indeterminate, fuzzy-logic, quantum-inflected Donald Trump would serve our purposes far better. According to all the computer forecasts, when the robot finally exits the scene, he'll be leaving behind a humiliated Pence, a poleaxed Republican Party, and a Newtopia rushing pell-mell toward secession."

"Ainsley, this is a terrible idea."

"Possibly. Will you help us out?"

"I need to ask my daughter what she thinks. Would the B.U.G. like us to Livestream our conversation?"

Thanks to President Trump's chronic inability to focus on more than one self-generated crisis at a time, the blood staining his hands and the dead bodies accruing to his policies never reached the maximum quantity imaginable. Future historians will be called upon to explain why, for example, Forty-Five did not start a thermonuclear war. Were the question put to me, I would point to Trump's probable conclusion that even the most basic sort of global H-bomb holocaust was likely to do collateral damage to his real-estate investments.

Throughout the first two weeks following his heroic deeds at the Alamo Reenactment, Mike Pence emerged as the Promethean figure that Forty-Five had merely imagined himself to be. The rumors came thick and fast. Before pushing Burgess Armitage and Elton Coates off the south wall of the Alamo, Pence had supposedly broken each of their jaws with a right uppercut (the corresponding doctored images soon appeared on QueueTube). In the case of Slack Kovich, it wasn't the Secret Service that brought him down but rather Pence, who'd grabbed a revolver from Agent Cassidy's holster and plugged the gunman through the heart (the deep fake immediately went viral). During a visit to St. Agnus's Hospital, Pence had allegedly cured two children of cystic fibrosis and sent three adult cases of lung cancer into remission. Exploiting his latent telepathic powers, he had alerted the F.B.I. to an imminent terrorist attack on the Statue of Liberty, with the result that thousands of tourists, and the Lady herself, were saved.

"You've become a legend in your own time, Mr. President. You played William Travis, but right now you're closer to Davy Crockett."

"I owe it all to you, Walker," said Pence, pacing around the White House chapel. "If I hadn't joined the Alamo Reenactment, some *other* Travis would've foiled the terrorists."

"To be precise, Mike, you owe it all to *Jesus*."

"Jesus, of course."

"And his Council of Angels."

"Some people say I thwarted only Elton Coates. They say you got Armitage, and my bodyguards shot Kovich. To tell you the truth, I don't remember."

"You stopped all three, Mike."

"I like what you said in your prayer about calling America the Republic of Jesus Christ."

"And I meant it." I cast a freighted glance at the Secret Service agents. "Mr. President, our Lord has yet another task for you."

"I am evermore ready to witness for Christ," said Pence, gesturing the T-men out of the chapel.

Not surprisingly, Celeste had pleaded with me to support the Techno-Doppelgängers, Inc. scenario. She said I was karmically obligated to play my part.

"This revelation arrived right before you got here." I pointed to the Palm Sunday scene filling the chapel window. "Our stained-glass Jesus gave me to know that your administration has reached a crossroads. Now is the time for Michael Richard Pence to show the world that Heaven has rewarded his moral purity with powers eclipsing even those of the divinely appointed Trump."

I informed an increasingly incredulous Pence that, as a first step, he must order the removal of Forty-Five's embalmed corpse from its resting place on Fifth Avenue, across the street from Trump Tower. Naturally I was among the thousands of former New Yorkers who regarded the Trump Mausoleum (plus Visitors Center and Gift Shop), with its outsized marble angels riding on faux-Egyptian sphinxes, as a vulgar and irredeemable eyesore, but today I refrained from offering my opinion—for it happened that the real Reverend Walker Lambert had championed the Midtown mausoleum by way of discouraging Trump from his preferred postmortem disposition (which would have involved evicting the remains of the eighteenth President from Morningside Heights, replacing them with Forty-Five's body, and changing the name of the sepulcher from Grant's Tomb to Trump's Palace). I explained that the corpse and its sarcophagus must next be transported to the Washington National Cathedral, where Pence would perform an unprecedented ritual, far more momentous than any state funeral or prayer service ever conducted in that mighty neo-Gothic edifice.

"The resurrection will last about twenty minutes," I said. "During that interval he'll bless the nation and impart a few words of wisdom from beyond the grave."

"Resurrection?" said Pence. "I don't understand."

"You're right, sir. We should reserve the word 'resurrection' for our Lord alone. Let's call it Trump Redux. You're going to bring him back from the dead."

"I don't follow you."

"On live television."

"Trump?"

"Trump."

"Back from…"

"The dead. For twenty minutes."

"I'm having trouble with this."

"Of course."

"But it's what our Savior desires?"

"He couldn't have been more explicit."

"What if something goes wrong?"

"God is the stage manager. What could go wrong?"

"I don't know, Walker. It all sounds…"

"Blasphemous?"

"Well, yes."

"Believe me, Jesus will know how to spin this—through his earthly emissaries, I mean, our team at Fox News."

A shroud of melancholy enveloped the President. He shuffled to the back of the chapel, kissed the marble lamb beside the Francis of Assisi statue (pre-Reformation Catholic saints being acceptable to evangelicals), and returned to the altar. As he fixed on the stained-glass Palm Sunday, his face blossomed in a seraphic smile. He heaved a sigh of relief, like a person realizing he hadn't sent that embarrassing email to the wrong recipient after all.

"You know something, Walker? I can feel the power of Christ vibrating through my bones."

"A power that will soon vibrate through the Chosen One's bones."

"I'm psyched."

"This will take considerable planning. I suggest you form an *ad hoc* Trump Redux Committee within your circle of confidants."

"Leave Congress out of it?"

"The Democrats' presence on the Hill might be negligible, but they'll still kick up a fuss."

"But how do I bring the miracle about? I've never done anything like this before."

"Neither has anyone else, except our Lord. Merely place your hand on the corpse's forehead and say the proper incantation."

"Sounds simple enough."

" 'Gather up the four winds, O ye angels of air, and breathe upon this man,' " I said, the words Ogden McQuaid had composed for the occasion.

"I can do that," said Pence.

"It continues in that vein for a few more sentences. I'll email you the complete text."

"I'm terrified, Walker. Terrified, exhilarated, dizzy, wonderstruck. Do you suppose this is what marijuana feels like?"

"Not my area, Mike."

"This is just like marijuana. It must be."

On March the 31st, 2036, Mike Pence revealed to a cadre of journalists gathered in the Rose Garden that he'd been directed by God to bring Donald Trump back from the dead, an announcement whose troublesome theological and political implications did not go unnoticed. Throughout the first two weeks in April, the scheduled miracle consumed the U.S. cable-news demagogues, the Pacifica information outlets, the Newtopia public affairs programs, the European press, the evangelical blogosphere, and even the Vatican's multilingual radio network. While every Democratic lawmaker in the U.S. issued statements to the effect that the President had evidently lost his mind, Republican members of Congress unanimously endorsed the Second Coming of Forty-Five, speculating on Fox News that Mike Pence, hero of the Alamo Reenactment, was about to fulfill the primary purpose for which Heaven had put him in the White House.

Although Ainsley and her bosses were hoping I could convince Pence to stage the event on Easter Sunday—April the 13, 2036—the Trump Redux Committee decided that would smack of sacrilege. Yes, there was only one Donald Trump, but then again there was only one Jesus Christ. In the end, the miracle was postponed a week.

On Saturday, April the 19th, the day of the scheduled run-through, I entered the Washington National Cathedral for the first time in my life. The abrupt change of zone astonished me, from the honking hurly-burly of Wisconsin Avenue to the vaulted serenity and echoing marble of America's unofficial house of prayer (nominally Episcopalian, but nobody pressed the point, not even the head of the diocese, Bishop Muriel Phelps). Technicians from Fox and the lesser networks scurried about everywhere, installing cameras, microphones, control consoles, floodlights, and reflectors. Dominating the central nave was the Jerusalem Altar, made entirely of stones retrieved from Solomon's Quarry in Israel, but what riveted my attention was the immense sarcophagus resting before the altar on a cast-iron catafalque. Earlier in the week, the Redux Committee had, with considerable fanfare, flown the great stone coffin out of New York City on Air Force One and then transported it from Reagan International to northwest D.C. in a nineteenth-century hearse drawn by four black horses. Unbeknownst to everyone at the run-through except myself, the mahogany casket within the sarcophagus contained neither flesh nor bones, the B.U.G. having switched the body for their automaton. Forty-Five's actual remains still lay in the Trump Mausoleum.

Although Ainsley seemed to believe that Techno-Doppelgänger's robots were incapable of violence against humans, my every instinct told me to steer clear of Forty-Five's mechanized twin tomorrow. When I informed Pence that I wanted no involvement in the miracle beyond the sort of brief invocation I'd offered at the Alamo pageant, he'd readily agreed. I was therefore dismayed to spot my name in four different places on the gold-bordered brochure the Redux Committee had distributed to the various reporters, journalists, and video directors milling around the nave.

THE WASHINGTON NATIONAL CATHEDRAL
PROGRAM FOR SUNDAY, APRIL 20, 2036

CARILLON PRELUDE
Danziger Choräle für Carillon, Johann Eggert (1728–1803).

ORGAN VOLUNTARY
Nun komm, der Heiden Heiland, Johann Sebastian Bach (1685–1750).

OLD TESTAMENT READING
Isaiah 2:1–5.

PSALM 122
The choir introduces the antiphon, then all repeat in plainsong chant.

NEW TESTAMENT READING
"At the last trump," 1 Corinthians 15:52.

OFFERTORY
Make checks payable to WNC.

THE LORD'S PRAYER
Ancient is the link between our daily bread
and the spiritual food we receive in the Eucharist.

BREAKING OF THE BREAD
The presider prepares the wafers in silence.

INVITATION TO HOLY COMMUNION
All who seek a deeper life in Christ are welcome. Please receive the bread in outstretched hands and sip the wine from the chalice, guiding it gently to your lips, or you may dip the wafer into the wine. Respond to receiving Communion by saying "Amen." Gluten-free wafers are available.

ADDRESS TO THE NATIONS OF THE WORLD
The Reverend Walker Lambert, Presidential Faith Counselor, on "What Brings Us Here Today?"

LIFTING OF THE SARCOPHAGUS COVER
Bishop Muriel Phelps, Bishop Lawrence Langford,
the Reverend Walker Lambert, Father Shamus Monaghan.

RESURRECTION INCANTATION
President Michael Richard Pence, 46th President of the
United States, opens the casket and raises
his predecessor from the dead.

RESURRECTEE'S ORATION
Donald John Trump, 45th President of the United States.

REENTOMBMENT
Bishop Muriel Phelps, Bishop Lawrence Langford,
the Reverend Walker Lambert, Father Shamus Monaghan.

INTERPRETATION OF RESURRECTEE'S ORATION
The Reverend Walker Lambert on
"What Did We Learn Today?"

THE NICENE CREED
The people stand as able.

THE BLESSING
The presider blesses the people, who respond "Amen."

CARILLON POSTLUDE
The Washington Ringing Society.

"Mr. President, I am bewildered to find myself featured prominently in the program."

Flanked by two Secret Service agents, Pence fixed on my unhappy face. His eyes were bloodshot. His lower lip trembled. "The Committee convinced me only you can properly frame this event. The world deserves to know every detail of your epiphany in the White House chapel."

To dramatize my distress, I crumpled up the schedule. Releasing a soft growl, I pressed my palms against the crinkled sphere as if molding a snowball.

163

"Did you hear harp music, Walker? Did a dove flutter above the altar? Does Jesus have a baritone voice, or is he a basso profundo?"

I jammed the snowball into my jacket pocket.

"All right, sir, I'll set the scene, but I'm *not* going to explain away whatever Trumpian invective comes out of his mouth. My specialty is prophesy, not exegesis."

"If not you, then who?"

"Yourself, perhaps?"

"No, Walker, that won't do. Colonel Travis has slit the earth with his saber, and now he invites you to cross the line. The republic needs you."

To this day I'm not certain why I agreed to play the roles of arbiter and umpire at the Second Coming of Forty-Five. Morbid curiosity? An unconscious desire to address the entire population—or something close to it—of planet Earth? Whatever the reason, I marched toward Pence and offered him a crisp salute.

"David Crockett, reporting for duty, Colonel Travis, sir."

"Good to have you with us, my buckskin buccaneer. Now let's get the job done."

V

DURING my adolescence in Teaneck, I received Holy Communion at least a dozen times, but the Methodists always made the ritual boring by using grape juice instead of wine. Although I never considered converting to Catholicism—there are simpler ways to get elevated on a Sunday morning—the Washington National Cathedral version of the sacrament proved strangely gratifying: I was finally drinking real wine at a Eucharist.

Outside the building, a ferocious storm raged and howled, weather that seemed better suited to a crucifixion or a Slaughter of the Innocents than to the Second Coming of Forty-Five. Hadn't God gotten the memo? Wasn't something miraculous about to occur, worthy of all the birdsong and sunshine the Almighty could summon? As the sacrament unfolded, I thought of my grandfather's favorite British horror film, *Taste the Blood of Dracula*, which had the vampire's disciple, Lord Courtley, bringing four nineteenth-century male sybarites to a deconsecrated church and leading them in a blasphemous parody of the Eucharist while lightning flashed and thunder boomed.

We drank the blood, we ate the flesh, and then it was time for my "Address to the Nations of the World." Upon climbing the spiral staircase to the great stone pulpit, I cleared my throat and, fixing on the teleprompter, told the story of my epiphany in the White House chapel. I concluded with a personal observation.

"Some of you out there believe that our current Chief Executive should not have sold Alaska to the Russian Federation. Others are unhappy that Mr. Pence awarded the Presidential Medal of

Freedom to the Sycamore gunmen. We must not forget that these actions were mandated from On High. Today the hero of the Alamo pageant will bless us with an incomparable gift—not in atonement for past errors but in testament to his exalted standing in the universe. My fellow Americans, I present to you Michael Richard Pence, servant of the Lord!"

I abandoned the pulpit and descended to street level. The President rose from his pew and, trailed by two secret Service Agents, solemnly approached the sarcophagus, where he was joined by the stout, stately celebrant of today's Eucharist, Bishop Muriel Phelps, her tall, rangy, African American confrère, Bishop Lawrence Langford, and a spindly, soft-eyed Catholic priest, Father Shamus Monaghan. Aided by a block and tackle, the three clerics and I lifted the massive cover and set it on the floor, nearly crushing our fingers in the process.

Mr. Pence leaned toward the casket and raised the hinged mahogany lid. The Fox News camera operator dollied in for a closeup. I glanced at the monitor. The President set his palm against the automaton's brow, thus activating the algorithms that would play out over the next twenty minutes.

"Gather up the four winds, O ye angels of air, and breathe upon this man!" Pence intoned. "Seize hold of the sun, O ye angels of light, and restore the radiance to his eyes! Dip thy gourds into the sea, O ye angels of water, and wash away the stone that sits upon his heart! Take Eden's clay in thy hands, O ye angels of earth, and mold for this man a new body, that he may walk among us once again! Donald John Trump, come forth!"

I'm still not sure why the man at the great Aeolian-Skinner organ elected to augment the Second Coming of Forty-Five with the Hallelujah chorus from Handel's *Messiah*, nor do I understand why the Men and Boys Choir was suddenly moved to supply the libretto. Obviously some uncanny inspiration had seized the souls of both the organist and the singers. The effect was astonishing. As the pipes sent piercing shafts of sound reverberating through the great nave, counterpointing the thunderstorm outside, and a hundred male voices proclaimed "For the Lord God Omnipotent reigneth," the tangerine-cheeked, golden-haired Donald Trump simulacrum, dressed in a dark blue suit and a bright red tie, sat bolt upright in its casket.

A half-dozen churchgoers fainted in their pews. Eyes gaping, jaw dropping, Mike Pence took a step backward.

"Hallelujah, Hallelujah, Hallelujah, Hallelujah!"

Muscle by muscle, valve by valve, cylinder by cylinder, the Techno-Doppelgänger climbed free of the sarcophagus and lowered itself to the floor. It wobbled like a gyroscope losing momentum, then lost its balance and fell on its pneumatic posterior.

"King of Kings and Lord of Lords!"

Slowly, spasmodically, Mr. Trump got to his feet.

"And he shall reign forever and ever!"

He rotated his head and, blinking under the glare of the television lights, surveyed the spectators.

"Hallelujah, Hallelujah, Hallelujah, Hallelujah!"

He abruptly pivoted on his heel and screamed at the organist. "Stop that damn racket!"

The startled musician lifted his hands from the topmost keyboard. The choir became suddenly mute. With the understandable awkwardness of a newly resuscitated corpse, Mr. Trump climbed the spiral staircase to the pulpit and, pursing his lips, scanned the audience.

"Hello, all you smart and terrific Ever-Trumpers out there! I'm told they've never had so many American citizens in this church before. Any Jews here today? A show of hands, please? No Jews? Where are my Jews? You people never appreciated me. After all I did for you, one scheme after another to protect your money, and you were never grateful. Let me tell you, Heaven is a wonderful place, not as terrific as Mar-a-Lago, but still great, and I would've ended up there if they hadn't slipped a bunch of fake documents into my dossier. I've heard the culprit was that Democrat Jew—I mean that *Demon*-crat Jew—you know who I mean, shifty Adam Schiff. Unconstitutional! Witch hunt! Hoax! Say it loud. 'Lock him up! Lock him up!' I'm not hearin' the chant, people. What's the matter with you? Pence got your tongue? You probably believe it was Pantywaist Pence who brought me back. Not true. I did it all myself. Me! L'il Mikey's not a necromancer nor any sort of romancer, I hear, very frustrating for his wife. Just look at the size of *my* hands. Unconstitutional! Witch hunt! Hoax! I actually enjoyed myself in Perdition Land. All the pussy you can eat. When you have fifteen people infected with the virus, and within a few days those fifteen will be down to zero, that's a pretty good job we've done. I see lots of black faces in the pews today. My African Americans, they love me. We used to say 'Negroes,' but they didn't like that, and once I got scolded for saying 'the coloreds,' as in 'I'm for the coloreds every time,' but 'people *of* color,' that's suddenly okay, '*of* color,' who would've thought one little adverb was such a big deal? Anyone who wants a test can get one. So there I was, lying in my casket in the Trump Mausoleum, which is much larger than Grant's Tomb and the Pyramid of Cheops put together, and I got to thinking about that LGBTQ emblem so many bad characters hide behind these days, and then it hit me: it looks like a sign you'd see in the Forty-Second Street Subway Station, not that I ever ride the fucking subway. 'Hey, mister, can you tell me how to get to Union Square?' 'Well, you take the L train, transfer to the G, then hop the B, but avoid the Q, it's full of fudge packers.' Unconstitutional! Witch hunt! Hoax! Could we try sticking it to Shifty Schiff again? 'Lock him up! Lock him up!' Silence. You people are pathetic. Screw you, Pantywaist Pence. *I'm* the one with the power over life and death and drones and interest rates. We have it totally under control. It's one person coming in from China. They say I'm a polarizing figure, but they also say I'm *de*-polarizing, because our great policies are causing the ice caps to melt. Make up your damn minds! Polarizing or depolarizing? All this crap about our planet being on fire—it's a swindle perpetrated by our corrupt deep-state news media, because only God can thaw a glacier, and if we *really* needed the ice, he would've let us keep it, but we *don't* need it: I've got plenty in my fridge. Unconstitutional! Witch hunt! Hoax! You think Lame McCain could've resurrected himself? Hah! Never! He couldn't even get out of a North Vietnam prison cell, and I heard the security there was very weak. You can take the N train, but never use the N-word train. I'm the least racist person I know. Ask any ten-dollar chocolate whore. The socialists out there can't even decide whether to call it the greenhouse effect or global warming, one day this, one day that, climate change, extreme weather, existential emergency—you name it—and next week they'll call it something *else*, mark my words. Actually, there is no N train. It's going to disappear. One day, it's like a miracle, the virus will disappear. And what about Crooked Hillary's emails? Lock her up! Lock her up! Sing it loud! No? Screw you all. She and Biden never got tired of kissing Obama's ass. Unconstitutional! Witch hunt! Hoax! Pantywaist Pence couldn't raise a gerbil from the dead. When I was down Gehenna way, I learned some great new words. Shizzing. You know that word? Shizzing? It means pooping and ejaculating at the same time, and that's exactly what I've been doing up here, even while I'm giving this amazing speech, but very high-IQ individuals like me, we can concentrate on many things at once, like shizzing and sermonizing. Give me a minute to hitch up my pants. There! Done! Poontang, taco hole, mustard slot, hairy oyster—they all mean the same thing! Looks like my time's up. This has been the greatest twenty-minute resurrection ever, am I right? Am I right? See you in the afterlife!"

The doppelgänger lurched away from the pulpit and gimped down the spiral staircase. Seized by a sudden burst of energy, it brushed past the two Episcopalian bishops, the Roman Catholic priest, and President Mike Pence, all four clustered around the sarcophagus in various states of mortification and dismay. The Chief Executive wept openly. Lawrence Langford was hyperventilating. Muriel Phelps and Shamus Monaghan seemed stricken with apoplexy. None of the three clerics evinced the slightest interest in returning the cover to the sarcophagus.

Shifting gears, decelerating from a sprint to a march, Mr. Trump moved down the central aisle of the nave. He glanced from pew to pew, evidently expecting people to reach out and touch him, or at least give him a standing ovation, but instead they recoiled from his presence. One old woman, wearing a mauve dress and white gloves, made eye contact with the resurrected President and vomited on her missal. At last he reached the cathedral entrance, then burst through the Gothic doors and disappeared into the storm. A minute later, the B.U.G. agents hoisted him into the back of their van—or so I assumed—and spirited him away at top speed.

Like a condemned man ascending a scaffold, the noose dangling emphatically above his head, I returned to the pulpit, one lugubrious step at a time.

"The program calls for me to interpret the late Mr. Trump's oration or sermon or whatever you want to call it, but I'm at a loss for words, and you probably are, too. Even though I hold a White House appointment as Mr. Pence's faith counselor, at this moment I'm out of my depth. If anyone from Fox or some other news organization accosts me outside the cathedral, let me assure that person I shall categorically refuse to answer his or her questions."

Somehow the congregation found the mental energy and the physical stamina to pursue the day's agenda. In low voices and with staccato breaths they recited the Nicene Creed. Bishop Phelps blessed the people. Cued by the program brochure, they responded "Amen." The Washington Ringing Society likewise did its part, so that a mighty carillon rolled forth from the dual bell towers, echoed across the plaza, and reverberated up and down Wisconsin Avenue.

And suddenly it was over. Trump Redux had actually happened—the Second Coming of Forty-Five had played itself out: but whether the faux miracle portended a bright new day for my adopted country or the beginning of Pacifica's end, I could not begin to say.

Although I spent the next two weeks avoiding news reports from any mass medium, preferring to play the recluse and binge-watch the final season of *The Bad Place*, my daughter insisted on bringing me up to speed through text messages and voicemails. She reported that a plethora of competing theories was consuming public and private conversations in the United States and Pacifica and throughout the planet at large.

Among churchgoers, the controversy turned on Forty-Five's apparent admission that he'd spent the past seven years in Hell. Christians from both political parties found this revelation disturbing. A few Republicans of faith, however, joined with Fox News in dismissing Trump's remarks about Perdition Land as yet another of his marginally amusing jokes (these were the same people who insisted Trump wasn't being serious when he'd publicly asked China to dig up dirt on Joe Biden), and he'd really spent his posthumous sojourn in Heaven. A small but vocal minority of GOP Christians insisted that, because Judgment Day had not yet occurred, Trump was thus far neither damned nor saved and therefore must have returned from some eschatological netherzone.

While the three interpretations—Heaven, Hell, holding tank—were mutually incompatible, conservative politicians and voters reached consensus on one point. Contrary to his boasting, Trump had not resurrected himself (such a kidder, that Donald). Rather, a bona fide miracle worker presently occupied the Oval Office, a fact that boded well for the future of the Republican Party. Indeed, for thousands of woefully sick and suicidally melancholic citizens, Pence's supernatural powers were beyond question, and so they began gathering daily outside the White House, hoping he would appear and heal them.

Meanwhile, people of a materialist and secular persuasion cultivated conspiracy theories. Donald Trump had never died—he'd merely gone into hiding. No, he'd died, but the person in the sarcophagus was his deranged twin brother. No, not the real Trump, not a twin, but a master illusionist, capable of simulating miracles through mass hypnosis. Not the real Trump, a twin, or a magician, but a look-alike actor. Not the real Trump, a twin, a magician, or an actor, but a hologram. Not the real Trump, a twin, a magician, an actor, or a hologram, but an Audio-Animatronics robot.

"Inevitably, somebody would get it right," said Ainsley, "but it doesn't matter, since the robot theory has no more going for it than the twin theory or the magician theory."

"Did your guys obliterate the automaton as planned?"

"They dissolved every last molecule. Onward and upward. Have you seen today's headlines?"

"I've been avoiding the news," I said, sipping a latte. "Likewise human contact, Twitter, Facebook, and all beverages except whiskey and Starbucks coffee, sometimes in the same mug. Trump Redux took a lot out of me. Celeste occasionally gives me an update."

"Did she fill you in about secession?"

A mourning dove cooed in a nearby cherry tree. I closed my eyes, savored the bird's lament, and shook my head.

Ainsley reached out and squeezed my forearm. "Polly, we've won. Every Newtopian state has left the Union—all except Maine, and it's expected to follow suit next week. We have you to thank, sweetie."

"Thank me after Pence *doesn't* respond by starting a civil war."

"According to our best intelligence, the President has become clinically depressed. He's turned most of his responsibilities over to Vice President Santorum, who, being some sort of Republican, is leery of foreign wars, even foreign wars fought on formerly American soil."

The border collie, the Yorkie, and the two golden retrievers came trotting down K Street, dragging their moonfaced and discombobulated professional walker. Whenever Ainsley and I met on the patio outside our habitual Starbucks, this same pack came loping past at exactly eleven A.M. You could set your watch by them.

"Do you think Pence might be about to resign?"

"It's possible."

"So all the news is good?"

"Well, not *all* the news. This just in from Fresno. The *real* Reverend Walker Lambert has … there's no way to sugarcoat this … your alter ego has escaped."

The Yorkie peed on the grassy verge.

"Escaped?"

"Uh-huh."

"Fuck. Does Pence know the world now contains two Walker Lamberts?"

"Yes, but he doesn't know which is which." Ainsley sipped her chai. "When you see him tomorrow—"

"Tomorrow? I never want to see him again."

"You promised Pence a final meeting."

"No, I didn't."

"Three o'clock sharp, the White House chapel." Ainsley caressed her tablet. "Would you like to see the email?"

"Feh."

"Be prepared for him to question your identity."

"Should I also be prepared for him to put me in jail?"

"The B.U.G. won't let that happen."

"Easy for you to say."

Ainsley took a long swallow of chai. She steepled her index fingers and brought them to her lips. "A couple of years ago one of Nicole Yoshida's Chippie bodyguards, Myron Flegenheim, lateraled her a flash drive from a disgruntled F.B.I. agent named Patrick O'Donnell. By Yoshida's reckoning, the O'Donnell dossier reveals, quote, 'a Pence administration that's essentially a wholly owned subsidiary of Vladimir Putin and the F.S.B.,' unquote. Evidently the White House is so beholden to the Russian Federation that even Pence's sycophantic Republican Congress might convene an inquiry—if they ever see the data."

"Will they?"

"As I needn't tell you, impeachment is a mug's game, but we're prepared to put the O'Donnell card on the table if it might keep one of our agents from harm."

"I guess I can stomach one more meeting."

"Three days from now we'll fly you from Reagan International to LAX, and you'll be a free woman. Meanwhile, we're shuttering Operation Epiphany for good. Mission accomplished. Honey, your country is eternally grateful to you."

Thanks to my daughter's bulletins, I knew to anticipate the huge crowd outside the White House, thousands of petitioners wracked by unquiet desperation and intolerable pain. Pennsylvania Avenue looked like the charity ward of a nineteenth-century hospital, the pavements and verges swarming with moaning wretches. I was soon engulfed by wheelchairs, crutches, oxygen tanks, portable dialysis machines, and cots holding terminally ill children. The scene might have held a certain apocalyptic fascination were it not so unbearably sad.

At this point in his career as the PFC, the White House security people were used to the comings and goings of Reverend Walker Lambert. Fearful that the throng of victims might turn unruly, the guards summoned an armed escort and told them to take me to the White House chapel. Within the hour I found myself alone in the sanctuary, pacing fretfully around the pulpit, the sun striking the stained-glass window and casting the Palm Sunday tableau onto the white marble floor.

On the dot of three, Mike Pence and a couple of Secret Service guys entered. The bodyguards eyed me with suspicion, as they might a vampire who'd tried misdirecting them by wearing suntan lotion (such a scheme had figured in a pretty good Polly Nightingale escapade called *Lusty Bloodsuckers of Transylvania*). I feared that the agents and the Chief Executive knew the current PFC was not all he seemed.

"Brian, Lloyd, you can go," said Pence evenly.

The agents backed out of the room.

"Good afternoon, Mike," I said. "Praise Jesus."

The Chief Executive accorded me a plaintive glance. "Who *are* you?"

"My parents named me Walker Lambert."

"There's a man sitting in the Rayburn Room right now who says the same thing."

"An imposter, no doubt."

"The F.B.I.'s fingerprint records and DNA samples suggest otherwise. I'll give you a choice. You can either tell me the truth, or I'll call back Brian and Lloyd, and before long you'll find yourself in the J. Edgar Hoover Building down the street, waiting to have your picture taken."

I was prepared neither to argue with forensic science nor to match wits with a bunch of G-men, even if my friends in the B.U.G. ultimately came to my rescue.

"All right, Mr. President. You win. I'm tipping over my king. Before I became your PFC, I was a movie actress named Polly Nightingale. I specialized in adult entertainment."

"My God. Are you saying you're a female?"

"If we must apply rigid categories." I removed my prosthetic Adam's apple and my dental appliance, slipping them into my pocket.

174

"You mean I've spent many hours in this chapel alone with a woman?"

"I won't tell if you won't."

"A porn star? Like that Daniels person?"

"Now that you're up to speed, would you mind if I got free of this damn boob harness?"

The President said nothing.

And so it happened that I performed a kind of striptease before Mike Pence, systematically shedding my name-badge lanyard, navy blue suit jacket, white cotton shirt, and beige silk camisole. I removed the spandex bra. The President gaped. He sneezed. His teeth chattered. I set the clothing on the altar, then draped the lanyard and the boob harness over the pulpit. Yes, there was more than a touch of malice in my performance, but I felt not a twinge of remorse.

"Here's what I must know, Miss Nightingale."

"Polly."

"This whole Trump Redux thing—it was a B.U.G. conspiracy, right? I don't really have supernatural powers."

Leaving the camisole and the jacket on the altar, I restored my cotton shirt, then engaged the bottom button and the two immediately above it. "In my opinion, nobody has supernatural powers, not even God."

"If that thing in the cathedral wasn't Trump, what *was* it?"

"Did you ever visit the Magic Kingdom?" I engaged a fourth button. "Did you go on the Pirates of the Caribbean ride?"

The President fleetingly surveyed my cleavage. "Are you saying that darn creature was a robot?"

"Built by Techno-Doppelgängers, Incorporated."

He fixed on the floor, idly moving his foot in and out of the projected Palm Sunday tableau. "All those ailing people on the sidewalks—they'll be devastated when they learn I was duped by the B.U.G. and can't cure them."

"True, but I think you should visit them anyway. They'll get some relief just from knowing their President *cares*, unlike Reagan after the AIDS epidemic had killed thousands, and unlike Trump after … you know what."

"I hate this job. I wish I'd become a man of the cloth."

"Maybe you should resign and make Santorum the President. He's always wanted it on his résumé."

As I'd seen him do many times before, Pence walked the length of the chapel and, reaching the back wall, kissed the marble lamb beside Francis of Assisi.

"What I'm about to propose will sound strange," he said, returning to the altar. "Until I figure out what to do, I want you to remain on my staff, advising me politically and spiritually."

"Haven't you been listening? I'm not a minister, sir. I'm not even much of a Christian. I'm a porn star."

"But I like you better than that *other* Walker Lambert. He creeps me out."

"I tried to be equally creepy."

"Without success."

"Here's an idea. Why not tell the people on the sidewalks that God placed severe but necessary restrictions on your healing gifts? Leave out the part about the B.U.G. duping you. It makes you look like … well, a dupe."

"Brilliant! See, you're a *much* better faith counselor than the real Walker Lambert. Darn it, Polly, you and I had *fun* together. Especially at the Alamo. 'Our flag still waves proudly from the walls!'"

"Sorry, sir, I can't stay on your team."

"Why not?"

"Because I detest everything you stand for."

"Spiritually and politically?"

"Your policies are an affront to common decency and make me want to puke."

"And for you that rules out our continued association?"

"Yes."

The President seemed to deflate, as if he were the Stephen Austin balloon in San Antonio and my *yes* a dart. He slumped into the nearest pew and heaved a sigh.

"We've lost Newtopia," he said.

"So I hear."

"I don't sleep anymore. I wander the halls of the White House."

"Like old Prince Bolkonsky."

He rose and touched the cuff of my half-buttoned shirt. "A strange notion just crossed my mind. As long as I'm alone with a woman for the first time—a woman who isn't my wife—as long as I've dishonored God that way, perhaps we could … no, I shouldn't be thinking such things."

"What things?"

"Such things."

"I agree, sir. You shouldn't."

"The chapel door locks from the inside. A President at prayer must not be interrupted. I find you very beautiful."

I started to undo a shirt button, then thought better of the whole idea. "Shortly after the 2016 election, you and your daughter went to see Javier Muñoz starring in *Hamilton* on Broadway." I buttoned my shirt completely. "Did you know he's HIV-positive?"

Pence scowled indecipherably.

"After the curtain came down and the applause stopped, the cast linked arms, and the actor who'd played Aaron Burr addressed you from the stage."

"I was not offended. I said so the next day on Fox."

I stuck the Adam's apple back on my throat and reinserted my dental appliance. "A black man who'd been cast as a white Vice President attempted to engage with you, a white Vice President-elect." I removed my suit jacket from the altar, my name-badge lanyard from the pew, and put them both on. "Brandon Dixon wanted you to affirm that a Trump-Pence administration would work on behalf of the diverse religions, colors, ethnicities, and orientations that have made America great. Instead of acknowledging the cast's *cri de coeur*, you allowed the Secret Service to hustle you out of the theater."

"Later that evening my daughter recalled that we'd been booed as we took our orchestra seats. 'Yes, they booed us,' I told her, 'and that's what freedom sounds like.' "

"Here's what I wish had happened that night. Before you got to the lobby, I wish you'd turned around and said, in a clear, ringing voice, 'All faiths are equal under the gaze of the American eagle. All sexual identities are precious in the eyes of Jesus.' Could I hear you say that now, sir?"

"No, Polly, I won't say that. It isn't biblical."

"Neither is bigotry. Actually, bigotry is ferociously biblical, John chapter eight and all that. Could I hear you say, 'Immigrants—they get the job done'?"

"I won't say that either."

"Because immigrants are all terrorists and rapists?"

"You know I don't believe that."

"What do you believe?"

"I used to believe in Donald Trump."

"I'm homesick, Mr. Pence. I have a daughter at Stanford, a theater troupe in L.A., and a reservation on a Friday morning flight to Pacifica." I pointed to my badge. "If I were to hop a cab to my Georgetown hotel, would anybody try to stop me? As you might imagine, I have friends in high places. One of them is the President of Pacifica, and her favorite paperweight these days is a flash drive called the O'Donnell dossier."

"Begone, Polly Nightingale! Away with you! Remember the Alamo!"

I gathered up the spandex bra and the camisole. "Part of me hopes you'll conquer your insomnia"—I started out of the chapel—"but mostly I hope you never sleep again. *Adios.*"

It took me forever to get the second half of my million-dollar salary from the B.U.G., a situation so aggravating that I lost all interest in pursuing a friendship with Ainsley Laveau. When it came to the author of the Alamo Reenactment script, however, the estimable Ogden McQuaid (who'd also composed the resurrection incantation and about half the tropes spouted by the Trump doppelgänger), I was perfectly happy to admit him to my life. Not long after the Two-Bit Players' latest production—a global-warming allegory titled *The Queen of Frabbejoix*—went into rehearsal, Ogden sought me out in our troupe's new venue, the Fantomas Theater in Mar Vista, which we were renting with an eye to outright purchase if the play did well.

"I just wanted to say how much I admire you," he told me. "A less talented actress never could've sustained Operation Epiphany for almost a year."

"And a less daring writer never could've scripted your over-the-top Alamo pageant. I'm convinced it would've sparked a Newtopian succession if those ideologues with the machine guns hadn't shown up."

Years later, after we'd gotten married, Ogden insisted that for him it was love at first sight. I told him it would have been love at first sight for me, too, but I had a show to put on.

Loosely—oh, so loosely—based on an obscure 1904 novella, *Le Monde dans le Monde* (*The World within the World*) by an even more obscure French science-fiction author, Guillaume Jaseroque, the play unfolded on Zanalog, a planet whose interior is largely hollow. When rampant industrialization and runaway climate change begin poisoning all six continents, the dominant sentient life-form retreats underground, bent on founding a subterranean utopia, Frabbejoix.

Because the Zanalogs never managed to shake their addiction to fossil fuels, the experiment is doomed from the start. Within two generations, the buildup of carbon dioxide, carbon monoxide, mercury vapor, and methane renders Frabbejoix uninhabitable. The solution to the crisis seems obvious enough. The descendants of the original settlers must simply return to the surface, which by now—surely—has become a post–Carbon Age paradise.

A great shock awaits them. Their ancestors' former home has been colonized by a hostile alien race that thrives on greenhouse gases. These galactic imperialists have kept their industrial fires burning continually, the better to maintain a benevolent atmosphere. The Zanalogs, to their eternal chagrin, have nowhere to live.

On opening night a curious incident occurred. As we were taking our curtain calls—I had directed the show and also played the Queen of Frabbejoix—a stooped figure stepped into the aisle and haltingly approached the stage. I couldn't make out his features, but his posture told me I was seeing a person bent with age and broken by sorrow.

I bid the audience to stop their applause, so we could hear what this playgoer had to say.

"Immigrants—we get the job done!" he shouted.

"Thank you, sir," I said. "Welcome to Pacifica. By the way, if you have any trouble obtaining your citizenship papers, we can probably help. You know where to find us."

Our forlorn patron turned and, moving his arms in a kind of enfeebled swimming stoke, as if he were navigating a lake of molasses, lurched his way out of the theater and into the lobby.

I never saw him again.

BECAUSE IT IS BITTER

Cat Rambo

THE electric bus was driverless, but you could see the shifting of the driver's wheel back and forth as it adjusted its course, as though someone invisible sat in the seat. Ernst still found the sight uncanny after a few years of it, even if it was supposed to be safer on the highway. Underneath his own seat, midway down the bus, he could feel the vehicle juddering its way southward on I-405, headed to Seattle's East Side and the GoogleSoft campus there.

The screen on his jacket sleeve showed that he'd cut the time close this morning, but he should make it. He scrolled through a few headlines and the latest updates for HeyYou; his coworker Natalie had posted a picture of their morning bagel and his manager's manager Kev had posted a status update in Comic Sans, "Pumped and ready for the week!" Ernst tagged both to show team spirit.

He looked back up as the bus passed another of the homeless enclaves scattered among the scrub pines on either side of the highway. Here, in the spring of 2040, many of the tiny encampments that had grown up along highway medians and in gutted woods had been around for two decades, elaborate structures made out of scavenged siding and old pallets among walls of wire-strung blue tarpaulins and mounds of waste-scattered blackberry vines. They fell away as the bus swung into the park-and-ride lot. As he and the rest shuffled off their ride, the twin flags of Pacifica and GoogleSoft, the first a subdued gray green with its three gold stars, the second a cascade of rainbow-colored rings, flapped overhead against the hazy sky.

Building 187 was a few blocks away. The campus had once been full of buildings quickly and shoddily constructed; interven-

183

ing years had treated most of those badly, but 187 and its two fellows, 185 and 188 (no one spoke of 186's silent hulk) still stood, and housed GoogleSoft's developers and researchers dedicated to their junior branch.

Ernst held his thumb up to the entrance's scanner. A second passed while it checked the microchip implanted under the skin, then the glass doors swung open to allow him in. The air smelled of disinfected surfaces and less scrupulously maintained bodies; water rationing was in effect again.

The elevators were broken again, so he went up the heated spiral of the nearest glass-walled stairwell. He reminded himself that even if the building was threadbare, it was a job—an actual respectable one among other scientists. At least, he corrected himself, some of them. The bulk of them actually worked in the enclaves up in the Cascades and had considerably more resources at their command than Ernst and his fellows.

Every once in a while, one of the scientists here chose to move on. The rumor was always that they had been summoned to the largest of the protected spaces in those mountains, a vast underground complex, powered by hot springs and other thermal forces, whose admission price was exile to the sterile atmosphere there.

It was true you never heard from any of them again. But in Ernst's experience, that was true of anyone in life. At forty, he'd seen a lot of changes in the world and people coming and going with them.

He got to his office just as an alarm bell rang. A general groan arose all up and down the hallway.

"Drill again? Big Henry said, appearing in his office doorway. "That's the third one this month."

"Supposed to be American spies around. Looking for corporate secrets." Natalie St. Clair was tall and lanky; they wore a brightly colored scarf around their hair today, something patterned with green turtles and yellow birds against blueness that could have been sky or water with equal facility. A transplant from the U.S., they and Ernst had come into the company on the same day; the platonic bond had weathered social awkwardness on both their parts and ripened into a dear friendship.

"That's just to keep us all on our toes," another coworker, Geidon, said loftily. The small black man was always ready to propose the worst of any event. "If we're paranoid, concerned with all the theater, then we don't think about the things that they don't want us to be thinking about. At night, we're supposed to just go home, hook into the Xbox, and smoke weed. While on the other side, they're hooking into the same media system and drinking 'luded beer."

"Not the same system," Ernst said, even while fighting back the urge towards pedantry.

"No, it's the same system," Geidon said. "Same corporation owns all of them, just under different names. You follow them back, and it's all the same. Everyone just wants us sitting back and making wealth for them. You'd think there would be a limit for it."

Natalie said, "You need to stop listening to crank channels. It's a lot worse in the US. I don't even want to imagine what it's like right now, gearing up for the elections." Natalie had come from the Midwest: Kansas City. They called it the Heart of Darkness—the few times they spoke of it.

"The dark web is the only place where true information can end up, nowadays," Geidon retorted.

Milling together, their cluster moved into the hallway and then out the door. They proceeded to their appointed quadrant in the parking lot. Clots of people formed and reformed, exchanging gossip as they waited for the all-clear signal. Geidon went over to speak to another friend.

"Are you still working on those water quality datasets?" Natalie asked.

"Yes," he said.

"Funny, because when I popped my head in your office last week, the papers on your desk made it look like you're goofing around working on your grandmother's project again, even though Loretta told you last week to knock that off."

Ernst flushed and stared down at the cracked pavement. "I am so close," he said. "It won't take much to put it all together. I just need a little bit of time."

"You'll have plenty of time if she catches you and fires you. All the time in the world."

"I always have the datasets out when she makes her rounds," he said. "And I just use Rachel's stuff for a break."

"And I repeat: you're going to have plenty of time if you get fired."

"You're right, you're right," he said.

Ernst took a deep breath of the air, avoiding Natalie's stare. They wanted him to say he'd stop working on Rachel's project. He *should* stop working on Rachel's project. *Should* start focusing on the work GoogleSoft paid him to work on.

Instead of looking at Natalie, he focused on his surroundings. This wasn't a terrible part of the day, he would have to admit, although if he hadn't been ready to get back to work, he would have found it more tolerable. Before the merger, Microsoft had gone to some effort to keep the campus green and pleasant, a tradition GoogleSoft had continued. The Cascades sheltered the regions from the worst of the smog and pollution coming over from the Idaho work camps.

"Campus looks nice," he said by way of diversion.

"They had the gardening crews through this weekend, I think," Natalie said. "I'm glad they started doing that rather than during workdays. Those guys creeped me out. I always thought one of them would stage an escape."

"They only pick ones that will behave," he said. "It's how they get them to pay for their prison rehab costs."

The parking lot jostled with people. The alarm's shrill whoop continued at intervals, pulling at the edges of Ernst's nerves. Natalie seemed much more relaxed. "Isn't that bothering you?" he asked.

"You learn to tune it out," they said. "Focus on something else. How's the ukulele playing coming?"

His face burned, and he cursed the impulse that had made him bring it in for the Company Follies a couple of weeks earlier. The Follies, a homegrown talent show, had been a popular part of their company meeting, and he'd played the ukulele and sang, to suspiciously more applause than he felt he deserved. He'd decided to pick it up as a hobby in order to have something to talk about, but people were way too eager to remind him of his performance.

"Still practicing," he said evenly.

"That was so great. Part of it's just that you're a big guy," Natalie said. "There's something just adorable about that tiny ukulele, and you strumming away like it's the most important thing you've ever done." Someone shouted, and they waved in reply. "I'll be right back." They slipped away through the crowd.

There was a tug at his sleeve, and he turned to see a lanky, ginger-bearded man.

"You were really good at the Follies," the man said.

"Thank you," Ernst said uncomfortably.

"That's what you should be doing," the man said with great sincerity. "It's an engaging role for you. You could have gone pretty far on one of the instructive channels. They're so much more interesting, in my opinion, although I know they're an acquired taste."

Ernst said, even more uncomfortably, "Thank you." He didn't think the guy was hitting on him, but the interaction was just *off*, as though there was some context he was missing.

"Well," the little man said. "I just wanted to tell you that. I hope to hear you play once more sometime. I'm sure we'll meet again." His face did not seem particularly pleased at the idea. He turned abruptly and wandered off through the crowd.

Natalie beckoned him over to where they now stood, reunited with Geidon. "What was that all about?" they asked.

"Got me," he said. "Another GoogleSoft 'strong personality.' "

They snorted.

Geidon said, "Anyway. As I was saying, they just pay the fine, and the rest of us can go to hell. A third of Seattle's budget is funded by parking fines, did you know that? It was a news fact in *Pacifica Today*."

He dropped his voice as Kev approached.

Kev was two years out of business school and cutting his teeth as a manager on their team. So far, they had noticed him clearly cycling through the chapters of his leadership texts in his approach. They'd learned to recognize a certain look that he got when implementing a new chapter, a peculiar forward frown at some internal vision that they could only guess at.

He greeted them cheerfully, "Morning, team."

Geidon eyed him hopefully. Lately, one of the techniques Kev had been trying out on the group involved pastries, and Geidon tried to reinforce that behavior whenever it manifested. Today, though, Kev did not seem to have the white cardboard box under his arm.

"Back inside, people," he said. Then added at some internal prompting, "You're doing an awesome job."

They filed into the building as the alarm coughed one last time, then died away into silence.

Back in the office, Ernst worked on his datasets for a while, but his thoughts kept straying to his other project. He'd give it a little bit of time after lunch, use it as a chance for a break. No one could object to that. He left a few minutes early for lunch at the cafeteria, trying to avoid the rush, but most of the other workers had had the same thought. He grabbed a seat at an already-occupied table; two women at its opposite end were talking so intently that neither spared him a glance.

Mai slid onto the bench beside him. As she put her tray down, he took a sip of water, trying to conceal the uneasy mix of friendliness and fear that coiled in him at her approach.

The younger side of middle-aged and Hispanic, Mai had come up from somewhere in Southern California a few months earlier to visit their team, then take the experience back to her own workplace. She was short but solid, with large dark eyes that he found appealing, and an overly vivacious personality that unsettled Ernst when her attention turned his way.

Ernst much preferred to watch her interacting with other people. She did it so effortlessly, remembering fragments of their lives, like the names of their children, or a sick uncle. Made them feel special. But when he faced that attention, he grew anxious and ill at ease.

As now. Her tray held rounds of falafel and a fluff of quinoa. One of the things he liked about the GoogleSoft cafeteria—beside the fact that the food was plentiful and cheap—was that they changed the food around, mixed it up. Silence stretched out between them. He had to fill it with something. He said, awkwardly, "How's life in corporate housing?"

Mai grimaced. "Don't tell anyone, but it was so miserable last night with the noise from the couple next door again that I packed everything up and went to the housing over at Redmond Town

Center. I lucked out and got a quiet room letting out on to the back, right next the fountain, so it's like my own white-noise machine." She laughed at his expression. "It's just for another week before I head home, so it's not that wasteful," she exclaimed. She used a fork to halve a falafel and studied it before eating it. "How's your project going? The secret one, I mean." She grinned at him.

He looked around to make sure Loretta wasn't around. "Shhh," he said. "I'm not working on it that much."

"LaPlante's not around," Mai said. "She has meetings all through the day. Some bigwig coming up from the city, they said maybe Gates himself."

"Unlikely," he said automatically. "You mean one of his surrogates."

"Same thing," she said. Everyone knew the robot surrogates; Gates used them on occasion to wander the campus, using its lenses to examine his domain from afar. No one had seen the actual old man in years; he supposedly lived in that special encampment in the Cascades, one of the few tech billionaires who weren't rumored to have fled off-planet. "Anyway, how's it going?"

"All right," he said evasively. The truth was, he wasn't sure he was going in the right direction anymore, but since he wanted to impress Mai, he let himself brag. "I've been making a lot of break-throughs." Mai would be going back to Silicon Valley soon anyway. He didn't need to live up to his words. He might as well look a little important in her eyes. "I think I'm almost there. Give me another week or so, and I'll have it cracked. Rachel did all the heavy lifting. My challenge was figuring out a production system that made it not cost an arm and a leg." He tried to make the admission careless, as though he was used to coming up with complex solutions to dif-ficult problems all the time.

It worked. She looked impressed. "I didn't expect you to say that," she said. There was genuine pleasure in her voice. Maybe she cared about him a little. He wasn't sure. He'd never been good with women. The trick was how to let them know you were interested without being creepy about it, and he was afraid, as always, that if he said to Mai, "How about getting together sometime?" she'd recoil.

She was waiting for him to say something. Now was the time to try it out. Her bright eyes were looking at him—was that expectation

189

in them? He opened his mouth, ready to hear the bold, confident words sail out to conquer. Instead he said, "Well, it's good to make progress," which had to be one of the most stilted and unnatural things he had ever said. He could have kicked himself.

"Yes," she said, "I suppose that it is."

He thought she might have been about to say something more, but just then Amanda from GoogleSoft Diversity sat down with them. Mai began to talk to her about some problem with Amanda's child and school.

"It's like the schools don't want to teach the little savages anything," Amanda said. "Just keep them healthy, who cares about their minds?"

The two women laughed. Ernst stared down at his food and excoriated himself mentally. *You'll never have anyone at this rate*, he thought. *You'll die alone and bitter.* He barely noticed when Mai and Amanda excused themselves and left the table.

But Mai came back. She leaned in. Her hair smelled like apricots. She touched his shoulder and said, "Hey, I was wondering …."

Self-excoriation flipped over into utter panic. "I need to get back to my office," he blurted out, recoiling and pulling his arm back. He crossed his arms in front of his chest, then unfolded and refolded them, feeling like a parody of himself as he did so and hating her—to a depth that surprised him—for making him feel so awkward—and here in the cafeteria no less, in front of other people.

A part of his head wailed in protest, *You're acting like you're not but you are, you ARE interested in that sort of thing, and she's even making it easy for you*, but he was committed to the movement now.

She blinked. "Okay," she said. Then, her tone hurt, "You know, I wasn't coming on to you." He started to protest that his fears had lain in the opposite direction but by then she was gone. He couldn't even see which way she'd exited in the crowd of coworkers entering.

He distracted himself by sorting through the papers littering his office. While everyone had access to the company's computing power here, no one really trusted the electronic form anymore. The Cloud Wars of late 2036, in which almost every existing server farm had been brought to its knees, wiping out masses of data across the world, remained fresh in everyone's mind.

It'd brought back the popularity of paper, though nowadays it was made from bamboo and recycled rags rather than cheap wood pulp. Paper lasted. Anyone who'd been bitten by that data loss—much of which was never recovered—had a jaded idea about the reliability of computers overall, let alone cloud storage.

The Wars had lasted six minutes. During the weeks after, everyone had moved as though they were in shock. They confided their HeyYou, QueueTube, and SexyPic losses to each other, the hundreds of photos and check-ins, status updates. Even the Library of Congress had been hit by that, and the years of Twitter tweets it had been saving were virtual dust, floating away on an invisible wind.

Nowadays, backing up your work meant on paper or a hard drive that you had control over. It wasn't a question of the web's availability. The Internet was paradoxically available everywhere—though you paid for it. If not in money, then in time spent watching advertisements. The unfettered access here meant he could cut out the commercials, as well as the web bots that tracked his preferences and messaged him about things they felt he needed to buy. All in all, he had it better than most.

He spread out Rachel's research on his desk. It was as he'd said to Mai. His mission was how to make the work that Rachel had done economically feasible, capable of being manufactured on a large scale. Her medicine changed oxytocin levels while lowering dihydrotestosterone. She'd called it "empathy serum."

She'd believed it would change the world.

Ernst usually kept an eye open for Loretta, but the thoughts of his lunch encounter preoccupied him. Before he knew it, she was there behind him, looking at the sheets of paper spread across his desk, the project management spreadsheet open on his computer with the label "ES Production Costs." There was no hiding that he was working on something other than his assigned project.

She said, "Put that away. We've spoken about this before, Ernst."

He scrambled to save files and close down windows, ransacking his thoughts for something, anything that he could say. She said, "I don't want to see it again."

He couldn't help it. He muttered under his breath, "Then don't come around looking."

She stopped and turned around. "Mr. Claymore, you know that I don't need this job for money, right? I could be at home, binge-watching *Johnny Gunwise* and smoking good Vancouver-grown weed. Or watching my grandchildren run around being themselves."

Embarrassment suffused him. He'd never heard her talk about her life outside the company.

"But I keep coming in, and that's because I believe in the things that we're trying to do here. And because I want them to succeed, I put my time and considerable—I repeat, *considerable*—expertise in managing technology projects to their success. And one thing I know how to do is distinguish a productive project from one that's not going to yield anything. I understand you believe in your grandmother, *and* that her death was a tragedy, but you're going to have to trust me on this." Her voice was firm. "Otherwise GoogleSoft is going to have to say goodbye to you. This is your last warning. I want you to pack up everything to do with this project, any notes you have, so security can take them to the archives in the morning."

He could see past her shoulder that several people were in the hall, pretending not to be listening. Natalie's bright scarf passed by, accompanied by the back of Mai's hair.

"Do you understand me?" Loretta said.

He let his anger stiffen his spine. "Yes," he said shortly.

She paused, but he added nothing to the affirmative. She sighed. "All right then."

People in the hallway scattered as she turned back to the door and exited. She did not close the door behind her, but no one appeared in it until ten minutes later, when Natalie's head popped around the door. "You okay?" they said.

"Yeah." He was grimly gathering up his notes and stacking them in a cardboard box. He didn't look around. His face felt tight with the lingering anger.

He wanted to curse, say something derogatory about Loretta, but he swallowed down the impolitic words. He liked his job here. He wanted to keep it. Could he replicate some of this work at home? Maybe lie low and wait a few weeks, then just run some datasets here every once in a while. They didn't closely monitor what the workers were doing, at least, he didn't think that they did. But now that he reflected on it … it wouldn't be hard to monitor for keywords outside one's project, or give managers graphs of where desktop time had been spent. He'd known people censured for too much social media time before, so there was at least someone looking at things.

"I warned you she was going to catch you at it," Natalie said.

"Don't be self-righteous, Nat. It's too irritating right now."

"Let's cut out at five and go for a drink."

He didn't want to have to make small talk. By now gossip about the scene with Loretta dressing him down would be flying throughout the group, and people would be pretending that it hadn't happened, while trying at the same time to extract as much information as possible, particularly if it could be used in any way to get more resources for their own projects. He didn't have the patience for that. Weed and *Johnny Gunwise* actually sounded pretty good.

"You can bribe her, you know," Natalie said. "Everybody does it with their managers. Get her a little sweeter on hearing your name. Bag of coffee beans, maybe."

"Fuck," he said. "Who has that kind of money?"

The rising heat across the globe facilitated coffee rust sweeping across Central America, wiping out its coffee plantations by the mid '30s, at the same time encouraging the coffee berry borer to invade Africa's shrinking fertile zones. Coffee was sold by the ounce now, rather than the pound. Like everyone else, he drank the CoffeeZatz GoogleSoft provided for free.

"It'd be an investment in your job."

"I'm going home early," he said, throwing the last notebook into the box.

"Think that's wise?"

"It's that or wander around here being an aimless dick," he said. "Or working."

His thoughts flip-flopped. Natalie was right. Going home now would be stupid, an act of unnecessary defiance. But he deserved a break, another part of him said. Loretta would have felt the tension of the scene as well, would know that it had taken a lot of emotional toll. She probably didn't want to see him any more than he wanted to see her. He said, "I need to think about what I'm doing with it. Get a fresh eye."

"And by it, you mean the project you're supposed to be working on?" they said cautiously.

"Yeah," he said. "I just have to shift gears and everything will be fine. Need to reset. That's hard to do here."

"All right," they said. "See you tomorrow."

Home, a.k.a. the cohousing project, Mandalorian House, lay to the north of Redmond, up in the Woodinville sprawl. It had been established twenty years earlier by a group of six families who had originally purchased the thirty-five acre tract of land together and built their separate houses on it.

Ernst had been lucky that his grandmother, Rachel, had left him the money to buy into a space within one of the two "bunkers." The monthly costs ate up a third of his salary, but came with Wi-Fi, water, and the communal kitchen, which saved him enough on food to make it worthwhile. Someday, when he wanted to cash out, he could sell his spot.

He got off the bus on the main road and walked up the long driveway to the little settlement. It was fenced off with barbed wire. One duty of the residents was to patrol and roust the homeless that encroached on its edges every once in a while. He automatically checked the fence as he walked, but saw no breaks among the clumps of nettles.

He entered the house he shared with three other GoogleSoft workers, passing through the common area and muttering a greeting at Sean and John. Both worked night shift. On this day, their day off, they were sitting on the ancient yellow plastic couch in VR helmets and playing Fallout 47: The Prehistoric World on the Xbox.

"You're home early," Sean said, his tone questioning. Ernst was better known for long hours at work than for short ones.

Ernst grunted evasively and went into his room. It was towards the back of the house and overlooked woods, real woods, something increasingly rare in the world. If he lost his place at GoogleSoft, he wouldn't be able to afford this place anymore. Being part of a co-op meant that you had to be a contributing member or else have put in the number of years of service that would buy him time. He'd gotten used to the luxuries afforded by this life, much more than he would have in most single apartments. And he'd lose the sense of family that pervaded this place, something that had been missing from his life ever since Rachel had died.

He could have passed into the system at the age of twelve when his parents were killed in a car accident; Rachel was his only living relative. She'd had him sent up to Seattle, where she could raise a sullen teenager with grace and goodwill.

And he'd definitely been sullen. He'd hated the world he saw falling apart around him. His grandmother had money—Microsoft had made investment in the educational system around Redmond a priority in those earlier days—and Ernst found himself challenged in a way he never had back home.

But he never rose to that challenge. He remembered exasperated conversations with his grandmother, her asking, "You had legal pot in California too. What's different about it here? Is there someone providing it for you on a regular basis, some store that will sell it to you?"

"No," he'd said, and hadn't explained how easy it was on the U Wash campus to find a student willing to sell. You had to watch them—more than once someone had vanished with his money—but he'd learned to go along with them to the store and hover within sight. It had been the same in San Jose.

But the thing was, why worry about the future when it seemed like the world was going to burn? That was the year more and more students started committing suicide—there was that whole cult of them—and then a few years later the insurance companies started pushing some of their own solutions, like the cash grab for college-aged seniors, allowing them to "opt out" of the system and get a lump sum in return.

He said, "I thought you'd understand. What's it going to be like by the time I'm out of college? What's going to be left?"

Rachel had never bullshitted him, that was one thing he had to admit. Had never pretended that she and the other generations hadn't royally fucked things up.

She said, "God, I don't know. Other human beings, maybe. But you can act like your life has some meaning to it or not, your choice. It's just that it's a lot more likely to feel like it has some meaning if you treat it that way. Can you trust me on that one, Ernst? I know your mind is telling you to reject what older people are saying right now, but there's a few ... a few glimmerings of wisdom left." She'd grinned at him wryly. "This is why I took you in, after all, just so I could lecture you," she said with dry humor. "It's so much fun."

He'd had to laugh.

"Work at things just a little harder," she'd wheedled. "It's only for a couple more years, then you're off to some other school and out of my hair." She'd flapped a hand at him. "Off to cause some other woman grief."

So he'd rallied enough to make it into community college. By then, there were no longer student loans to be had, and he'd been lucky to have her ready to plunder some of her savings "as an investment so you'll come visit me in the old-age home," she'd said. He hadn't realized how lucky he was until his tenth-year high school reunion. Despite the affluence of the area he'd grown up in, only half had gone on to higher education. Part of it was the malaise of the times, sure. But plenty of it was about the Benjamins, or in Pacifica's case, the Baracks.

Rachel had been an old-school hippie, called herself a bleeding-heart liberal although she'd always been one of the most pragmatic and dispassionate people he'd known. She'd filled her tiny garden with plants and herbs, and composted everything. She'd even had two beehives, perched up on top of the garage, a location that had kept the hives safe and unmolested. Her pride was passing out jars of the golden honey in clear mason jars with honeycomb suspended in them. He'd loved chewing bits of the raw comb; the flavor of summer, the bright taste of the sugar, the flakey slide of the wax against his teeth.

Then one spring, the bees had all died to some new pest that had come in on the wind, apparently from Japan: tiny red spiders that bred and bred till they smothered the bees. He remembered a shelf of honeycomb furred with them, like bloody mold. Rachel had cried for her bees that night, after a couple of late whiskies, thinking him in bed. He'd never seen her cry any other time, even when he'd come close to flunking out of college that first year. She'd been disappointed in him, certainly, but not to the point of tears.

What would she think of him now? She'd also believed her hobby work might save the world. Then she'd died at the tail end of the most recent pandemic.

He used up most of his water allowance with a prolonged bath. He deserved it. He'd worry about laundry later, or resign himself to paying a little extra. He toweled off and smoked a joint on the back porch. The sunset was crimson and purple. One thing about pollution, at least it made for pretty sunsets, and right now, before wildfire season started, the air was breathable.

Ambling into his room, he sagged into a chair to flip on the view screen. There it was. Loretta's mention hadn't been idle; like most of the people on the continent, she loved this particular show.

Johnny Gunwise was in its eighth season right now, and popular enough that many people watched it weekly, old-style, rather than binge it. Johnny was not the human hero of the detective series, but rather the advanced AI governing his weapon, an impressive steely pistol with various robotic augmentations that would periodically appear on it. Johnny was a smart-ass, and rabidly anti–gun control, where his wielder was not. Both, though, were very fond of shooting first and asking questions later.

It was more interesting than most of the other shows, mostly because it was one of the few that still had human writers, whose material tended to be both quirkier and more complicated than machine-generated fiction. After it was over, he skipped over *That's So Pacifica*. Usually he found the way they poked fun at known foibles of the liberal nation entertaining, but lately the jokes had seemed a little too insistent that Pacifica was all about unimportant things like free-range chicken in children's school meals and sorting your recycling.

He wasn't sure how to balance that silliness against the demonizing of the United States the show did at the same time, such as saying that to be gay there was to risk public tarring and feathering, or shunning by one's neighbors, let alone the denial of simple things like the right to get married or raise children.

The United States had stood behind the resurrection of Donald Trump, and actively embraced the various conspiracy theories around it, while at the same time upping its game as a "Christian nation" under the leadership of what some claimed to be an animatronic Pence.

Their television channels featured plenty of mindlessly grim reality shows, documenting people forced into artificial situations, made to act out insane scenarios. Sunclear Broadcasting's latest— shown in Pacifica in the name of freedom of speech—was the televised punishment of doctors brought back from Pacifica and Newtopia for performing abortions, despite complaints from both countries and the censure of the United Nations.

The news wasn't much better, full of the usual disasters. Another epidemic, this time arising in Australia. A rogue AI crashed three planes when the airport system it had infiltrated refused to give in to its demands. A community down in Danville, California, that was still trying to secede from Pacifica, this time led by a failed politician working to jumpstart her career with indignation. By now, though, the majority of conservative Californians had left the state, unable to put up any more with the increasing encroachment of liberalism on their freedom, and the state's alarming imposition of things like vaccines and education on their children.

Another piece mentioned a small skirmish near the Idaho border checkpoint, a bunch of teens clashing. It was still unclear who'd started what, just that three of them were dead, two from Pacifica, one from the United States. The usual intonations by politicians followed condemning the violence and twisting it to their own agenda; the tragedy either meant guns should be rejected or embraced, it seemed, depending on how you wanted to read it.

Johnny Gunwise made a public service announcement reminding people that if they saw something suspicious, they should report it so the authorities could check it, even if it seemed small and innocuous at the time.

None of this distracted Ernst. He kept hearing Loretta in his head. *Otherwise GoogleSoft is going to have to say goodbye to you.*

"Fuck," Ernst said to the empty air, and then followed it with a second instance, more resigned. "Fuck." He was going to have to face facts. He would have to give up working on his grandmother's project for at least a while, maybe permanently, if he wanted to stay employed. Loretta would continue to watch him. He couldn't lie to himself about that anymore.

Well, so that was that. He'd ship the project off to the archives and focus on his own work. He'd be a good team player, someone Loretta would want to keep. Rachel's work could wait. He had his own life to live after all. His own priorities.

So what if Rachel had thought her empathy project could change the world? That was delusional at best, and an example of how overwhelmingly arrogant she could be. Like you could save the world with a single thing, push a single button and change everything, say a single word and have it be the magic spell that made everything work differently. That was stupid thinking. The world was big and complicated and hopeless, but he could keep his head down, plod along, do his job, fill in his years, and retire when it was time to do so, and follow Loretta's suggestion for a perfect day.

He went to bed resolved in his spirit, and he didn't dream that night. The same determination buoyed him up the next morning, filled him, carried him all the way along to the campus, his building, his hallway, his office.

When he walked in, at first, he thought he'd entered the wrong room. It hit him in the gut like a blow. His office in shambles, chaos, everything out of place. The files in the cabinet had been dumped out on the floor, drawers pulled out and thrown aside. The backup drive for his computer was gone, wires dangling. Every book on the shelves had been taken down to riffle through.

All he could focus on was a single cinematic detail. The plant in his window had been dumped sideways, soil scattered as though searching for anything hidden there. Black dirt had sifted down onto the carpet.

Natalie, coming up behind him. "What the fuck?" they exclaimed.

A scattering of quick words from somewhere else. He was frozen. He wasn't sure what anyone said. All he could do was stand there. He'd never been robbed before, never had someone enter space that he thought of as his, no matter whether or not technically it belonged to GoogleSoft, and pillaged it.

"My work," he breathed out. The box holding Rachel's files lay on its side. The papers that had been in it, along with the scattering of flash drives, were all gone.

Kev, summoned by someone, was standing beside him. "This is a very serious thing," he was saying to Loretta. Ernst heard the two of them talking as though he was very far away, as though the words were coming through layers of glass.

Kev touched his shoulder to get his attention. "I've called security," he said. "Stay here." He studied him for a moment. "Have him sit down," he told Natalie, as though Ernst couldn't understand his words, as though Natalie would have to interpret. "Get him some CoffeeZatz with plenty of sugar in it."

Kev finally wandered away, and Loretta came to survey the damage. "Huh," she said. She looked at Ernst, and he wondered for a wild second if she thought he'd done it, ripped off his own notes in order to keep working on it, in order to persuade her that they had been worthwhile.

But he must have been being paranoid. All she said was, "Have the secretary set up a security interview with you so they can debrief you."

She looked at everyone else in the hall. "This is why we take precautions, people," she said, raising her voice. "This is why we password protect our machines and make sure things are locked up at night."

"But I'd done both of those—" Ernst told her.

"I'm sure," she said. "But it doesn't hurt to emphasize it when something like this happens. Go do your interview. The sooner you get that all cleared away, the sooner you can start getting things back to normal."

Security was on the southern side of campus, a three-story building whose doors all bore the sign, "RESTRICTED ACCESS." Ernst signed in at the front desk. A guard showed up almost immediately and escorted him to a small room, its carpet gray with dusty age, holding a small table and two chairs set in opposition on either side of it. Ernst took one and tried to scoot it away from the table; it was bolted to the floor, placed so you couldn't see the door behind one's shoulders opening or closing.

He tried to access the net only to get a warning that he was in a secure building, and it was not available. He waited, wishing he had brought something to drink with him, or a book, or something to write with. He looked around at the walls, directed his gaze to the pattern of dots on the acoustic tile overhead, and finally settled back and thought about Rachel's project, trying to picture some of his lost notes in his head. His fingers itched with the need to write them down.

The door opened and someone came in. Ernst twisted around in order to look at them. The burly man in a GoogleSoft security uniform was abnormally broad shouldered, as though he spent a lot of time lifting weights. He made Ernst feel willowy and undeveloped. He sat down in the chair across from Ernst and took out pen and a form to fill out, laboriously noting several details before he addressed Ernst.

He didn't introduce himself, just said, "Ernst Claymore, huh? Tell me in your own words what happened."

"I came in this morning and someone had rifled through my office."

"Rifled and took stuff?"

"Took a lot of things."

"All right." He wrote some more in silence while Ernst waited, then said, "Tell me the list of things they took from GoogleSoft."

"All my project files. My hard drive. My notebooks. For two different projects."

"Two projects, huh? That normal, for someone to be working on two projects at once?"

"One's a hobby, really."

"I don't give a crap about hobby stuff. Any personal items, you'll need to fill out a special form for that. I'm only concerned with company property. So now—who did you talk to outside of work that might have known what you were working on?"

Ernst felt even smaller. From the way the man was glaring at him, it seemed as though he thought Ernst had been responsible. "No one," he said. "All of my friends are people from my team."

"All of your coworkers come to work this morning?"

"I don't know. I came straight here when my manager told me to," Ernst said.

The man glared as though this was an unreasonable answer. "This is corporate espionage," he said. "And GoogleSoft is one of the things that keeps Pacifica—keeps the world, really—running. Spies don't just threaten the company, they threaten our country when they come to steal innovations from us. What about your friend from America, this woman Natalie?"

"They're nonbinary," he said automatically. "They came for asylum."

The man rolled his eyes but moved on. "And this guy, Geidon. What do you know about him?"

Ernst stammered something, and the man continued down his list.

All through the interrogation, Ernst felt cold and shaky. He kept seeing the scattered papers in his mind's eye. It had been a violation of a kind he'd never experienced.

It seemed that security thought it had been Mai. When someone came in to talk with the man, he heard her name several times in their quiet discussions at the back of the room, saying something about an empty room.

But, by the end, he realized they were going through the motions, that someone, probably Loretta, had let them know that his project was of little consequence, that it didn't really matter if the intelligence was on its way east. Mai had been here and was gone now. They were more interested in fixing the holes to keep anyone else from coming in through that route than pursuing her.

They let him go, eventually, although not until the day had stretched almost its way through.

On the walk back to his building, he thought about Mai at lunch, saying, "I had to switch rooms." There would only be a couple by the description she'd given, towards the back and near the fountain. Would it be possible security had overlooked that she'd moved her belongings there?

He took the bus over to Redmond Town Center rather than home. The corporate housing bordered Lake Sammamish, its waters overgrown with algae. In the middle of the lake, bobbed some of the squatter islands, floating shelters that the police cleared every few months, towing them in behind small barges, loose platforms built of old inner-tubes and nets full of sealed plastic bottles. The complex's name was Lake Vista; it had been built in the late '90s and had not weathered the transition into the twenty-first century well. One building had slid halfway down a slope; its abandoned sides bore signs optimistically pronouncing it a fixer-upper investment opportunity, and chain-link fence encircled it, almost buried in the verdigris- and grime-colored blackberry leaves.

As Ernst made his way to the back, he glanced around for cameras, but saw none. The fountain burbled as he checked the two rooms near it. Only one looked occupied, and through the window he could see a GoogleSoft bag on the desk. The older lock yielded to a credit card, a skill he'd learned in high school, sneaking back into his grandmother's after his curfew. He felt something of the same thrill of worry, down deep in his belly, as he eased the knob open. What if it wasn't just that security had overlooked this place? What if Mai was still here as well?

The hotel smelled like old laundry and dishwater that had steeped too long, but in the bathroom he found apricot-scented shampoo and conditioner.

There were two big suitcases in the closet and clothes still in the tiny bedroom's closet. The refrigerator in the kitchen held a take-out container half-full of noodles and a container of egg-substitute. A minimal handful of spices sat by the electric stovetop.

The tiny room had little in it to distinguish itself. The bed was made; did that mean she'd left last evening without going to sleep? He thought it must. He opened each drawer in the bureau and the bedside table. Scattered garments, things she must have chosen to leave behind. He went back into the bathroom. The towels were cheap; one lay crumpled beside the shower door. Studying the toiletries and the drawers, he thought that there seemed to be gaps enough to suggest the packing of an overnight bag, as though Mai had been traveling light.

The desk had a scattering of papers, and he went through these with greater care. Surely there must be some clue to her presence here. He pulled a blank pad of paper over and looked at the top sheet. Taking a pencil, he rubbed the side of the lead back and forth until the indented words emerged: *5:30 PM, VRA—June 3, Kansas City.*

A week from now. And in Kansas City. Center of the US. The Heart of Darkness itself.

"Follow her? Into the US?" Geidon said. "Are you out of your fucking mind? Do you know what that place is like? Everyone has guns. Have you ever shot a gun?"

"No," Ernst said, "But I don't think they actually have *mandatory* guns."

They were at the Rock and Robin restaurant near the Google-Soft campus. Once called Red Robin, the chain's name had changed after climate extinctions led to the unfortunately catchy nickname, Dead Robin.

Its menu had remained the same. Nowadays, though, burgers were protein disks made of vegetable matter and adorned with various configurations of condiments. Ernst took another bite of chana dal burger.

Gideon shook more Parmesan dust onto his Italian burger. "You're being stupid," he said.

"You said the acronym, VRA, meant it's a virtual auction. How's that work, if it's virtual?"

"Actually, it's virtual auction *space*," Geidon said. "You go and plug into *their* VR system. That way you're totally anonymous when bidding. It's not like you're going to be able to bid."

He ignored that. "But it'll give me a lead to Mai. She'll have to be there too. And then I can confront her."

"And do what?"

"I don't know. Something. I just have to know."

"Know *what?*"

"I have to know what's going to happen to Rachel's work. I don't care if she sells it. In fact, if she sells it to someone with more re-sources than I have, maybe it'll get out into the world and change it sooner. Maybe they'll hire me, since I've worked with it already."

"You'd emigrate to the US?" Geidon said with horrified fascination.

"What? No! Just get a work visa or something." How could he explain how much this meant to him? He just had to make sure that someone would develop it, that they wouldn't get discouraged by the same factors that had kept it at the bottom of GoogleSoft's priority list.

"Why not go to Natalie?"

"Because they've tried to cut all their contacts to the US, they said. On the other hand, *you* keep talking about all your dark-web research and knowing who and how to bribe. You were talking last week about bringing duty-free cigarettes over, and how you knew someone making a killing on it. Was all that just you posing?"

Geidon shook his head and leaned forward. "Okay, so what you want are papers that get you across the border, but you don't want to have to wait the thirty days they'd normally take to process. You can't afford *their* speed-up fee, but I have a friend that can get you what you want, papers with your name and credit that basically say you're going over as lower-level skilled entertainment. We'll make it the ukulele since you can back that up, unless you've got some other skill I should know about?"

When Ernst failed to supply any, he continued. "I'll get you a bus pass to the border checkpoint in Spokane. After that, you'll be on your own to get to Kansas City, but I can give you some leads that may be able to steer you the right way."

Ernst felt ashamed of having made fun of Geidon's hacker talk with Natalie in the past. He'd hoped Geidon would have had some of the resources that he'd hinted at, but when approached, his co-worker had revealed that he'd actually been showing only the tip of the iceberg. He swallowed and said, "Hey man …."

"You sure you don't want to involve Natalie? They know that area; it's where they grew up."

"That's why," he said. "Security was already asking about them. I don't want to do something that causes trouble with their work visa."

Geidon said, "All right. Like I said, you can't afford the government speed-up fee, but you're going to need to be able to afford mine."

"What is it?"

"I want your spot in Mandalorian."

"Done," Ernst said without hesitation. He felt a twinge of regret as they shook hands, but ignored it. He'd find another place. Co-housing was the norm nowadays if you didn't have family to live with; the trick was finding a group you could coexist with. Mandalorian's geeky mélange had suited him, and he'd miss it, but who knew? He might not be coming back anyway.

The Greyhound bus smelled like pickles and the ghost of vomit, and it had a human driver rather than one of the more expensive machine units. Ernst pushed his way towards the back and put his backpack and the ukulele's case on the luggage rack, then settled in next to the clouded window overlooking the Seattle bus lot.

A teen sat on the sidewalk, playing a homemade didgeridoo made of PVC pipe, hat in front of their feet, cheeks pulsing as the instrument droned. Hazy sunlight filtered through the glass, uncomfortably warm. Ernst watched as the bus filled up with other travelers to Spokane. Most seemed like fellow Pacificans, but there were a few tourists on their way back, laden with suitcases. It was illegal to bring most things back from Pacifica, but Geidon had told him there was a standard bribe system in place.

"Won't save you if your name's on a government list, of course," he'd said. "But there's a lot of Americans. They can't afford to watch them all. That's why they have that LoyalEye app. You see someone taking an image of you, they're probably putting you up on that. They score points if someone gets fined or arrested, and points buy them tickets in the national lottery. I installed it on that burner phone I gave you, but you won't be able to report them. It's just so you can get the notifications if someone's posting about you."

"This seat taken?" Ernst looked up to see a thin man wearing a sailor's cap. His face was grizzled with salt-and-pepper stubble and sagged like an old sack.

"All yours Ernst said. The man nodded, slung his rucksack into the rack beside Ernst's gear, and sat down. He pulled out earbuds for his phone and began playing TapTapBoom on it.

The bus coughed out black smoke and started out of the lot, headed for America.

The trouble didn't hit till three-quarters of the way up the mountain, when the black exhaust thickened, and the bus began to emit a high-pitched whine that reached inside one's eardrums and plucked away any chance of dozing. The patient driver coaxed the bus all the way to the top, but at the rest stop there, he announced that they'd be getting out.

"Passengers who purchased travel insurance should stand on that side of the lot," he said, pointing. It took a while to unload the bus and sort the luggage, but eventually, they all stood in their various groups. Ernst and his seatmate were both in the uninsured group.

When the new bus arrived, there was a ragged cheer mixed with unease at the crowd realized that the new bus was significantly smaller. The passengers who had purchased insurance were loaded into the bus along with their luggage. Their bus driver stood in the bus's doorway, addressing the group still standing by the bus.

Ernst had presumed he'd tell them a second bus was on its way, but instead the man said, "Well, you're on your own folks. If you can get down the mountain, there's another bus station there. Your ticket will be discounted fifty percent for the inconvenience. Good luck!" The bus door closed after him before the stupefied crowd could respond.

"Can they do that?" a woman said plaintively. "Really, can they?"

"That's why they're the cheapest option," someone else told her.

Some stayed in the lot; a few having managed to call friends or family in the area. Others started down the mountainside. A few optimistic souls kept trying to signal trucks to hitch-hike, but the self-driving vehicles that comprised most of the ones whizzing by were not programmed to stop, and the few human truckers working at competing with their mechanical counterparts were in too much of a hurry to stop.

Ernst found himself walking beside his seatmate. They fell into step, moving in silence. The sky was hot with sun, and the gravel crunched under their heels as they walked. It was more labor than he was used to, but there was a pleasant effort to the motion, to the descent, that he found himself enjoying.

"I'm Bob," the other man said abruptly.

"Ernst." He thought about offering his hand to shake, but the other seemed disinclined. They just kept moving forward.

After a half hour though, Bob seemed more ready to talk. "You visiting the US?" he asked. "Some kinda musician?"

"Yeah, I'm going in for a temporary job," Ernst said.

"Huh," Bob said. "Some would call that impolite."

"What?" Ernst said. He adjusted his pack. Walking was less pleasant by now. He could feel blisters starting on his heels and smallest toes, and sweat ran down the small of his back.

"Just saying, they could be hiring American musicians," Bob said, his tone flat, eyes facing forward.

Ernst searched his mind for responses, decided to try to find common ground. "I'm just going where they offer me gigs," he said. "Hard to find them anywhere, these days. So, I take it you're coming back to America? Were you visiting Seattle?"

"My sister lives over there," Bob said. His shoulders unstiffened a little. "Had to talk about what to do with my mom, she's getting older."

"That's hard," Ernst said.

"Well, she's been living with us all this time," Bob said. "Time for Alethea—that's my sister—to take her. We can't afford her medicine. But now it turns out there's all sorts of hoops to jump through, if we want to do that. Paperwork and fees and such, and

Alethea's all, 'I got a job I work, I don't have time to go around chasing down forms.' "

"Oh," Ernst said. They trudged along in more silence. Ernst considered his blisters in detail and wondered why he hadn't worn better socks.

Well, that was reasonable, he told himself. No one had warned him about the bus, although, now that he'd had time to consider it, he remembered some stories from people coming back from the US. He hadn't paid very close attention, but hadn't Amy from Google-Soft Verb complained about something similar happening in Arizona? You were always hearing horror stories about Arizona, that was the problem.

He tried to take his mind off his blisters. "Did you do any sightseeing in Seattle while you were there?"

"Not much," Ernst said. "Felt like hostile territory to me."

"Because of Alethea?"

"Because y'all aren't real Americans, but you pretend like you are, and we're supposed to go along with it."

"Yeah, well," Ernst said. He didn't want to pick a fight if he could avoid it, even when Bob seemed to be waving one in front of him. "I bet I'll feel that way going into Idaho. Anything I should look out for there?"

When they spotted the barn by the roadside, Bob's suggestion that they grab the chance to nap in its shade and continue down when it was later and cooler seemed like a good one, particularly since it gave Ernst a chance to change his socks.

When he roused himself, sticky and sweaty a few hours later, he found the contents of his pack dumped beside where he'd laid sleeping, the majority of the contents plundered. His ukulele was gone. He was glad he had stuck his currency in his belt at Geidon's advice; he took it out to reassure himself, then stuck it back in.

All right, he told himself. *So my resources are more limited than I'd hoped*. But he could walk still, and Bob would be ahead of him by now, and hurrying, so there probably would be no chance of further confrontation.

He wished he'd brought more water. At the time he'd been out-fitting himself, he'd been thinking about weight, but now he regretted his choices. *Mistakes were made.*

If anything, this would make his story more convincing. He had enough bank credit to make them let him through, but they wouldn't find it suspicious if he spent time looking for the thief. And that sort of looking would take place in the same sorts of places where you might be able to find out who trafficked in stolen data, and who they might have sent into Pacifica, and where that data would be headed, once it had been auctioned off.

Ernst approached the bus station in the foothills well after dusk.

As he'd moved downward into the mountain's shadow, looking eastward, he'd seen expanse of flat and dust, studded with wind generators. In a few months, the hot summer would strike hard here, stretching for months of weather in which it'd be dangerous to go outside for any length of time, another killer summer that would trim one side of the population with heart attacks and strokes among the elderly and the other with a rise in infant mortality.

People would cake themselves in sunscreen and carry brightly colored parasols to reflect back the sun's sizzle and dazzle. West of the Cascades, what had once been the state of Washington, remained damper than most of the world, but the summers on its eastern border were as dangerous as any desert.

The bus station looked like an immense aluminum cylinder, sliced sideways and laid on the ground. Near it spun three enormous wind turbines, their blades a dull gray-brown.

By now, the agent had dealt with the bulk of the other passengers before him and was unapologetic about his treatment. She did point him to the tiny shower available to customers, and he waited in line for it until his turn to set the timer and race to sluice himself off before it ran out.

Ernst felt better after that, and took his seat on the bus in better spirits. The next stop would be the border checkpoint, he thought, and swallowed down his reservations. This was something he had to do. It was more meaningful than working on datasets that anyone could process. *No*, he told himself again, looking at his reflection in the window as the half-empty bus lumbered away from the station. *No, this is the right thing to do.*

The officials at the border preprocessing station were hostile to him, even after he explained that he had been robbed along the way. The sight of his papers did seem to reassure them, and after some intense conversation among themselves and number of expectant pauses where he was forced to signal that because of the robbery, he had no means of bribing them, he was allowed to endure a long series of waits in various rooms, and then eventually pointed in the direction of the actual border checkpoint.

The buildings that lined the roadside here were once-temporary, low-slung shelters that had been rendered more permanent by additions of concrete-block walls. Barely visible in the darkness, angles of razor-wire gleamed atop the high wire fences marking the line between Pacifica and the United States.

The air smelled overpowering and sweet, the smell of the nearby ethanol plants. The Midwest depended on its corn, and vast monoculture farms stretched across the state. Pence had declared wind farms carcinogenic a few years back and demanded that the state tear down all its existing turbines; the ethanol plants had sprung up to replace those

The American border officials made him strip down and go through a series of showers, decontaminations, for hours before he was reunited with his clothes, warm to the touch from their own decontamination process, in a small room on the other side. It might have seemed outrageous once, but nowadays, when anyone could whip up a virus in their basement—let alone the natural ones rising in the close quarters of major cities—every country required certain safeguards and none more strict than the xenophobic US, which led the pack in number of deaths in every pandemic.

He was unsure how much his indeterminate racial status helped him; he was from a mix of Iranian and Swede and simply looked like, as Rachel had once said dryly, "a very hairy white man."

The officials never addressed him directly, just spoke to the air in half sentences, telling him what to do, where to go: "Down the hall." "Through that door." "Strip; dump clothes there." They talked back and forth among each other, details of a bowling game the night before, how drunk a coworker had gotten. It was as though he was a ghost, standing there naked as they ignored him except to say, "Next shower."

After he felt unspeakably, painfully clean, they let him into a new room, where he passed his wrist under the eye of one scanner and then stared into another, wireless electrodes suctioned to his temples, answering the questions that the machine asked him while it measured his voice for stress. He was glad, for once, for the tame existence that he'd led up until this point; no, he had never been jailed; no, he had never been convicted of a felony. Asked for his reason for visiting, he said, trying to keep it even, "To find my friend Mai and talk to her."

It seemed a lifetime of waiting, expecting for the machine to denounce him, before the green "cleared" sign flashed, and he was directed on to the next station. He ate his lunch from a vending machine; a packet of processed vegetable paste rings and a Coke, licking crumbs from his fingers and feeling it all insufficient.

Around 3:00 P.M., after a final verbal interview with a bored official that took his fingerprints and DNA sample, he stepped out of the building. He was in the United States now.

It didn't feel as different as he had thought it might. On the Pacifica side, the flag flapped above a building painted with its colors: the muted gray-green, goldenrod-colored trim, and the bushes were trimmed and tidy. On the US side, the buildings were in worse repair, but the sprawls of red, white, and blue petunias out front were just as fierce. At both the rest stop on the Pacifica side and the US one, pairs of volunteers oversaw the distribution of cups of Coffee-Zatz and packets of creamer and sweetener.

A steady stream of people flowed in and out of the building behind him; one jostled him, forcing him to the side and into the shade.

His phone crawled along at a tenth of its usual speed. Had they installed some virus on it? He scrolled through one of the articles Geidon had loaded on his phone.

10 Things You Should Know Before Visiting America

1. *Guns of all shapes and sizes are entirely legal, and people are not required to advertise that they're "packing heat"! Laws also back up their right to shoot if they feel threatened, such as the famous "Stand Your Ground" laws of Florida, Kansas and Texas. Avoid arguments and places where judgment may be impaired, such as bars or public gatherings, and you'll be fine.*

2. *Everyone's got a side hustle, probably more than one. This is particularly true in the border towns. Many of these are illegal, and they will not hesitate to rope an unwary foreigner, particularly if they are not white, into a scam.*

3. *You will not be given access to health care while in the United States unless you have financial surety. While the US government will allow you in without this, hospitals themselves will not give you treatment without assurance they will be paid. Instead, you will be taken to the nearest border checkpoint. You will be charged for your transportation.*

4. *Don't drink the water! In fact, ask not to have ice in that drink. Sodas and other bottled beverages are fine, and you might as well take advantage of the wide range of sodas the US is known for around the world!*

5. *If you are gay or lesbian and traveling with your partner, public displays of affection are a major faux pas and may even put you at risk depending on your surroundings. Play it safe—no smooching!*

6. *Stick to major brand names when buying foodstuffs. Erratic and unenforced food labeling laws mean that most of what's written on American packaging is meaningless, even when it's an assurance like wheat- or peanut-free. Be safe—assume nothing, and check wrappers to make sure they're not past their expiration.*

7. *Americans love to show off their country! Ask them what they're proud of, and you'll find them eager to show you the corners of wilderness and parts of history that still remain.*

You'll particularly find challenges for the adventurous eater, whether it's deep-fried candy bars at the local state fair or the Buffalo chicken wings available at the neighborhood bar. Ask the Americans you encounter where they go to eat and, you'll find yourself rubbing elbows with some of the most interesting people around.

8. *Tip well! Most of your servers are not actually paid a wage, and some even pay a small fee for access to the job. Remember that giving them your Pacifica currency is illegal, and that someone can earn a bounty for turning you in for illegal activity.*

9. *Some phrases won't get the same reaction that they would back home, such as "Happy Holidays," which you should replace with either "Merry Christmas" or "Happy New Year," as appropriate.*

10. *If someone offers to pray for your soul, it is polite to offer a small tip. This is one way many Americans get around labor laws. You will find such laws are already relaxed or unenforced, such as child labor, overtime, and safety precautions deemed too expensive.*

Ernst looked up to see a teenage girl with her camera pointed at him. She didn't make eye contact, just snapped the pic, and turned to walk through the doors behind her.

He felt a buzz on his phone and looked at it. A LoyalEye notification, bright red with blue and white stars bordering it. He opened it to find a picture of himself with the note, "Just standing there casing the place. terrorist???" It was followed by a flood of comments that seemed divided about fifty-fifty as to whether he really was a terrorist or not. He decided to move on before more people took his photo.

Luckily for him, his wrist-chip still worked to show his bank balance, despite all the various horror stories about them getting extracted for other people's use here in the States. He would get food and then think about what to do. The missing ukulele certainly would be a lack, but maybe it was just as well that no one would be asking him to play it to corroborate his story.

Stopping in a drugstore whose door promised REAL HUMAN SERVICE!!!!, he wandered through its aisles in search of bandages for his blisters. Every aisle was capped with red, white, and blue displays crammed with merchandise.

He paused to examine a rack of key chains labeled with the sign Crammed with Presidential Luck!!!!, a scattering of oddly shaped orange and pallid white things that he thought were mushrooms then abruptly realized they were thumb drives in the shape of cartoon penises, each labeled with the name of a recent American president. Smaller print on the labels read "Guaranteed to contain 100% pure luck from your favorite president!" Other merchandise was also branded with *Trump* or *Pence*, while one shelf held the candidates who had surfaced to challenge Pence this year. Other merchandise was labeled "Republican-approved" or "Official brand of the GOP."

He found a pack of soft-gel bandages a few aisles on and took it to the counter, where a dispirited teen at the register was smoking while tapping on her phone. He had to say, "Excuse me," before she set the phone down, exhaling an exaggerated sigh that treated him to the smell of clove-scented tobacco. Her name tag read "Marlowe."

She rang up his purchase and pushed the chip-reader at him so he could hold his wrist over it. When he did, it flashed amber. He poised for panic, but she just huffed out a deeper sigh and picked up a scanner beside the register, and flashed it at him, then put the bandages in a bag and shoved that at him in turn.

He said, "What was that?"

She had already picked up her phone anew. She looked up from it to make an interrogative sound at him. He wondered if she could actually talk.

"What was the light?" he said.

"Notta citizen, gotta take a pic," she said, and took another drag to blow out smoke just as he was about to ask more, setting him coughing. Another customer cleared their throat behind him and he stepped aside.

Outside the door, he sat on a bench long enough to apply the bandages, despite the three times his phone buzzed with comments like, "Gross!", "This dude don't give a shit gonna get him some RELIEF!" and "The homeless problem has really gotten out of hand."

He looked around the intersection. It really wasn't all that strange in terms of the restaurant and shop names, he realized. McDonald's, Jack-in-the-Box, KFC. A few that were less familiar like "The Cracker Barrel." A couple of small chains. A few blocks down was a Rock and Robin. A touch of familiarity in a strange land.

Heat gathered on his shoulders from the sun as he walked along the street; the restaurant's shade was welcome. A waitress found him a table, and he surveyed the menu before deciding on just coffee. It startled him that more people were smoking in the restaurant. Back in Pacifica, tobacco use was rare. Here a cigarette machine squatted near the register and every table held an ashtray.

Most of the menu items were the same, though it seemed as though someone had gone through and removed most of the spicier ones, which puzzled him a little. He asked the waitress, a thin blonde named Mika, her arms striped with patriotic tattoos, about it.

"That's for religious reasons," she said. "Some folks don't believe in foreign food." She lowered her voice a little. "Best not to ask that sort of question, honey. Someone will Eye you for religious intolerance."

"But how is that intolerant?" he said, puzzled.

"You're making them feel uncomfortable about their religious choices," she said patiently, as though explaining something to a six-year-old.

He subsided and ordered a Pilgrim burger, which was turkey-flavored and came with a side of cranberry rings. It was clear that he was not the first Pacifican she'd dealt with, and through the rest of the meal, she answered questions for him. He had the list of contacts Geidon had given him, but he thought that, here, perhaps his own people skills would be enough to get him through, rather than needing to rely on Geidon's stratagems. He'd save the contacts for another time.

First things first. He needed to get to Kansas City. His money was limited. Would someone let him hitch a ride? He asked Mika about such an arrangement but to his dismay, she shook her head.

"If you do that nowadays, the ride services get on you," she said, "so most of the people going any distance don't want to risk it."

216

She hesitated. "Well, there's someone I can ask. You got anything against Muslims?"

"No," he said, and bit back the words, "Of course not," because of the earnestness on her face.

"All right," she said, sliding her order pad into her apron pocket. "She isn't a Muslim, really, but most people don't know the difference. Let me go see."

He watched her go across the diner towards a heavy-set, older Sikh woman sitting by herself, an e-reader tilted as she ate. They exchanged words, and both women glanced over at him. He tried to look harmless and worth helping. It must have worked—or maybe it was despite it—but the waitress came back to him. "She says she'll be ready to go in ten minutes, if it suits you."

Her name was Amina Patoha, but she said to call her Patsy. Her truck was bound for Kansas City, hauling grapes from Oregon, and she was moving fast so the heat wouldn't strain her rig's air conditioning. If he was willing to talk along the way, keep her awake, she was happy to take him into the city and drop him off wherever he preferred.

She apologized for having to keep the radio on, but said that if she kept it on, her gas got a Sunclear discount at the fuel stops, and that it added up.

"Are there a lot of people like you from Pacifica driving trucks?" he said. "Don't you run into trouble? I mean, in all the TV shows, this place is super racist. And there was that documentary about the temple that got shot up."

Patsy shrugged. "Some. But you gotta make a living. Certainly there's one thing the TV programs don't prepare you for, and that's ICE," she said.

"What? There's so many shows about them."

"There are. And none of them are accurate. Even the ones that claim to be reality based. Those lapel cameras that they all talk about, right?"

"The ones that are legally required?"

"In Pacifica, they are. In the US they aren't, and they get 'accidentally' turned off all the time. Keep some money in your wallet where a police officer can slide it out without being too obvious about it, and you'll be prepared for most of the shakedowns. But if you're on a list, don't expect that to help any. That's how people get disappeared. You don't want to spend the rest of your days working off vagrancy charges in a prison."

"I'm not on any lists." Or was he? He wondered if Mai had the power to put him on one in case he followed her. If she was working for the government, she might. But the way the note had been phrased, the fact of an auction—surely she was some sort of independent agent. And would she have realized how determined he was and expected him to come chasing? He didn't think so. No, she would have underestimated him. He felt a grim satisfaction at that.

"You're going to need to remember some stuff," Patsy said. "One, don't drink the water."

"I knew that," he said indignantly.

She looked over at him. "No, they tell you that and then you tourists think you know what's what. When I say don't drink it, I mean, not a drop. Don't brush your teeth with it, keep your mouth closed in the shower. And when you're eating, try to stick to the big brand names. There's no laws anymore about food, and labels aren't required to tell you anything. I have a cousin who's allergic to corn, and he packs his own food all through here. You should stick to Rock and Robin. They're pretty safe."

At the next rest stop, the urinal in the men's room was hazed with graffiti involving who was doing what to who and a scattering of apocalyptic quotes. He was noted in LoyalEye twice for taking too long to wash his hands. The comment "Casing da joint much?" got eight likes. He was acquiring a following, apparently.

As they descended into Kansas, the Colorado mountains still stretching upward behind them, they moved through the hills, the landscape growing flatter and flatter, the vegetation sparser and sparser. It became hotter, and the wind picked up, swirling dust that danced along the roadside, coating the electric wires that accompanied the road.

At lunchtime, they found another Rock and Robin. Waiting to sit down, he smelled fake meat and fat-sizzled potatoes and thought nostalgically of home, of the meals he'd eaten there from the same chain. His mouth watered.

"This far away from the border, you always want the restaurants you sit down in," Patsy said.

"Why?" he asked. Uneasiness stalked its way up and down his spine with the deliberation of an angry cat.

"Tastes better." Their waitress led them to bench and table formed from extruded yellow plastic, scuffed and dulled, the surface smelling of disinfectant. He followed her and sat down, feeling with distaste the grippy stickiness of whatever invisible stuff it was that coated the seat.

"Tastes better how?"

Patsy flicked a thumb up and over her shoulder. "Chemicals piped into the air here. Smells good and makes the food taste better. Believe me, it's worth sitting here."

His look skittered over the crowd in the restaurant, and she laughed. "Lucky for you everyone will think you're nervous because you're with me," she told him, tapping her headscarf. "If there's a choice, I stick to the Sikh restaurants, but the one close to here was firebombed lately."

Her matter-of-factness surprised and appalled him. "Is there an upsurge in that?" he said uncertainly. He looked at her food, "You can eat here?"

Again her look required no words. She gestured at him to eat. "It's all vegetable-protein based," she told him.

The first bite was nothing like food back home, somehow delicious and yet chemical-tanged. The flavor intensified as he chewed. He swallowed before he was quite ready to, feeling the food solid and weighty in his throat.

"It's good," he said, astonished.

"Of course it is," Patsy said with patience. "You think people would pay for food that wasn't good? This is America, there's free choice." The wry twist to her lips made him think she wasn't convinced by her own words. "Just be aware there's a low-grade euphoric in it."

"What?" he said, startled. "It's drugged?"

"Most processed food is," she said. "Low grade. It won't affect what you do. Just makes you more content. Less prone to troublesome thoughts."

He looked at her. "You don't mind eating it?"

"I have an implant that filters it out," she said. "Best two grand I ever spent. If you go back to Pacifica, be aware you're going to have withdrawal the first two weeks. But you're not thinking about what happens when you go back, are you?"

She looked at him, and he felt as transparent as a pane of glass, all his worries and ambitions written on it in indelible marker. He felt the urge to confess everything to her, to ask for her help in tracking down Mai, but he said, weakly, "I'm just looking for my friend. But maybe I'll settle here."

"Ah huh," she said. "I'm convinced this place will seem so much better to you that you'll stay."

"I couldn't get a job in Pacifica," he lied. "So I came here."

"Sure," she said. "Sure. You look like a guy with no skills, you bet." She pointed down to his hands. "Those are the hands of rough labor, sure," she said pointedly.

"I play the ukulele," he said. "It just got stolen."

"I'll let you off at a place where there's a flea market in the evenings," she said. "You can probably find one there, along with clothes that don't say 'tourist' so clearly."

"You think I should do that?"

She smiled. "I *know* you should do that."

Patsy directed him to a Sikh-run motel in Kansas City, but said she wasn't staying there herself. "Gotta get this delivered then push on for another load," she said, gesturing at the truck. "Good luck to you."

The market wouldn't open until midnight. He ran through her advice in his head. "It's not entirely legal, but the vendors pay enough to keep the police away. The thing to watch out for were video drones because that means some reality TV shit is going on, and you never know when that's a crime show."

"But they can't film reality TV without releases, can they?" he'd asked

By then, he'd gotten used to her bemused, *what the fuck does this guy think he's doing?* look. "You and I both signed releases in order to get into the country," she said. "Sunclear owns the rights to broadcast us; anyone else has to pay them licensing fees. Anyhow, you should be fine. That doesn't happen much."

She dropped him off, and he watched the massive trailer truck move away.

The hotel was called the Sunflower Inn; it boasted brown and gold trappings, most of them faded now. The tiny room smelled of ancient cigarettes and the clear plastic covering the chair's upholstery. The rug was pitted with old burns and piebald with suspicious stains. The single window overlooked the parking lot and the scattering of pedal-cars and older vehicles in it. The most up-to-date thing was the giant television set across from the bed, and that didn't even have a gaming rig. Perhaps an evening watching it would be his best bet for acclimating.

But a few hours later, he was more confused than ever. First, he'd watched a comedy about prison existence, *Life Behind Bars*, about three prisoners, trying to outwit the prison system. The jokes seemed grim to him, involving insects in the food or an ongoing joke about rats living in the toilet, while the laugh-track blurted out applause and giggles every time the rats were mentioned. Two channels over was *Johnny Gunwise*, defeating a gang of eco-terrorists sabotaging the government's Nebraskan grain fields.

That was comforting. Plenty of the same shows as back home. That was one thing that the new world hadn't lost, much like social media. Television had settled into an uneasy detente between nations, though America had implemented censorship boards intended to "keep propaganda out of the film and television industries."

A few channels further, an aging wrestler oversaw *Senior Battles*, letting elderly people compete to double, triple, sometimes quintuple the payout cash grab. Most of the time the challenges were humiliation or mental, but there was at least one physical challenge each episode, the course and the challengers chosen to create the most drama possible, usually with a story so bathetic that it *had* to be crafted, others involving grandchildren or great grandchildren, derelict and/or drug-addled parents, and often some sort of medical condition.

After that was something called *The Happy Hour*, which was stories of heroic citizens helping their fellows. It felt inspirational,

221

but underneath it, he thought, there was a sense of desperation. Rachel had always hated this sort of news story, saying it was designed to hide the fact that the government wasn't helping people in the first place.

He flipped through half a dozen more channels, each dedicated to prayer and exhortations to the viewer on how to maximize the power of their prayers by paying the church to have them amplified. The Cathedral of Lilies leader, Preacheress Aimee, and her husband Noah—both Aryan blond and with wide blue eyes that had to be cosmetic lenses—were providing a special rate on "prayers from the heart of our own blooming Garden of Love." An organ played some crescendo in the background. He felt some rumbling in his bones, as though the TV were sending out subsonic signals and realized he was fingering his wrist-chip, thinking about sending in a contribution. He'd heard about the hypnagogic powers of midwestern television, but hadn't realized how easy it would be to fall prey. He turned the TV off and tried to catch a nap before the flea market.

Ernst thought he wouldn't be able to sleep, but when his wrist buzzed with his 11:45 P.M. alarm, he blinked out of shallow sleep, his mouth sticky and sour. He brushed his teeth and went out onto the street. He wanted fresh clothing, but more importantly, he hoped for a lead on Mai's whereabouts and the virtual auction.

The flea market was supposed to be in the parking lot of what had once been billed as the world's largest Costco before the chain got gutted by fines for overcompensating their workers in the late 2030s. It lay bordered by an overpass's shadow on one side and a walled freeway's unseen sizzle of traffic on the other.

Even at this time of night, the street was busy, and the pools of light under each streetlight glinted with broken glass among the scattered bits of trash, and cigarette butts. The black asphalt still held the fevered warmth it had accumulated during the day, burning up at him as he crossed it.

He could hear and smell the market before he got to it: the bubble and stink of vat-grown meatpulp, popcorn mingled with a touch of burned kernels, and a candy sweetness from some deep-fried snack. The parking lot was clustered with tables laid in irregular aisles. Portable lights were set up every few tables; blinking signs advertising wares augmented the visibility. Up above he could see drones. He remembered Patsy's warning, but he didn't feel like he had a choice. What was the worst that could happen to him now?

Red, white, and blue bunting was strung from cheap aluminum and plastic pipe frameworks, flapping in the cooler night breeze. People were everywhere, vendors talking with potential customers, holding out things to coax a buyer's touch. Teens were moving on skateboards off in one corner of the vast conglomeration of parking lot, focused on their own dance while a cluster of small children watched them. Swarms of cars and RVs filled one parking section, most of its streetlights dead.

Ernst passed among the tables of old clocks and tableware, placemats made of wine corks, and kitschy soap dishes shaped like tiny bathtubs or cat litter boxes or Trump's hairpiece. One table held nothing but empty glass food jars—the good, old-style kind, the kind he remembered from childhood. He remembered the names and commercials. Nowadays, food came in plastic sacks that you stuck in a heater before decanting.

A table of old coffeemakers, obsolete now that everyone used CoffeeZatz. He liked the look of some of them, though, like squat little robots, grimly determined to create coffee or die in the process. Tables of old embroidered linens, some stained or yellowed, others plastic-bagged and marked "non-smoking, non-smog area, pet free." A herd's worth of plastic horses corralled on a larger table with the little animatronic animals that had been so popular a few years back before most of them had been returned because of the shortness of their battery life. Disposable, like everything, everyone around him.

He spotted a ukulele buried in a clutter of other musical instruments, obscured by a tambourine and bongo drum that seemed to be locked in carnal pleasure. He extracted it and looked for a price label.

"Fifty bucks," the woman behind the table said.

He raised an eyebrow at her and set it back down. She waited until he'd fully released it before she said, "I could make it less. What would *you* think is fair?"

"Twenty," he said.

She scoffed but let him talk her down to twenty-five plus the case, and smiled at him in parting in a way that made him think that he hadn't gotten the best of the deal. He bought clothes at another stall: two bright T-shirts with *The Happy Hour* lettered in flowers and jeans that were closer to the unfitted ones the men here seemed to be wearing, which didn't stand out the way his khakis did.

He coughed as he passed a cluster of smokers, and someone called out, "You too pussy to breathe a little tobacco?" in his wake.

He didn't look around.

They shouted, "Hey, hey you, I'm talking to you! I recognize you!" Footsteps behind him, then a shove at his shoulder that made him sidestep in order to maintain his balance. Bob. He wore a red baseball hat reading KAGA KORPS. He moved up and into Ernst's space, breathing out a sour stink of beer. "I *said,* you too *pussy* to breathe a little *tobacco*, boy?"

Ernst backed away and realized too late that he was near one edge of the market and being driven into the darkness among the cars.

"You Pacifica social justice asshole, come to sneer at good American citizens?" Bob said, taking another step forward. "Come to see how real Americans live an' die? Claim we're just scum and thieves?" There were other men behind him, wearing similar hats.

"No," Ernst said desperately. "I'm not anything like that. I came here because I wanted to leave all that behind." Some dim part of him was watching himself plead with disbelief. *You're better than this,* it said to him. *If you stood up for yourself, then he'd back down. He'd see you're serious.*

But he didn't want to get punched in the face, didn't want them to fall on him and beat him. The thought of it paralyzed him. He hoped he wouldn't piss his pants. The violence, the readiness with which the men had moved to anger, was something he'd never encountered back home.

Bob drew a gun from inside his jacket. To Ernst it looked as large as a cannon. He'd seen them on soldiers or police, but he'd never been so close to the barrel of one, or had it pointing at him. For the first time, he thought, *I could die in this place.*

"All I gotta say is that I thought you was menacing me, and I'm in the clear," Bob said. "My cousin shot three Canadian blackies last year that thought they'd get smart with him, running around with all their fancy aboot prancing." Behind him, his friends grinned in confirmation.

"Please don't shoot me," Ernst said, and the fact that he was able to keep his voice steady made him feel even steadier. Dull fatalism settled over him. Whatever happened, happened. He might as well go out with some dignity. The distant side of him that had been watching all of this from the sidelines cheered.

Two drones danced down from the sky and hovered. For a second, Ernst thought that he was saved, but from their positions, they were simply recording the incident, rather than intervening. All three bore the Sunclear News logo. The man and his friends paid them no attention.

"Look," Ernst said, pointing at one. "They're going to record you shooting me in cold blood. You'll go to jail."

"No I won't," Bob said with confidence. "I'm an American citizen, exercising my free rights. You're not on your native soil, therefore you're fair game. No one cares about shooting foreigners. Hell, there's a bounty on some countries. Are you Iraqi? You're worth five hundred bucks to me to shoot if you're an Iraqi and don't have a work permit to be here."

"I have a work permit," Ernst said. "I told you that."

"Then show it to me."

"You think he leaves something like that in his pocket?" a new voice came. It was oddly familiar. A thin, tall man, dressed in worn jeans. A face that Ernst recognized. How was that possible? A brother or cousin somehow?

The lookalike stepped forward. "He's one of my workers. Just went astray. He's new. Shoot him, and you're paying me a fine." A casual tone, as though they didn't care much whether the result would be the money or Ernst.

But clearly the fine mattered to Bob. He scoffed and tucked the gun away. "We could still beat the shit out of him." he blustered. "You should be taking better care when bringing dirty foreigners into the country."

"Sure, sure. But is that worth the fine? Because I got full insurance on him."

After a little more grumbling, the men dispersed. Ernst faced his coworker.

"Natalie?' he said uncertainly.

"Jesus Christ, Ernst," Natalie said. Now that Ernst was looking closer, he could tell it was definitely them, though dressed in male gear. "What the fuck would you have done if I hadn't come along?"

"Gotten the shit beaten out of me, probably," he said. He bent over and rested his hands on his knees, trying to calm his heart and slow his breathing.

"Come on," Natalie said. "You know I had to threaten Geidon before he'd tell me where you went? Kept saying things about freedom of choice until I said freedom of dumbassery and threatened to tell Loretta about the darknet server he's been hosting on his office computer. You know I grew up in this area. Why wouldn't you ask me for help?"

"It seemed like an awful lot to ask," he said.

That took them aback. "Well," they said, "wouldn't you do it for me?"

"Maybe?" he said.

"Maybe?" Their voice tilted upward with incredulity.

"Well, sure," he said. "Sure."

"What the fuck ever," they said. "Let's go grab coffee. I've arranged for you to meet someone."

This iteration of the Rock and Robin was next to an army recruitment center, which meant they'd stepped the patriotic decor up to levels that Ernst hadn't witnessed before. The artificial plants growing in the window boxes had red, white, and blue leaves as well as petals, and the music loop was set to military-boyband-pop, a genre that Ernst was not fond of.

"What's with the music?" he asked as they slid into a booth in the corner.

"This area supplies more soldiers than any other area in the world." Natalie studied the menu. "When it stopped being able to supply so much grain, they decided that training schools were the next best thing."

"Who's coming to meet us?"

"My second cousin, Paisley." They signaled to the waitress. "Two Patriot burgers, cauliflower extrude on the first, salad-surrogate on the second."

Ernst ordered an Alamo burger with an extra side of Pence-cue sauce for his fries. "Why her?"

"She has connections in the virtual world."

"You don't?"

"I moved away. More than that, I left this country. A lot of my old friends still see that as a betrayal. And she's from a different branch of the family, richer than mine."

"I didn't know you came from money."

"Technically I don't." Their lips quirked at some interior joke. "But I'll let you see for yourself. Ask her about being an heiress."

He expected someone who looked like Natalie, but the twelve-to thirteen-year-old that sat down bore little resemblance. He was no judge of women's clothing, couldn't tell from those cues where she stood socially, but her teeth were straight and white. Her face, though, had an odd lopsidedness to it that he couldn't decipher. She compensated for it by twitching her left shoulder upward as though to balance its pull.

"Paisley, Ernst," Natalie said. "And vice versa. He wants to find some big virtual auction being held somewhere here on June 3, Pais. Know anything like that?"

"Hello to you too," the girl said, but didn't pause long enough for Natalie to reply. "There's a couple events like that. I can ask around."

"How long to find out?"

"Half an hour, depending on whether people are up to snuff. Maybe faster if you're willing to back it with some FastWallet cash." She eyed Natalie with an interest that sharpened when they nodded. "All right. 'Scuse me while I glaze."

She leaned back, and Ernst looked over to Natalie in confusion.

"She's in VR space," Natalie said. "I'm going to go wash my hands."

By the time the waitress brought their orders, Paisley's attention had returned. She said, "I've got some agents out, I'll tell you when they report in. She pulled her Patriot burger towards herself and began eating it with neat, efficient bites. "Hang on, I got quick chores," she said, and set down the burger to tap at her data sleeve for a few minutes. From where he sat, Ernst could see cartoon animals and fruit and oblique rounds of gold coins dance across the fabric.

"Natalie says you're some kind of heiress," he said.

The girl's look was not entirely friendly. "Sorta, yeah. My family lives off our CoolCoolKittyPets," the little girl said. "We have the largest CoolCoolKittyPets enclave in the world. It's the only one that survived the Cloud Wars."

"That's a game, isn't it?" he asked.

"My grandfather was part of the initial beta, and then his kids all played it," she said. "That's a lot of clicks over the years, and with the people who pay to play, they can afford to lose interest and drift away. My family knows the developer team working with the company; we do a lot of testing for them, particularly economy-level stuff. We have pieces of some other holdings too. My cousin's the number three TapTapBoom player, worldwide."

"So that's what she meant when she called you an heiress?" Ernst said, incredulously.

Suspicion throbbed in her narrowed eyes. "Yeah, and what's that to you? It means I got a little more cash than most people, that's about it. I can trade stuff in the game for things I want."

He hunched his shoulders in defense and shuffled his feet under the table. "It's imaginary, all of it," he said. "Just pixels."

"Like money's not?" she said scornfully. "Can you use your Pacifica script over here in the stores? Or can I march into one of your stores and buy a loaf of tofu?"

She twisted the word scornfully.

"You'd have to go to a moneychanger," he said. "But the financial systems do that. The Pacific Coast Stock Exchange, the Chicago, and the New York one—they all interact. They agree on a specific value for money.

She shook her head stubbornly. "Just as 'maginary." She dimpled suddenly. "You can't argue with me, I'm too cute. Just give up."

Despite the dimple, there was a shrillness to the sentence that did not bode well to him, a sticky edge of temper tantrum and malice that made him want to move on.

"All right," he said, as agreeably as he could manage. "So, you're a CoolCoolKittyPets heiress. Which means what?"

She eyed him as though waiting for more, then shrugged. "What it means," she said with condescending emphasis, "is that I also have more access than a lot of people to computer resources. Most people have slow-web. That's why Natalie brought you to me."

"Is that what's been going on with my phone?" he said with a trace of relief. "I thought it had been hacked."

"It probably has," she said. "All the phones tell the companies where you are. We stay here long enough, an informant will show up, try to make friends with you, try to find out what your business is."

"How long is long enough?"

She pointed with her chin at the doorway. "Just play it cool and act like you're here to talk CoolCoolKitty," she said.

"I really have no clue what that is other than an online game that's been around a long time," he said.

The woman who paused beside them was a middle-aged white woman with sun-streaked blonde hair. "Well, hello," she said in a vibrant tone that made him think she must know him from somewhere. "Are you new to Kansas City?"

"I'm a tourist," he said.

"I'm not," the girl announced. "He's here buying a CoolCool-Kitty from me. Trade in virtuals is legal as long as I pay taxes on it. You're interfering with my free trade."

The woman smiled at the girl. "Well, aren't you just the cutest thing," she said. "Shouldn't you be in school, sugar?"

"I'm homeschooled." The girl turned her attention away from the woman and put her phone between herself and Ernst. "You see that purple shading on the feathers?" she asked Ernst, acting as though the woman had become invisible. "That means it's one of the originals. You can't get them anymore except through trades like this. If you want to check the value on Auction-bay feel free. My prices are reasonable. Nobody complains."

He could see Natalie coming back and noticing the woman at their table. They paused and studied the cigarette machine near the front, looking as though they were debating between brands but angling themselves so they could see the interaction.

The woman took out a phone and balanced it meaningfully on her fingertips, but Paisley shook her head. "I know my rights," she said. "I'm a minor; you can't post about me on LoyalEye."

The woman slid her phone back into her purse and took out a data card instead. "Here," she said, handing it to Ernst. "Here's my contact info if you ever find yourself needing someone to talk to about the local sights."

"Get along, get along," Paisley jeered. The woman retreated with enough dignity to make Paisley's mockery seem like hollow defiance.

Natalie came back to the table.

"Was that a close one?" Ernst said.

Natalie and Paisley both laughed. Paisley took several of his fries, stuffing them in her mouth. "Pass me that card," she said indistinctly. He slid it across the table, and she picked it up and snapped it in two.

"Hey!" he said, startled.

"You don't even want to know how many trackers and sniffers are built into that," she said. "Cheap shit, though."

"She'll just tell the drone network," he said, feeling hopeless.

The girl's look was scornful. "Most of the drones are privately owned," she said. "You think the government has enough money to have drones running around watching everyone? As long as you haven't given any of them reason to think you have money, they won't latch on to you."

Ernst grimaced. "Look," he said. "I don't understand anything about this place."

"Is it really that different from Pacifica?" she asked.

Natalie maintained silence.

He looked around at the faces and said, reluctantly, "Not all of it. People are people. But I'm used to being able to talk about things."

"You can talk about things here," she said.

"Really?" he said. "In the television shows, people here are always getting dragged away by the secret police."

"I'm not saying there isn't a secret police," she said. "But I don't know that they're all that secret. And if you have the money for a payoff, you don't have to worry about it."

"So who gets dragged off? What happens to them?"

"The people who are lazy and don't have any money," she said. "They're not contributing anyhow. So they're put in prison, where they can work and give something back to society."

At a ding, Paisley paused to consult her sleeve. "Okay," she said. "I know where your event's taking place."

"So it's definitely in a physical location?"

"More secure that way. The only truly secure computer is one that's unplugged," Paisley said.

"Meaning?"

"They want you on their network, but their network isn't part of the Internet. It's housed on an internal server, and there's chip-nullifiers so you can't access the Internet, even small smart-body devices."

Ernst blinked. "Very retro."

"It's fucked up, if you ask me," Paisley said. "People act like the Internet's something you should hide from, when it's more like air." She shuddered. "Anyhow, the real event's not till tomorrow. You're going to need a place to hide him."

"I thought Aunt Susan might," Natalie said.

Paisley shook her head. "She took the grab."

"What? She always said that was a racket."

"Kenny talked her into it by saying the grandchildren could afford college if she deeded it to them. You know who would do it? Laurie's running her place still, and they AirBunk the visitor's quarters. Want me to check?" She tapped at her sleeve, then said, "She's got it open, she says."

"Ugh," Natalie said, then, reluctantly, "But yeah, that would work. Man, Ernst, you are seeing the whole seedy underbelly of America."

"Where are you going to take me?" he said.

"We've got a place to stay tonight," she said. "But you have to do some work in exchange."

"What kind of work?"

"It's an old-age home. Old-age things. Maybe work in the kitchen or the laundry. They always need workers, and they're not monitored because if they were official, they'd have to pay more taxes on them. Cheaper just to bribe the city to not notice the workers.

There're quarters in back that no one's supposed to be using. Tomorrow, we'll go to the auction, and you can find out more there."

Outside the diner, three children had set up camp under the shelter of a green awning that read in straggly white lettering, *#kids4kids* and underneath, "As featured on *The Happy Hour.*" They were selling palm-sized plastic bulbs. Customers bit off the tapered ends and stuck them in their mouths to squeeze out the bright red, blue, or cloudy white liquid. In front of the kids, plastic cases contained clusters of the bulbs, a medley of colors, others a single flavor.

All of the kids were sunburned and sweaty. The oldest was almost a teen, the two with them perhaps eight or nine. All were blond and overweight, faces marked with angry red pimples. They stared expectantly at Ernst as he and Natalie passed.

The oldest said, "Mister, hey mister, aren't you going to buy something?" Their gender was indeterminate, their body sagging with flesh, but their face was drawn.

He shook his head, trying to avoid eye contact, but one of the smaller ones darted out from behind the booth to stand in front of him.

"Mister, if you buy one, it buys a kid a school lunch, and we'll pray for you," she said with painful sincerity. Natalie paused, watching him as though he were a zoo animal on the other side of glass, and they were curious as to what he might do next.

He turned back to the booth. "How much for just one?"

"I can't sell you just one, but I have three-packs," the oldest said.

He didn't want to argue any more, didn't want to draw attention to himself. In Pacifica, the government fed the kids, even if there were arguments sometimes about things like local sourcing and whether potatoes were a vegetable. He said, "What happens if you don't make enough to buy the kids lunches?"

"People split sometimes," one child said. "My prayer group does that. Divvies up whatever they have."

The other little kid shook their head. "The big ones grab the food," they said with a fatalistic sneer. "That's how it always is, my dad said. You have to be fast and tricky if you're little."

"And are you?" Ernst asked them. "Fast and tricky, I mean?"

They scowled at him. They wore a faded tank top with Johnny Gunwise's gun facing outward and the words "Don't tread on Johnny" in scrollwork lettering, drooping down over black athletic shorts and cheap flip-flops. "Fast and tricky enough," they said with a belligerent swagger.

"This is a scam, right?" he said. "You kids must get *some* kind of school lunch."

They just stared at him. He could see disbelief and calculation flickering in their eyes.

"It's real sad, mister," one said. "It's hard to learn when your stomach's growling."

He gave them the rest of his change from the meal and left carrying two three-packs of bright liquid.

"Is that true?" he asked Natalie as they walked on. "Kids have to buy their own lunches?"

"Not if their parents can afford to buy them and books, they don't," she said.

"What if they don't have the money?"

"Then they go hungry. I had a classmate who used to eat paper until the teacher caught her. She said it at least made her stomach feel like there was something in it. It's why a lot of people belong to the mega-churches, because they'll qualify as part of their food-pantry programs and such."

He'd thought Pacifican poverty was bad. There was nothing about this on television from America. He'd always thought life over here would be more modern and glossy. That Pacifica had intentionally gone woodsy because they were embracing a touch of being backward, outside the norm. Embracing *That's So Pacifica*, and its goofy kindness. He said, "Is that why you went to Pacifica?"

Natalie lowered their voice. "Maybe not something to advertise," they said. "My family still thinks I'm just visiting. But no. I could have gotten a job here as a tech of some kind, probably. But they don't believe in being nonbinary. If you're gay here—or god forbid trans—you get out, as soon as you can, before someone finds out and lists you on LoyalEye as a sex offender."

Their voice held bitterness that Ernst didn't want to ask about.

233

"My cousin Pam is picking us up," they said. "She'll take us to Laura's."

"How many cousins do you *have*?"

"A lot," they said. "Used to be more of them, a lot more."

Again, the unexplained bitterness. He looked sideways at their expression, but it was shuttered and did not invite further questions.

Susan was an unexpectedly vivacious woman, driving a small van. When they got on, he saw she was a paraplegic, strapped into a special driver's seat. As they took their seats, she launched into a barrage of updates about various family members, ignoring Ernst. He got the impression he was an unwelcome reminder of the fact that Natalie had chosen to live elsewhere. But Natalie's refusal to reply except in monosyllables eventually wore her into silence.

He watched the bleak landscape as it rolled past. Like Seattle, there were people living in the medians, in encampments that had by now become almost permanent, but he saw signs of differences as they rolled along: police cars surrounding one such encampment, officers overseeing its occupants being forced to dump their possessions onto bonfires, which sent thick, black smoke roiling up to the heavens like a clumsy appeal to an unknown, primitive god.

"Must have pissed someone off," Natalie said, noticing the direction in which he was looking. "Most of the time, it's like Pacifica, and police don't bother with them."

"What do they bother with?" he asked.

"The things they're paid to do," Susan said.

"Serve and protect?"

Her sideways look was sly. "That's General Robotics' motto, isn't it? Their security units are too spendy for this part of town."

Ernst lapsed back into silence, feeling himself at odds with the world, and alone. Why had he chased Mai this far? What did he hope to accomplish? He thought of his grandmother, and her sincerity, of her conviction when she said, "I think it might change things back. I think it could change the world." In retrospect, that feeling only struck him as hopelessly naïve.

They got off at the outskirts of town, near a series of gray buildings and cinderblock patios surrounded by fast-food chains, mattress stores, and tattoo shops. Dispirited cedar bushes edged the artificial lawn; you rarely saw actual grass lawns anymore. It was a single-story sprawl, and looked as though originally it might have been one edge of a strip mall whose only surviving remnant was a tilted sign, reading, "Prairie Wind Food Court."

They did not enter through the front, but took a cement walkway, by now shimmering in the heat, around to the back, to enter to the kitchen.

His first impression on entering was steam and even more overwhelming heat. Three women filled large metal trays with food, working quickly. Natalie went to one lady, who stopped in her labor long enough to exchange words. Her look over at Ernst was appraising and, apparently, she didn't like what she saw, because her eyes narrowed. She said something in rapid Spanish.

Natalie turned back to him, looking amused. "She says white men are lazy and make bad workers."

"I'm not," he said. "Tell her I'm thankful, that I'll work hard for her. All I need is a place tonight."

They spoke again; the woman shrugged.

"All right," Natalie said, "I'll see you in the morning."

"You're not staying?" he said, startled.

"My family wants to see me. I said I would go have dinner with my parents."

There seemed be no question that he would not be accompanying them to that dinner. He felt an edge of irritation and bewilderment. They had followed him here to help him, but didn't want him meeting their family?

"You don't want to," Natalie said, reading his face. "Believe me. Uncomfortable for you, uncomfortable for me, and just plain confusing for them." They patted his shoulder. "Everything will make more sense in the morning."

The kitchen overseer set him to dishes, rinsing the food scraps off the plates before sending them through the industrial-level dishwasher. Once that was done, she had him sweep up, then hoist the trash out to the curb. Afterward, she gave him a plate of thick yellow noodles garnished with lumps of lab-grown chicken meat. Salty and spicy, it was tastier than he expected, or perhaps it was the savor of the hard work. He hadn't done anything like that for a long time.

Another of the kitchen workers took him to where he could wash up and sleep. They passed through a lounge of oldsters watching some virtual show, three-D masks making them look like gargoyles. The halls smelled like urine and disinfectant.

In many of the doorways, the room's occupant sat in a wheelchair, watching the hall with solemn resignation. He felt their stares as he passed.

Everything was patterned with golden wheat on a brown background: rug, curtains, wallpaper. The effect might have been elegant once, but the fading made it seem smudgy and uneven. He washed up in a men's bathroom shared by two elderly men quarreling with each other near the empty paper-towel dispenser. There were three stalls, two of them empty and one at the end occupied by someone wearing bright orange sneakers, never moving the whole time he was there.

The tiny bedroom was crowded with two single beds, a bedside table crammed in between them, and looked long disused. His disinterested escort brought him there, gestured around, and told him to be at the kitchen by six A.M. There was no television, and the Wi-Fi was erratic and slow.

He texted Geidon, "Kansas is dull as pants."

A few minutes later, Geidon replied, "Pants can be exciting." Then in a few minutes, "Want to call?"

"No," he texted back. "Signal's too flakey. Any sign of Mai?"

"None. Everyone says she vanished."

He felt a grim satisfaction. He'd known she meant no good, somehow. That was why he had rebuffed her, surely. A corollary occurred to him. Maybe she had come on to him because of the experiment.

But what had she been after? The US couldn't want the empathy research to become widespread, for people to learn how to spread that quality, become more empathetic. Were they intent on suppressing it somehow? Then why have it go up for auction?

He wished that Natalie were there to talk to, or anyone, really. He got up out of bed and went to the window, which was covered with pollution's gray film. Outside, the wind scoured the earth and drove red dust in waves across the sidewalk, caked the plastic roots of the fake greenery lining it.

Finally, he went back to the bed and lay there, wishing desperately for a sleep that did not come.

In the morning, tomato-colored light filtered in through the curtains, and he got up. The same orange shoes were in the third stall, and he wondered uneasily if the occupant had died, but then one of them moved slightly. He waited a little while to see if the person would emerge, washing his hands several times, but they did not.

He gave up and went down the hallway, smelling the same smells as the night before, mingled with a sickly sweet smell that turned out to be the white paste cooking in vats on the immense range top.

Again, he worked, first helping lay the tables and then to clear away the dishes and detritus left by the elderly occupants before he was allowed any food of his own. This time, he was not forced to eat what the elderly had consumed, but got the same meal that was being doled out to the nurses when they came in for their midmorning breaks: a crude biscuit, a lump of flavored lab meat stuck on top of it along with a comma of whitish gravy. It was less palatable than the night's meal, perhaps because by the time it was served to him, it had cooled and congealed. The same salty flavor of the night before was there. He drank orange liquid and wished he had coffee. Or at least CoffeeZatz. This came from cartons marked Fauxfee.

Ernst spent the morning working under Natalie's cousin's eyes, trying not to seem lazy. He remained unconvinced that he lived up to the example of the women working around him; every time he turned around, they were doing something else, and they seemed indefatigable, chattering away as they moved the elderly people—primarily whites, he noticed—from dining room to lounge to the rooms and back. He spotted the man with the orange shoes, a tiny, withered fellow in a blue shirt who said to Ernst, as he passed, "My daughter's coming today. She's going to get me out of here."

"Of course, she is," Ernst said politely, and tried to move past, but the man was solidly in his way now, staring into his face.

237

"Do you know her?" he demanded. "She has blonde hair and hazel eyes. She's a doctor. She said I could come home with her, but she can't mind the place sometimes. You need to go get her. Tell her if she doesn't come get me soon I'll report her to LoyalEye!"

His quavering voice grew louder and louder. Several other old-sters moved towards the pair, drawn by the commotion. Then another of the capable Hispanic women was there, coaxing the old man back to a chair and calming him. She cast a reproachful glance back at Ernst over her shoulder, as though blaming him for the old man's outburst. Ernst tried to look calming, a good influence.

Nonetheless the original woman who'd said he looked lazy pushed him out the door to wait for Natalie, pointing towards a shaded bench. He didn't want to sit out there, where it was a good fifteen to twenty degrees hotter, but she would not allow him back inside, just shut the door in his face. Red-faced and embarrassed, he went to the bench and sat watching the passersby.

Many of the cars were cheap, self-driving ones; others were older and evidently repaired. He saw more buses and noticed that they were not public. Each sported a different logo, advertising some business. Few people were on foot. Those who were, were inevitably either walking a short distance between their car and a business or else pushing either grocery carts overlaid with sacking, their belongings jutting out through the wire sides, or homemade go-carts, their wheels scavenged from other vehicles. Occasionally, someone went by with a dog trotting at their heels. All seemed to be going somewhere else, as though this neighborhood were so poor, it wasn't worth begging in.

A car pulled up to the curb and disgorged Natalie, who didn't wave to the driver as the car moved away. They looked tired and worn, as though they'd had even less sleep than Ernst. They came up to his bench and sat down beside him.

"Ready?" they said.

The virtual auction was supposed to start at dusk, and it was in another of the vast buildings downtown, now abandoned. The clear walls of the building were starred and spider-webbed with impact marks that had cracked but not shattered the thick plexiglass. Desiccated corpses of pigeons that had strayed into the plaza's heat during the deadly noon hours to be killed by the focused heat lay scattered like clots of feathery dry leaves on the sidewalk. The same daily heat kept the space clear of squatters. Someone had fastened a string of LED lights in purple and green to mark a side entrance, the only sign of habitation.

Ernst went in by himself, as they'd agreed. He swallowed as a bored-looking guide led him along a corridor and to a VR cradle before scanning his wrist-chip and socketing him in. Paisley had said they wouldn't care whether or not he was a citizen, just whether or not he could pay for any bids he made. That was strictly monitored, and he wouldn't be able to bluff.

That was all right. He was just here to see the auction and look for Mai. And Natalie would be watching outside; if Mai got past him, they'd follow her. He felt resolute and determined as the attendant fastened the data helm and gloves on him.

The rig clicked. Ernst smelt alcohol for a second as the scent filters fired up and felt a faint rumble through his body as the cradle adjusted itself. Crowd noise came to him, surrounding him, as though he stood blind in the middle of a huge room of people, before, suddenly, the visuals kicked in, and he saw the space.

Whoever had designed the room had monetized it heavily: advertisements crawled over the pillars around him and small clips buzzed like bees from one person to another, checking preferences and settling in for a spiel whenever they found a good match. He set himself on data neutral before any could move in his direction; a few stirred at his arrival, but there were plenty of other people to draw their attention.

Avatars ranged wildly but most people had picked from the defaults; he saw a number of Trumps, Pences, and Grahams, along with caricatures of Nicole Yoshida and Dakotah Ng. Three different Johnny Gunwises.

Someone pinged him. Could it be Mai? He looked around to find the avatar, then spotted it. As an ironic touch, she'd taken on their old manager's Kev's appearance, he noted with wry satisfaction. He piped over to stand beside him. Was it her? It couldn't be Kev, that didn't make sense. No, she'd be counting on Ernst, and only Ernst, to recognize that face.

Before he could say anything, whoever it was established a peer-to-peer private link and said, "ICE is on its way. There's a tip-off. You already can't log out without getting to the settings reset chamber." They pointed across the enormous space.

Was this some kind of diversion? But why would she have pinged him, drawn his attention, when she could have just slipped away through the crowd? He said, using the same private connection, "Mai?"

"There's going to be a shoot-out," they said. "Just get going." They flickered and were gone.

Moving to the setting reset meant going point to point rather than a direct line. He started in the right direction, moving through the milling avatars, pushing his way past a Pence and Trump yelling angrily at each other in language that made it clear they were spouses.

Everything shattered into blue light and alarms. Text and voice barraged everyone. "This is the ICE. Do not attempt to disengage from the network."

He moved faster. ICE would have to lock things down from inside, and he'd had enough warning that he could beat them there. He wasn't the only person to have this thought, but at least he had the jump on the majority of the crowd, and those clustering behind him slowed ICE in turn.

He slammed back into real space and stared at the face hovering above his. It wasn't Mai.

"Kev?" Ernst said in a daze.

"Mmm, yes," Kev drawled. "I'm afraid there's been a bit of a change of plans overall. Come with me."

Shouting echoed all around them, accompanied by shots, but Kev led Ernst away into quiet, down a deserted hallway. They emerged out into an equally deserted parking lot. The ICE wagons seemed to be clustered on the opposite side of the building; the only thing here was a large armored car. He and Kev both got in; Kev leaned forward to speak to the driver. "Station please," he said. He opened up a compartment and took out two bottles of water, handing one to Ernst. "Drink this. VR is so dehydrating."

The bottle was marked with the Rock and Robin logo. The water inside was slightly cloudy but tasted unremarkable.

"What's going on?" Ernst said, lowering it.

"You have plenty of questions," Kev said. His stare was abstracted the way Paisley's had been. "I need to take a quick meeting first. It's best if you sleep."

"What?" Ernst said, but then everything went away.

By the time the world returned, the car was driving up into mountains. Had he been gone minutes, hours, days? He didn't know. Wherever they were, the sun was setting behind them. He twisted to look.

The road led up into the mountains, higher and higher. Halfway up, the thin haze of smog parted before them, and they emerged into the clearer air. From up here, the world looked nightmare and feverish. Processing plants smoldered in the valley's cradle, the chimneys sending gouts of blue flame up into the air at intervals. Lines of lights led back and forth over the earth. Kev was motionless beside him, apparently lost in his meeting still.

Paved road gave way to gravel under the tires. Up above, the stars were bigger and brighter than Ernst had ever seen them. The trees here were ragged fractals against the deepening violet of the sky. They were going slow enough that he could roll down the window. The driver glanced back, but made no objection.

"What are you doing?" Kev asked, stirring.

"I wanted to smell the pines," he said. "It reminds me of home. Lots less moss though."

Kev snorted. "Those are all artificial."

"What?" Leaning out he took a breath. The air smelled of dust and stone, not of greenery. "What are they?"

"Surveillance, solar, broadcast," Kev said. "And weapons, should the peasants ever decide to storm the citadel."

"Who are we going to see?" he asked again. "Is this a Google-Soft project?"

Kev shook his head. "I would tell you if I could, you know that."

"I don't know that," he retorted, "particularly since you're not telling me anything now." He rolled the window back up and folded his arms. The seat was astonishingly comfortable, but he refused to relax into it.

Should he ask about Natalie? Was she part of it? Part of what, though?

He'd been ... what did the spy novels call it? He'd been "made," that was it, and now he was being taken for interrogation by someone disguised as his former boss's boss. They knew he was from Pacifica, and now they didn't just have his research, they had him as well. He'd been a fool. He looked at the door handle and thought about opening it, flinging himself out onto the gravel and shale. He looked again at the black, jagged edges of the pines and wished he'd made different choices in life.

They pulled up to gates flanked by two guard posts, but they did not hail the guards inside. Instead, the driver flashed a card out the window at the sensor, and the gates swiveled open, admitting them. A half-mile farther on, they pulled up in front of an unremarkable door set into the rockface.

"Bringing you in through a service entrance," Kev said. The door swung open to reveal a humanoid robot in neat red and white livery. "Go with the bot, Ernst. Do what it tells you. I'll be there soon as I can."

Before Ernst could respond, Kev pushed at his shoulder, and he found himself standing with the bot. It regarded him with unblinking eyes, and then reached to press the button on the panel beside it. He realized they were in an elevator as it began to descend. After a few minutes, his data sleeve stopped working entirely.

The panel didn't show numbers, just a bar of light across a longer panel. It sank as they went down and down, farther than he would have thought possible. Then the doors opened, and he was handed out to other servitors.

Their touch was impersonal but meticulous. They scrubbed away the dust accumulated during the last few days, shaved him, and braced the freshly exposed skin with toner and moisturizer. His hair—everywhere—was trimmed and conditioned and his nails buffed with a pale gold polish applied.

Earrings were found for him even though he hadn't worn any since college, and the outfit they put on him was a suit that had money woven into it both figuratively and literally in the form of strands of gold thread that gleamed in the light. They took his old data sleeve but gave him no replacement. His shoes were slippers, their soles so thin he could feel the grooves in the tile floor he stood on, as well as its slight but pleasant warmth.

A door whirred open, and Kev was there. He wore an outfit much like Ernst's though colored in a ruddier gold. A red and white rose grew from his lapel.

"There you are," he said. "Let's go."

Ernst wouldn't have known they were underground from the auditorium-sized chamber, edged with sculpted alcoves and curves of white-paved stairs that led upwards to a second-floor balcony that lined the room, showing glimpses of more curtained alcoves and doorways leading elsewhere. Along one wall, a fountain splashed jets of water horizontally a few inches out before gravity dragged the streams downward in a constant flurry of water noise.

Underfoot, the floor was marble, inlaid in an intricate pattern laced with iridescent wire. It shone as though it had been put in place that morning and no foot had ever touched it.

But there were plenty of feet touching it, moving back and forth in the room. They were mostly pale, and tall, and uniformly beautifully dressed in silky, long-sleeved fabrics whose delicacy looked as though they might tear away with a breath. Everyone's skin was perfect, as were their teeth when they showed them in bared-teeth smiles. Their voices were modulated and smooth, the women's tinkling like wind chimes, the men's bourbon and gravel growls.

Then Ernst and Kev moved into another room, and his astonishment redoubled. The space that stretched before him was so vast that there seemed no way it could be contained under a mountain—an underground lake, with a pier in which a large floating raft was docked. It spanned thousands of feet across, the tessellated surface glowing in mother-of-pearl patterns.

Little tents occupied it, placed here and there. Cushions and couches were heaped in them, their upholstery sparkling in jewel-bright colors. Overhead were projections of blue clouds, a color he hadn't seen overhead since California childhood, and gulls cried out back and forth, lots of them. Nostalgia grabbed his throat and would not let go.

Kev led him down the hillside, and they passed the guards on the dock, who nodded deferentially at Kev. The floating raft was stable underfoot, despite the appearance of give. Servers passed among the groups, with plates of food bites and shining flutes, some filled with clear liquid, others with frosty white. Kev snatched two glasses as a server passed, handed Ernst a white one. Unexpected fire nipped at Ernst's lips when he took a cautious sip. Kev laughed, drained his own, and handed the empty glass to another server.

The ubiquitous drones that hung in the air overhead dipped down every once in a while to catch a close-up or snatch of conversation. Whenever such moments happened, the focus of the drone's attention would pose a little self-consciously, their gestures become just a hair more dramatic, their smiles a little wider, their frowns holding an edge more of gravitas. Two drones moved to either side of Kev and him, their round lenses trained on them.

Kev smiled.

"Ladies and gentlemen," he called, making the people around them hush and turn, "May I present Ernst Claymore of Pacifica!"

There was a murmur of conversation that, to Ernst's astonishment, simmered with approval.

"How do they know who I am?" he muttered in an undertone.

"You'll find out," Kev said. Despite the toothy smile, his voice was tinged with unhappiness. "They decided to call you in early. That's one of the problems with … well, you'll see. Come, the Trumps want to meet you. And then the others. Zuckerberg's very keen on you. You'd think he'd produced you, the way he talks about your 'ambitious drive.' Come on."

He pulled Ernst over to a small group of very blond people, whose white teeth, flashing at him in smiles, made him think of feral animals. Some of them he knew from watching politics: Ivanka's smooth mask was well known, as were the paunchier Trump boys, giving way to their father's weight patterns.

Everyone seemed an odd combination of age and youth. Their skins glowed like pearls rolling in morning dew. Their shining, well-brushed hair was full of wave and luster. Their faces were young, but their hands were old.

They all seemed delighted to meet him, greeting him as though he were a family friend. The world around him felt surreal, a dream in which he was expected to know everyone already but had somehow forgotten.

"There's a presentation later," Kev said from beside his elbow. "Just stay out of trouble till then."

"Aren't you going to stay by me?" he said, panicked.

Kev was watching a dapper young man across the room and the dapper young man was looking back. "No," he said absently, "it's not like you're any use to me anymore. They've spoiled you, all for the sake of an evening's fun, when I could have gotten months more out of your line."

"I don't understand."

"You will. In the meantime, just enjoy yourself. There's plenty of booze and pills, and you won't get food like this anywhere else in the world unless you're in some other fancy enclave. Chocolate, peanuts, seafood. This is the midwestern hub. A bunch of them flew in from either coast, and you've even got some of the international set."

He looked around. There weren't just America notables, though. Here was a stiff looking Buttigieg, arm in arm with his husband, and Sanders, sagging jowls, glowering up from a mechanized wheelchair. Now that Ernst looked around, he could see other American elite here and there in the crowd, as well as leaders from Newtopia.

Where was he?

Someone jostled him from behind, and he turned to see a pair he hadn't been introduced to yet.

"Fresh meat!" the young woman said happily. "Are you enjoying yourself, fresh meat?"

She was bright eyed. Glittering dots of light moved up and down her skin under the loose knitting of her dress, which showed more of her flesh than he was used to seeing in person. Her lips held the same dots of light, moving across their surface, but clustering closer and closer. She smelled like something sweet and berrylike, like a fruit plucked from the sky.

245

Her companion shared her features. Ernst thought they were probably twins. He had the same lights, but his moved across his face like a mask, swirling over the skin around his eyes, while others gloved his hands. His outfit was made of black ribbon, woven together, small gaps showing his own taut flesh. They looked like something out of an haute couture fashion magazine.

She reached out and grabbed Ernst's face, pulled him to her for a kiss. He had never been kissed like that before, ruthlessly, with no regard for him, only the pleasure seized from him, and his hard-on was so instant, it was almost painful, because it was a kiss that promised next steps, like taking him then and there, on the marble floor.

He felt a hand on his back, the other man crowding close, nuzzling along his neck.

"I'm sorry," he said, feeling barely coherent, and amazed that he was managing to string words together. "I'm not bi."

"It doesn't matter," the young man said, and his tone was reassuring and calming, making Ernst's heart start to slow. Then he added, "We don't care." His tone made Ernst's heart start to hammer even harder. The young woman was pulling him back into one of the curtained alcoves, the young man's hand resting in the small of his back, pushing and insistent. But before it could go any further, they were interrupted.

"You two should move along," a new voice said. "If you damage him before the presentation, everyone's going to be upset with you."

The interloper was tall and of indeterminate sex, sparse-fleshed almost to the point of emaciation, their hair a bleached white stubble obscuring a haze of black lined tattoos, curlicues of writing, across their skull. They wore shreds of torn and faded plastic wrappers on a network of silver wires that looked like barbed wire, although the knots of wire faced outward rather than biting into the papery flesh. They wore simple paper slippers, of the sort he'd had to wear while enduring the border decontamination.

The two vanished. Ernst said, politely, "I didn't catch your name."

"My name doesn't matter," the person said, their voice snippy and bordering on shrill. He suddenly realized it was the voice of Johnny Gunwise, "You won't need to remember it." They sneered at him. "I was just saving the twins from their own appetites. They're skating on thin ice nowadays."

Ernst returned a blank look, at a loss what to say.

The person continued. "I don't have anything against the spy-reality art form, of course. There's something to be said for working with the amount of randomness it injects into the narrative. But people make allowances for it because the protagonist doesn't know what's going on, as though that excuses them. Take your conversation with the children, for example. It felt preachy, and should have been edited out, except that the rules prohibit it. I'd love to know how many viewers you lost there.

"None," Kev said from beside him, his approach unexpected. He toasted the tall person with an abrupt gesture of the glass he held. "Not a one. Picked up seven-point-two percent, actually. So it's not like you know anything about art," he said. "You're archaic. I could replicate you with another animatronic Pence like the one in charge now and get twice the laughs out of a canned laugh track. Go back to the Stone Age, you hack. My art's aimed at the people that really matter, not feeding pulp to the masses."

Their hands fluttered, shaping a series of gestures that flowed too fast for Ernst to understand; the drones swooped low to catch every twist of motion. They said nothing more, dropped their hands to their sides, and turned away.

Ernst turned to Kev, wanting to ask the meaning of the encounter, but the man had vanished again.

Standing to one side, he noticed that the food trays had colored bands around their edges. Apparently a system to denote their contents, because he noticed Kev sticking to the gold and copper bordered trays and avoiding those banded with silver or a pinkish rose gold. He was used to systems like this—Pacifica marked food according to vegan, kosher, halal, and all the other differentiations that affected choices. He wished he understood this one better but he was lucky, he had no allergies or dietary restrictions.

An ancient wizened woman in red velvet stopped him as he stepped back and jabbered something at him in a language he couldn't identify.

"I don't understand," he told her and tried to move on, but kept her hand tight on his sleeve, forcing him to pause beside her as she spoke at length. She seemed intent on having him try everything, stopping various servers as they passed in order to press more bites on him: a roasted fig stuffed with some sharp white cheese, drizzled with a tangy syrup; rounds of flatbread sprinkled with tiny citrus-scented seeds; cubes of marinated meat, so tender that it was almost falling off the tiny silver skewers that impaled them.

Each time she gave Ernst a morsel, she said something that he presumed was its name or some preparation detail and paused expectantly to wait for him to nod his approval. Each bite was more delicious than the last.

"**word**," she said, and stopped yet another server, whose tray held curls of smoked pork, glistening with red sticky sauce, each wound around a thin reed. She plucked one of the curls from the tray. Ignoring his efforts to intercept the offering, she popped it into his mouth. The meat had a fatty savor to it, complemented by the sauce's bite. He chewed and swallowed. Her eyes glittered at him like black beads.

"Did you like?" she said in English.

"Delicious," he said politely.

"I knew you would appreciate it," she said. "They came from your region. What you call free-range, rather than kept in cages."

"Lucky pigs!" he said, and chuckled.

"Not pigs," she said, and followed his chuckle with her own.

"What then?" he asked.

She was about to answer, but just then, Kev was there yet again, and pulling him along. "Time for the presentation," he said.

Kev led him off the raft structure and through a large archway, out into yet another huge chamber. He realized its starry ceiling was a projection and the trees and flowers around him grew in pots. Underfoot were more pebbles, but they were fixed in place and made of some material that gave way easily, so those of the women and men wearing high heels were in no danger of falling. There was a half circle of sunken pit in the middle of the chamber. Tiers of benches surrounding it, an inverted stage like something from an old Greek theater. The men and women moved to the benches while Kev tugged Ernst down the stage.

"Am I going to have to make a speech?" he said, worried. The rich food spasmed in his stomach with a surge of bile. He wished he had a glass of water. Maybe Kev would send a server to get one if Ernst asked.

"Don't be ridiculous. I'm the one responsible, at least, even if they've chosen to pick you before your full time," Kev sniffed. "It's not like I didn't anticipate them moving early," he said. "But I expected to have a little more time. So much remains unresolved."

They reached the stage and moved to the center. The audience paid no attention, chattering among themselves. Looking at them as they sat in graceful poses, drones in an aerial ballet above them, Ernst felt small and shabby and a little dirty. They seemed larger than life, every one of them flawless.

"Ladies and gentlemen," Kev said, and then repeated it a little louder. The lights in the room dimmed and a single spotlight picked him out. The room quieted. Kev let the silence grow before speaking.

"I have, I would like to think, brought you multiple enjoyable storylines in the course of my tenure as major producer," he said, "including many of the wonderful absurdities of 2036 and 2037, but the success of my latest, more gritty, endeavor came as a pleasant surprise. Less pleasant is the fact that you found my protagonist so gripping that you wanted to meet him. Who knows how it might have all ended?" His smile reminded Ernst a tiger whose prey is being snatched away. "But you spoke, and here he is. Hero of *Chasing the Spy From Pacifica.*"

Applause rose from all around them.

Ernst looked at Kev. "I don't understand," he said.

"You're entertainment, dear fellow. You're the star of the series I scripted."

"You scripted?" Ernst's head throbbed. "But you're a Google-Soft manager."

"I am one of the foremost practitioners of spy-reality series," Kev said. "The foremost, if the truth be told. You're the star of the latest."

There were eyes staring at him from all around.

"They've enjoyed the show. They wanted to meet you," Kev said.

"So Rachel's project wasn't real? None of this was real?"

"Oh, real after a fashion. We use the material we're given, that's something I pride myself on. She thought it was real enough. But over here, they already had access to the technology. They use it all the time."

"Impossible." He thought of what he'd seen, of the children working to buy their own lunches, the ancients shuffling through the retirement home's cubicles, the smog hanging over the prison camps. "You're telling me they've increased their empathy?"

Kev laughed outright. "Of course not." He gestured around himself, at the rows of beautiful people in their benches. "They remove it," he said. "The whole room is nothing but well-socialized sociopaths. And they love a good spy-reality show." He lowered his voice so only Ernst could hear him. "They like to pretend that they understand what it means," he said, and grinned. "And now they want to talk to you."

He released Ernst's arm and stepped away. The occupants of the benches surged to their feet, came forward, and inundated him with questions. They'd been holding back out of desire to not spoil the surprise, he realized, and now they didn't care. They asked him whether he was attracted to Mai—the love story was so muted, one woman said. "So deliciously muted and understated."

"I'm just shy," he said uncomfortably.

"Of course, of course." She beamed at him as though he had proven some point and then moved away to talk to someone else about her theory.

"Such a shame." He turned to see who had spoken and saw the ginger-bearded man from the GoogleSoft parking lot, days ago. "I told you," said the man. "Such potential. And they bring you in and spoil it all." He tsked. "Well, I'm glad to have gotten the chance to meet you before they spoiled you. Good luck."

Before Ernst could even answer, the ginger-bearded man was jostled aside by a woman coming forward to speak.

She said, "Kev didn't tell you, but there are some of us who don't eschew empathy." She pressed a hand to her heart. "No, we cultivate it in ourselves, so we feel deeply when we are watching you. I myself have suffered along with you at every moment."

He thought of the thirst and sweat of the road, of the menace of the men and women from the flea market. "At every moment," he echoed.

She failed to perceive the irony in his tone, but a server, passing by his elbow, paused and held out a glass to him, unsolicited. He started to wave it away, but a tiny motion, a jerk in his direction, of it, stopped him. The androgynous server looked him square in the face, trying to convey some message that he could not read. He took the glass, and they bowed, then moved away through the crowd. He watched them go, trying to pinpoint something about their appearance that would allow him to pick them out of the crowd.

He sipped his drink, looking at the woman's thirsty, sympathetic eyes, the thin smile tacked on her mouth. He said, "Excuse me," and fled down a hallway, looking for a place to vomit. Someone guided him, a hand on his elbow, to a cool, tiled space where he knelt and spewed up the contents of his stomach into a white porcelain bowl.

When he looked up, he saw the person was the server. They stood beside him quietly.

Ernst said, "I'm surprised the drones don't capture this." He wiped bile from his mouth.

"You're exclusively available to the people here tonight," the server said. "The ones from outside this enclave have paid well for the privilege. They don't often get a chance to spend like this. It would dilute the privilege if anyone could tune in and watch you now. They have to wait for the recording later."

Ernst's head pulsed and throbbed. His mouth tasted like greasy ashes. "But that's why they brought me here. I'm just entertainment," he said. "Just a scenario getting played out as part of some huge reality show."

"Now you're getting it," the server said in a kindly tone.

"It's too big," Ernst said. "I mean…."

"No," the server said. "They didn't create it. It just evolved that way. The crazy times rolled around and the truly rich pulled themselves into their enclaves. Not like the world outside was getting any more appealing, with its smog and bad water. And then they got bored. The only thing to play with was either each other or us. And they can still bite, so they turned their teeth on the ones that can't fight back."

"Why are you telling me all this?"

"Because you've got a lot of fans," the server said. "Not just among them. Among us."

"Who's us?"

"The people that keep things running. The service technicians. The managers. The accountants that make sure money flows from point A to point B. Even a few of the people like Kev and his kind, who craft the narratives that keep you all quiet, like a man and his pet gun, so you'll think of guns as your friends. It's not a good action sequence unless a few bullets are flying, so *Johnny Gunwise* is there to make it all normal."

"Why do you help them, if they're so bad?"

"Why do you think? For most of us, it's simply the smartest choice. Collaborate and serve them or be part of the flock they prey on. And when I say prey ..." He hesitated, "Well, we've been providing them with sport for years." He put his mask back on. "But for a few of us, it's the only way of gathering intelligence so we can strike back someday."

"I can help you with that," Ernst said. "If what you say is true, and they really do like me."

"You still don't understand," the server said. His voice was patient. "They called you in. They want to rub elbows with you tonight, say they were part of the latest craze for spy-reality. But there's plenty of other actors waiting in the ranks. Ones that don't know what's going on. You see, it spoils everything if you know what's going on. You know you're performing. The Actors Guild passed rules long ago about that. They didn't want the competition. Few enough of them make their way up high enough to get a place at the table. To have your sort horning in, untrained and unqualified, would have been more than they could bear."

"So what happens to me?"

"You're no use to them after tonight. Someone will probably take you home as a fucktoy, after they auction you off. That might buy you a few more days. But that's the only reason someone would take you. You don't have any performing talents, that's been made clear. The thing everyone likes about you is your sort of clueless innocence. It's very endearing. But I can see it getting shredded away right now. It won't survive the night."

"So they'll just throw me outside then."

The voice was still patient. "No. You might go warn someone else. That's unallowable."

Ernst swallowed. "So they'll kill me." He managed a weak smile. "Surely, I'll get stuffed or eaten or something. My organs salvaged."

"They grow all that. They don't want all the chemicals you have in your body, even over in Pacifica. And it's worse over here, with the junk they cram in the food."

He thought of the old woman saying, "They're free range" and found himself doubled over the toilet again.

"So why tell me all this?" he said dully. "Are you just trying to tie things up for some story in your head?"

"Because they made the mistake of giving you a real project."

"Rachel's?"

"We've got a way of making it go viral now. Production costs were the stopping point. You've gotten us further along. Now we're ready to infect them all."

"But they live in isolated enclaves."

"They mix much more often than you would think. What's the point of being rich if you can't show it off to other people? Because we'll mix it in with something. A technology that slows the growth, makes it take years. By the time they realize what's happened, they'll all be infected."

"And what happens to me?"

The dark eyes held more sympathy than Ernst felt he deserved. "You've done something meaningful. Something that changes the world. Isn't that what you wanted, why you've been chasing your grandmother's research all along?"

The server had said he'd done enough, but it didn't feel that way. He rinsed his mouth and moved through the crowds. The encounters

253

seemed all the same, faces flashing with perfect white teeth, false smiles that could have hung in the air like Cheshire Cat grins. He ate more food. He drank more wine. He took three small pills offered in a bone-white cup.

He was standing next to the empathetic woman again, and she was expanding on the exquisite nuances of her existence.

"So you'd do it again," he said.

"Oh no," she said. "I make the most of it, but it's so painful to be this sensitive. It's as though other people's pain were *literally* echoed in my body."

"That must be very distressing," he said politely.

"Human beings can learn to cope with anything," she said. She paused, raising her arm up to bring it against her forehead in a theatrical gesture of despair that seemed rehearsed, but not enough to actually be smooth.

Several people swirled around him, and someone pulled her away. "Dear Mary, you absolutely must come speak to David, he's beside him…" floated back through the crowd.

Ernst forced a smile at the newcomers and their small talk, taking another drink from a passing tray without meeting its bearer's eyes.

By the time of the auction, he was drunk and sullen. He stood on the dais in his rumpled clothing. "Make him strip!" someone in the crowd called out and much to his embarrassment, two handlers removed his shirt but allowed him to keep his pants. He felt himself flabby and small in this room of engineered, pampered bodies.

Silence greeted him, then a chorus of voices. The booze and drugs sang in him and when someone grabbed at them, he swung. There was a chorus of screams and shouts.

A price was proposed, and no bids made, so a second smaller price was proposed and met with the same fate. In the end, they pulled him down from the stage, and he was taken to a small, bare room with only a chair in it and told to wait. There was no door handle inside.

He waited an hour before he went to the door and listened at it. Nothing. He banged on it, raising his voice. "I'm thirsty. Can I get a little water at least?" The alcohol was surrendering its grip on his system, and he tried to relax back into its embrace, but it ebbed away, taking his courage with it. He could have smiled. He could have pretended. Now, he would be killed, and his death would be pointless, not even recorded by the drones.

Footsteps in the hallway. He waited, listening. Someone fumbled with the door, and he stepped back, preparing to launch himself at whoever entered. He wasn't going to go down without a fight.

But he checked himself at the sight of who stood in the doorway.

Natalie said, "Let's go," and without further explanation, wheeled and started down the hallway. They wore a servitor's uniform, in the same colors as all the rest. For the first time, he realized they were the red and white of Rock and Robin.

He stammered out, "I thought you were gone."

"They pulled me out before ICE surrounded the building. But I couldn't get word to you. They said you were being monitored too closely."

"Lucky you," he said. "Now, I'm too worthless to monitor."

"Jesus Christ, *now* is not the time to go all despondent," they snapped, and stopped in front of a doorway to fumble with it. "This leads to an access tunnel to the surface. From there, we can walk down the mountainside, and there'll be a ride waiting to take us into town. They'll get us back to Pacifica. Once we're there, we can figure out how to expose all this and move against them. How to get the infection spreading. This is a real fight now."

They focused on moving along the tunnel. He felt washed clean with relief. Natalie was here. Everything was okay now. There was nothing they couldn't face together.

Sunlight dazzled him as they threw back the upper hatch. Natalie grinned at him and grabbed his hand.

Together, they started down the hill. Far above them, golden sunlight turned the drones into metallic bees as they recorded their journey from multiple angles. Someone would sort through the streams for the most dramatic angles and lighting later.

It would definitely be a series worth binge-watching.